Praise for the Novels of Connie Johnson Hambley

THE WAKE

"What a wonderful read. Connie Johnson Hambley does a masterful job of weaving the incredible healing power and positive impact of the horse into an edge of your seat story. It's very clear that Jessica's healing–both emotional and physical–is intertwined with horses. But that is just one of the facets to this multi-layered story that keeps you riveted throughout the tale."
– KATHY ALM, CEO of PROFESSIONAL ASSOCIATION OF THERAPEUTIC HORSEMANSHIP INTERNATIONAL

"In *The Wake*, Connie Johnson Hambley delivers a fast-paced, emotional conclusion to *The Jessica Triology*, a series that focuses on competitive steeplechase rider Jessica Wyeth and her search for answers to long-held family secrets. The political background of a divided Ireland and acts of terrorism on behalf of nationalism make this an especially timely book, and horse lovers will fall in love with Hambley's powerful portrayal of the deep, healing bond between horses and humans."
—HOLLY ROBINSON, AUTHOR of *FOLLY COVE*

"For fans of high speed suspense, international political intrigue, and strong female characters, Connie Johnson Hambley delivers on all fronts in *The Wake*. This third book in the *Jessica Trilogy* is as exciting as Hambley's first two titles, and Jessica Wyeth is a compelling heroine that lives on in the reader's imagination. A terrific read!"
– LAURA MOORE, AUTHOR of *ONCE TEMPTED*

THE TROUBLES
Winner Best Fiction, EQUUS Film Festival Literary Award

"*The Troubles* is a sweeping narrative that travels across generations and continents to paint a richly textured, historically accurate picture of a troubled country fighting to find its soul amid clashing loyalties and political chaos. Hambley skillfully unfolds several urgent mysteries at once, while giving us complex characters, gorgeous settings, and a prose that sings with the cadences of Ireland. (As a bonus, *The Troubles* also boasts the best descriptions of horse races you'll find anywhere.)"
—ELISABETH ELO, AUTHOR OF *NORTH OF BOSTON*

THE CHARITY

"*The Charity* reads like a wild cross-country ride...complete with twists and turns, stomach-lurching drops, and the steady thrum of adrenaline...It's the thrill of the unraveling mystery, a hint of romance, and a terrifying glimpse into the clandestine terrorists in our midst that will keep readers glued to the pages of this thriller."
—*MASSACHUSETTS HORSE MAGAZINE*

"I enjoyed the plot and the twists it took along the way...It's rare for a mainstream novel to seamlessly incorporate an equine element, but Hambley did just that."
—*THE CHRONICLE OF THE HORSE*

THE JESSICA TRILOGY ~ BOOK 3

THE WAKE

WHEN TRUTH
WON'T
DIE

CONNIE JOHNSON HAMBLEY

Published 2017 by Charylar Press in the United States of America
Copyright 2017 by Connie Johnson Hambley
Library of Congress Control Number
2017909647
Hambley, Connie Johnson
The Wake/Connie Johnson Hambley
p. cm.
Paperback ISBN: 978-0-9991154-0-4
Ebook ISBN: 978-0-9991154-1-1
1. Family Secrets—Fiction 2. Adoption—fiction
3. Northern Ireland—Fiction
4. Irish Republican Army—Terrorism—Fiction 5. Horse Training—Fiction I.
Title.

This is a work of fiction. Names, characters, places, and incidents are the
products of the author's imagination or are used fictitiously. Any resemblance to actual events, locales, or persons, living or dead, is entirely coincidental. The opinions expressed within are solely the opinions of the author
and do not represent the opinions or thoughts of any other person, corporation, or entity. The author has represented and warranted full ownership
and/or legal right to publish all the materials in this book.

Charylar Press

DEDICATION

To Andrew.
Gone far too soon. Never forgotten. Always loved.

ACKNOWLEDGMENTS

This trilogy falls inside the violent years before the Good Friday Agreement determined how Northern Ireland would be governed. Unrelated world events on both sides of the Atlantic shaped this book's characters and plot. The Centennial Park bombing at the 1996 Summer Olympic Games in Atlanta, Georgia was a horrific event that took the lives of two innocent people and injured many more. The bombing is part of our collective experience as Americans and happened at a time before we feared unattended backpacks in public places. Terrorism has many facets and my prayers go to all people impacted by that atrocity and far too many more since then to count.

My thanks go to Windrush Farm Therapeutic Equitation Center of North Andover, Massachusetts and to Mandy Hogan for allowing me to use their names in this work. I've spent many happy hours volunteering as a horse handler at Windrush and am always amazed at the impact their programs have on the lives of so many children and adults. Windrush offers hippotherapy treatments in partnership with licensed physical, occupational, and speech therapists to supplement their array of therapeutic riding programs provided by certified and licensed instructors. Any misrepresentation of the process of equine-based therapies or Windrush's facilities is all due to my own over-active imagination and my desire to tell a good tale.

Special thanks go to my law school classmate, Kurt Hughes, for his invaluable help in understanding adoption issues. Kurt received national recognition as an Angel of Adoption by the Congressional Coalition of Adoption Institute, and his work will live on through many happy generations of Vermont families lucky enough to have his counsel. Once again, any factual errors or misstatements are to be blamed on the squirrelly machinations of this fiction author's mind.

Where would I be without my Betas? Elaine G., Anne M., Gerry M., Laura M., Philip M., Susan O., Elaine P., Jessica R., Lis S., and the Supreme Commanders of all Betas, Linda Doll and Lisa Frieze.

Every crime writer has her go-to expert on guns, munitions, raid strategy, and more. My thanks go to a certain retired captain of a large regional police department and S.W.A.T. commander, for his invaluable assistance.

Last, but never least, thanks and love to Scott for supporting this crazy life I've chosen.

JESSICA WYETH'S FEET hadn't touched the tarmac before she knew returning to the States was a mistake. The twin engine Gulfstream IV made her an easy target as she paused before descending the jet's airstairs. Arriving at the private corporate terminal didn't stop reporters from finding her. Questions pelted her from the group gathered at the edge of the chain link fence. Dark stains under their arms appeared each time they raised their cameras, proving the hot and humid Kentucky summer could be as oppressive as they were. They strained to grab their piece of her—the fugitive who had stopped running because she had no place to hide.

Someone must have leaked that Northern Ireland had kicked her out and questioned if the U.S. would take her in.

She was news.

Strike that.

She was their meal ticket.

"Why did you flee the United States?"

"Are you worried about other charges being pressed against you?"

"If you're innocent, why hide?"

Each click of a shutter was an electric jolt pushing her dream of a quiet return farther away. She yearned to greet the world on her own terms; bruised, but cleansed and new. Thick air, laden with the stench of jet fuel, hot tar, and sweat, pushed against her as she stood in the passageway. The cool air of the Irelands faded to memory as if it had been years since she roamed its hills rather than hours.

She hugged herself and wished she could get them to see that she had been a victim of a terrible accusation and left the country in the secure embrace of a man who loved her. Michael's men being there to greet her would have been a welcomed sight.

She sighed. Maybe not. Michael M. Connaught, whose initials graced the jet's fuselage, added to her situation's complexity.

Two police cars, flanking a large black SUV, pulled up and blocked the jet's path. The gold seal of the U.S. Immigration and Naturalization Service proclaimed their purpose and the array of flashing lights ensured everyone knew it. A man with shorn hair opened the SUV's passenger-side door and leaned his heft against its frame. His head angled toward the jet as he spoke into a radio mic pressed to his mouth. Aviator sunglasses shielded his eyes. Self-importance oozed out of him. Red patches blazed up his cheeks, betraying his excitement even as he tried to hide it.

Jessica suppressed a smirk. What were they protecting? The public good? Or something else? The gaggle of reporters evidenced that few thought she was worthy of protecting, or all that good. The familiar urge to flee tickled the back of her neck. Uncertain and afraid, she backed into the cocoon of the jet.

A man in his late twenties, dressed in a crisp uniform with "MMC, Ltd." embroidered on the chest pocket, held her suitcase. Cabin Steward Devins avoided her eyes as he spoke. "I'm sorry, Miss Jessica. The captain's just learned there's an issue with your re-entry. I'm afraid that beefy lad doesn't want your dainty toes on his soil," he said, soft brogue keeping his inflection light. "May I suggest you wait here 'til you've got clearance."

"Here? As in Louisville?"

"No, Miss. I'm afraid if you disembark you'll be detained."

"Whoa. You're telling me that as soon as my feet hit the ground, they'll handcuff me?" Her back thumped against the hatch frame in disbelief.

"Not so much handcuff you as provide an escort, but an armed one at that. I've not seen the inside of the terminal, but it's a fair guess you'll be more comfortable with us. We've been told the authorities' presence is all quite routine."

"Routine enough to send three police cars?" She dared another peek out to the tarmac. The staccato ticks of camera shutters trilled. "No. Something's up."

Devins' expression darkened long enough to trigger acid to pool in the pit of her stomach.

She pinched the bridge of her nose. *Don't show fear. No one knows. Everything will be fine. Michael will help me.* "How long will this take?"

"We're hoping for a few hours at best if everyone cooperates. Longer if suspicions are raised."

"Give it to me straight," she said, voice steady. "Are you saying days?"

"That's exactly the issue, Miss Wyeth." Jessica turned to see the pilot standing inside the cockpit door. A pin of gold wings with "Capt. Lisbeth Laramie" engraved in block letters rested on her uniform's navy blue lapel. The salt and pepper bun at the nape of her neck sat as neatly as it had at the beginning of their nine-hour trip from Belfast.

Captain Laramie drew in a short breath and squared her shoulders. "The only information I have is that officials in Northern Ireland contacted their counterparts in the States to inform them of their findings while we traveled."

"What findings? Those guys are from immigration! I'm *returning* to the States." What was happening? *Immigration? Oh, God.*

"I'm not one to quarrel with the officials, Miss Wyeth. When one country expels a person, no other country must take them in until they've completed an investigation. As long as you remain on board and don't deplane, we're cleared to take off."

The pocket of her blouse pulsed in time with her heartbeat. She crossed her arms in front of her chest. "What do they think they know?"

"I'm very sorry. I only know what I've been told. Detaining you for questioning is within their rights. They don't have to state a reason to detain you other than another country placed you on a watch list."

"If greeting me with a press corps and a couple of overweight officers was all they could pull together on short notice," Jessica said, forcing an upbeat manner, "they must be stalling for more time. But why?"

"I understand that as long as they do not place you into personal custody, this is, um, how do you Americans say no official records would be made?" The captain's brows furrowed as she struggled to find the words. "Ah! Off the books. Informally detaining you on airport grounds keeps this off the books for them. I've seen people kept from entering the country for days until matters were resolved."

Jessica shrank into the shadow of the door as she looked at cruisers, agents, and reporters. The theater was too perfect. Images of the inevitable headlines of the evening news tracked across her vision, marquee style—*Murdering Heiress: Resurrected to a Life on the Run.* She began to feel very small against the forces at work. "Stalling gives

3

more time to push out skewed facts against me. I've been trashed through the news, and the reporters out there tell me I'm about to sell more papers. Truth. Rumor. Doesn't matter. But, if I can't leave, you can't either."

"You can leave the U.S., you just can't enter. You're welcome to stay aboard while the craft is serviced. We're not needed for another flight or you'd have to wait in a secure area inside the terminal. You must stay on the airport's premises." The lilt of the captain's words did not soften their message. "We will remain on the ground for as long as it takes. I'm told legal teams in Belfast and Boston are working on your situation now."

"Is that what this is? My *situation*?" Jessica laughed at the ridiculousness of her circumstance. Her situation, as the captain deftly stated, required nothing less than legal teams in two countries trying to talk logic to bureaucrats.

They'd have more luck making pigs fly.

Devins secured the door. A soft whir of the airlock sounded as the hatch sucked into place. Vents hissed. Cool, filtered air replaced fetid airport fumes.

A chime sounded and the captain reached for a phone corded to the cockpit wall. She motioned toward the back of the jet. "There's a call for you. A gentleman from Ireland," she said with a knowing smile. "You can take it in the private quarters."

The only clues Jessica was in a small jet instead of a posh hotel were the curved walls and oval windows. Deep leather seats, fashioned to look more like high-end club chairs than airline seats, swiveled to surround a small conference table to form conversation areas. The rear section of the aircraft held a bedroom, shower, and another smaller seating area.

Devins brought her to a lacquered console containing a small desk, computer terminal, and phone.

"Press the lighted line when you're ready to talk." He set down a small tray holding a glass of ice with a wedge of lime and a green bottle of sparkling water. He looked out to the SUV. "Clever men, these American officials. Lying in wait for us to land, they were. It's as if they know everything even before it happens." He pulled the shade down and motioned toward the phone. "The line is as secure as we can make it." He didn't need to say more, and clicked the door quietly behind him as he left.

Once seated, Jessica grabbed a paper and pen from the drawer and reached for the handset. Her hand trembled above the phone for a moment before she drew it back, shaking it to stop her tremor. The light blinked steadily. She poured a mouthful of water, sipped, and answered the call.

"Michael! I'm so glad you called! What's going on?"

"Tisn't Michael. Murray here. Did you get my scones alright?"

The shock of hearing Michael's butler's voice stilled her before she broke out into a grin. She had spent the better part of a month under Murray's loving care at Ballyronan, Michael's home, on the shores of Lough Neagh, the lake that dominated the center of Northern Ireland, and knew Michael's trust in the cherubic man was well placed. "Murray! You know your scones are my favorite. Thank you! Why isn't Michael calling me? Is he okay?"

In the pause before Murray responded, her heart leapt to her throat.

"Aye. He is, and he gave me firm orders to make sure you have everything you need. The Irelands are a sadder place without you here, Miss Jessica. I'm hearing you're having a bit of trouble with your homecoming."

Devins' caution tempered her from asking more about Michael, but disappointment crept up her arms and she hugged herself to keep it from reaching her heart. She pushed the tension out of her voice. "Geez, I'd say. Captain Laramie says it's best I stay on board until things get sorted out."

The hollow sound of the phone receiver pressed against his chest filled the line. "Ah. Here's my pen. Tell me exactly what's happened. Has anyone approached you or contacted Captain Laramie?"

She pulled the shade open an inch and pressed her head against the window frame for a better look. "Two police cruisers and a federal immigration agency SUV blocked the jet as soon as we touched down. No one's contacted me directly. Can you tell me what's going on?"

"Strikes me as a lot of saber rattling and spotlight mongering. Word from our sources is that you were expelled from Northern Ireland due to suspicions you're linked to terrorist activities."

Terrorist activities? Sweet Lord. "That's crazy and I wasn't expelled! My training job was over and I was leaving Northern Ireland anyway!" Her lie tumbled out, easily, without thought or effort, the warning of eavesdropping freshly imprinted. She could put her own misinformation out, too.

She would keep the truth to herself. Hours before, in a dark terminal, a grim-faced man in a wrinkled suit thrust papers in her face while muttering something in a thick accent she couldn't understand. Michael had taken the papers from her as he kissed her good-bye, promising he'd take care of it and all would be well.

Murray continued. "If they had anything more firm than a bunch of hearsay, they'd've dragged you off in cuffs. Master Connaught's about to eat the head of the eejits in Stormont who think they know what's what."

"Stormont? That's Northern Ireland's Capitol Hill! Why would anyone there be interested?"

"Och. It was lousy timing the day of the steeplechase you rode in coincided with that terrible shopping center bombing in Manchester."

A subtle shift in tone made her pay attention to each of Murray's carefully chosen words. Her official reason to be abroad was to train horses for a private race at the Aintree Racecourse in England. Horses and all of the feed and gear traveled with her from her training location in Ireland to an airport outside of Manchester, England. Reports in one of England's notorious tabloids concocted a story that she was the mule for the explosives that gutted a city block in the Arndale shopping district. The Irish Republican Army claimed responsibility for the bombing, and the investigation by England's MI-5 and Northern Ireland's Security Branch in Stormont had turned up nothing. Frustrated authorities were getting desperate for results. Her mouth dried.

Her unofficial reason for leaving the States was that she was drummed out of the country. Power beyond her comprehension had framed her for the murder of Gus Adams. The press dubbed her the Murdering Heiress and determined her guilty. Seven months ago, she had emerged from years of hiding to reclaim her name and her innocence. Doing so nearly cost her life. The crowd of reporters outside her window showed few believed—or cared—she was blameless. Then or now.

Murray's tone told her he shared her concerns as he continued talking. "International security is not to be trifled with."

"Anyone who thinks I was involved with the Manchester bombing is a headline-mongering lunatic."

Murray chortled. "Say what you will, but you Yanks have a phrase, 'Guilt by association.' I'm afraid it may be fitting."

"Jesus, Murray. Why should I be investigated? My life's been under a microscope for months. Today I counted five news vans and about twenty reporters. I'm really afraid this means history is about to repeat itself." She took a gulp of water and drew in a deep breath. When she continued, she lowered her voice and slowed her words. "I don't trust reporters to be objective about my innocence and I trust authorities even less—especially when collaring me would make their career. Something has whipped them up into a frenzy. This response can't only be about me being at the wrong place at the wrong time."

She could hear Murray stifle a cough. "Michael's knackered getting counsel to straighten out those sleeveens. Sit tight. Won't be too much longer for you."

"Sitting on my hands in a fishbowl makes me feel even worse." Being powerless to control what would be said about her was especially frustrating. Being raked over the coals with hyped-up rumors was painful enough, but her trip to Ireland uncovered facts she needed to stay buried. A band of tension tightened behind her eyes. "I wish it would all go away," she said, voice barely audible.

"You wish to be *Manannan Mac Lir,* you do."

"Who?"

"The god of the sea who had a magical horse called Splendid Mane and a suit of armor that could make them invisible. Ah, I only wish I could do that for you."

Murray's wit softened her. He always knew how to talk with her in a way that lessened the pain. She could see why Michael trusted him above all. "I'm sick of disappearing. It's their turn to get out of *my* way!"

Murray whooped. "Och! I can see the blood of a rebel in you."

His words hit a fresh wound. She doodled dozens of little circles in the corner of the paper.

Murray filled the silence, his voice soft with concern. "And you're well? I sent more food to the galley than scones. You won't go hungry for a while yet."

"I'm okay. Really," she said, trying to believe it. "Can't I get off this plane? I'm going to go crazy being locked in here."

"I'm sorry Miss Jessica. Michael says there's no other choice for you."

"Will he call?" The question spilled out before she could stop herself.

"He'll be in touch. Of that, I've no doubt. I'm signing off now. God speed, Miss Jessica."

She held the phone to her ear even after the light blinked off. The cabin felt empty. Too empty. Michael's absence filled every cranny.

Devins knocked before entering. "You're set, then? We're taxiing to another hangar. Should get us out of view for a bit."

Jessica's shoulders sagged as she glanced out to the fence protecting the tarmac. Reporters craned their necks to see around the cruisers. Beefy Boy and the Bubbas remained diligent. "Isn't there something we can do about them?"

"I'm afraid not. Lads are doing their bit to protect the public."

The officers leaned against their cars, relaxed, and settled in for their shift. The immigration official stood with them, in full display, with his thumbs in his belt at just the right angle to pull back his jacket and expose his holster and badge. As she watched, he turned, giving the cameras a good shot. The pose subtle, but obvious to her.

She walked around the cabin and pulled down every shade.

Wednesday, July 3, 1996
Belfast, Northern Ireland
United Kingdom

BISHOP KAVAN HUGHES poured tea into a fine china cup rimmed with gold and thanked his housekeeper for her day's work with a nod, a signal that solitude was what he needed now. Rosalie moved silently around the sitting room, tidying stacks of discarded files, before she slipped away, easing the door shut behind her. Gray-haired and capable, Rosalie kept his flat in visitor-ready condition since politicians and statesmen of every calling could appear at any hour of the day. A man of the cloth is expected to be available to his flock, but Kavan's world had another dimension. His duties to the Catholic Church paled when pressed into service for his country. At least that's what he wanted them to believe. He was the unofficial conduit between the Irish Republican Army and the government, a reality that placed him more in the role of mediator than spy. Then again, the difference was only a matter of perception and politics.

Kavan was known only as *an Sagart*, the Priest, to anyone outside of a selected few. As *Sagart*, he had access to the thoughts and hopes of both sides of the unification conflict. The loyalists wanted the six counties of Northern Ireland to remain loyal to the British Crown and remain in the United Kingdom. The nationalists wanted one nation on the island of Ireland, not two. Either in a confessional or a pub, men and women sought his counsel. First as an inexperienced and freshly ordained priest, then through his ascension to bishop, he listened and advised, keeping his own passions mute. Without tipping his hand, he honed the brawn of the impulsively violent and inflamed the hate of the passive, all the while taking pains to keep both sides engaged with words, and away from bombs and bullets, but keeping the threat of such fresh and clear. Some say his gift for mediation was God-given. He knew his success was due to the love of a woman.

Bridget Heinchon, a woman vibrant with beauty and intelligence, claimed his heart long before he was betrothed to the church. Together they orchestrated the resistance of the powerless against the might of the powerful, always cautious to keep the union of their hearts private. Kavan was the invisible bond that kept the coalitions together. Bridget, too impatient to work alongside thickheaded politicians, was the force and the voice of Northern Ireland's civil rights movement. Her brothers, legends in the IRA, were killed by the British. Bridget spent years in a U.K. prison before Kavan was able to free her. The cost of her freedom was to be forever banned from her homeland as a terrorist.

Bridget and Kavan shared the hearts of all who knew them and the secrets of revolutionaries. No one saw them as a couple and never once did she betray him. Not as a girl sneaking him censored books, nor as a woman when her belly grew large with his child.

She forbade him leaving the priesthood, insisting his work in brokering peace was more important than following her into exile. By the time she was freed, their child was over five years old and never knew either of them as a parent. Only because Bridget's sister Margaret, and Kavan's best friend Gus Adams, did a better job at parenting than he ever could have, did he finally relent and remain in Belfast and in the Church. Bridget had been right. His work at keeping all sides of the conflict talking saved countless lives.

A harsh fact in his world of brokering peace—success is invisible. Only the failures make the headlines.

A soft knock at the door disturbed his thoughts. Rosalie entered, followed by a squat man with a sanctimonious air.

"Deputy First Minister Bragdon is here to see you, Your Excellency." She backed out of the room, giving a small bow with her head.

"Reggie! An unexpected pleasure." Kavan drew a smile on his face and forced himself not to flinch when he pumped the clammy hand of his visitor.

The top of Reginald Bragdon's bald head barely reached Kavan's shoulder and he tilted it back with an arrogant bearing to look Kavan in the eye. "You're kind beyond words to see me again. I admit I've grown accustomed to dropping in on you at all hours and will miss our impromptu visits. I'm not privy to the celebrations within the Church, but I certainly want to be among the first to congratulate you on your ascension to Archbishop when the time comes." Predator eyes, moist and marbled with red veins, scanned Kavan as if looking for a spot to sink sharp teeth.

"My appointment will not be formalized for several months yet, and no public announcements have been made."

"And Rome?" Bragdon asked, looking at the stack of boxes waiting to be filled.

"As always, you seem to know the inside bits of information. Rome is a temporary assignment and I've time before the movers come and pack me away." His voice did not betray his irritation. As head of Stormont's Special Branch, Bragdon had more than enough access to intelligence and didn't need to pester Kavan with inquiries on trivial details. Modeling himself after the U.S. Director of the FBI, J. Edgar Hoover, Bragdon's thirst to know everything hinted at a hunger for control.

Kavan continued. "Stormont's a thrumming hive since the Manchester bombing. What's it been now? Not even three weeks? Any breaks in the investigation yet? Papers are filled with speculation, but empty of news. Lord High Mayor of Belfast and a few worried parishioners have been busy wringing their hands on my doilies, as if I could help them." Habit and caution stopped him from telling Bragdon anything he wouldn't have found out on his own. Keeping what looked like open lines of communication worked in Kavan's favor. Recent events left him in a state of vertigo, his fate uncertain. He steered the conversation to familiar ground.

"Those IRA vermin think they can wage a war with trucks filled with explosives and win the hearts of the citizens by calling in warnings, protecting the populace in the same breath they use to kill." Bragdon took in a ragged breath, shuddering his jowls. "I don't know what I would do without your sage advice. You always have a way of bringing sanity to an insane situation. We're lucky to have you." His lips pulled back in a smile, showing rows of square and yellow teeth.

Kavan ushered him to a chair. "Nonsense. Just doing my part."

"Contacts at MI-5 say all leads on the truck and men seen leaving the scene have turned up nothing. One of our sources said those thugs are claiming victory because no one died. *Victory!*" The word spat out. "Brass balls on those goats." Bragdon's face flushed and his eyes focused in the distance. "Incompetent asses, each one. *I* want to be the one to crack that case. I have to be."

Kavan beamed his most disarming smile, knowing that when ambition combines with ruthlessness, dangerous men are made. "And you will be, of that I've no doubts. Tea?" He settled a cup on a saucer and poured steaming amber liquid over the two cubes of sugar he knew his visitor enjoyed.

"They're gloating about the terror they inflicted. What've you heard?"

The sudden question was one of Bragdon's interrogation techniques. Lull the suspect into thinking the conversation was going in one direction, then zing them with a pointed question and watch for the millisecond of facial twitches to get your answer. Kavan answered easily, his face impassive. "I knew nothing of the attack. I'm quite firm in my anti-violence position. I'm the last person the planners would confide in." He cooled his tea with a noisy sip.

"No solid leads. Nothing but speculation swirling about. Have you noticed," Bragdon asked, gesturing with his head toward the stack of newspapers, "that the story has slipped from page one? No more than a single column deep inside. Only the rag sheets carry on with speculation." He peered at Kavan over the rim of his cup.

Kavan pushed out his abdomen to fill his lungs, willing himself to be calm and to keep the color from rising in his cheeks. Respectable United Kingdom newspapers, such as *The Telegraph, Guardian,* and *Financial Times*, printed verifiable news and the Manchester bombing story was an embarrassment of paucity. The investigation was stumped with dead ends and leads that went nowhere. Less respectable papers, like the *The Sun* and *the Daily Mirror*, trumped fact with bald-faced lies, and stories of conspiracies and *femmes fatales* bloated their enviable circulation. "And speculation it is. Fine people have their lives ruined for a few pounds earned by shoddy reporters. I don't pay them any mind."

Bragdon puffed. "Oh, but you should. One rag hag has it the young American girl brought the explosives to England with her damned horses. It's the same girl accused of murdering that Gus Adams fellow you were boyhood chaps with. Jessica Wyeth."

Kavan's skin began to shimmer. He replenished his tea and raised the pot toward Bragdon, inquiring. Bragdon declined and reached for a biscuit. Kavan settled the pot back onto the tray. "I've heard of her, certainly. She was cleared of all charges when Magnus Connaught was indicted, and the case made her a celebrity. A cheap way to sell papers is to feather-dust with the facts. She was already a *cause célèbre* by any measure, and linking her name to the bombing is too tempting a way to sell newspapers to be ignored."

"True enough. Such an unfortunate mess." Bragdon's shoulders and head sagged in a pose of deep remorse. "Having to do with the murder of your friend, I thought you may have heard something."

"It's no secret I knew Gus Adams, but we lost contact years before he was killed." A lifetime of hearing confessions without showing judgment rehearsed his expression to a plain of serenity even while his heart pounded in his chest. Bragdon was fishing and calibrating Kavan's trustworthiness by lobbing facts or falsities and watching for that subconscious wince or tightened jaw that would expose a traitor. Did he know Gus and Kavan had shared the love of a remarkable woman? What would happen if he learned that the last words Gus ever spoke to Kavan were, *It's a girl*? "It was a sad surprise to learn of his horrific death. May God rest his soul. But why so much interest in this American?"

"You know I take what the tabloids say with more than a little salt, so I checked a few facts through my channels. In fact, Wyeth had traveled with crates of gear from Ireland to Manchester via private jet. That much is true, but it's unconfirmed what was in those crates. Just having her name crop up so soon after the murder allegations were settled was enough to dig further. The first flag for me was she had traveled to Gibraltar, a well-known terrorist hotbed, immediately upon leaving the States, before she went to Ireland." His lips smacked as if anticipating a meal.

"Seems a bit rash to be booted because of her poorly timed travels." *What did he know? More importantly, what was he trying to find?* "I heard she got tangled up with that Connaught fellow. That would be enough to put the Queen Mum on your watch list."

"Right you are! The jet she traveled on is owned by Connaught enterprises. I don't have to tell you what a sewage pit that Connaught tribe is. They've long been the money behind heinous crimes. First the grandfather, then the father. Now the son is wallowing in the shite-pit." He raised his hand to stop Kavan from speaking. "I used her association with the Connaughts to complete the petition for her departure."

"*You* issued the petition?"

"It was at the behest of the head of the investigation." Bragdon gave a sheepish grin behind tented fingers. "These networks criminals use are not to be ignored. Her passport had only recently been reissued—on false documents, no less!"

"*Re*-issued?"

"After Adams' murder, she faked her death. When she resurrected herself to clear her name, her passport had to be issued again. There was so much sympathy for her plight, not one official paused to consider the veracity of the supporting documents." He ejected the words, impatient to move on to his main point.

Kavan would not yield. "Many people have their passports reissued. I'm not an expert on such matters, but I see no crime here. So why did you *invite* her to leave?"

Bragdon's eyes narrowed. "Officially, she was invited to leave Northern Ireland because she had traveled on false documents. I expedited her departure for suspicion of, and affiliation with, terrorist activities."

Kavan kept his voice like warm honey. "Paranoia doesn't befit a strong country. If Norn Iron skittered at every shadow, our streets would be empty."

"But safer, for sure. I only have the power to investigate direct threats. Now that she's left the country, I don't have the resources to do more. That's why I mention her to you. The Irelands are a small community and the church even more so. If you could make some inquiries to learn more about her, I'd be indebted."

Kavan brought his cup to his lips and feigned sipping tea. "You said it yourself. She's no longer here and not a threat, direct or otherwise. What could you possibly learn about her that could affect the security of this country?"

Bragdon's expression, hooded and knowing, made Kavan's skin crawl. "The birth certificate her passport was issued on bothers me. Birth certificates are reissued, certainly, but bureaus are able to verify questionable certificates by researching hospital records and matching the information. It seems that one child was born to her parents of record, Margaret and Jim Wyeth of Hamilton, Massachusetts, and that was six years later."

Kavan interrupted. "A cursory search of *hospital* records leaves too much open to assumptions and rumors." He beamed. "I have it on rather good authority that life events can be documented by the church as well."

Bragdon flicked his hand, dismissing the alternative. "It didn't take much effort on my part to learn that Margaret Wyeth was Bridget Heinchon's sister!" His voice rose for emphasis. "After Heinchon's expulsion from Northern Ireland, she moved near Boston. If it's true Margaret had only one child, it's feasible Margaret helped hide Bridget's illegitimate daughter."

"Well now, I have to stop you there." Kavan flashed his most disarming smile. "You've nothing that says Bridget ever had a child." He paused, calculating, using his body posture to encourage Bragdon to do the same. "The Wyeth girl is in her late twenties. Bridget would have been in prison when she was born. Birthing a child behind bars would have definitely been part of an official record somewhere. If what you're saying is remotely true, then not only did no one in the prison system note a laboring woman, but an infant was spirited out of the country. I'd say you're grasping at straws."

Bragdon's face reddened and he sat forward in his seat. "The reissued birth certificate is a fake, meaning the passport is faked. That's a felony according to U.S. law, and entering our country with such is a felony here." He jabbed his finger into the palm of his hand, motions jerky with excitement. "You can see the impact this has on national security. We need to get to the bottom of this passport forgery and stop the free flow of terrorists!" He nearly shouted the last words.

"Reggie. You're a powerful man with a tremendous record of achievement. I've been honored to be in your counsel. I hope you've benefitted from my support." He spoke slowly, using the time to allow Bragdon to gather himself. He waited until Bragdon acknowledged agreement to his carefully spun words. "All you've said is nothing but conjecture. So Margaret and Bridget were sisters. That doesn't make them both terrorists and it certainly doesn't make the child one. A cursory search of hospital records is just that—cursory. You're too smart a man to pin your reputation on thin-to-no evidence. Spending your valuable resources on this girl takes you away from your core duties. Use your talents to find the heathens who bombed Manchester. That girl has had more scrutiny than Princess Diana's marriage. As most see it, her worst crime is her choice in men. Don't let this titillation distract you away from what you do best."

"Are you afraid of me digging deeper?" Bragdon moved his barrel-shaped chest forward in his chair. The droplets of spittle, trapped in the corners of his mouth, coalesced into strings of white foam. "You're connected to this girl by Gus Adams. You reached out to me to release Heinchon from Maghaberry prison for compassionate and humanitarian reasons as her health declined."

They had not spoken about Bridget's release in over twenty-three years, and Bragdon's whining tone dredged up the sludge of compromise Kavan had to swallow to set her free. In the years since her release, never did Kavan speak about *why* she was held. Bragdon was the prime power behind her incarceration. Any commoner knew then, as now, holding a person without leveling proper charges and without the process of a trial was ill-suited for a country that proclaimed to be strong and fearless in the face of words and ideas. Bridget's only crime was to organize resistance against oppressive policies of the United Kingdom. She dared to empower people to question why six counties of the island of Ireland had to be amputated and grafted as a limb under the crown. In the prime of her youth and beauty, she was branded a criminal and hunted like an animal. Firebombs lobbed at her by order of the military maimed her for life and nearly cost the life of her unborn child. The edges of Kavan's vision clouded and he focused inward to calm himself so his outward visage remained calm and placid. Nothing more could be done for the dead, but for the living he prayed for strength.

The hammering of his heart lessened and he resumed listening to Bragdon.

"You surprised me by convincing her to accept the condition that her freedom hinged on her immediate expulsion from Northern Ireland. I was happy to help, but where does she end up? Near Boston with Adams and her sister. All of these relationships are not a coincidence. I wager this Wyeth girl isn't who she says she is, and she has the support of more than just the Connaught clan. I want to find out all I can about her." On that, he rose, looked Kavan in the eye. "And I will." He gave his good-byes with a flourish Kavan found nauseating.

Kavan remained motionless. Jessica Wyeth, suspected terrorist, was nothing of the sort. He should know. She was his daughter.

The teacup rattled on its saucer as he placed it down on the tray. The room felt small as he paced the carpeted floor. Bragdon was on the scent and Kavan could feel the hunt close in around him. Everything Kavan had worked for was in jeopardy. The scandal of being a father was one thing. Bedding a denounced terrorist of the IRA was another, and then having that child be the Bonnie to Northern Ireland's Clyde was ruinous. Every word he had ever uttered in support or condemnation of terrorist violence would come into question. The cease-fires he had brokered, the compromises he had mediated, and the future peace talks—among Sinn Fein and all other political parties of Northern Ireland, government representatives of both Irelands and the United Kingdom—would disintegrate like the ash of a cigarette.

His whole life's work and the loss of the love of his life would be for nothing.

16

Could it be only a few days ago that he had assured Jessica he had made peace with the consequences if his paternity was exposed? They had met in the Holy Cross Convent, on the rocky coast of the North Sea, just outside of Belfast. Jessica's birthplace. The nuns could tend to the matter of birth, but not her mother's injuries. They sobbed when circumstance forced them to deliver Bridget into the hands of the authorities at the hospital equipped to save her life. The nuns' vow of silence was never more challenged nor more valued.

Bragdon's homing in on the truth unsettled him. Jessica had the support of a powerful network within the church to help Gus spirit her out of the country to a new life in America. The rumors of using the gear of horses to transport bombs to Manchester were not that farfetched. Gus had used his experience in transatlantic horse transports and connections in shipping and customs to bring the infant Jessica into the waiting arms of her Aunt Margaret. The plan was hatched and executed without anyone outside of their tight circle knowing the truth; a pregnancy faked in the U.S., a newborn smuggled out of Northern Ireland. Kavan's fingers grew icy as he acknowledged that the more people who knew the truth, the more vulnerable he became.

Once tormented, he had confessed his paternity to men inside the church who had vowed to protect his privacy. Together they prayed, and as one they determined his sin was merely to experience the whole of human love with a woman who gave herself freely to him without siphoning him from the church. Worse scandal had touched other priests. Their reprehensible acts were inflicted on children unable to protect themselves. Those priests had survived scandal and retained their titles, although their careers derailed and hopes for better futures imploded. Kavan's steady presence, good looks, and otherwise spotless record brought him to the attention of cardinals who supported his rise through the ranks. Fatherhood made him a better priest as he understood that sin often flowed from a well of good. He counseled sinners and mediated strife with insight and care as no other priest before him did. His was the fastest ascension to archbishop in generations.

He wanted Rome. He deserved it. The tart taste of ambition coated his mouth.

What could happen to his daughter? Northern Ireland deported her and authorities dusted their hands of the matter. The paranoid and unsubstantiated reaction would be dealt a lethal blow by the legal teams Connaught-the-younger no doubt had working on it. An

American citizen deported on the basis of innuendo and fear? *Bosh*! If word leaked that she was the child of Bridget Heinchon, considered a subversive and feared by the British, the conspiracy mongers would become insatiable. Add the fact that her father is the priest long loved by both sides for his even-handed management of serpentine politics, and a feeding frenzy of epic proportions would ensue. Only heads rolling in the streets would satisfy the mobs. His would be the first. Hers the second.

Bragdon was right. Jessica's passport—issued by the United States to evidence her American citizenship—was a fake. Born in Northern Ireland to citizens of Northern Ireland, only the blood of her homeland flowed through her veins. Any proceedings—with lawyers, courts, and outside officials—risked too many questions. With her mother formally deported, was his daughter a woman without a country? He and Bridget never considered this possibility when they planned her life. What if his network failed him? What if Bridget's and his careful plans unraveled and became a noose instead of a safety net?

But his child had placed her own head in that noose. Her relationship with Michael Connaught was nothing he could have foreseen. She had the power to live her life as she wanted, yet she allowed the gossamer threads of the Connaught's sticky web to hold her fast. The thought that he may have guided her to the illusion of safety goaded him. What choice did he have? Then or now?

His life hung in the balance of her choices. The same was true for the hundreds of people who trusted him with their souls.

He stopped pacing and listened to the sounds of his flat. The mantel clock chimed six o'clock, signaling Rosalie's departure for the day. He waited until he heard the click of the outside door before he walked down the hallway to his bedroom, stepping around half-filled boxes earmarked for Rome. Shutting the door quietly behind him, he drew the shades and curtains. Reaching his hand between the mattress and box spring, he felt for the packet of letters. The sight of Bridget's careful handwriting warmed him as it always did.

A light powdery scent drifted from the pages. He untied each packet, slipped the brittle and yellowed pages from their envelopes, and ran his finger over the careful script, trying to absorb the last of the life force of the author through his skin. He passed the next hours reading as the memories of a younger man flowed over him and through him. At times he laughed aloud, other times he wicked away a tear with a corner of his cassock. When finished, he pressed each letter to his lips and held it there, longing for the moist warmth of her skin, feeling only the dry scratch of paper.

It was well past midnight when he poured himself a final Scotch, neat, and raised a glass to the pile of papers in the hearth.

He sipped the smoky liquid as he watched the flames lick the pages and turn his memories to dust.

Thursday, July 4, 1996
Beacon Hill
Boston, Massachusetts

THE RESIDENTS OF Boston's Beacon Hill didn't care if their homes had been built on a lowly cow pasture or that part of their hill was used by their forefathers to fill in the tidal swamp that became Back Bay. Brick townhouses hugged narrow streets patched with layers of asphalt over cobblestones. Baskets of fuchsias and ivy hung from streetlights made to look like the quaint gas lamps of long ago. Palladium windows, thick with layers of preservation and paint, graced the top jams of oak doors. Whatever the residents needed to keep their conclave current and safe, the Commonwealth of Massachusetts would provide through metropolitan renewal projects, historic preservation, or private grants. No project was so big or expensive that it would not be funded by lawmakers whose ancestral roots dated back as far as the swamp.

William Wyeth sipped his gin and tonic—tall, extra lime, cracked ice—and looked out over the Charles River. Perched on the most prominent point of Beacon Hill, William could see a flotilla of sailboats from the city's recreation department drift with limp sails close to the barge filled with fireworks for the evening's celebration. Boats of all colors clogged the river jockeying for the perfect vantage point. Mothers and nannies pushed strollers laden with picnic items along the Esplanade. Fathers and boyfriends hurried toward the Hatch Shell looking for a spot to listen to the Boston Pops and see the timed display of Roman Candles, Ground Spinners, Peonies, and Horse Tails. Storrow Drive had closed to traffic, altering the sounds of the city that drifted up to William's rooftop terrace. He set his glass down on a wrought iron table, paint peeling in rusted flakes, and tugged his shirtsleeve over his pale wrist. He had time for a refill or two before the sun set and the fireworks began.

For all the history his view held, today's scene looked surprisingly new to him. The papers were alight with news that Boston's most infamous citizen had returned to the States. His phone had not stopped ringing, but he resolved not to answer it until he knew which manner to adopt. Was he the relieved uncle, happy that his brother's daughter was safe? Was he the cautious and protective brother incensed that his patrician family had been victimized by a series of horrible crimes? Was he the concerned everyman, wanting to comfort a woman he had known since birth? He didn't know how to play his role, but knew his future depended upon it.

The last thing he wanted his neighbors, let alone any reporters, to get wind of was that he wished Jessica Wyeth had stayed dead.

He grabbed his glass, yanked too hard on the roof deck door, and cursed when the doorknob came off in his hand. He jimmied it back on, finished his drink in one gulp, and headed down the stairs, wooden treads creaking under his weight. As he rounded the corner to descend to the second floor, the bedroom door on the right flew open. Heavy curtains inside the room were drawn against the late afternoon sun.

Connor Battington looked in no mood for niceties. His hair rioted in greasy spikes and his button-down oxford shirt was barely buttoned or down and bunched under his armpits. Tiny blue lobsters marched across his boxers. "Oh, shit. It's you."

William's upper lip curled into a smile. He made a show of glancing at his watch. "Good morning to you, too, Mr. Sunshine. Waking in time for cocktails, I see."

Connor braced himself against the jam, resting his head on his forearm. "Those fucking stairs make the whole place shake. Hell of a racket to wake up to."

William smirked. "I'd be happy to move your room to the servants' quarters in the cellar. It's much quieter and you won't have to deal with that pesky afternoon sunlight."

"When are you going to get them fixed?"

William bent and retrieved a gray sock and dangled it in the air. Connor's pinched expression proved that eyes the color of claret could function outside of low-lit bars. "When I don't have to pick up after you anymore."

Connor snatched the sock, studied it for a moment, and tossed it on the ground. "Not mine," he said and shut the door.

I'll teach that little snot a lesson, William thought, but quickly lamented that hoisting his tenant out to the street would have to wait. He continued down the stairs to the front hallway. The day's newspapers lay strewn on the oriental carpet. Worn hand-knotted fringe adjacent to a faded oval patch evidenced generations of visitors entering through the massive door. A pair of crystal sconces flanked a gold-framed mirror hanging above a marble-topped table. Prisms, milky with grime, surrounded dusty candles with untouched wicks. A silver dish, a gift from silversmith Paul Revere to some family member or another, which once collected calling cards, sat tarnished and empty. Takeout menus yellowed in the corner.

Stooping to gather the newspapers made his head throb. Light coming through the transom was too dim to read by, so he shuffled his way to the living room. The formal room was designed to surround visitors with enough comfort to leave little question of how privileged they were to sit there. Blue and white Delft tiles surrounded the hearth, framing the brick opening with scenes of windmills and dykes. Bookcases, once jammed with first editions and photographs, sagged precariously forward. The Seth Thomas mantel clock ticked its arrhythmic beat and displayed a time no one paid attention to anymore. Pictures filled every available wall space. Larger paintings dominated the center of the walls. Smaller ones dotted down their sides and filled the spaces above doors. Lesser-known works of John Singleton Copley graced the walls alongside pieces by Winslow Homer. Rectangles—visible only by the grimy shadow bordering vibrant wallpaper, dotted the wall or loomed nearly hidden behind a tall lamp—revealed spaces where art once hung.

Family portraits showed the same room—dust and cobweb free—with children, aunts, uncles, cousins crowded around. Other photos showed the Wyeth boys on either side of their father during their prep school days at Exeter. Eight photos displayed a progression of years from Jim's freshman year to William's senior. Jim, the oldest son, stood on the right, William the left. Gradually Jim's round and child-like face morphed into a study of angular adolescent indignity at being posed. Jim stood perceptibly farther away from him and their father each year, the distance evidencing the growing gap in their worldviews. Pictures of Jim stopped after that. Except for one.

The photo, taken at Christmastime, showed Margaret and Jim standing arm-in-arm, with their daughters Erin and Jessica seated in front of them on a large tufted ottoman. Margaret wore a long red plaid skirt and white blouse, the toddler Erin a red plaid romper, and eight-year-old Jessica a matching jumper, starched white shirt with a Peter Pan collar, and polished Mary Janes. The fact that Jim's tie was the same plaid made William grunt with satisfaction. Jim always did know how to put on the proper Wyeth face for the public. The Christmas tableau was also the only image of Margaret that graced the shelves, even though she had lived in this townhome since she had turned fifteen. Straight off the boat, she had no idea being a nanny and living in a moldy basement marked her as low class. Jim could not have pissed off his father more with his marriage to a servant girl than if he had lost the family fortune shooting craps. Well, almost. William should know. He was glad their father was long dead.

He continued to scan the shelves, searching for a picture of himself with his niece. The back of his mind played with the fact that having photographic proof of their bond could prove useful. The only one he had was of him holding an infant Erin. A six-year-old Jessica stood beside him, body angled away as if repelled by his presence. Her face closed in a frown, with clenched fists pressed to her thighs. Her bright blue eyes and the set of her jaw easily identified her as the same woman in the day's papers. His face, not yet bloated by drink and weathered by sun, was less recognizable; but the family resemblance to Jim would be enough proof of family ties. He huffed on the glass and dusted their faces on his butt.

Returning his attention to the day's papers, he switched on the light and scanned the headlines. The most recent editions of the *Boston Herald* and *Phoenix* blared about some murder in Dorchester. Interior stories provided nothing more, and he threw the papers to the floor, kicking them aside with impatience. He grabbed the day's edition of the *Globe*, slipped it out of its plastic sleeve, and settled deeper into the sofa. William snapped the paper open and needed to look no further than the front page.

JESSICA WYETH GROUNDED
Special by *Boston Globe* correspondent Colleen Shaunessy-Carillo

LOUISVILLE, Ky (Associated Press) - Jessica Wyeth, known to many as the Murdering Heiress, resurfaced at the International Airport in Louisville, Kentucky, where she has been detained by immigration and customs authorities.

Newspaper accounts in the United Kingdom speculate Wyeth's presence at a private steeplechase event in the United Kingdom is tied to the recent bombing at the Arndale Shopping Mall in Manchester, Eng-

land. The Irish Republican Army has claimed responsibility, but no arrests have been made. British authorities continue to investigate.

Wyeth was expelled from Northern Ireland on suspicions linking her to the transport of the explosives used in the bombing, allegations which American authorities decline to comment on. Sources state Wyeth refuses to leave the private jet she arrived on due to concern of being remanded into custody if she disembarks.

Wyeth's notoriety began nearly eight years ago when top thoroughbred trainer and manager of the renowned Wyeth's Worldwind Farms, Gilchrist "Gus" Adams, was found brutally slain at her family's training facility in Hamilton, Massachusetts. No formal charges were brought against Wyeth, the primary suspect in the murder, as she was presumed dead in a tavern explosion days afterward.

The case of the Murdering Heiress should have faded from memory. Instead, Wyeth resurfaced in Boston in December of last year. She was the subject of one of the biggest manhunts in the city's history as reports of her appearance were confirmed by the attorney general at the time, the late Owen Shea.

In a stunning turn of events, she had contacted Attorney General Shea with information that led to a grand jury indicting Magnus Mikevy Connaught for Adams' murder. Connaught's indictment cleared Wyeth of homicide suspicions. Connaught, a successful businessman loved by Boston's Irish community, died from complications of a lengthy illness shortly after his indictment. His death ceased all court proceedings related to Adams' murder. Without the exacting fact discovery and disclosures which would have occurred during a trial, some still question Wyeth's innocence and Connaught's indictment.

Connaught was the rumored head of a powerful organized crime syndicate known to insiders as The Charity. The sprawling multinational network, comprised of both war- and peace-related enterprises, has long been suspected as the key funding mechanism behind the terrorist activities of many groups, most notably the Irish Republican Army.

Attorney General Shea's grizzly murder in Boston shortly after Connaught's indictment is considered by local law enforcement officials to be retribution.

Wyeth's involvement and connections to organized crime have come back into question. After her name was cleared, Wyeth again disappeared from sight earlier this year. Sources close to British authorities claim her reappearance in the proximity of the Manchester, England bombing is not a simple coincidence.

Details of Wyeth's life on the run while presumed dead are few. What is known is that she used a variety of names and identities to stay hidden from authorities. Most sources indicate she traveled extensively in the western United States, working seasonally on ranches or at ski areas. She was recognized early last fall after winning an equestrian event in the wealthy enclave of Perc, Kentucky.

Wyeth's fame continued to grow despite her attempts to remain out of the public eye, an act made more complicated by her purported relationship with Magnus Connaught's son, Michael. The younger Connaught is said to have taken over running the family's global enterprises. Whether he follows in his father's footsteps or breaks free from his family's legacy remains to be seen.

Sources familiar with the situation state that Wyeth could return to Boston. Calls to family members to confirm her return have remained unanswered.

William shifted on the lumpy cushion, silently cursing Duncan Phyfe. He folded the page over on itself, careful not to err as he tore out the story.

"What to do. What to do," he muttered to himself as he tapped his fingers against the sofa's winged arms.

The afternoon hours slid by as William read and re-read every shred of information he could find about Jessica and the Connaught clan. He cursed the money he had spent to claim his brother's estate as his own. The maddening array of blind trusts and hidden accounts thwarted his every turn. Private investigators. Lawyers. Financial advisors and financial sleuths. His fingers itched at the closeness of the millions. Hell, he even used psychics to suss out what the obstacles were. Should it have been that hard? He could have saved himself a bundle if he had known she was going to pop back into her life with neon lights and fireworks showing her whereabouts.

The story carried a picture of Jessica, laughing, arms around the neck of a horse. He jabbed his index finger into her eyes and gouged.

A knock on the front door—a powerful hammering of a lion-gripped ring against a tarnished brass plate—brought him out of his reverie. He sat motionless for a moment until he grabbed the file and scuffed to the kitchen knowing the shades and curtains protected his motions from discovery. Weeks of dishes filled the sink. A stench of rotted food hovered in a nearly visible cloud. He rested an ice cube in his hand and cracked it with the back of a spoon, the process repeated until the glass brimmed with small chunks. Beefeaters and a splash of tonic followed. He shrugged when the only lime he could find was shriveled and brown and rolled around in the crisper with solid thuds. He jabbed a hole in its rind and pressed a few drops of liquid into his glass. After taking a long pull, he sifted through his file, but he was well familiar with its contents.

Jessica Wyeth's problems were of no concern to him.

Right?

This time the knock came from the courtyard door. A shadowed head bobbed on the other side of the transom. Sheer curtains blurred details. He tried to hide a little longer and didn't answer. The rapping increased in tempo and force.

"Mr. Wyeth? Is that you? My name is Colleen Shaunessy-Carillo. I'm a reporter with the *Boston Globe*. I'd like to speak with you about your niece."

He froze.

"Mr. Wyeth? You remember me. We've spoken before."

With incremental movements, he drained his glass.

"I can see you standing by the sink. Your niece is in some kind of trouble. She needs your help. Please, can I speak with you? Off the record?"

Avoidance was futile. He tucked in his shirttail, rubbed his face with his hands, and pressed his hair down, frustrated what little of it demanded to cluster in greasy spikes. He poured another drink on the remains of the last and opened the door.

"Ms. Shaunessy-Carillo. The pleasure is all mine."

Colleen looked up at him with round milk-chocolate eyes. A linen shell the color of oatmeal over a black knee-length skirt exuded a professional air. Sweat plastered a strand of dark hair to her cheek. Ballet flats did nothing for her legs and less for her height. Even mile-high stilettos would not have brought her to his eye level. Trembling hands juggled a notebook and recorder. Her green canvas messenger bag, of the cheap military surplus variety, hung diagonally on a mesh strap from shoulder to hip.

He remained in the doorway, signaling she was to go no farther, and blocked her view inside.

She sighed with relief. "Thank goodness you're home. I've been trying to reach you for days."

He raised his eyebrows in response.

"You might not have heard the news. Your niece has been expelled from Northern Ireland and the U.S. is considering whether or not to allow her reentry. Colleagues of mine in Kentucky say she's stuck on a private jet."

He stifled a smirk. "Is that right? I hadn't heard." With his right hand, he flicked the file closed.

Colleen's eyes followed the movement. "Newspapers are full of speculation, but I wondered if she had reached out to you."

"No. Why would she?"

"You're family, of course. Being supported by someone of your stature would be helpful. I can bring you to her. She doesn't have any support. She may need guidance."

"Guidance? Hardly. She's a grown woman with a mind of her own."

"It's her mind some people are worried about."

"If you're here to tell me news I don't care about or to dig around for salient gossip, I'm afraid you're wasting your time." He moved to close the door.

The door stuck on her propped-up toes. "What are the odds that she clears her name of murder and runs smack into the middle of the very organization that ruined her life to begin with?"

William shook his head. He well recalled the wild-eyed and hollow-cheeked wisp of last winter's paparazzi photos when Jessica first reappeared. They showed a stark departure from the vibrant child he once knew. "I only remember her as a beautiful young child, full of life and happiness. I'm sorry, but you're wasting my time and yours."

"Give me one minute. If you're interested, give me another five and I promise to be direct."

He sniffed with amusement. Being direct was not one of her lesser skills. "Thirty seconds. What's this nonsense about her mind? I'll not have the Wyeth name associated with harmful innuendo."

"I have access to the country's foremost experts on psychological trauma. I've spoken with everyone from Post Traumatic Stress Disorder experts to psychiatrists who've worked on the Patty Hearst case."

"Patty Hearst? I've not heard that name in years. Wasn't she the publishing tycoon's daughter who was kidnapped by the Symbionese Liberation Army and surfaced a year later helping her captors rob a bank?"

"Yes. The doctors I've spoken with say Jessica's ripe for the picking for that kind of mind control. Certain things have to happen for a person to be indoctrinated into a terrorist network. Many psychologists believe brainwashing techniques are similar to techniques used in prisoner interrogation. Most commonly the practice is referred to as thought reform."

"Brainwashing? Thought reform?" He touched Colleen's elbow and tried to guide her to the steps. "These are words for fiction writers and cults. I'll not be a part of this."

She shook her arm free. "Just hear me out. Please. Give me five minutes. If you still think I'm grasping at straws, fine. I'll leave and not bother you again."

"Ever?"

She grimaced and shifted her messenger bag. "Maybe not forever, but I'll agree to call first."

She's got spunk, he mused, a quality he detested. "Okay. I'll listen."

"The first step is to isolate the target. This happened when Patty Hearst was kidnapped and cut off from everything she knew. For Jessica, she cut herself off from her identity by hiding to avoid arrest for murder. Think about it. Parents? Dead. Sister? Dead. Aunt? Dead. Anyone who could have helped her was either dead or corrupt. Isolation produces introspection, confusion, and a distorted sense of reality. She was already softened by this experience when she met Connaught. Are you familiar with him?"

William searched the ceiling for an answer. "Connaught? Isn't that the fellow who was finally indicted for the Gus Adams murder?"

"That was Magnus. I'm talking about Michael, his *son*."

His lips pursed in thought. "I seem to recall hearing about the son." He tucked his shirttail into his trousers. A droplet of moisture slid down the side of his gin and tonic, inviting him in. His mouth twitched. "Go on."

"Okay. So she's been traumatized and somehow rallies enough to get her name cleared. What's the first thing she does? She enters a relationship with the son."

"Relationship?"

She rummaged through her bag and retrieved two pictures of Jessica and Michael. The first was at a fall event, the foliage accented their formal attire and decorations of a jockey statue holding a lantern exposed Kentucky roots. The next was more recently taken at Aintree Racecourse after the steeplechase. Jessica stood slightly behind Michael. His arm was in front of her, as if stopping her from moving away.

She continued. "I think he offers her the appearance of protection. Her isolation from community continued when he brought her to Ireland." She put the photographs back inside her bag. "The next step is induced dependency. This is where all security and sense of self is molded around the captor. Special talents are devalued to confuse the victim or are commandeered for the benefit of the captor. Connaught is definitely supporting her horse habit, thereby increasing her dependency on him. Plus, she's surrounded by bodyguards, making it impossible for anyone outside of Connaught's circle to reach her. No doubt, the only thing she's experiencing and hearing is what he wants her to experience and hear. He's controlling every minute of her life."

"What does all this do to a person's memory? Surely they don't forget who they once were or their entire life's circumstance. Wouldn't they reach out to past friends or family?"

"Trauma can erase or suppress memory and influences can change them. Once dependency is complete, the last piece is dread. This comes from fearing what happens to her when she steps outside his bubble. Anything she does outside of his influence is met with some kind of detriment. If she steps out of line, she's hounded by press or is at risk of harm by disenfranchised members of his father's organization. She becomes dependent. Reasonable and sensible actions trigger unreasonable and escalating reactions. She begins to dread interacting with institutions which could help her. Only extreme measures remain. Who knows what kind of experiences she's had because of him."

Colleen stepped back and eyed him expectantly.

"This is all very amusing, but I fail to see why my niece would be the target of such unfathomable measures."

"I can't be silent on this any longer." She stopped, mouth screwed shut around a thought she would not say. After a moment's deliberation, she continued. "She's clearly being manipulated and being used as a shield to deflect attention from his activities. There's been speculation in some tabloids that she was on the flight that likely carried the explosives for the Manchester bombing. The jets she traveled on were owned by one of Connaught's enterprises—MMC, Ltd., a sprawling multinational behemoth. Officials inside the U.K. believe his organization used her and her horse transports to carry out a terrorist attack. Even if she was completely unaware, she'll have an impossible time proving her innocence if any hard evidence surfaces that she knowingly participated in such transport. Think of it, she leaves the States to be with the ringleader of an organized crime group. Maybe she knew about his connections, maybe she didn't. It doesn't matter because she's physically present at each stage of the planning and the final attack. The circumstantial evidence is damning, and she's already being deemed culpable. Her case would be career making for anyone who arrests her and successfully prosecutes."

She paused, expression melting to a beseeching expression. "She'd have to be crazy to fall for a guy whose father destroyed her family and whose family businesses support such crime."

"But to what end?"

"Maybe Michael wants to expand the family business. The father pulled the strings for global terrorist groups. He didn't stop at the IRA and his influence didn't stop at writing checks. Magnus created terrorists by finding and training individuals willing to die for a cause. But Magnus was old school and his son is savvy, visionary, and smart. American extremists—especially beautiful blond ones—are hard to find."

All of the doubts of the past days and months disappeared as a switch flipped in his head. He dropped his chin to his chest and let his shoulders sag. "I'm beside myself with worry about how to help her."

"Have you contacted her?"

"No. I've not spoken with my niece in quite some time."

"Why not?"

William's eyes narrowed before he forced them to widen. "I've tried many times, but—as you can imagine—she's been difficult to reach." His fingers twitched toward the waiting cocktail. "But why do you care? You've never met her."

Colleen hoisted the messenger bag to her front. Papers bulged from every pocket. "I have requests for updates from every news agency in the country, which is why I want to bring you to her. People are claiming they're witnesses to her erratic behavior. Her whole story is being told by people who never knew her, so no one is hearing the truth." Her eyes rounded to chocolate pools. "I . . . I can't stop thinking about this."

Neither could he, but that tidbit he'd keep to himself. A world of alternatives opened just when he thought he had nothing left.

He swore he saw a well of tears. That was the first time he noticed the dark circles under her eyes. "Ms. Shaunes–"

"Colleen. Please call me Colleen."

"Colleen," he said, name coming out slowly with discomfort, "As I said, my niece is a grown woman, free and able to make her own decisions. Generations of Wyeths have lived in this very home that she herself visited as a child, albeit infrequently. She knows how to contact me and she hasn't. I really don't understand how I can help her or you."

Colleen's lips pressed into a red slash across her face. "That doesn't surprise me. In fact, it fits the scenario I've described. She must be about ready to crack."

"I don't see how this involves you or how the *Globe* could allow you to spend this much time on a story that is more suited for the *National Enquirer*."

She looked down at her feet. "I'm here because she's your brother's daughter. You're her only family. You have a responsibility to reach out to her and reconnect her to reality."

"As I said, I don't know how to reach her."

"I do. I have a contact in security at the airport where she is now."

He tried to hide his surprise. He could be face-to-face with his niece in a matter of hours—if he wanted to be. "And what do you want in return for this act of family togetherness?" Air filled his upper chest, and hovered there, suspended.

"Exclusive rights. Photos, video, interviews. I get first dibs."

He deflated. "I'm sorry. I really don't th–"

"And for you? Fees. The *Globe* won't pay for stories, but I know organizations that will pay. Big."

William looked down the length of his nose at Colleen. "I could take offense at your implication, Ms. Shaunessy-Carillo. I hardly think implying my story is something that could be purchased is going to make working together feasible."

As quickly as Colleen stammered, she composed herself. She smoothed back the damp tendril of hair, absently twirling it around her index finger. "I didn't mean to imply that your motives for speaking with us could be monetarily driven. Such a thing would only tarnish the Wyeth name you've so judiciously protected." She fidgeted with the flap on the canvas bag. Her eyes moved from looking at her hands to staring directly into his face. "I only meant to say that your time is very valuable and your family name stands for something. You are on the boards of different community organizations. I'm thinking that *donations* made to those groups in your name might help balance some of the time you'd spend discussing your niece and offset any ill will that may start to swirl. Also, perhaps donations to the private charities and non-profits that you head could be of benefit. Bolstering your position in the community can only help you." She opened the top of her bag as far as the canvas would stretch. Inside were files of photographs, notes, camera, and voice recorder. "I've done a lot of research on the Wyeth family, but no one wants to hear it from me. I'm sure you'd want to clear up any inconsistencies with a book of your own. Maybe two. I'd bet publishers would clamor for it."

"I simply don't see how I–"

"—and advances. Publishers would pay advances for this story. Big ones."

He grabbed his cocktail and raised it in salute. "Well now. Here's to protecting the Wyeth family name."

JESSICA SNAPPED OFF the TV as soon as she saw her face promoting the upcoming evening news. Every channel carried some form of her story. Local stations showed the line of news vans on the airport access road, telescoping antennae and satellite dishes crisscrossing one another. Since her story was not considered hard news, national coverage focused on celebrities affiliated with organized crime and people-on-the-street interviews. She was relieved to hear some people supported her right to travel as she wished and they admonished the press to leave her alone. Others fretted over the risk she posed and gave the evening's money shot of mothers hugging their children, shielding them from the murderer roaming free. And a terrorist? Is anywhere safe?

Analysts spun her story in any way they could to keep the camera on them. In little more than forty-eight hours, her story had saturated the news cycle. Few outlets touched on the international policies keeping her in limbo.

Agitated, she stood up too fast and struck her head against the curved walls of the fuselage. She was caged aboard the jet, but her feeling was nothing compared to how trapped she felt by circumstance. She hadn't asked for any of this and wanted the nightmare to go away. Now.

First Officer Andrews placed a tray on a stand with a Caesar salad and grilled chicken and a glass of white wine. His white shirt was still crisp and his manner upbeat. "The captain and Mr. Devins have gone forth into the land of the Burren, Miss Jessica. They've decided to brave the wilds and take care of airport business. Usually, only one of us is needed for that, but we thought it best for no one to be alone. Did'ye see them on the news? Swarmed as soon as they hit the terminal, they were. Flies to honey, at that."

"I'm so sorry about all of this. I had no idea my arrival would trigger a frenzy."

Andrews raised his hand, palm out. "Enough now. We don't take your sorries. It's all a bit of a romp for us. Those boggers with their cameras think they're all that, but a manky bunch they are." He pushed his chin up with his index finger and turned his face to profile. "How do you think your American friends will take to me? My mug's ready for Hollywood, don't you think?"

The first smile she had in a day tugged at the corners of her mouth. "I think they'll find you quite dashing." Daylight outlined the drawn shades on each window. Additional light came from long tracks folded into the ceiling, giving everything a pinkish tinge. "You'll have a chance to get out, though, won't you? Kentucky is beautiful. If you've never seen it, you should take some time to explore."

"Och. Flyin' over this countryside will be enough for me. Your Master Connaught's requested one of us to be aboard with you at all times, and he's hired additional security. Snug as bugs we are." With efficient movements, he spread a white tablecloth on a small table and placed the salad, wine, and silverware next to a bouquet of pink snapdragons, daisies, and black-eyed Susans. "You won't be needing for anything, he'll make sure of that. And the crew is happy to be of service."

The pager in his breast pocket began to vibrate. He looked at the screen and opened the hatch. Immediately, the high whir of idling jet engines and loud voices filled the cabin. The captain and Devins entered looking wilted and frazzled from the combination of the humid Kentucky heat and American journalism at its hungriest.

"Jaysus! I've not experienced the likes of that and I shan't want to again," Captain Laramie said as she straightened herself with a tug on her lapels. "This should all be a memory for you soon enough." She looked over Jessica's head to Andrews. "We need to be serviced and fueled and are cleared to leave once we're ready." Her eyes darted around the cabin and out to the tarmac. Her hands—that typically fell calmly to her sides—wrung one another, reddening her skin. "You've got yourself a visitor."

A man stepped into the cabin. He did not offer his hand in greeting and only uttered, "Declan Cleary."

The captain bustled. "Mr. Cleary's arrived from Boston. I'm told he's the man who can help."

Instinct, or something else, made Jessica put as much distance between herself and the visitor as she could in the tight quarters. She'd seen too many men preen themselves with self-importance to let her guard down now. Declan looked every bit the ambitious attorney on the rise. His dark auburn hair and softly mottled complexion hinted at an Irish ancestry if his name wasn't enough. He held his ground like he owned every mile below his feet and above his head.

Her throat closed and eyes heated. With effort, she pulled her stare away from Declan to interrogate the captain. "Told? By who?"

"Mr. Connaught himself before we left Belfast. He gave me Mr. Cleary's number with orders that if there was trouble when we landed, I was to contact Mr. Cleary first off." The calm and unflappable captain looked ready to faint.

"Mr. Cleary." Jessica's greeting hit the right note of cold. "You need to explain all of this."

"Your entrance to the States is being questioned for security reasons. No one questions if you can leave as you are considered a passenger on a jet that is being refueled and serviced. Typical courtesy for all international flights. An offshore safe haven has been arranged for you."

Jessica recoiled in surprise. "What is it those . . . those *immigration* agents think they have on me? I'm not going anywhere until I talk to M-Michael. They think they know what they're doing blocking my return, but trust me, they don't." The words came out in halting spurts as the reality of her confinement firmed. Her bravado faltered. "Michael will have their heads."

"Maybe so, but not before they have a go at you first. Michael Connaught wants me to act as your counsel . . . just in case."

"Just in case of *what*?" The sides of the cabin closed in on her. What once felt like an oasis of calm and security took on a prison-like feel with her one route of escape blocked and guarded. "I've done nothing wrong," she said aloud, but inside her heart the words circled, *except be born.*

Declan motioned toward the tarmac and the crowd pressing against the fence. "Do you think that matters?"

Did it? She was raised to share her toys and to ask permission to stay out past curfew. The worst thing she ever did was skip school a few times. Well, quite a few times, actually. Not to get high behind the barn, but to have as many hours of riding in a day as she could.

Monthly minutes in a confessional—kneeling and confessing her four cuss words, five stolen cookies—and giving penance of ten *Our Fathers* and ten *Hail, Marys*—to satisfy Bridget that her cleansed soul would enter heaven. Did all that matter?

"Hell, yes. It matters."

He glanced at his watch and his mouth screwed up to one side, making it clear explaining more was a waste of his time. He hammered at facts that sealed her fate and had begun the series of events that brought them to this moment. "Your circumstance, affiliations, and proximity to a criminal element were enough to raise eyebrows. Northern Ireland is especially sensitive to anyone who could be planning to do them harm. You triggered three important alarms." He raised his index finger. "One," he focused on his task, confident he had her full attention.

Jessica's eyes moved from his finger to the starched white cuff secured with cufflinks monogrammed with "DC," and up a navy sleeve.

He continued. "Routine protocols flagged your passport as having been newly issued within six months of a hostile event. Two," he raised a second finger.

Her look continued to his perfectly tailored lapels and a white pocket square. A free-spirited salmon-colored tie clashed with his body-contouring suit. His height forced him to bend his head forward in the cabin to a stooped and humbled position. The posture didn't suit him.

"You had traveled to areas known for Irish Republican Army activity prior to your arrival in the Irelands." When she raised her eyebrows in question, he answered, "Your visit with Mr. Connaught in Gibraltar."

Her skin flushed at the memories of a brief and beach-filled vacation.

He continued, "And three," he said, holding his pinky down with his thumb.

Jessica allowed herself to look at his face. Irises the color of peat were framed with thick lashes and betrayed no hint of emotion. He didn't blink.

He finished his enumeration. "Officials in the Special Branch of Stormont uncovered information indicating issues with your passport. These factors triggered an investigation. I'm afraid your affiliation with Mr. Connaught tipped the scales to expulsion."

She found her voice. "Being expelled from Northern Ireland has nothing to do with my re-entry to the States." In a smaller voice she added, "Right?"

"The summer Olympics begin in Atlanta in a little over two weeks. International security is in overdrive. In the past, the United States had identified and issued diplomatic warnings on IRA operatives who returned to the United Kingdom, only to have them walk off planes or boats and never to be seen again. This show of force sends a message to the international community that information received through intelligence channels will be taken seriously. I doubt they have any criminally damning evidence or other reason to deport you. If they did, they would have forcefully boarded and taken you into custody. Most of what you're seeing now is posturing, pure and simple."

Anger pushed blood into her cheeks. "*Posturing*? You're telling me that the United States government sent officers for a photo op based on nothing more than rumors?"

"Without knowing exactly what information they have, I believe your celebrity is being used to further their agenda. I doubt they care who you are, except your situation fits their current political needs well. They know your face is going to sell papers and any news associated with you will penetrate deep into the populace. Novel news angles are exploited in the run-up to the Games. Part of our government's security strategy is to make a show over how much might they can throw around—even if it's for a nonsense threat like yours."

A trickle of sweat down her back made her shudder. "What facts do they think they know?"

"The possibility of bomb materials being transported with your horses to the Olympic venue in Atlanta triggered a massive response, and you're a wildcard."

"I'm no wildcard," she said.

"Authorities don't like it when a person has been presumed dead. A lot has to happen to make them un-dead. The process takes time and you are being afforded all of the rights and protections any U.S. citizen would enjoy."

"And the fact that immigration officials are here has nothing to do with the validity of my citizenship and passport?" The question had rattled around inside of her since she saw the immigration seal on the SUV. The truth of her birth roiled inside. What little she knew about naturalization told her she was not a U.S. citizen. If that was true, what protections did she have?

Declan looked at the crew, taking the measure of each. "Perhaps we can continue our conversation as we travel."

She pulled her arm out of his reach. Events were unfolding too rapidly with too much unseen and unknown by her. "If I jet off before I know why they want to detain me, I'll look guilty."

Declan cocked his head. "Guilty? Of what?"

"I don't *know!*" Her face heated. "If I march down these steps, immigration will grab me and escort me somewhere—into the terminal or their cars. It doesn't matter. I'm damned if I stay and damned if I leave. With half of America watching this on live TV, the court of public opinion will determine me guilty. No. I'm not becoming chum for the piranhas." Everywhere she looked, MMC emblazoned each surface. The crew. The fuselage. Hell, even the damned napkins. "Michael can't want this."

"He's well aware of the costs to you, but I'm afraid he sees no alternative and has directed us to leave."

The promise of safety and normalcy was only yards away, on the other side of the hoards. She could run again, be on her own, trusting no one, and lying to all, but she had lived like that before and hated the deception and isolation. She yearned for a life without the albatross of her past and wanted back the dreamy world of her childhood. She wanted to return to the one place she could call home and to be surrounded by open fields and barns filled with horses. Michael promised her all of that without the complications curious and judgmental people presented. He populated training facilities with the world's best horses and hand-picked each employee. He surrounded her with everything she wanted or needed. Horses. Privacy.

And bodyguards.

Choices narrowed, the easy path was to blindly follow Declan, trusting that Michael would help her each step of the journey, but panic stopped her from relinquishing the last scintilla of choice she had. "There's got to be a better way," she said to no one in particular.

Declan began to speak, and she raised her hands, palms open and pushing the air in front of her to silence him. She needed to think, to cobble together a solution using whatever tools she had, with her own resources and someone who knew at least part of her truth.

She turned to the captain. "I need to make a phone call."

Footsteps trotted up the airstairs amid increased shouts of reporters. Two women entered the cabin. The first, dressed in a fuchsia linen suit with matching hat and carrying an oversized purse, pushed past Captain Laramie and threw her arms around Jessica.

"Sweet Caroline in the sunshine! My Gawd, child! The wake of fury that follows you!"

Momentarily stunned, Jessica stood rigid and blinked. The onslaught of warmth and friendship shocked her back to the world of loving contact. She thawed and returned the embrace, happy to be enveloped in a cloud of Channel No. 5. "Electra! I can't believe you're really here!"

Electra Lavielle, Perc, Kentucky's unofficial mayor and human hurricane, was the only friend Jessica had. Miles and time may have separated them, but their bond was strong and instant. A year's friendship forged a lifetime of trust.

Electra spoke softly into Jessica's ear. "Did you find what you were looking for?"

Even as Electra's eyes shone with a lioness' urge to protect her cub, Jessica would never utter her truth. Her imperceptible shrug and tensed body telegraphed a willed silence as her thoughts raced. A few weeks was not enough time to adjust to her vertigo-inducing reality of being a bishop's bastard. She stumbled to form an answer. How could she begin to voice that she was lied to from birth? Good people with good intentions remained mute fearing that if the truth became known, carefully constructed peace talks would topple and countless lives would be lost. Her landscape had shifted to one with fuzzy borders.

Jessica pressed her lips together and looked at the crew, forcing a change of subject.

"I'm here when you're ready to talk." Electra tightened her embrace before extending her arms, holding Jessica's shoulders. "I've been busier than an old biddie at a county fair since you called. There wasn't a minute to lose." She gave her head a little shake as if rattling pieces of information into place. "Michael called not long after you. That man of yours wouldn't rest until he knew what was up my sleeve. Lordy, he nearly insisted on an armed escort. I daresay, I felt I needed one getting into the airport."

"Michael called you?" Jessica brushed Electra's cheeks with a quick kiss. "I shouldn't have doubted that."

"I worked his badgering against him and learned all I needed to know to cobble together a solution for you." Electra dug around the inside of her purse, pulled out a handkerchief, and dabbed her forehead. "Gracious child. This is so much drama! You've got to get away from here before those hyenas eat you alive!"

"I think you're a couple of days late. Every newspaper in the country is picking away at me."

"They can pick lint off a sweater forever without it unraveling. What's important is getting out in front of public opinion and controlling the message."

"That's why I called you. Time to put your daddy's media empire connections to work and call off the hounds."

"Empire?" Electra began, head bowed and eyes downcast in a stance of studied humility. "Hardly, child. He was fortunate in his life to be well placed, if not well funded. Bracebridge Thadius Lavielle," she pronounced each syllable as if reading from a scroll, "would roll over in his grave if he saw those heathens out front. In fact, if he were alive today he'd take each one–"

Captain Laramie cleared her throat to interrupt what promised to be a familiar and lengthy diatribe and motioned them into the cabin. "We've a checklist to attend to and we've no time for entertaining visitors." She waited for introductions. When none were offered, she motioned for Andrews to close the hatch.

Electra used the moment to grab the arm of the other visitor. More girl than woman, she was tall, about Jessica's height, with a riot of dark hair. A polyester blouse and ill-fitting pants struggled against her ample frame. She fumbled with an oversized portfolio and satchel. "This is Ellen. She's agreed to trade places with you for a while."

Ellen's eyes rounded with excitement. She suppressed a giggle. "Glad to meet you," she said, voice breathless with awe.

Jessica took her hand and slowly shook it, looking Ellen up and down. "Not quite what I was expecting," she said abruptly. "What about the other details?"

"Didn't that henchman of a lawyer talk to you?" Electra looked at her watch and shook her wrist with impatience. "He was supposed to be here this morning."

"He was, but left while the jet was being serviced."

"The intimidation tactic of involving immigration worked to keep you here long enough for reporters to descend on you like a pack of ravenous dogs. They got what they needed." She stepped forward, grabbed the satchel, and handed it to Devins. "Would you be kind enough to place Jessica's belongings in here? Please," she said, uttering the last word as an afterthought.

Jessica wasn't fooled by Electra's smile and rounded eyes, nor was Devins. Electra's genteel warmth tempered her steely resolve, but denying her would be a mistake. He took the satchel and disappeared into the back cabin.

As Electra spoke, Ellen took off her wig and shook it out. Sweat matted her hair to her head. "Damn. Wearing this thing is killer. Wait 'til you're a few miles from the airport before you take it off." She stole a lengthy look at Jessica before she blushed and looked away. "I can see why Electra called me. Same height and weight. Just about the same coloring, but without the wig my hair's a bit more blond, but I don't think it will be noticeable." In a spurt of confidence, she added, "The padding was something I added to keep the smarter ones guessing a while longer." She held her arms out from her sides, posing, hoping for acknowledgement. Receiving only cool stares, Ellen slipped off her blouse, showing a body suit padded with rolls of foam. "This suit made me sweat like a pig. I hope I didn't pit it out too much getting here."

Jessica clenched her jaw as she absorbed the information. Her eyes never left Ellen, but her question was directed toward Electra. "How many calls did you make in finding a decoy?"

"One. Direct to Ellen. Her parents are dear friends and I had promised Ellen a wonderful prep school graduation gift. A trip was perfect. I filled her in on the way here." Electra took Ellen's discarded clothes and placed them on a seat. Reaching inside her oversized purse, she brought out a sundress and sandals. She motioned for Ellen to change and continued talking. "I barely had time to make all those calls you needed."

"I couldn't speak freely, but I knew you'd figure out exactly what I was trying to do as soon as I mentioned Tess White wanted to see you," Jessica said, mentioning the alias she used when she first met Electra.

"I'm so grateful you called. I knew you had a germ of a plan, but if you want to get back to that mountaintop scrub you call a farm, you need to think again. Not only is it woefully inadequate to address your horses' training needs, that place is impossible to secure. Perc is already crawling with reporters and curiosity seekers. If you think this crowd is bad," Electra said, motioning toward the tarmac, "wait until they know you don't have a security fence around you."

"What's the alternative?"

"My plan is to buy ourselves some time by having people believe you've left the country again. But we can't make a move yet. Marching you outside before all the legal details are taken care of would certainly encourage those local yokel officials to grab their fifteen minutes of fame."

An intercom chirped and the captain opened the cockpit door. Sunlight poured through the curved windshield. An array of dials and switches blinked. "You've another visitor," she said, working the main hatch.

Declan entered, lowering his head to clear the frame. Still crisp, he seemed impossibly immune from Kentucky's heat. In a northerner's way, he ignored Southern conventions of greeting and tilted his head toward Electra. "You must be Mrs. Lavielle."

Electra bristled at his lack of manners.

"It's *Ms.* Lavielle, and you're late, Mr. Cleary."

"Unavoidable," he responded, voice flat. "The heightened security around the Olympics is making reactions unpredictable. Your phone calls to your pals, the Feds, acted like a dentist drill on a raw nerve."

Electra gave a satisfied smile. "Exactly. I knew I could help expedite things along."

Declan's jaw muscles pulsed. "Expedite? Escalate is more like it. Your involvement increased confusion and therefore concern. Despite your help, we cleared Jessica for entry to the U.S." His expression remained impassive. "I question your strategy to get her off airport grounds."

Electra straightened her skirt and didn't look up. "You mean Michael questions it."

"Michael believes getting her out of the country is her best option."

"He has no part in our plan and neither do you. Safety might be his concern, but my friend's ability to live her life as she wants to and not be hounded by lies is mine." Electra placed her open hand against her chest and lowered her head. "My daddy, rest his soul, was a master at pre-emptive strikes of strategically placed information. I'm going to reshape her public image from a wanton *Murdering Heiress* to a hapless woman who craves privacy. Public opinion from her last splash in the media softened considerably with my help." She sniffed and fingered her oversized pearl necklace. "Rotten timing of thoughtless acts can derail even the most astute campaign. I'll have no part in a strategy that would throw her to the wolves without thinking things through."

I'm right here. I have a name, Jessica wanted to shout, but she knew she wouldn't be heard.

Electra took a step closer to Declan with her eyes fastened to his as she spoke. "I will be proactive."

Declan would not be cowed. "And doing so risks an even bigger fiasco."

Electra's eyes narrowed. "I know what I'm doing, Mr. Cleary."

"I find that hard to believe, *Ms.* Lavielle."

Jessica watched the sparring match with growing dread. An image of a cat tormenting a mouse before the kill popped into her head. She indentified with the mouse.

Electra placed her hand on Jessica's arm and lowered her voice to a conspiring tone. "When you're ready, you'll tell me your whole story. Daddy would always say, 'Satiate the lions and they won't eat the Christians.'"

"Wait. What?" Jessica pulled away. "Tell you the whole story?"

"Nothing's worse than hearing bits and pieces and not knowing how it fits in the whole. You have my word nothing gets printed without your approval."

"Nothing good ever happens when my name gets in the news." Jessica groaned in frustration. The *whole* story. Kavan's face floated before her. He had spent the last twenty-eight years following her life and using his contacts in the church to provide for her as best he could without her ever suspecting the truth. He had protected her in ways she could not see. She wanted to protect her privacy, but she wanted to protect him more.

"How do you see this will help keep reporters from hounding me?" Jessica prodded.

"They want a story and a scoop. If we feed them a story that's filled with truth, keep them happy and away from the sensitive issues, they no longer need to scour the cage looking for tidbits. We can't stop the rubbish from being printed, but we'll establish trusted sources. I'll have you sit for interviews with them." Seeing Jessica's expression change, Electra paused. "Our message will be direct and clear. You won't have to field any wildcard questions that you're not prepared for."

"You mean, we will tell them the exact facts and story line we want them to know and that will stop them from searching for more?"

"Exactly!"

"I don't see how the stories can be controlled. These things feed on one another, and before you know it, something has been said or reported that re-ignites the flames. You can't put the genie back in the bottle."

The challenge made Electra give an enigmatic smile. "You can if you control the genie."

Jessica's palms slicked with sweat. Either she trusted Michael's plan that had her leave the country under a veil of suspicion and guilt, or she resorted to old tricks and placed herself in Electra's care that plunked her squarely in the center of controversy. Controversy she could live through. Being viewed through a prism of suspicion and guilt would get her killed.

"It's the genie I'm worried about," Jessica said, trying not to think about what would happen if an overly curious mind started digging into her past.

Cabin Steward Devins returned with the satchel filled with Jessica's belongings. "Here you be, Miss," he said as he placed the satchel by the hatch.

"You are so kind. Thank you, er," Electra looked at his nametag, "Mr. Devins." She sat in a leather-clad seat like a queen descending upon a throne. "Now then. What's a lady to do about a drink around here? Do you Irish drink sweet tea? I'd love some iced. With bourbon. And mint. Can you?" She projected the epitome of Southern manners, but the set of her jaw and shoulders made Devins scurry to help.

One corner of Jessica's mouth pulled up in a smile. Electra was where she liked it best—in the middle of the action and in full control.

"You're sure you want to do this?" Declan stood upright with his hands clasped in front of him. Jessica tried to read him, but his façade was bulletproof.

"I don't want to flee the States to any safe haven and I don't want to get pecked alive by reporters. Electra's plan is the only way I can stay in the country and ditch the press. What choices do I have?" She squirmed under his unyielding gaze.

"We're waiting for final word from Immigration and Naturalization Services," Declan replied. "Nothing needs to clear in through customs, so that will save us some time. Once I'm assured authorities up and down the chain of command have acknowledged their overreaction, and orders have been given to not intervene, the jet will leave. Then the trick will be getting you off airport grounds before word spreads. As for the reporters," he let his voice trail off as he pulled a shade back an inch and peered outside.

Jessica reached out and took his hand off the shade using only her index finger and thumb. The plastic material snapped back against the window. "Getting me somewhere where I can't be reached is my main concern."

"Mine too." Electra sidled closer to Jessica to form one body of unity.

Declan examined his hands, opening and closing his fingers.

Jessica turned to Electra. "You think this is a solid plan?"

"I do. I've seen too many situations where someone on the inside of an organization makes a little extra cash by selling a tip before a press conference can convene."

The pieces of the plan fell into place. Jessica searched Electra's face for any trace of worry as she spoke. "Okay then. The reporters saw you, an assistant, and Declan visit the jet and will see the same three people leave, only I'll be in Ellen's place. The jet will depart, destination unknown to the reporters, and will drop Ellen off on an island hopping adventure."

Electra smiled. "I've notified some photographers to be at the airport when she arrives in . . ." She looked at the captain for confirmation, "Grand Cayman?" Receiving agreement from the captain, she continued. "Maybe she'll draw attention away from Jessica for days or weeks, maybe not, but Ellen acting as decoy will allow you to slip out of the airport now."

Tension hunched Jessica's shoulders. "I hate using old tricks, but the only way to play this game is on my terms. Before we act, I need to know that Mr. Beefy out there knows not to detain me or stop me for any reason. I don't want him pissed that his nightly news debut was scuttled." She looked at Declan. "Can you make sure of that?"

"Consider it done. I'm waiting for one last confirmation."

Cabin Steward Devins returned with a tall glass filled with ice, reddish-brown tea, and green mint leaves on a small tray. A wedge of lemon sat beside a nip-sized bottle of Jack Daniel's bourbon. Electra cracked the seal, poured the contents into the glass, and took one gulp. "Much better, thank you." She settled deeper into her chair with a satisfied air. "All we need is time to get you to my farm unnoticed." She motioned to Jessica and Ellen to sit.

"Your farm? I thought you said Perc was already crawling with reporters?"

"True enough. Rest assured my property is quite secure. In fact, when I first met Michael years ago he offered to outfit it with perimeter sensors and the like at such an outlandishly cheap price I couldn't refuse!" She puffed with pride. "It's one of the benefits of having a business partner who owns a security conglomerate."

A sound, deep and growling, came from Declan. "You think that's enough?"

"I do. I have experience with paparazzi. I've kept more than one starlet out of the public eye while controversy swirled. She'll be fine with *me*." She turned her body away from him, closing the conversation.

Less than an hour later, Declan received confirmation. Within minutes, Jessica pushed the last of her hair under the wig. The foam morphed her body from lithe to heavy-set. She addressed Ellen. "And you'll be okay? Do you have plans once you get there?"

Ellen hugged herself with excitement. "I'll be fine. The money Electra is giving me will let me wander the islands for a few weeks and I'll be back before classes start. I have the addresses of friends and hostels. I'll know how to sail, too, so I can crew from island to island." Excitement radiated off her. She handed Jessica a pair of sunglasses. "That's it. You're good to go."

Electra gripped Jessica's shoulders, turning her slowly and scrutinizing every detail. Then she walked to the back of the cabin to assess her from a distance. Buttons on the floral blouse pulled slightly over large foam breasts. Pull-on pants in an unnatural shade of blue clung to a dimpled butt. Brown hair cascaded in tight kinks. Thick-soled shoes matched the brown vinyl portfolio and satchel. The transformation to no-nonsense assistant was complete.

She hugged Ellen good-bye and shook hands with the crew. Jessica gave each a kiss on the cheek and her thanks. With a nod, she showed she was ready.

The wig itched. The foam torso was damp from Ellen's sweat and its unwieldy proportions made her waddle. Sunglasses slid down her nose. Her chest tightened as Andrews opened the hatch. Electra and Declan led the way. Within two steps, she was engulfed in blast-furnace heat. The immigration agent approached them. Her breathing suspended. He was supposed to keep away from them, not get closer. What was he doing?

The sound was deafening. Jets rushed down runways and taxied. The airport was a hive of activity, but the tarmac surrounding the private terminal was unnaturally calm. No baggage trams buzzed. No maintenance people hovered. Declan shouted something in the agent's ear, words masked by ambient noise. The agent shook his head, and then strode toward Jessica, covering the distance over the tarmac with a dramatic flair. He stood so close she could smell his over-spiced scent over the tar and jet fuel. He scrutinized her, turning his head side to side, eyes boring through the layers of foam.

Declan brought his face within an inch of the agent's face. "Not here," he commanded. He looked toward the jet, bringing the agent's attention to the hatch.

Ellen walked past the open hatch long enough to draw attention. A stiff breeze whipped the sundress around her legs and she used her hands to press it down. Windblown hair obscured her face. She made herself visible, and then dipped back inside. Rapid-fire clicks sounded as cameramen struggled to get the best picture for the news cycle's money shot—Jessica Wyeth fleeing, again. All eyes were drawn to the jet and the sudden bustle surrounding its departure. The airstairs were folded up, wheel chucks removed, and engines warmed up.

Declan nudged her forward. Her feet rooted in place and her skin tingled with a sense that things were going terribly wrong.

The pull to witness the surreal was too strong, like rubbernecking at an accident site. Jessica tried not to look at the reporters, but she couldn't help herself. Cameramen on stepladders and heat-wilted reporters pressed against one another. Each face turned toward the jet.

Except one. Beside a petite reporter with bobbed black hair craning her neck for a better view, a man studied the trio of Jessica, Declan, and Electra, his face notable for its oval shape and starkly pale skin. No reporter gave an overweight secretary, with unruly hair struggling with satchels and purses, a second glance as she walked to the terminal, but the man nudged the woman next to him and motioned toward them. His face triggered a checklist of names to scroll through her head. Declan touched her arm again. The trio walked into the terminal.

The agent followed.

Declan entered the terminal first. He stopped, looked around, and motioned for the group to continue.

Once inside the terminal, the agent said, "You're damn lucky you have powerful friends." He spoke too loudly, almost as if he wanted to be overheard.

Jessica shrank away. "I want to be left alone. You have a job to do. Stop wasting your time on me."

He looked toward the jet. "My job here ends as soon as that jet leaves. No one trusts that guy," he said, motioning with his head toward the MMC letters on the jet's tail. "And we're not so sure about you."

"I . . ." she started to speak, her voice barely strong enough to be heard, "I'm not a part of all this."

"Like hell you aren't."

"I. Am. Not. A. Part. Of. This," she shouted, almost a shriek. The whine of the warming jet engines whisked her words away. "I've not done anything to deserve this."

The agent expelled a sharp breath through flared nostrils. "Sometimes it's not what you do, but what you don't that stinks." He stepped back as if her presence repulsed him. "Go. Leave. But don't think we're done with you."

Electra put her arm protectively around Jessica's shoulders. "Pay him no mind. Let's go." She glared at the agent over the top of Jessica's head.

They continued to a waiting limousine. No one stopped them.

Safe behind smoked glass, Jessica removed her sunglasses and observed the circus outside. All cameras pointed at the jet. The pale man pulled the reporter toward the limousine.

Declan sat facing the rear. The dim light of the interior flattened and blanched his features, making his eyes two black pits. Beads of moisture on his forehead shimmered. He didn't look at her, but she was aware of the tension in his body. He pressed his head against the headrest and braced his arms against the seat.

They were stuck behind a line of news vans clogging the exit. The limousine inched forward. The jet started to move, and the crowd migrated toward the fence as one unit, clearing a path to the exit. Jessica refrained from pushing her face against the window to see if the man was watching the limousine or the jet. Why was he so familiar?

The Gulfstream taxied to the end of the runway, paused, then accelerated, heading away from them.

Declan turned and rapped his fingers on the partition separating the passengers from the driver.

"Get a move on." His voice was husky, almost a growl. "Now."

From the corner of her eye, Jessica saw an airport fueling tanker lumber toward the runway. Something wasn't right. Why was it there, now? Couldn't the driver see the runway was active? She leaned forward, grasping the armrest in her hand. The tanker's driver seemed disoriented by the setting sun, raising his arm to shade his eyes below the lowered sun visor. His other hand worked the steering wheel back and forth. Beside him sat another man, bearded, with a baseball cap, brim turned to the back. One camera perched precariously on the dashboard and another held out the passenger window. The tanker swayed, then hesitated before it turned onto a surface road that cut across the jet's path. She imagined the crew and Ellen, buckled into to seats and listening to the whoosh of air and the whine of the engines as the jet accelerated. The tanker swerved onto a collision path.

Jessica gasped. The only sound was the roar of blood rushing through her ears.

The jet's wing and tail flaps moved as it tried to pull up. It lumbered down the runway, accelerating. Any effort to stop was too late.

Memories of a tavern engulfed in flames exploded in her head, disorienting her from past to present. A woman's charred body found in the tavern's ashes gave Jessica seven years of cover. Memories from Gus' murder flooded her thoughts, triggering a desperate need to flee. Flashes of knife blades and riflescopes danced beside an Irish cop who wanted her dead for what she knew. People she was supposed to trust wanted her dead. Was it happening again? Lies, deceit, and ambition surrounded her then, but she hadn't known it. Now? She knew even more. Plus, she knew their names.

Would Ellen's charred body found in the wreckage of the jet give her freedom or take it away?

Electra stared intently at her fingernails, the media maven with the decade's best story sitting beside her. Declan pressed his back into the seat, eyes closed. Who was he? Irish. Boston. Connected.

Did they agree to the details of this escape together or did their agendas clash?

Her knuckles blanched with the force of her grip on the armrest. The thinnest spark of heat ignited somewhere deep inside her head.

The whine of twin engines collided with an explosive roar.

"No! Oh, please! No!" Her fingernails dug into the upholstered door. She squeezed her eyes shut, unwilling to witness the tanker careen into the jet's side.

She waited for the heat of the vibrant orange fireball to scorch through the smoked glass.

She screamed.

"Jessica? Jessica, dear. Are you all right?" Electra patted her arm.

The pressure to deceive, the lies, all she had been through was too much. A physical pain, almost a scalpel's slice, streaked through her brain. Only a steady flow of screams lessened the pain. She opened her eyes to see the Gulfstream carve a smooth arc through the air, wings dipping slightly. The tanker truck continued on its way.

"I thought the truck . . . I saw the . . . I was sure they were going to collide and then they would have found Ellen's body and thought it was me faking another death—like the tavern, but the tavern wasn't an accident and my friend was there by mistake, looking for me, but they thought her body was mine—and the reporters witnessed my escape and it would have looked like I planned it all." She grabbed her head, panting, and slumped back against the seat. "I'll never be able to live my life. It's not my fault! None of this has been my fault!" The last words keened in a deep-chested wail.

Electra and Declan looked at one another and back at Jessica. Electra laced her fingers through Jessica's, lips puckered with worry. "I haven't the foggiest idea what you're talking about."

Saturday, July 6, 1996
Boston, Massachusetts

COLLEEN SHAUNESSY-CARILLO took the T to the *Globe*'s offices before heading back to her apartment. Once William had agreed to travel to Kentucky, she hadn't left him alone for a minute. She made flight arrangements while he packed and kept him close the entire trip to Logan Airport, Louisville, and back, only freeing herself from him when she paid for his cab back to his home. Colleen almost cursed her fascination—no, *obsession*—with Jessica Wyeth. Almost. Her reporter's spidey sense was on high alert that the Wyeth clan—and its proximity to the Irish Mafia—would keep her in stories for a long, long time. She'd need more than smoking-gun evidence to pull the trigger on a string of damning stories against Jessica, and time spent with William helped solidify her relationship with him for future access.

William was too arrogant to suspect she had her focus on a bigger story.

She'd hoped to use the day to work uninterrupted. Reporters, rushing to meet deadlines for Sunday's paper, sat hunched at desks. She spent hours combing her email for nuggets of information. Her voicemail overflowed with people trying to reach her. Some wanted to give her tips about the fugitive, most wanted to get some.

"I saw Jessica Wyeth in the Caymans and have pictures to prove it!"

"How did you learn she was in Kentucky?"

"You claimed she remained in the States after her jet departed. How did you know that?"

"When are you going to stop looking at Connaught and start focusing on Jessica?"

Her stock in the newsroom was rising and she needed to plan her moves exactly right so she could cash in. The bounty she was looking for was a place in journalism's highest echelon. A Pulitzer. Any story starring William was too gossipy and not newsy enough. Wayward niece. Cash-strapped uncle. Squandered inheritance. Intriguing, but not hard-hitting news. A Berger Award for outstanding human interest reporting would do. Nicely.

But, damn. A Pulitzer sure would be great. She thought she kept her ambition hidden, but her editor was on to her.

"That last story you wrote on Wyeth only made it to page five. Are you missing seeing your name on page one, above the fold along with the other stories on the Olympics, terrorism, and security?" Maxim Collier loomed over her. The sleeves of his blue oxford shirt were rolled up, exposing his skinny and hairless forearms and hiding the grime, frayed threads, and missing buttons on his cuffs. Two splotches of dried coffee—black, no sugar—marred the otherwise perfectly wrinkled front. He'd been newsroom editor for five years and had a reputation for smelling when a reporter was determined to keep their name in the by-line and associated with a hot story. Colleen wasn't surprised he waited for her to return.

She shrugged, trying to appear impartial. "Are you saying if I had written Connaught's actions more prominently in the article I would have made the front page?" The coordinates of her heat-seeking missives for Jessica Wyeth and her no-good boyfriend were locked in, and her aim was getting better every day. If she had her druthers, Michael Connaught would have no shelter and a Pulitzer would be hers. At last.

He hoisted the bag on her desk. "You're doing the legwork needed to connect Wyeth's name to the dark side of the Connaught clan. It's the kind of association that a person never recovers from. It's also the kind of bias I won't let on my pages."

Impartiality be damned. "I'm not biased," she snapped. "Michael Connaught reminds me of that twelve-year-old kid who took his daddy's Maserati Quattroporte and was clocked on the Mass Pike at one hundred and twenty miles per hour before he could figure out how to stop. Only blind, dumb luck kept that kid alive. Same is true for Connaught." She scowled. "He wields more power than a nuclear fusion chamber but has no idea how to use it. There's a big story in the connection between Wyeth and Connaught. I'm vetting all my facts. Don't worry."

"The courts stopped investigating anything connected with the Connaughts after Magnus died, but you didn't. First you looked at Magnus' brother, Liam, but decided the power resided in the next generation and focused on Michael. That's a hell of a leap. Did your sources inside the FBI tip you?"

"Sources? FBI?" she exclaimed, wide-eyed. "You know those guys are as tight-lipped as ever." True enough. Her FBI connections never uttered so much as a peep—even as they slipped copies of documents into her car or dropped the name of a person she should talk to. She could investigate in ways they couldn't and they used her as much as she used them. Her last meeting before she left for Kentucky and her first connection when she returned was with her buddies. With the dance of deniable contact fully choreographed, information flowed. Max was no fool, but she'd protect her source with her life.

Regardless, the investigation into Connaught enterprises was as active and hot as ever.

"Michael is trying to play all innocent, like he doesn't know where the piles of his father's shit lay before he stepped in it and tracked it all over the place," she said, face heating with anger. "You've said it before. Ignorance of a scofflaw is no excuse. Rather than minimizing suspicions, everything he's done exacerbated them. He ignored requests for interviews by authorities, stonewalled investigations, and disregarded subpoenas—which, in fairness, is pretty easy when you're in a different country. But not helping unravel his father's mess makes him as much a leader of organized crime as if he created the mess himself."

"Okay," Max said, leaning forward. "For argument's sake, let's say he's tracking shit all over the place. That doesn't mean he makes it. If the FBI determines the money is the fruit of an illegal enterprise, they'll simply freeze the assets and seek ways to permanently claim it. They already froze most of daddy's inheritance to keep it out of Michael's hands."

"Damn it, Max! Are you saying that it doesn't matter if the father laundered embezzled cash and murdered innocent people who wanted out of his organization? How can anyone turn a blind eye to the organization when the son takes over?"

"Word on the street is the organization is in chaos, running in circles like a chicken with its head cut off. You can't assume the son is participating in illegal actions. You've said it before, the courts stopped caring after Magnus died."

"You and I are on the same page in wanting to ensure Michael goes to jail on his own actions, not the actions of his father. If the son had kept his head down and played his cards right, he'd have been able to live a happy life on his daddy's millions. But *nooooo*, he wanted more and I'm going to get the evidence to prove it."

"Thanks to Wyeth?"

"Thanks to Wyeth," she affirmed. Stating she worked on stories for the *Globe* opened more doors than Home Depot sells and her research flowed. "I was able to compile a database of MMC enterprises matching flight plans with financial records showing international money flow. Since Magnus Connaught died, wherever Michael has flown in his private jet, Connaught money follows—pushing money offshore and hiding assets. He's been glad-handing charities with one hand and taking freshly laundered money out of their pockets with the other."

"And the connection to Wyeth?"

"Wherever her horses go, his jets go. And where Connaught money goes, civil unrest erupts. It's no coincidence that MMC, Ltd. is suddenly interested in Arabian horses—from the Middle East. It's not a coincidence that an MMC company is one of the major sponsors at the upcoming Olympics with a special focus on equestrian events. You're the one who tells me to trust my instincts. A serendipitous confluence of events usually isn't a coincidence."

Max hitched his hip on the corner of a desk and crossed his arms, listening. "You gained access to William Wyeth by portraying his niece as a hapless victim. Are you sure you want to follow that narrative?"

Colleen grimaced with discomfort. "Okay, fine. You got me on that one, but saying she was a Patty Hearst-esque terrorist in the making got me into the Wyeth inner circle. The most likely scenario is something different. Jessica is a bright, resourceful woman who knows how to survive. The fact she plugged into the Connaught clan willingly was more shocking than getting struck by a bolt of fricking lightning."

"So, run me through your narrative again—from the beginning." He swung a wooden chair in front of him and sat, legs straddled with his arms resting on the back. The age of the chair was apparent from the layers of black film on its slats and the groan of its legs as it protested Max's weight. "Take me from what the public already knows about her and how you're digging for something different."

"The public first met Wyeth as the Murdering Heiress who had been exonerated for the Adams murder by the indictment of Magnus. Resurrecting from her presumed death was sensational enough to keep her in the headlines, but then news hit that she was injured during last winter's search for a boy with special needs. Who organized the search? Michael. Then some goon ended up dead during her rescue. The public couldn't get enough stories on her, so I kept digging. I'd been fluent in Magnus' dealings for years, but I had no idea the son even existed. When news of Wyeth's injury reached me, I was shocked to learn about the connection, so it was easy to transfer my interest to the son rather than investigating Magnus' brother Liam.

"Anything relating to Magnus piqued my interest, but the son had an untarnished reputation as a local sheriff. I would have given Michael the benefit of the doubt if the deaths of Magnus and the goon had been separated by years or months rather than days."

"Let me see if I follow you," Max said, counting the points down on his outstretched hands. "Michael was a model citizen in a small town. Law abiding. Well-regarded and well connected. He established the perfect appearance of an estranged son trying to carve his own life outside of his father's world. Your opinion was clear that Magnus was a rich conniving lowlife—a modern day Machiavellian bastard. When Magnus died, your research into his life became irrelevant."

"I let the facts speak for themselves. I didn't spin anything." Her jaw jutted forward, indignant at the implication.

Max raised his hand to quiet her as much as to calm her. "I recall our conversations at the time. Your interest in Michael intensified when he claimed the goon's death was due first to exposure, then to an animal mauling. The conflicting stories prompted you to dig further."

She chuffed. "A bullet in the head was the last thing I expected to see in the final autopsy. He was a law enforcement officer protecting a citizen. If the death was due to a permissible shooting in the line of duty, why the smoke?"

"I know you, Colleen, and I know how you think. The direction you're taking is that by becoming a sheriff and parking himself on the fringes of his father's life, Michael gave himself a license to kill. At least in Kentucky."

"If Michael had just played his cards right, I might not have investigated the death further and stumbled on the information that the goon was Magnus' henchman. Sonny-boy stepped right in the middle of daddy's shit and made a pile of his own. It was just one more damned coincidence, right?"

Max closed his eyes. His lips pressed into one line forming the expression all the reporters in the newsroom knew too well. His encyclopedic brain was sifting through facts and angles, looking for the best possible route for the story and any barrier to its publication.

"So, you put pressure on Michael by writing hyped-up stories–"

"They weren't hyped-up," she barked.

His withering look cowed her back to silence. He continued. "Hyped-up stories about a hoax search and the mysterious death. You wanted Michael to step forward and defend his actions even though you knew a line-of-duty shooting to save the life of an innocent is the stuff that makes legends and careers. He saved Jessica's life."

She couldn't contain herself. "Right! And instead of smiling from the cover of *People* magazine, he fled the country. I can only imagine the bullshit cover-up story he fed Jessica to entice her to leave with him," she said, gripping her head then throwing her hands in the air. "Jessica had been cleared of murder and was free. Why the hell was it so important to run to Ireland? He fed me, and anyone who read my stories, lies. There's a story in why and I'm going to be the one to break it." Her cheeks blazed crimson.

"God damn it, Max! Think of the time line," she continued, full throttle. "Magnus Connaught's death enjoyed some damned fortuitous timing as far as Michael is concerned. A bit too fortuitous if you ask me. That's why I pulled Magnus' coroner's report and pinged every person I knew for more information. I came up with nothing. Yeah, the old guy was sick and all, but he croaked a few short weeks after being indicted for Gus Adams' murder. A freshly freed Jessica fell into Michael's arms—as did hundreds of millions of dollars. All Michael had to do was keep his nose clean for a few years and he could live a trouble-free life with one hot babe."

"I allowed you to pump out stories about Magnus' and the mountain guy's deaths because they were fact-checked and we were both hoping the stories would prod investigations. Nothing happened."

Colleen shifted uncomfortably under his glare. "Okay, fine. Nothing happened because every potential avenue was blocked by his stateside lawyer."

"Lawyer? Who's that?"

"Some Cleary guy from Southie," she responded, irritated at the interruption. "Michael Connaught fled the country for no good reason that I could see." The hidden story was complicated further by what she did not tell Max. One key target of her stories was Michael's connections to businesses in Kentucky, and Electra Lavielle was one of his major partners.

When she tried to get Lavielle to go on record about their business dealings, Lavielle scuttled the information trail as only an experienced media maven could. Colleen had intimated that the stalwart and upright Lavielle name was connected to a larger scheme. She should have known better than to suggest Bracebridge Thadius Lavielle's daughter was implicated in a cover-up of organized crime. She took a chance and it backfired.

What happened? The story was trounced by Lavielle.

The loss cost her the Pulitzer.

Undeterred, she had to get another way in to Connaught's businesses. That's where Wyeth fit in.

Max was one step ahead of her, as usual. "The best thing that came out of the whole search was the overwrought attention the public provided his alleged sweetie, Miss Wyeth."

Colleen beamed. "Right! His actions proved he knew it, too, right down to the first thing he did with her. He brought her to Gibraltar and covered her with terrorist stank!"

"Go slow with me on this one. What are you saying?"

"There is no way any self-respecting freedom fighter for the Irish cause would *not* know Gibraltar is the hub of planning, training, and networking. Agents of England's MI-5 gunned down IRA operatives there to stop the spread of terrorist contagion. The Rock, as it is affectionately known in certain circles," she said, proud of her insider's knowledge, "is home to a U.K. military base and was crawling with insurgents and wannabe thugs right under the crown's jewels."

"You're saying from that trip forward, Jessica Wyeth was knowingly participating in Connaught's plans."

"Yup," Colleen smirked, victory within her grasp.

"Not so fast. The reader is thinking Michael Connaught is using Jessica as a human shield. Saying Jessica Wyeth has gone rogue will be a tough nut to crack."

"My gut isn't any different than our readers,'" Colleen defended. "I can't fathom how an innocent woman would be anywhere near Connaught. The only rational explanation is Jessica Wyeth is training to become a terrorist. I'm building my story carefully, but the Manchester bombing and her participation–"

"*Alleged* participation," he corrected.

"C'mon! If the bread crumbs were any larger, you'd have whole loaves filling the streets."

"So, in light of the Manchester bombing, you're building a case against Wyeth, knowing it will lead you straight back to Connaught. Why not just focus on Connaught and leave Wyeth out of it? Connaught's story is more appealing to a national audience than Boston Brahmin William Wyeth losing his inheritance," Max pressed. "You have two things working against you. The first is that the public fell in love with the spunky Jessica Wyeth and the second that is Michael Connaught is cultivating an impeccable image as a big ticket donor at international celebrity-filled charity events. He befriended upright citizens with unquestionable integrity who will no doubt vouch for him. You're going to have a hard time pinning anything on him."

She had to agree. His cover was nearly perfect. But Michael lacked the finesse needed to keep her off his trail.

"I'm not giving up on Connaught. I've tried researching him directly, but I'm stopped at every turn, so Wyeth is my way in. I'm careful with my research. Everyone here knows that," she said with a wave of her arm. The motion brought her attention to the other reporters in the cramped room. She had been too engrossed in her conversation to notice others had stopped working to listen. An uncomfortable hush filled the room.

With cheeks blazing, she gathered her belongings and left.

The clang and screech of the Orange Line train as it accelerated out of the Forest Hills station faded as Colleen thumped her way back to her car. Driving in Boston on the Fourth of July is impossible, so she had parked her car at the T station nearest her apartment. Her trip with William was a pleasant surprise and was worth the parking tickets that were sure to be tucked under the wiper for leaving her car unmoved the past two days. Her messenger bag grew heavier with each step and papers bulged from each pocket. She barely had room for the toothbrush, mascara, lip balm, hand sanitizer, and clean thong she always carried for unexpected overnights. Assignments included.

Massachusetts' humidity had nothing on the clinging soup of Kentucky, but by the time she had cut through the *Globe's* parking lot to the JFK/UMass stop on the Red Line, sweat plastered her hair to her face. She yearned for a cold beer, a shower, and clean clothes.

Her intuition tingled to watch her back, and she scanned the platform and deserted station. She couldn't shake the feeling of being followed, and searching for an air-conditioned car when she changed trains served the dual purpose of observing who was around her. Being back in Boston amplified her feelings of unease. She admonished herself for becoming as paranoid as she was obsessed.

The strap cut into her shoulder, and she shifted the messenger bag to carry it more on her back than hip, pulling the strap in front of her to keep the bag in place. Was it the summer heat that made it feel so heavy or were her fears weighing her down?

Even a few hours of cooling dark did nothing to firm the sidewalk under her shoes. Squishy asphalt muffled her footsteps, making it easier to hear the sounds of the night around her. The working class neighborhood of triple-deckers captured the heat. Windows were flung open with curtains limp in the breathless air. Fans whirred in darkened houses. She ducked into a doorway and scanned the street, smiling to herself as the grubby pavement and yellowed streetlights wrapped her in welcome.

She loved her city, especially when gems of the past and present revealed themselves in surprising ways. In the heart of Boston, gleaming walls of glass and chrome reflected centuries-old graveyards of founding fathers and brave minutemen. The red brick Freedom Trail meandered around the cobbled star of the Boston Massacre and past doors of the best damned cannoli bakeries this side of Italy. The Swan Boats drew families to play a short distance from where the Boston Strangler roamed. The city lured her and lulled her with its Janus face, just like what Connaught is doing to Jessica, she mulled as she continued up the barren street.

Maybe her Pulitzer isn't that far-fetched. If she could only be certain she was on the right track, she would know where to focus her energy. Michael? Jessica?

A tingle shot up her spine as she weighed the celebrity fluff of Wyeth's stories with the hardcore facts of dogged research.

The tingling became more pronounced as Colleen savored the dreams of rewards her stories could bring. The stinging grew to a welt of hot pain as she walked. Then her knees buckled and the sensation coalesced to a spot between her shoulder blades. The sights and sounds of the street sharpened with the flood of adrenalin. The hum of air conditioners and the drip of condensation from rusted window units blended to sound like the growl of an animal. Mortar between filthy bricks, glimmering with flecks of mica, turned on a kaleidoscope hinge. Moist summer air thickened as she struggled to catch her breath. She pulled her messenger bag to her front and felt the scrape of something sharp pull across her skin. Her muscles weakened and shook.

A figure ran down the street. Dirty jeans, sneakers, and a hoodie vaulted over a parked car and turned the corner out of her sight.

What the hell was that? She looked around for help or to find a witness. Strength returned to her legs. Her hands shook as she nearly fell against her car with relief. Trembling fingers fumbled through the bag's pockets for her keys.

What she found was no monkey-knot key fob. A dagger was sunk into her bag up to its hilt. The point protruded from the other side by a half inch, just enough to cut her, but not enough to kill. Her heart stilled for a moment knowing she was damned lucky it hadn't been stilled forever. The thick canvas of the messenger bag combined with the volume of pages from her obsession stopped the blade from going further.

Using a tissue, she plucked the dagger from the center of her bag. The ornate Celtic design engraved on the quillion shone in the dim light, the blade and handle richly polished. Dusting for fingerprints would be useless, but she'd bring it to her buddies in the FBI anyway. Irish trinket shops carried dozens of the cheap knives, and she knew they'd have a devil of a time tracking its owner.

She felt the lightness of it in her hand. With the other, she reached around and fingered the tear in her blouse. A trickle of something down her back made her shiver. Blood? Sweat? Both? Her hands were shaking so badly she could barely poke the keys into the ignition.

Was she getting a knife in her back because of her relentless research of Connaught dealings or because of her never-ending stream of articles on Jessica? Fruits of her obsession, the volume of papers in her messenger bag, saved her life and firmed her determination to bring down Michael Connaught and anyone who supported him. Jessica was no innocent. Her time to extricate herself from the Connaught clan's clutches had run out.

Why target Colleen now? She'd been a thorn in Magnus' side for years and one in Michael's for months. What was happening that forced their hand to try and scare her?

The Olympics? Her stomach sank at the thought.

She wrapped the dagger and placed it in the glove compartment, mind parsing through details. Throwing a knife from a distance meant someone didn't want to get close to her. The figure vaulting away looked to be in his mid-teens, suggesting whoever ordered this attack considered her a low-level threat. Intimidating her into silence would start with a young Turk who wanted a larger role in Connaught's organization. If they wanted her dead, she'd be dead, so keeping her alive must serve some kind of purpose. But what? What was it that she was supposed to be doing?

Swiveling her head and body and peering into her mirrors, she looked for any movement or shadow. She didn't know who or what was out there. She only knew the next time she dropped her guard and someone from Connaught's team got that close to her, she wouldn't be so lucky.

Pebbles sputtered in all directions as her car fish-tailed down the street.

FLECKS OF LATHER fell from Kilkea's mouth as they flew over the ground. Jessica pulled hard on the right rein, drilled her leg into his side, and demanded a hairpin turn with a change of lead. The end of the three and one-half mile course was in sight and water jumps, oxers, and brush-topped walls faded behind them. With tunneled vision, Jessica calculated the strides to the next obstacle, a five-foot high log wall, and tried to correct their approach by checking their speed. Chunks of airborne turf dotted their wake. Kilkea slipped and his haunches dropped before he scrambled his legs underneath them and catapulted forward.

"*Heyo, horse*. I'm in control here. Trust me," Jessica said in a commanding voice. Kilkea flicked an ear back and worked the bit, refusing to obey. In three strides, they vaulted over the wall at a poor angle. Jessica's balance was thrown off. She gripped his mane as she dangled over Kilkea's side, one foot tangled in a stirrup and the other leg hooked over the saddle. Confused, Kilkea pulled up and reared, nearly unseating her. Determined not to fall and using all of her strength, she forced herself upright. Balance recovered, she turned her upper body, pulled his head and launched toward home.

A man, compactly built with a body of muscle and brawn, and a head of shocking red hair, calmly stepped inside the field. Jessica and Kilkea skidded to a stop.

"Jaysus, lass! You're not ridin' as if you're listening to the animal at all! I'm daft wonderin' who you're trying to kill. You or the horse?" Jax moved forward and gripped the reins. He stroked the horse's neck and murmured in calming tones. Kilkea slowly relaxed, head dropping and sides heaving.

"Miss Jessica? Did you hear me?" Jax and two other grooms had been chosen by Michael to help Jessica rebuild her training business and farm. Not only were Jax and his men consummate horsemen, but their ability to discern and deal with physical threats hinted at military-type training. Handpicked due to their unquestioned allegiance to Michael, Jessica was not foolish enough to think they were mere grooms.

Jax's brows furrowed. He patted her leg. "Miss Jessica?"

Jessica's eyes blinked and focused. "Oh, right. Yes. One more horse. Is another ready?"

He stepped back as she swung her leg over the horse's neck and hopped down. Her rubbery legs gave underneath her and she grabbed the stirrup leather for support.

"No. You're pushing yourself and the animals to their limits. Ease off. Your judgment is skewed and that near crash proved it. Take a rest."

She bit back a snappish reply and willed her voice to be even. "Fine. I'll ride more tomorrow."

"No you won't at that. You need to talk with the owners and make sure your training goals are aligned with theirs. You've been riding hard and crazy and I'm not sure it's all been about the animals for you." His voice lowered with concern. "Breathe deep and think, Lass. Look at this animal."

Kilkea's red sides, streaked black with sweat, heaved like a bellows. Jax continued. "He wasn't trained like this for weeks while he was quarantined at the air transport facilities."

Jessica blinked. "Right. Weeks." Focusing on his words didn't clarify their meaning. Too many fears crowded out rational thought.

"You know as well as I," Jax said, "that there's no quibbling with the authorities when they want to ensure transatlantic sicknesses aren't imported with the livestock and nothing so much as the sniffles is spread. Exercising them while in the quarantine facilities would have risked exposure to other animals. An isolation period is mandated even if your horses are as healthy as, well, a horse."

She almost smiled. "You're right. I should have taken that into consideration. Maybe we should have demanded he be with

Bealltainn," she said, referring to the horse on loan to Ireland's equestrian team that was placed in the quarantine barns at Georgia International Horse Park outside of Atlanta.

"Aye. 'Tis a thought."

Keeping her mind on business kept it off of her. Her body ached, but her heart more so. Traveling to Perc was to be her homecoming and she had been excited to return. The enclave of Perc sat inside the river-lined valley of the Pine Mountains in a remote southeast corner of Kentucky. The two-hundred year old town offered picture-perfect beauty and residents resolute about maintaining their privacy. The steep mountain walls covered in dense forest and a single winding country road through a treacherous pass kept all but the most determined from finding it.

When she first moved to Perc over a year ago, she had hoped to put down new roots and carve a home for herself hidden away from prying eyes. Instead, moving there became the first domino in a series of discoveries. What led to her finally being able to reclaim her life now became her bluegrass-lined prison.

And with her reclaimed life came bodyguards and paparazzi. She hated both.

She pressed her eyes shut in an effort to concentrate. "Bealltainn's training has continued without a break in readiness for the Olympics. I guess they thought since Bealltainn won at Aintree, an Olympic event was the next logical step for him."

Jax sneered. "That horse is no more Olympic material than I am. You Yanks have the craziest ideas of what's possible."

"It was the Irish team's idea. They're struggling to stay top-ranked over Germany," she said, regaining her focus. "The interest was not so much in having Bealltainn compete, but it was felt one of their riders would benefit from additional training on him. Seems the guy had a nasty fall and lost some of his nerve. His coach felt riding Bealltainn would be enough to shake the fear out of him while conserving their other horses for competition."

"Or make that poor lad never want to ride again. I can't say I agree with their training strategy, but if you feel Bealltainn's in good hands, that's enough for me." He scuffed his toe into the dirt, inhaled as if to say more, and huffed with a shake of his head.

"What aren't you telling me?"

Jax worked his mouth, as if sampling what words to say. "Did Missus Lavielle tell you every piece of equipment you transported with the horses was scrutinized to the fullest?"

She exhaled, puffing her cheeks. "I get it. If they couldn't get to me they'd get to my animals. Right?"

He let the question lie in the air. "It's just barn talk, but a horse being shipped to the Olympics directly out of your care fed the fear of another terrorist attack. Feed sacks were ripped open. Poultices examined. I heard one report that Bealltainn himself was X-rayed."

"That's ridiculous paranoia. I'm glad I'm not going to show my face there. I can only imagine the insanity my presence would start."

He shrugged. "They'd say their actions are from an abundance of caution. I'd say your horses can't so much as pass an air biscuit without someone worrying about your evil genius at work transporting explosive gases."

A smile crept into the corners of Jessica's mouth despite her foul mood. "If I'd known they wanted to examine my horses that closely, I wish I started them on a bean diet."

Jax broke out in a big grin. "Rolex is ten months from now," he said, mentioning a major three-day event known for establishing—or ruining—careers and horses. The event focused on cross-country, dressage, and stadium jumping, testing the ability of horse and rider to adapt to various demands. "Kilkea and Planxty were penned up in quarantine for weeks without a decent training schedule. It doesn't tax your noggin to know their conditioning suffered. Michael's syndicate may forgive an injury, but the other owners won't. Run Kilkea like that, and he won't be competing at Rolex. Mark my words."

She turned her head away knowing Jax was right. Planxty was Michael's favorite horse, a big gray with an even bigger heart, whom she rode daily, but not as hard as Kilkea. Ignoring Kilkea's condition and riding to his limit was a selfish act and she hated herself for it. "It's just that . . . I mean I only wanted . . ."

"What you're yearning for isn't for the taking. You can't buy people's friendship, but you can buy privacy. Michael's makin' sure you've got all you need of that."

She heard his words and knew the meaning behind them. Her polite acceptance by Perc natives disappeared with the arrival of satellite trucks and an increased demand for caramel lattes. Isolation is welcomed when invited, but not when forced. As much comfort as she should have felt at being in Michael's protective shell, she felt increasingly uneasy.

Where words failed her, doubt filled her. She still reeled from her episode at the airport. Could she read a situation clearly? Jax's intervention made her question her ability to judge an animal's condition and create a training regimen. She felt uncentered and fragmented any time she was off the farm. She hid her yearning to be welcomed and accepted behind reserved nods and pleasantries, and wasn't surprised when her manner was rewarded with reluctant hellos and stiffened shoulders. She cringed at each whisper and flinched when women spoke to neighbors behind backs of hands brought up to mouths.

Horses became more her oasis than ever. Riding hard was the only way to make sure she could breathe. Unsure of what her future held, she found solace in focusing on her animals.

Chastened, she looked at Kilkea. Sweat and lather dripped from his sides. The humid Kentucky summer did not give either of them a respite. A yearning for Ireland's cool air surprised her with a pang of homesickness. But where was home?

She draped an arm over the horse's neck and pressed her face into his mane, a motion meant for affection as well as to hide the tears that stung her eyes more often than she wanted to admit.

Jax wasn't fooled. "Give yourself a rest. The horses need it, as do you." He looked past her to miles of rolling green pastures lined with black wooden fences made from four horizontal planks nailed to four-by-four posts. Fields dotted with weeping willows and flowering trees surrounded a compound of three barns, one indoor arena, an outdoor ring, and cross-country course. "I like it here well enough, but I won't be blamed for overtraining the animals or under caring for you. It's life's short straw you pulled. Either you get yourself together or those buzzards you call reporters will pick you to the bone."

"No matter what I do, they're everywhere. Maybe Electra is right. If I give them what they want, they'll leave me alone." The few stories Electra had shared with her had been withering, with the *Boston Globe* leading the way.

"Och! You're talkin' daft. I heard the paparazzi were being paid in bags of gold for pictures of Princess Diana and her boyfriend despite their holding interviews."

She snorted. "I heard one of me earned them more."

"I don't want to find out. Me and my men are kept busy ousting the lot, including misery mongers who want to get a closer look at you. Some've dubbed you the queen of the Irish Mafia."

"Is that all? I thought I was the devil incarnate who helped orchestrate Whitey Bulger's disappearance."

"Who?"

She smiled to herself. "A Boston politician's crime boss brother who vanished a little over a year ago. I feel like the press is intent on ballyhooing rumors over facts."

"'Ballyhooing' you say? Sounds like a bit of the Irelands came home with you after all." Jax flashed a wide grin, showing a gap-toothed smile.

Humor rolled off her. She didn't miss a beat, "'Rumor' is what polite company would refer to. Lies are what others would say."

"Fair enough, but lies are more interesting than truth. I'm losing count of the false alarms. This farm has been wired with motion sensors and cameras in the same way as Master Connaught's home in Ballyronan. Surrounded by love and attention, you are." Inflections in his voice hinted at being amused even though neither of them were.

The fact that each piece of security equipment bore the brand "2100, Ltd.," depicting Michael's "MMC" initials with numbers instead of Roman numerals, added nothing to help her feel protected or loved.

Jessica brought the reins over the horse's neck, loosened the girth, and ran the stirrups up their leathers, tucking the looped end under the irons to secure them. Jax secured a halter and took the saddle, pad, and bridle.

"I'll walk him out." She turned away and took the long path around the barns.

Training at Brandywine Farm was Electra's idea, and it had everything that horse or human could need or want, including the recent addition of a heliport. Jessica had everything, except the feeling of home.

After she cooled him, Jessica turned Kilkea out in a paddock. He shook his head free of the halter and rolled, rubbing his back into the grass and letting his legs flail. She propped up her leg on the bottom rail, rested her chin on crossed arms, and watched him. After he shook himself free of dust, he plodded over and nuzzled her pockets. She couldn't stop herself from laughing out loud. One minute he was a keg of dynamite, and the next he was nothing but a big dog who wanted a rub and a treat.

Kilkea pressed his head against her hand as she rubbed his forehead. In the few minutes she had allowed herself to empty her mind and observe the simple pleasure he received from a good roll and a rub, she forgot her worries. The increased distance to her troubles hinted a normal life was there for the taking if she knew how to put the past behind her.

She walked up the dirt road to the barns to check on the training schedule for the coming week. She entered the feed room and was surprised to see a young girl, about eighteen years old, glaring at her. A collie mix dog panted at her feet.

She extended her hand. "Hi. I'm Jessica. I don't think we've met."

Eyes lined with cobalt stood in sharp contrast to white skin. A dozen earrings dotted up her ears. Any hair that wasn't tortured into cornrows or shaved off, stood stiff in black spikes.

"Yeah. Hi." The girl eyed the outstretched hand warily and took a step back.

Jessica rubbed her empty palm against her leg. "And you're?" Her voice trailed off.

"LeeAnne." Almost as an afterthought, she added, "I do the night feedings and turnout." LeeAnne reached for a stack of buckets. She put them in a line on the ground, glanced over the clipboard of instructions, grabbed a scoop, and began mixing different feeds and supplements.

Jessica leaned forward and gave the dog's ears a rub. "She's a sweetie. Yours?"

LeeAnne grunted.

"What's her name?"

The question was met with a stare and a head cocked to the side. "Ginger."

"Hey, Ginger." Jessica gave the dog's back a scratch. "I can give you a hand with the feeding, if you want."

LeeAnne continued to work with her back to Jessica before she answered, "No. I'm good."

"You must go to the high school I saw in town. Nice that you're so close."

LeeAnne's actions slowed. "I'm done with school," she said as she continued working with the efficiency that came from a familiar task and place.

A few minutes of silence passed. Jessica searched for something to say and felt stupid for trying. Instead, she reviewed the training notes and turnout schedules. LeeAnne gathered up the buckets, three on each arm, and pushed past, bumping into Jessica without a grunt of apology. Jessica bit back a reprimand when she noticed LeeAnne's arms were crisscrossed with straight lines—some white from scarring, others still angry and red.

The scars told a story Jessica was far too familiar with. They showed LeeAnne had something in her life that was too painful to deal with consciously and directly. Cutting allowed her physical control over when, how, and how much to hurt, rather than go through the emotional equivalent of open-heart surgery without anesthetic to parse out the reasons for her pain. Talking was hard. Cutting was easy.

LeeAnne put the buckets in front of the stalls. The dog trotted beside her, shadowing her every move. The hungry and impatient horses whickered and kicked their doors. Rather than yelling at them to quit, as many stablehands would have done, she entered each stall and spoke in a soft voice as she delivered the feed. She didn't rush, but gave each horse a moment of time. It wasn't long until the only sound was contented munching. The harsh lines around her eyes and mouth softened and LeeAnne began to look like the teenager she was rather than the hardened adult life circumstance had made her.

Jessica ventured across the gulf. "The horses like you."

LeeAnne rested her forearms on a stall door, back turned. "I feed them. They're just hedging their bets."

Jessica raised a brow. "'Hedging bets'? I've only heard that phrase around racetracks. Someone you know race?" She half smiled, hoping to get the conversation on a pleasant track.

LeeAnne's eyes narrowed. "My father was a stockbroker. Never been to no track."

Still trying, she asked, "Do you have your own horse at home?"

"No home."

No emotion. Stark. Was there any way to get the conversation on good footing? Jessica ventured a weak, "I know the feeling."

"You don't know shit." LeeAnne pushed herself off the stall and faced Jessica, the motion pulling up her sleeve to expose more red lines, some crusted and new. "Don't come in here and be all buddy-buddy with me like we have anything in common. Look around," she said with a sweep of her eyes. "This whole place revolved around you from day one. You check on the horses. People check on you." Her tone rose, mocking. "'How's our girl this morning?' 'What are Jessica's plans today?' Missus Lavielle watches everything you do. Those grooms you brought can't take a piss without making sure someone's looking after you. You so much as look at a horse, and someone runs to bring it to you groomed and tacked. You say anything, and men drop in their tracks to obey. You have power, so don't come in here and even hint at you know what I'm feeling. You don't."

Jessica stepped back, bitten. LeeAnne's visible scars did not mean she wanted the world to see her emotional pain. They were her yellow-zone, a warning to keep away. LeeAnne was right. Jessica didn't know a thing.

LeeAnne kicked the buckets aside and strode out of the barn. A few yards down the drive, she stopped and lit up a cigarette. Her chest swelled and collapsed at each drag, her back turned. Ginger flopped at her feet.

LeeAnne alternately flicked ashes on the ground and stubbed her booted toe on the gray ash. Jessica couldn't trust herself to explore her own inner world, let alone someone else's. Once again, silence proved to be her only protection.

A beat-up red pickup truck with a mismatched blue fender lumbered up the drive. LeeAnne watched it with guarded eyes and shoved her hands in her pockets. The door squeaked open and a marionette of a man emerged. Long arms and legs, clad in various shades of filthy denim, unfolded from the cab. He was no more than twenty-three years old, shaved head, with a body of hollowed-out skinniness seen only in the very sick or very addicted. Toothpick legs ended in a pair of buff colored work boots, the kind that construction workers favored because of their steel toe. With a wag of his head he motioned LeeAnne to get into the truck.

"Not done." She took a hesitant step toward the barn and stopped when she saw Jessica standing in the door. Ginger stayed close, tucking herself behind LeeAnne's legs.

He pressed, undeterred. "You wanted a ride back and here I am."

"You're early, Rudie. I said later." She looked at the empty paddocks. "Can you wait? Won't be more than another forty minutes."

"Fuck that no. I ain't waitin' and I ain't leavin' and coming back again. Getting in here is hard enough without me doin' it twice."

LeeAnne shrugged. "I gave security your name. You didn't have no problem."

"Like hell I didn't. They sniffed me up and down like I was shit." His head moved in a slow arc as he looked at the barns and house. The door to the barn office was open. A compressor and a tool kit were visible. He looked at the back of his truck as if calculating how quickly he could carry each and make a clean departure. Only after he lit a cigarette and leaned back against his truck did he see Jessica standing in the shadows.

His grunt and lowered head said her presence disrupted his plans. He ground out his cigarette with his heel, straightened, and pulled the fabric of his jeans at his thighs, settling his pants lower on his hips. As he walked up to LeeAnne, Jessica's heart began to thrum. She had been the target of too much violence not to recognize his menace. The small insight into LeeAnne and her relationship with Rudie made her heart break. LeeAnne's powerlessness was palpable in his presence. An urge to protect ignited.

He gave LeeAnne's shoulder a rough shove. "Hurry it up." LeeAnne scuffled back to the barn. He tried to follow.

"She'll work faster if you don't get in her way." Jessica walked forward, putting her body between theirs and blocking his entry into the barn.

"I said she's done working today."

"LeeAnne said another forty minutes."

Most men would have looked into the face of a person who confronted them. Instead, his eyes went first to her chest, then down her legs. When they finally settled on her face, his expression changed from hate to one of recognition. "Huh. You're that rich bitch folks been talkin' about. Seen you on the news. Better enjoy your freedom while you have it, cuz I hear they're coming after you." He brushed past her toward the barn.

"I said no." Jessica moved with him to block his path again. She looked him up and down, mocking his gaze, and wrinkled her nose. "Horses are sensitive to stench."

The next seconds passed in a blur. He pushed his open hand against her chest with such force her head snapped forward and she scrambled to keep her feet under her. Again, she managed to block his path. When he grabbed at her shirt to toss her out of his way, she raised her arms up and across the center of her body—between his gripped hands—throwing his arms aside and forcing him to release her. Angered, he kicked his leg out and tripped her, a classic move hinting at too much drunken brawl experience.

Something inside her clicked. Jessica may have been the target of violence, but she was never a victim, and now was not the time to start. Her fatigue vanished. A red haze filled her vision and her blood heated, filling her body with a survivor's strength. She drew herself up on one knee, gathering her muscles to launch into him. Each small motion froze in its own snapshot, progressing with incremental frames. He was slight and wiry, with a high center of gravity. She was shorter, but coiled strength. He may have viewed her as a nuisance, but she saw him as all the opportunities lost to protect herself and stop the inevitable. Rational thought failed her, only the knowledge of kill or be killed was clear. She brought her other leg behind her, tucked into a runner's starting position.

Jax was on him before she could launch. He threw Rudie face down and pulled his arm up behind him in half Nelson. The barnyard filled with action. Jax's men ran from around the side of the building and hoisted Rudie to his feet just as Jessica vaulted at him, fists clenched. Stunned, Rudie struggled as the men held him by his arms.

Her breath came in short deep gasps as she planted her knee in his groin and landed solid blows to his jaw, neck and chest before Jax took over and buried his fists into Rudie's gut. Multiple times. Rudie grunted with each punch and would have doubled over if the men had not held him upright. Jax's face showed no anger or fear, managing the event like a typical day at the office. Ginger yipped and circled, adding to the confusion. Horses grumbled with worry.

Jessica stepped back, panting from exertion and adrenalin. The urge to inflict more pain paused as the red veil lifted from her vision. Pieces of her environment came back into focus, along with a dull throb in her hand.

"Ow! Crap!" Jessica held her right hand against her chest and hunched over. The rushing sound in her ears was replaced by thuds and grunts as Jax continued his pummeling. Sanity slowly returned. "Jax! Stop it!" Jessica implored. "Enough!"

Jax stepped back but did not signal the men to release Rudie.

"You all right, Miss Jessica?" Jax looked from her to LeeAnne. "And you Miss LeeAnne?"

LeeAnne, pale and shaking, hugged herself in the shadow of the door. "Ah, shit, Rudie. What'd'you go and do that for?" A track of mascara flowed down her cheeks. She gave a shrill whistle and snapped her fingers. Ginger bounded over and sat at her feet, ears back. "He didn't mean it. It was an accident. Those guys jumped him."

Rudie started to speak. "That's right! You tell 'em, LeeAnne. I was jumped. I'll f–"

His sentence was cut off with an elbow to his chin.

"Shut up, feckin' Yank." Jax patted hay and dirt from his hands. "You won't be coming here again and you won't be causing any more trouble for these ladies." He looked over at LeeAnne and addressed her. "We'll get you to where you need to go, so you won't be needing a ride from him, but you best be reassessing your friends. We'll be escorting him back to whatever hollow he's come from. Sean?" he spoke to one of the men, "drive him in his truck. Alfie? Get your truck and follow them out." The heavier set man released Rudie and disappeared around the side of the barn.

A few minutes later, two pickups clattered down the drive. Sean drove with Rudie slumped in the passenger seat of his truck.

Jax examined Jessica's hand with more than a little enjoyment. "A little ice will do you fine. Next time you try to give a bloke a right cross to the jaw, make sure your fist is closed as tight as you can make it and don't tuck your thumb in or you'll be sporting a cast for sure."

She flexed her fingers. "I . . . I have no idea why I did that."

"Don't you now? I doubt that. Most lasses would attack with fingernails as an eagle's talons, but you went at him like a prize fighter."

She opened and closed her hand, wincing with the movement. "Maybe I'll try that next time."

"Next time? Ah, you won't at that. Fightin' with a closed fist means you've less fear and fight to win. But putting me out of business, you are. My job is to make sure there are no more 'next times.'"

LeeAnne began to furiously clean the stalls and turn the horses out for the night. What the hell just happened?

Jax lowered his voice to not be overheard. "I told Missus Lavielle that having that girl here would bring bad news, but she didn't listen to me. You might think you can keep yourself safe, but my job is to make sure of it and havin' access to the farm while you're on it is something Master Connaught has ordered me to control. You best tell your friend I'll not be having filthy dicks within a hawk's sight of you. And for the girl?" He paused and looked over his shoulder at LeeAnne. "I'm sorry for her woes, but she needs to get sorted out on her own time."

Jessica waited until Jax left to approach LeeAnne. LeeAnne's face was red with exertion and she had rolled up her shirtsleeves. Above the crisscross of thin scars were faded bruises. If Jessica needed any more proof LeeAnne was an abused woman, all doubts faded. "Are you okay?"

"I don't want to talk about it."

"There are people who can help. You don't have to go–"

"I said I don't want to talk about it. Leave me alone."

Jessica looked up toward Electra's sprawling house. "Don't talk, then. Just listen. You don't have to go back to him. I'll ask Electra if you can stay here. She has more than enough room. The choice is yours, but please be safe."

LeeAnne's lower lip quivered and she looked at Jessica with tear-filled eyes, but said nothing.

"At least give yourself one night. Longer if you want, but just one night. You deserve that much." Jessica yearned to reach out and hug LeeAnne, but knew better than to touch an abused woman without consent. Doing so, even in friendship, perpetuated feelings of power-lessness in the abused. "Rudie needs time to cool down." She made a point of looking at the bruises. "You know his pattern. He'll probably blame you for what happened. Tonight will not be a good night for you to be near him. Don't go back home."

Her words were met with silence. She tried another tack.

"The horses like it when you're around and that tussle unsettled them. At least hang out here for a few hours and calm them down."

LeeAnne wiped the back of her hand across her nose and said nothing.

"Alfie will drive you wherever you want to go tonight. You don't need to put yourself at risk by taking rides with Rudie. Is there any-one else who can help?"

"My truck's in the shop. Only need rides 'til it's fixed. 'nother day or so."

"Let me take care of you." She spoke the words before second thoughts could pull them in. Her voice caught, startling her with its potency. Caring for someone outside of her problems gave promise the semblance of a normal life could be hers. "At least, um, at least please take care of yourself."

She waited for an answer and received only a turned back. LeeAnne grabbed a handful of lead ropes and walked into the barn.

A dull ache teased at Jessica's temples. She had done all she could and knew she would do more if LeeAnne would let her. Suddenly ex-hausted, she decided to see if Electra was back from her errands. She had walked only a few strides when a Mercedes sedan pulled up the drive and parked in front of the main house. Electra emerged, fluffing herself to look presentable. On seeing Jessica, she walked over and linked arms.

"Gracious child! You look like a wrung out dish towel."

"You have no idea." A whiff of Chanel No. 5 pushed her away. "Careful! Get too close and I'll contaminate you with horse hair and Parfum d' Manure."

Electra pulled her closer. "Dirt is a small price to pay for time with you! Why don't you get cleaned up and I'll cook us dinner. Looks like some food'll do you good."

Jessica squirmed under Electra's probing stare. "Good idea. I've had a hell of a day."

"Bad day training?"

"Yeah, and I met LeeAnne and her boyfriend."

"Her boyfriend! Rudie? What was he doing here?"

As they carried bags of groceries to the kitchen, Jessica filled Electra in on the highpoints and only hinted at Jax's pummeling. She explained an ill-timed approach to a jump as her need for an icepack on her hand. As much as she wanted to unload her worries by confiding in someone, years of hiding calloused over the ability to do so. "Seems I can't do anything right in the animal or human world today." The air felt heavy around her. Her shoulders rounded with the weight of it.

Electra produced a tissue from her purse, motions uncharacteristically deliberate.

Jessica tensed. Electra was a human radar, one of those rare people whose empathic abilities made it impossible to hide anything from. She watched as Electra blotted her cheeks and forehead with a genteel flourish as she peered into Jessica's face. "Seeing Rudie treat her like that must have been terrible for you."

Jessica shrugged.

"I can't imagine how you felt to see a young woman overpowered by that lunk."

Electra's grey-blue eyes bored into her. She looked away.

"You look like a wreck," Electra said. "You need to take better care of yourself."

Jessica shifted the icepack and used one fingernail to scrape the grit from under the others. Seeing her knuckles were raw and red, she placed her hands in her lap. "I'm fine. Really."

"That outburst you had when we were leaving the airport told me you're anything but *fine*. If I had any doubts, those purple half moons under your eyes would erase them, and now this."

"Electra, please. I'm–"

"Last time we spoke, you weren't sleeping. Since you've been here we've all made sure to keep the outside world away from you so you can get some rest. Are you getting any?" Electra reached over and raised Jessica's chin. "I love you as my daughter. Having you back in Perc has filled this empty house as if I had my own children. Whatever it is that's bothering you, one day I hope you can talk to me like family."

For what felt like the hundredth time that day, hot tears pricked at Jessica's eyes. They flowed not just from sorrow and fear for all that had been lost, but from a yearning to connect in the exact way Electra offered. But the meaning of family was complicated, for imbedded in it was an iron core of loyalty, and silence was the only way she knew to function with what little family she had. The blood of a civil rights activist and a pillar of the Catholic Church ran through her veins. The least she could do was honor that legacy, and silence was her testament. She held Kavan safe inside the void.

Now was not the time for her to pull a scab away and bleed her secrets.

Jessica sniffled and squeezed her eyes dry. "C'mon, really. I don't want to talk about me. Is that okay?"

Electra enveloped her in maternal folds for a long moment. "For now, yes. No promises for later," she said, pouring juleps into tall glasses heavy with extra ice and mint. She ushered them to the shaded front veranda. "Tell me, how is LeeAnne?"

They watched LeeAnne lead two horses to a paddock and give them a vigorous head rub before setting them free. After she looped their halters on a fencepost, she propped a leg up on the bottom rail and leaned against her arms in a posture of deep thought. Ginger sat at her feet. Jessica felt connected to her in a way she couldn't understand.

"She's good with the animals. Kind. They respond to her. Me? I think she'd rather puke than be in my presence."

Electra chuckled. "Well, at least she didn't curse at you. That's a good start."

"Ha! That's what she'd have done if she didn't like me?"

"You must have made a good impression."

"I'm not so sure. What's her story? Why is she here?" When Electra struggled to answer, she prodded. "I saw the scars."

"LeeAnne is the cousin of a dear friend of mine. Her scars are her armor. Showing them is like a lion snarling his teeth at you. It's a warning to keep away, yet at the same time, I think they're a cry for help. She's had a rough home life. Her father is a drunk and abused her."

"You wouldn't think a stock broker would be the type."

"She told you that? I'm impressed you two had a conversation.

Jessica picked at the wicker on the rocker. "I'm not sure you'd call it a conversation. More like a telling off. She says the way the farm revolves around my every whim puts the two of us on different planets. Her life must have been pretty tough for her to cut herself up like that, and Rudie should be jailed for what he does to her."

"Her mother did nothing to help when she was being abused by her father, then LeeAnne escaped only to be brutalized by that scum of a boyfriend. I'll make sure he never sets foot on this property again."

"I think Jax is a step ahead of you on that one."

Electra widened her eyes. "By God, I'll bet you're right!" She looked toward the barn, as if he might appear just at the mention of his name. "My friend was hoping that working with horses and having a safe place to go would help LeeAnne regain some control over her life."

"She's not going to heal as long as Rudie's in her life. He's a controlling and abusive monster. She said her truck's in the shop, so she might be more comfortable here if she doesn't have to worry about getting rides back and forth. How about your guest house?"

"My thought exactly!" Electra exclaimed.

They were pleased and more than a little relieved when LeeAnne agreed. They settled her into the cottage behind the barns, then returned to "the big house" —as Electra liked to call her home. The clapboard mansion was impressive in size and looked even more imposing because of the four two-story tall white pillars that supported a portico and shaded the wide porch—or veranda, as Electra called it—where their cocktail glasses sat beaded with condensation and forgotten. Each window was trimmed with heavy casings and flanked by shutters painted a green so dark they almost looked black. Wings jutted off the main house at a slight angle as if to hug the curved drive and courtyard. A tiered fountain burbled freely in the center garden, lush with red and pink roses and hibiscus flowers. They walked along the brick path and entered the front door. The main foyer was dominated by a sweeping staircase and brass chandelier, area bright with white painted wainscoting. The height of the ceilings helped to keep the interior cool.

They ate a light dinner of steamed greens and chicken, sitting in the kitchen rather than the cavernous dining room. Electra tried to engage her in conversation, but Jessica could only summon a wan smile and steered clear of her questions.

"I'm so tired, I can barely string two words together. Tell me more about what's gone on in Perc since I've been gone."

Electra prattled on, catching Jessica up on local personalities. Plans were in gear for another Harvest Hunter Pace and the hardware store owner was crowing with delight over his horse's growing reputation. Jessica should have been pleased that a horse she had trained was winning championships, but nothing she heard stuck. Exhaustion pulled at every fiber of her being. Physically, her muscles ached and joints groaned if she stood too quickly after sitting. Tears stung her eyes even when she forced them away. Her skin no longer fit. Only after her head bobbed forward and she hoisted heavy eyelids up over gritty eyes did she excuse herself for bed.

She hardly noticed that the sky was still streaked with fading hues of purple and peach when she pulled the covers over her head.

What is it about sleep that overwhelms a person when they least want it and eludes capture when craved? Jessica willed sleep to come. Memories mixed with dreams as images dissolved and coalesced. The scenes from the barn played in a loop in front of her eyes. Again and again she saw LeeAnne's eyes change from guarded to fearful and back. In slow motion Rudie's hand came up and pushed her aside like a chit in the wind.

"I hear they're comin' after you."

Coming after who? For what? With strobe-light movements, Alfie and Jax seized Rudie and throttled him. Freeze frames of LeeAnne's face flickered as she recoiled in fear, razor-thin scars red against her white skin.

These were the worst moments of the day, when she was alone in a bed that wasn't her own, yearning for the escape of sleep. The shadows on the walls jerked and slid in front of her closed eyes and infiltrated her dreams. Emotional balance slipped away in the riptide of physical exhaustion. Memories that pushed to be heard during the day, only to be thwarted by the demands of a conscious mind, soared as dreams teased her with feints and dodges. In the half-sane world between wakefulness and sleep, she thrashed, then paced, muffling her steps and cries. Sleep must have come, for when she woke she was bathed in sweat, in a bedroom flooded with light from every lamp, and chairs wedged against doorknobs. She punched her pillow, rolled onto her stomach and pushed her face into her hands to stop her lower lip from trembling.

Echoes of her conversation with Electra at dinner reverberated.

She could once again feel her hands drawn into Electra's own. Perfect oval nails painted a deep pink contrasted with Jessica's nibbled and dirty ones.

"Shoot, Darlin'. No one would blame you for having nightmares. After what you've been through, it's a wonder you're not a raving lunatic."

A lunatic. Was she a lunatic? Are lunatics born or made?

"I've been reading about something called Post Traumatic Stress Disorder. You can't keep the stress of what happened to you bottled up inside."

"I don't. I ride." At once, she was galloping on a white horse in front of a boiling wave of snow, intent upon keeping the avalanche of memories and feelings from burying her.

"Hard enough to get you or one of those animals killed! No, you need to talk to someone. If not to a doctor, then to me."

The delirium of a sleep-deprived night swirled on. "Maybe you need something to take the edge off your worry and help you sleep and then we can talk. Everything would be off the record. No recorders. No notes. You have my word I won't talk with a soul." With dreamy X-ray vision, a digital recorder glowed in Electra's purse.

A soul. Her mother's soul. Bridget's soul. Was that gone forever? Kavan would know. Jessica gave a silent wail in her pillow as grief swelled and rotted inside of her. How could she grieve for a mother she had only begun to know after her death? Would Kávan be enough to anchor her to the present or to show her how to love?

Love. Loved. Always loved. Michael loved her and killed because of it. Twice. Protecting her.

Or was he?

Had he killed more?

She shuddered awake, or had she been awake the whole time? Was being told she was loved enough to keep the pain away? Her brain needed sleep to categorize information and make connections. But when sleep is broken, are the connections sound?

Her whole being ached as she acknowledged she had been hunted and harmed by those who had sworn to keep her safe. The foundation of who she thought she was—the oldest child of a loving and cohesive family—crumbled as she realized she was collateral damage in a war she knew nothing about. She was raised as an American, educated but not politicized. Wars meant camouflaged soldiers, heavy artillery, and airdropped bombs in jungles and deserts, not dungaree-clad men parking explosive-filled trucks on busy city streets. Those she trusted lied to her.

And the man who loves her? Does Michael lie or does the love itself lie? Silence. His silence. Her silence. She didn't want to pull back the surface, fearing what she would see in the underbelly of truth. She couldn't shake the feeling that maybe she wasn't loved or protected, but a pawn in an invisible game. What could exposing her true parents mean to the brokers of power? The pain of grappling with her past meant coming to terms with certain truths and she simply wasn't ready to be still long enough to sift through her experiences. Doing so would force her to acknowledge she was fully awake when the nightmares unfolded and that she failed to see the warning signs.

Shadows slithered along the ceiling. They darkened and spread as her thoughts skipped along the surface of slumber. The shroud of sleep lifted as a hand smoothed up her hip and cupped her breast. Another hand slid up her inner thigh. She jerked awake to feel breath on her face and her body yearning. The room was silent. The red numerals on the clock said four-fifteen, and she was still alone, tortured by sleep and thinking of Michael. It was Michael's hands that brought her body to life. It was Michael's life she stepped into when she reclaimed her own. One blessing of the hallucinations of sleep was she could smell his scent. Clean. Masculine. Hers. He had built a cocoon for her. Filled it with everything she needed or wanted. He grieved for Bridget with her and allowed her time to weep for a mother she barely knew. She clasped her hands over her nose and mouth to capture his scent, but he was gone before her eyelashes flickered.

Another hour passed with enough time to burrow her secrets and fears deeper inside. No casual observer would ever stumble upon her secrets, nor would one think to extend a hand to someone with a beautiful and placid exterior. She didn't look like she needed help. Her scars did not streak down her arms in shades of white and crusted red. Her scars were not hues of purple and yellow. They were inside, safely hidden from view.

Jessica shut down. Being still on the inside was difficult. Being still on the outside kept her alive. Although she no longer had to hide in plain sight in disguises and false names, instinct told her to be wary of displaying emotions or thoughts lest doing so would tip her poker hand.

The alarm screeched and she pulled herself out of bed.

Saturday, July 13, 1996
Brandywine Farm
Perc, Kentucky

JESSICA DIDN'T WANT to acknowledge the additional sandbags of fatigue each day added. The sun rose and set in a relentless march that provided no respite. Her feet dragged along the ground and her boots tripped her as she walked the barn corridor. She was ill-prepared to deal with animals, let alone humans, and she fell short of the training goals she had set for the horses. Mornings slid into afternoons. LeeAnne continued to avoid her and Jax questioned every move of her training, keeping her well within the confines of safe riding.

Her confidence eroded and insomnia made her sloppy. When Declan emerged from a car parked in Electra's driveway, she didn't turn and run.

The spark to survive is a funny thing. Some animals react to a shift in wind direction in less than a second, leaping away with blurred speed. Others hope their spotted coats will blend them into dappled shade, not playing dead, but fooling the predator's senses to believe no prey is near. Still others inhale the fear, letting the chemical change sink deep within their bodies, waiting for the moment to become a predator themselves.

A stealth-like calm settled in Jessica's gut.

Declan, out of his lawyerly attire, wore a Bostonian's version of Kentuckian casual wear—cream linen shirt with the top buttons undone, no tie, and topsiders without socks. Pants, freshly pressed that morning, were no match for the South's sticky heat and clung to him in deep creases. Not hidden by a suit jacket, the power of his chest and back was evident and balanced that of his lower body. His was not an equestrian's body, supple with determined strength. His was the body of a machine.

Electra walked over to them, fussing with clippers, gloves, and a basket filled with flowers. Her wide-brimmed hat and Lilly Pulitzer print shorts—in shades of bright yellow, citrus green, and hot pink—were a perfect match for her pink rubber garden shoes.

"Declan. I wasn't expecting you." Jessica's voice was surprisingly calm despite the heat the sight of his body ignited in her. Cursing the sleep deprivation that allowed her primal brain to rule, she willed herself in check.

Electra smoothed her hand down her matronly frame. "No? I'm so sorry! I thought I told you over dinner last night."

Had she? No memory bubbled to the surface. Functioning at a reptilian level of intelligence had its disadvantages.

Electra gave Declan a stony look. "You were supposed to call before arriving."

Declan's demeanor was a study in neutrality. His gaze swept over the barns and arenas, to paddocks and back to the homestead before finally landing on Jessica. "Where are your guards?" A fly buzzed around his head. He didn't notice it.

Jessica motioned her head toward the barns. She became too aware of her filthy breeches and sweat-soaked T-shirt. "Why are you here?"

Declan shunned small talk and jumped directly into the business at hand. Normally, she liked directness. Today wasn't one of those days.

"Are you ready to talk?"

"I'm not ready for anything but good news." She looked at her boots and grubby knuckles. Anywhere but at him.

"I have to be back to Boston tomorrow afternoon. I have business matters to go over with you."

"I don't have any business with you."

"Yeah. You do."

Was that a smirk that flickered on his lips? "And?"

"We need to go over a few facts."

"What's to go over? What facts?" Electra tried to wedge herself between them, using her body as a shield.

Muscles worked along Declan's jaw. "I think it's best if you're not a part of our conversation."

Electra bristled. She waggled a pair of pruning shears in the air as if fending off an attack. "Can't you see she's at her wits' end? I don't know what's so important you couldn't talk to her by phone."

How could the earth's gravitational pull have increased ten-fold in a few minutes? Declan's presence evidenced things were not going well. Jessica struggled to hold herself up under her worries' weight.

"I wanted to lay out exactly what the process has been behind the scenes to regain your legal standing." He angled his head away from Electra.

The hairs on the back of her neck vibrated. "Okay. Let's hear it."

"There have been some inquiries into your background."

No one spoke for a half beat. Electra's eyes darted from Declan to Jessica and back. She linked arms with Jessica and escorted her toward the manse, bringing her mouth close to Jessica's ear. "You don't have to talk with anyone you don't want to. Tell me if you want him gone."

The urge to run was strong, but Jessica straightened her back. "No. I'm good. I want to hear what he has to say."

She knew Electra was assessing every inch of her for clues on how fragile she was. Electra commanded them forward. "If you're going to have a conversation, at least be civil about it. Don't stand out here. Come to the house."

Their footsteps crunched on the gravel drive. Inside, the air felt fresh as they walked through the main living room and dining room into the kitchen, their motions sounding too loud in the quiet rooms.

Jessica washed up as best she could while Electra made a plate of cheese, fruit, and bread, and a pitcher of ice tea. A glass overflowing with freshly picked mint sat beside a covered silver ice bucket. The trio walked to a small patio off the kitchen made cool by the climbing vines of bougainvillea, heavy with purple blooms. Tall and densely leafed green boxwoods lined the perimeter. A fountain, a sculpture of a mare and foal with water cascading around their feet, graced the corner. Hummingbirds buzzed among flowers and feeders.

Jessica took all this in as she paused at the patio door, hands on hips and shoulders back.

"You look like a girl ready for battle," Electra said over the brim of her glass.

Jessica grabbed a drink off the tray and sipped, immediately aware of Electra's heavy hand with the bourbon.

Declan took a long pull, swallowed. Then took another.

Electra began a patter of small talk in a gentlewoman's way to put the conversation on lighter footing. Jessica had seen the technique enough times to know it was a way to give guests time to quietly assess one another without confrontation. Electra bantered, skillfully steering the conversation around current events and local weather, but neither Jessica nor Declan engaged. The flow of words finally stemmed, and uncomfortable minutes passed in a soundless standoff. Declan remained motionless, unyielding in his unspoken request for privacy, clearly signaling any attempt that brandishing Southern manners and shaming him into compliance would fail. Defeated, she turned to Jessica. "I'll be inside if you need me. You'll be all right," she said in a tone meant to convey confidence, but missed.

Declan watched Electra leave and refreshed Jessica's julep. "Here. You're going to need this."

"Why?"

"You're in trouble."

Her mouth dried. "What kind?"

"The heightened response provided by your welcoming party of immigration officials is due to more than just your arrival's proximity to Atlanta and timing of the Olympics."

She crossed her arms in front of her chest to hide her pounding heart. "You said I was used to test U.S. response to a terrorist threat. My arrival helped them to stage a publicity stunt. They should be finished with me."

"Responses like that don't just happen and they don't simply evaporate without some kind of lasting impression. Northern Ireland's government wanted to learn something from the United States' response. Ditto for the U.S."

"What more is there to learn?" Sweat formed along her upper lip. She wiped it away with her shoulder. "They got their headlines from a stinking coincidence. What more could they possibly want?"

"They determined the birth certificate your passport was issued on was forged." He looked at her long enough for her to begin to squirm. Less than a second passed. "That's a felony. Formal charges could be brought against you."

She huffed. "Just in time for the evening news." False bravado edged her voice. How could she stop Declan from probing for answers she wanted to keep hidden?

"We worked every channel we had to ensure your problem-free reentry to the States. No doubt who we contacted and how was of great interest to the authorities. Don't be lulled into a feeling of security thinking countries don't spy on each other. All communications come under scrutiny. Even Electra's calls to her friends in the Feds when you arrived did not go unnoticed. Who did you contact before you left Belfast and once you arrived in Kentucky?"

"I didn't call anyone before I left Belfast. Michael made all of my travel arrangements. I only made one call out to Electra once I arrived." Cataloging additional conversations was easy. She received one from Murray. None from Michael, a fact that ate at her.

"You initiated contact with no one else?"

"No. Any other contacts were made to me, not by me. I can't believe a government would waste their resources on something like this."

He dropped his head down and tapped the pads of his tented fingers together as he weighed what to say next. He shook his head and looked at her. "Northern Ireland has determined you're the real deal. A terrorist."

Ice encased her. Her mouth worked but no sound uttered.

"With falsified documents, it's only a matter of time before the U.S. thinks so, too."

"Th-that's ridiculous! Y-you know more about me than most people. If you believe that g-garbage, I'm not saying another word to you."

"Michael confided in me that you were connected to the men and transported the explosives used in the Manchester bombing exactly as the tabloids had conjectured, but the mainstream press couldn't prove so didn't print." When she gasped, he raised his hand to stop her protest. "He says the bombing was his father's plan and he knew nothing about it. He's worked hard to suppress inculpatory evidence. His network is very good." He paused, waiting for her to absorb this information. "There's nothing actionable against you—yet. But the growing circumstantial case should be a concern of yours. A terrorist uses violence and threats to intimidate and coerce. The most likely person to promulgate terrorism is someone with extreme political beliefs cultivated over a lifetime, or someone recently radicalized. Prime targets for radicalization are individuals without strong or stabilizing ties. You fit the personality profile and your recent travels provide evidence of radicalizing opportunity."

"I traveled to train horses! It's crazy to think otherwise!"

His unblinking gaze settled on her. "Gibraltar?"

"Christ! It was *Michael's* idea to go there! He made all of the arrangements. It was the first time I'd ever been on a private jet and I thought it was fun! You know, beaches? Sun? Foreign country? It was a *vacation!*"

"Your presence there amplifies concerns and supplies hard evidence that you have been radicalized."

Hunched and hugging herself, she began to pace back and forth. "No, no, no."

"You need to talk to me. I know what I've been told by Michael and what I can discern from public records. You have nothing to gain from being silent. There's more to your story. I need to hear it directly from you."

Declan tried to rip away her anchors and to make her reliant upon him. How desperate would she need to be before she confided in him? About Kavan? Never.

Prey have eyes on the sides of their heads, allowing them to see to their sides and back with spare movements. Predators have eyes facing forward, a fact hunters use to their advantage when they suddenly find themselves facing large carnivores. Jungle survival lore is filled with stories of lone humans escaping a lion's wrath by facing the cat directly and waving their arms to look bigger and deadlier than their opponent. Prey, at the last moment of life, turn to face their predator head on, in a last ditch effort of attack and survival. Jessica didn't wave her arms, but stopped pacing and drew her shoulders back, keeping her knees loose as she looked directly at Declan. "There's nothing to hear."

Another fly landed on his neck above his open collar. He didn't flinch. "I need to know everything."

Everything? "No."

"As a U.S. citizen, you are being afforded all of the rights, privileges, and protections due." He paused, and leaned forward a few more degrees, resting his forearms on his knees, his posture calculated to convey he was someone she could trust. "Tell me about your parents."

Her eyes narrowed and she looked at a spot near his feet. "What's to tell? Margaret Heinchon, my mother, came to Boston when she was fifteen as a governess to care for Paul Wyeth's children after his wife died. Jim, Paul's oldest son, was eighteen when she arrived. They fell in love and got married. Simple."

"Not simple. Margaret and Jim were not your parents." He clasped his hands together and sat upright. "If I'm going to be any help here, don't bullshit me. You're suspected of criminal involvement, but a terrorism charge puts this on a different level."

"I have nothing to say."

"Your identity is being questioned. If your birth certificate was faked, who knows what else was faked, and that puts you smack in the middle of a shit pit."

Her years of running taught her to respond to questions with answers that people expected to hear. Doing so thwarted other questions. Danger came in the moments when the person asking the questions knew more than he or she let on.

Declan knew more than he was saying. But what? Swallowing didn't loosen the knot in her throat. In a convent outside of Belfast, on the rocky coast of the Irish Sea, Jessica learned her truth. What choice did she have? If she spoke of her mother, would it keep her father safe? Declan needed to know how to diffuse the situation if an official in Northern Ireland stumbled upon the truth. She began to talk slowly, calculating her words.

"Bridget Heinchon Harvey and Margaret Heinchon Wyeth were sisters. Bridget did what she had to do so I would grow up free from her troubles. She faked a marriage so her pregnancy would not be questioned in Ireland and Margaret faked a pregnancy in the U.S. and took me as her own. Both women are long dead. Are they trying to sort out my citizenship or Bridget's past?"

Declan remained silent for too long. "What makes you think the authorities are interested in Bridget?"

Did she really have to speak aloud what her heart wanted to hide? He remained motionless, black eyes staring straight ahead, but every inch of her knew she was being assessed. Was she weak and easily conquered? Would she turn and run? She became prey in a field of snares. Traps were being set for her and she didn't know where safe footing was.

Irrational anger grew as she thought about the harsh treatment her mother endured and all her father would lose if she was careless. Bridget was jailed in the late 1960's without formal charges being brought against her. History proved that many imprisonments were unlawful reactions by the U.K. government to speeches and activism. Bridget wanted to educate and mobilize the citizens of Northern Ireland to their rights as humans. She wanted bans lifted which prohibited the teaching of Irish history and the native Irish tongue in schools, both lessons to keep the Irish heart beating inside a weakening body. She wanted the discrimination of Catholics to cease, and for jobs and housing to be available for all regardless of their accent or religion. In America, Bridget's actions would have been regarded as her right to freedom of speech and assembly, but in the U.K., her actions were considered radical expressions of terrorist ideals and a threat to the country's security.

Jessica's words came slowly. "When I was in the Irelands, I learned that Bridget and her brothers were three of England's most hated revolutionaries for their efforts to reunify the island by trying to force the United Kingdom to relinquish control over the six counties that once belonged to the Republic of Ireland. Bridget was the brain and the power behind Northern Ireland's civil rights movement. Her brothers were the brawn behind many bombings of U.K. buildings and monuments. England killed her brothers and branded my mother a terrorist before throwing her in jail. She sat there for five years without charges ever being brought. Eventually they expelled her from Northern Ireland on her promise never to return. I didn't know any of this growing up. I learned the truth this spring."

"How?"

One word. An unanswerable question. Because Kavan had followed her every footstep throughout her life via the insular community that is the Catholic Church. Because he was so loved, anyone would do anything for him—even sending him word on a 'troubled runaway daughter of a close friend' who may have recently arrived in their parish. Easy to spot. Blond and striking. Good with horses. Because his trove of Bridget's diaries finally found her, and from them the truth of her parentage bloomed. Because Kavan never abandoned her even when she thought she was alone. Because he wept when he asked for her forgiveness, saying all Bridget and he ever wanted was for her to live freely and be loved.

She would not be the one to abandon him.

Her breath hitched. "The island of Ireland is a small place. I met someone who knew my mother and told me about her."

"Who?"

Kavan. Her mother's journals. "A family friend."

One corner of his mouth snarled upward. "As much as you're trying not to talk about your mother and her connection to the unrest and violence in the North, leaks will happen. Don't think your silence buys you safety. I don't give a flying fuck about your rebel DNA. Get over yourself."

She drew in a shocked breath. "How can you . . . I don't see how you . . ."

"I have no evidence that you are a child of a U.S. citizen. Do you have any documents that show who your parents were or where you were born?"

Bridget and Kavan lived their lives in the city where they were born. Belfast never had two people who loved their home more. No matter how she looked at it, birth made her a citizen of the United Kingdom. She thought of her torn and yellowed parchment birth certificate she had discovered behind a silver-framed picture. Bridget. Kavan. Northern Ireland. Baby girl. Her. "No."

"Do you have any document showing Margaret and Jim's adoption of you?"

The scent of the flowers became unbearable. Their colors dimmed. "No."

"Do you have any document showing any scenario in which you were naturalized?"

"No."

"Attention by U.S. Immigration is because they see you as an affiliate to terrorist activity, and in their eyes that makes you a terrorist. You know the drill," he said, eyes boring into her, "Innocent until proven guilty. If you are considered an illegal immigrant, you do not enjoy the same rights. As an alien, you are in the U.S. as a guest and, as such, your permission to be here can be revoked at their pleasure."

"Revoked? What are you saying?"

"The felony of a forged birth certificate combined with other verifiable facts put you at risk of being deported from the States."

"Deported! What? To where? I'm a U.S. citizen!" Even as she blurted the words, she knew they were false.

"Yeah? Well unless you can prove that, deportation is going to be pretty damned easy. Look, the fact of the matter is you can't change who you are and you sure as hell can't hide it. Learning your mother's history was a shock. I get it." He wiped his mouth clear of the snapped words and sank his head into his shoulders. He continued with a softened tone. "The risk here is allowing other people to define you by filling in the blanks of your past with their spin of the facts."

"You sound like Electra," she scoffed.

"Yeah? Well maybe it's one of the few things we agree on. If someone else discovers this truth, it will look like you were trying to cover it up and affirm suspicions that you have terrorist leanings. I'm worried that the constant barrage of articles quoting your uncle will fuel an investigation that could stumble upon the real story."

She pulled her head back in confusion. "I don't have an uncle."

"As far as the Wyeths are concerned, and the rest of the world, you do. William Wyeth is determined to see you."

She thought of the face she saw at the airport. Her lip curled at his memory. William Wyeth was pathologically predisposed to suck up all the limelight and free drinks he could. "I haven't heard anything."

He waved his hand in an exaggerated circle. "How could you? Inside this bubble? He's keeping your name and his face in the news playing the 'concerned uncle' card."

Hope faded that interest in her would wither because of her silence. She had steadfastly refused Electra's imploring to sculpt a public relations campaign designed to keep the most intrusive inquiries away. But Declan made it clear that William and the reporter from Boston had been relentless in their pursuit of a meeting, or at least a quote, about the Wyeth's family ties. But who is William to her? Only faint memories of a pale and sweaty man who caused Jim and Margaret no end of grief remained. Jessica refused to dignify the lie of her childhood with any acknowledgement of him.

"I'm not going to talk about the Wyeths."

"I think that's a mistake, but suit yourself. What do you know about your father?"

The question startled her with its change of the conversation's direction. She felt Declan's eyes scan every muscle twitch and eyelash flicker as she struggled to answer him.

Bishop Kavan Hughes. How many lives had he saved by being the calm voice behind the winds of hatred? Bombs weren't placed because of him. Riots didn't start. People paused and listened to his gentle voice. His message of reason and reconciliation shamed the powerful into humility and silenced the gangs into selfless thought. He was able to seat opponents at a table because he was the trusted link on both sides of the conflict. He wore his neutrality as confidently as his robe and Roman collar. If his paternity became known, all his good would evaporate as a drop of water on a heated skillet. She could only imagine the hunger for his demise by the governments in the United Kingdom.

Bridget's and Kavan's driving desire was to see their island made whole again, to be one nation, not two. Kavan wanted oppositional parties to sit at a negotiation table and use words to come to terms, not violence. How could she find fault in any of their actions?

Would this cause become hers? Would she care enough to protect Kavan to sacrifice herself for him? As pieces of her life sifted through her fingers like sand, she wondered if this was what it felt like to become radicalized.

Gooseflesh puckered her skin. What had she learned about her parents' lives? Enough to know they thought ahead. Planned. Built alliances and contingencies. The throbbing began again and she forced her thinking to clear. She knew the answer. She only needed to calm herself before she spoke, blowing the dust off childhood memories. Another memory flickered to the surface. Kavan and she sitting in the chapel of the convent. He, nervous as a schoolboy on a first date. She, awed at meeting her father and feeling the power of their blood connection. She hung on every word he spoke and remembered his imploring eyes when he said, even in death his best friend protected him.

"Gus Adams received his citizenship in the early 1960's."

A truth and a lie in one statement. Somewhere, in a dusty church basement, amid the cobwebs and discarded catechisms, a document existed that showed Gus was her father.

Declan's motions slowed. His head pivoted on his neck to look straight at her, body and shoulders motionless, eyes betraying nothing. His stealthy gaze struck a nerve at the center of her heart. "The laws are clear that any child fathered by him after the granting of his citizenship would be considered a citizen of the United States regardless of the country of birth."

He paused and muttered something that sounded like, "Well done."

He drained his drink and poured another, raising the pitcher toward her with a question, and stopped when he noticed her glass was still full. He topped off his drink letting ice cubes clatter into the glass and splash its contents over the rim.

"That's it then. All you wanted to know?" She brought her drink halfway to her mouth and lowered it, unable to add anything to her roiling gut.

"I'm hired to clean up the messes you and Michael are in. I'm not here to play hide and seek with the truth. Deportation on lack of citizenship will not happen unless the authorities have firm evidence. At least I know to look for a document, most likely a baptismal certificate that shows Gus is your father. That narrows my search to churches in the Boston area, most likely Hamilton."

The tucked-in edges of his mouth said he didn't buy her story, but would follow through regardless.

"I don't have to fear deportation now. Right?"

"Facts can be worked with."

The layers of deception surrounding Jessica's birth deepened. Other's knew her truth and lied to protect her. She sensed Declan knew more than he admitted and wondered how much of his pushing her was a test to see how far she would go to protect her father. Would he participate in the deception or would he use the truth against her—or Kavan?

She was ready to live her life as Jessica Wyeth. But as Bridget's daughter? And all that meant? Her resolve weakened. "I ... I don't want the public to learn about Bridget. She ... she kept this secret to her death. Let people believe William is my uncle." Tears stung her eyes. "Please."

Their uncomfortable silence was broken with voices from inside the house. Electra's voice rose and fell, followed by two male voices. She was shouting. Her words were clipped. Sentences short. One man spoke in faux-calm tones. The other man sounded impatient.

Jessica turned toward the noise. Her instincts hummed.

Electra's voice boomed. "You are *not allowed* in my *home*. I'll say this again, I do *not* know where Miss Wyeth is. She's *gone* for a *ride* on a horse and it could be *hours* before she returns! You have my word she'll be in contact with you as soon as she does."

Once again, sleep deprivation made her sloppy and she remained still as her brain chugged to catch up with events. With feline silence, Declan closed the gap between them. He grabbed the glass from her hand and threw it into flowerbeds. Thick mulch muffled its landing. She gave a little gasp as he spun her around and shoved her through the box hedge. She scrambled into a sitting position behind a hydrangea, tucking her body deep into the brush, and hugging her knees. He brought his index finger up to his lips with one hand and motioned with the other for her to stay put.

"This is preposterous! How dare you come barging into my home!" Electra's voice came nearer.

A man's voice. "I'm sorry, ma'am. You invited us in."

"I did no such thing." Electra's words dripped with indignity mingled with fear.

Declan returned to his seat one second before Electra burst onto the patio, feet tripping over the threshold as she tried to block the men's entrance onto the terrace.

Both men were fit and wore blue suits, white shirts, nondescript ties, and thick-soled black shoes. One was beefy, with a thick middle and a closely shorn head. He looked familiar. The remaining fuzz hinted at a receding hairline of dark brown hair. The other man, shorter with a more powerful build, had cropped salt and pepper hair with blunt-cut bangs that fell across his forehead in an unflattering Caesar-like line. Seeing Declan sitting there, they gave a quick look at one another and turned to Electra.

The beefy one spoke. "Mrs. Lavielle, you've been most gracious to invite us into your home."

"I didn't. You came to my kitchen door and asked if you could speak with me. I said yes."

Caesar piped in. "I beg your pardon, ma'am, but we asked if we could come inside. You agreed and led us to your patio."

Electra sputtered. "Well I couldn't leave you standing on my stoop for heaven's sake!"

Declan cleared his throat and glared at her. If a gaze across a room could be visible, two red beams would have been seen just before Electra disappeared in a poof of smoke. He slowly unfolded himself from his chair, expression changing from studied aloofness to something close to welcoming.

Jessica watched from the bushes. Recognition made her breath catch. From the airport. The immigration official. She pressed her knuckle to her lips to stifle a gasp. Fear filled her.

Beefy looked back and forth from Electra to Declan taking in every detail from head to toe, but Caesar's head never stopped moving as he scanned the windows of the house, potted plants, tops of tables, and shrubs. His vision seemed to pierce through the vegetation as if his eyes had heat sensors and could see the yellows, oranges, and reds of a warm body among the blues and greens of cooler trees and flowers. Their suit jackets bulged slightly on the left, ineffectively hiding shoulder holsters and handguns.

The three men shared a presence. The same energy emanated from each. Take charge. Control the area. Presume cooperation.

Declan extended his hand. "Declan Cleary. Attorney. Boston. And you're Agent . . ." His voice trailed off.

"Baxter," answered the taller one. "And this is Agent Sanford."

Caesar shook Electra's hand. "Charles Sanford. You know my father, Richard, from Keeneland. In fact, he's the one who made sure I was assigned to this case after he received your call. He passes along his regards."

Declan cocked his head. "Assigned? It's rather unusual for immigration officials to do field work." He looked at the offered identification, only raising his eyes after the others shifted uncomfortably. "You're not immigration."

Sanford coughed into his closed fist. "FBI. Louisville. We assist other agencies when requested."

Electra blinked rapidly and her mouth, slack-jawed and open, remained frozen, too stunned to thaw into the relaxed smile of Southern warmth. She plucked the offered business cards and dismissed additional identification with a wave of her hand. "Agent Baxter. Agent Sanford. What's the meaning of this?"

Agent Beefy Baxter turned to Declan, ignoring Electra's question. "Boston, eh? That Clemens is a hell of a pitcher for the Sox, but I'm a Braves fan myself. They're having a great season. You see any games this year?" Baxter poured on the charm, playing the role of good cop. Bad cop Sanford began to stroll around the patio in a failed attempt to look nonchalant as he patrolled the perimeter.

"I don't like sports," Declan said making it clear he wasn't going to play ball. Electra moved as if to speak. He stopped her with a look. "Were you expecting visitors?"

"Of course not! I would have mentioned it." Another look blunted her to silence.

Baxter stiffened and turned back to Electra. "We know Jessica Wyeth is your guest. How long have you known her?"

Electra stammered. "I don't . . . I don't see how th–"

Declan interrupted. "This is not an interrogation, nor are you presumed to be a witness to any crime. You don't have to answer any questions. Isn't that right, gentlemen?"

Patches of crimson crept up Baxter's cheeks. "We can ask questions of anyone we deem fit."

"And they don't have to answer."

"We came here to ask Miss Wyeth a few questions."

"Regarding?" Declan moved to stand between them and the house. Both agents watched him, right hands stretching and flexing as if itching for use.

"What brings us here is we understand she had an altercation with a young man," Baxter said as his lips pulled back in a shark's grin. "He says she ordered him beat up. We'd like to get the facts on that altercation."

"That would be an inquiry for local police, not you." Declan's eyes narrowed.

"Like Agent Sanford said," Baxter replied, "we assist other agencies when asked." He shot a look at Sanford, who responded with a curt nod of his head. Baxter continued, "And we've some questions about her recent travels."

Declan moved toward the open door and tripped. His sudden movement kept the agents' attention on him with their backs toward the gardens where Jessica cowered. He addressed them. "Then I suggest you go back to wherever it is you're from and wait for Miss Wyeth's call. That is, if she wants to speak with you. You can be assured we'll let her know of your visit."

Baxter ran his hand over the top of his head and scrunched his eyebrows, a theatrical gesture hinting at a sudden thought. "You're asking us to leave? I believe it's Mrs. Lavielle's place to welcome or dismiss guests."

"You didn't ask my permission to barge in here and Declan doesn't need my permission to ask you to leave." Electra sprang at the opportunity. "Gentlemen," she said, sweeping her arm outward, "good-bye."

Declan and Electra, flanking the two agents, disappeared into the house. Jessica gripped her hair in her hands and rocked back and forth, making silent wails of worry and confusion. Minutes passed when she could not hear any voices, and she brought herself back into control. Finally, the faint crush of gravel signaled a car departing down the drive. She waited for Declan to reach his hand through the brush before she allowed herself to breathe.

She patted the mulch and leaves from her seat, knees, and hair as she emerged back onto the patio.

"Do I run now or later?"

"You don't," Declan replied sending a chill down her spine. His eyes were dark and expressionless, like two black holes where light entered but nothing escaped.

She waited for him to say more. Instead, Declan sipped his drink and made himself another cracker layered with a thick tomato slice and cheese. His motions were slow and deliberate, allowing time to pass. He chewed for a moment, eyes never leaving her face. She shifted with discomfort.

Electra spoke, flustered with his silence. "You're going to have to speak with those agents. Maybe tonight, maybe in a week, but it's inevitable."

Jessica swallowed. "So?" Her attempt at bravado sounded hollow to her own ears. She could only imagine how it sounded to Declan.

His eyes moved to her bruised knuckles and scabbed hand. "You went after a man with your bare hands?"

Electra gasped. "What! You didn't tell me this! What happened?"

Declan ignored her and turned to face Jessica. "They are going to ask you a series of questions. If you lie to a federal agent or are caught in a discrepancy, you will be seen as uncooperative at best and criminally participating in a cover-up at worst. Trust me when I say this—the cover-up is always worse than the crime."

"What am I covering up?" she demanded. "I haven't done *anything!*"

"Even if you cover for someone else, a lie is a lie."

"Great. No lying. Box checked." Defiant, she flicked her index finger down, then up in a quick gesture, checking an imaginary box in the air. The conversation changed from confident strides to steps of slicked moss over river rocks. Behind his words loomed the specter of Michael. What did she know? What was she supposed to not know?

"Don't be ignorant of the resources supporting you. If you choose to lie, choose carefully."

His eyes bore through her. Was he trying to help or set her up? She reeled with the implications of all that remained unspoken. Terrorists lie. The innocent tell the truth. And men who love their women protect them.

Electra raised her chin and pulled back her shoulders. "What is Jessica supposed to do? She has to speak with those agents!"

He let silence gnaw at her nerves before he spoke again. "You are within your rights not to talk to them without counsel. I would recommend you call them tonight to schedule a time for an interview. Do it when I'm able to be there with you."

"Schedule? When?"

His mouth twitched in a smile. "I'm leaving tomorrow and my schedule is quite full. It may take a week or more before we find a convenient time for all parties. Delaying when we will actually meet, while appearing cooperative, can only work in your favor by giving me time to find out what it is they want to know."

Declan looked in the direction of the barns. His implication was clear. Her innocence didn't matter. She was placed under the watchful eyes of Michael's minions where her every move and contact could be scrutinized.

Michael said he loved her and, on those spoken words, she imprinted all of her hopes and expectations. He placed her in a castle and surrounded her with care, but she felt anything but cherished. Bridget taught her that actions speak louder than words. When was the last time he spoke with her? When was the last time he reached out to her directly? At the airport in Belfast, more than three weeks ago. Her heartbeat slowed at the realization.

In their last conversations, Michael claimed he was frantically expunging his organization of all criminal ties. She wondered if doing so without official scrutiny or transparency begged the question of his true motives. What were his motives in forging a relationship with her? Perhaps he had chosen wisely. She wouldn't be seen as an innocent caught in a web of deception. She had lived under false identities and fooled authorities. Then, she willingly traveled with the son of a money-laundering murderer. Her word would be not considered unquestionable truth. If presumed to be a terrorist, everything she said would be discounted and cherry-picked for indictable nuggets against Michael and anyone working for him—including Declan.

Michael had isolated her, building walls around her for her own security. Was she being placed in safekeeping until the moment came when she'd be more useful as a scapegoat than a lover?

By supporting Michael, she would receive protection against any attempt to discredit her as a terrorist. She hoped that by ensuring Michael's safety, she would ensure Kavan's.

The chess game became clear. The authorities would arrest her for traveling on a faked passport. They'd investigate. She was worried about exposing Kavan, and Michael knew she would lie to protect her father. Declan was worried about her exposing MMC's and 2100's connections to organized crime and was using Kavan as leverage to keep her silent.

Would she lie to protect Michael or Kavan? The answer lived in her heart.

"Michael says he loves me and would do anything for me. You being here is proof of that, right?"

She fixed Declan with a gaze she hoped looked confident and strong.

Monday, July 15, 1996
Boston, Massachusetts

DECLAN RUBBED HIS eyes and rolled his head in circles. The words on the pages spread across his desk had begun to run into one another. Hours of work remained ahead. He stood and stretched his back to get blood moving again.

Boston's streets, sleek from a downpour, reflected the taillights of the few cars moving at that hour into red lines. The sky over the harbor flashed from clouds heavy with the mid-summer storm. A bass rumble vibrated through the glass walls of his office. He braced his arms on the windowsill letting the cooled air from the vents blow up his sleeves and push away the smell of ozone and tar that seeped in from the street below. His eyes traced the roads as far as he could see, the rest he did from memory. Congress Street led to Atlantic. From there the road brought him to South Station and Southie— South Boston—and the heart of the city as any Irishman of mettle would attest.

His boyhood home was blocks away and a world apart. He only had to close his eyes to fill his heart with the aroma of stout and greasy chips from the Whiskey Priest down on Northern Ave. The tinge of brine and diesel from the docks was never far away. His father, rest his soul, was a longshoreman, with dancing blue eyes that could cut more sharply than the knife he kept in his boot. His mother was a saint, with hands raw from washing and worry, who never let her kids feel they were without.

The Cleary brood was as diverse as the threads that wove the fabric of Southie. Irish dominated, certainly, but after that, they ranged from honest to dishonest, educated to ignorant, pious to atheist. Whatever their differences were, he was tied to them by blood and the oaths of faith and fidelity. Loyalty knew no better man than Declan Cleary.

Discretion and silence brought him the biggest job—and fattest bank account—of his life. The corner of his office held the boxes of his former life. The bisque walls, bookcases, and glass-topped desk had not accumulated the clutter of a settled self. Bookcases sat empty. Dust dulled the glass table. He was not in a rush to curate the details of his new life and position them in view for others to see and judge. A few artifacts would suffice to convey unquestionable power while giving away the fewest hints of the personality that owned them.

He shook his arms out and felt the newness of his office surround him, wondering if this was what it felt like to arrive. His jacket hung on a wooden hanger, but his shirt sleeves were not rolled up nor his tie off. He felt his new office needed the respect of attire. A detail. The right touch would project an image and a truth. The wrong one, a weakness, and his lie. He reached into a stack of pictures, pulled out his framed diploma from Suffolk Law School, and hung it in the center of the wall. Magna Cum Laude. Law review. Next to that he hung his diplomas from Boston College High School and Boston College itself, reflecting his ascension from Southie to power. Perfect.

He looked through the other pictures. Images of the Cleary clan at communions and weddings commingled with pictures of charity dinners and beaming politicians shaking the hands of red-faced constituents. The faces were familiar to him, but their hearts were strangers. Clearys mixed with Bulgers, Shaunessys, Coogans, Sheas, and Connaughts. History mixed amongst them all and memories surfaced of boyhood bonds with Michael. He repacked them with bubble wrap and tagged them for storage as if warehousing his past would help him control his future.

He seated himself at his desk, tugged his cuffs, and folded his hands. If someone had looked in at him, he would have been mistaken for a praying man—head bowed, sitting on the edge of his chair.

One a.m. Eastern Daylight Time. Six a.m. Greenwich Mean Time. The telephone rang.

"Declan here."

"I appreciate you making yourself available." The secured line's clarity was impressive. Michael's voice was loud enough to make Declan pull the phone away from his ear. "This was the only time I could talk. Line sealed?" he asked, using a coded phrase to ask if security on the line was sealed from eavesdropping or recording.

"Yes. We can speak freely."

"Good. I'm pressed for time. I'm on my way to Geneva. How's your ma?"

The inflection of Norn Iron's dialect in Michael's speech irritated him—he's been in Northern Ireland for what now, less than four months? "Fine, thanks. Good of you to ask."

"And the new offices? Have you hired staff yet?"

"Settling in. Interviews soon."

"Good. Good. Did you get the papers I sent?"

"Yes. There are a few more signatures needed to settle your father's estate. Most of the liquid assets are frozen, but you still have access to real property. Formalities. I'll send the documents to Ballyronan. They'll be there upon your return."

"I'd much rather be on my way to the U.S."

"No. The timing is wrong. Regardless of how neat your legal house is when you return to the States, you're going to be forced to answer a lot of messy questions."

"Still, I want to see Jessica. Has she asked about me?"

Declan couldn't decide if Michael sounded hopeful or heavy. "No," Declan responded.

"She must be questioning why I'm keeping my distance."

"She's well aware of the problems you face. If you arrive before we're ready, you'd be subjected to the same subpoenas that can't reach you in Northern Ireland. I'm making sure arrest warrants aren't part of the welcoming package. Let's talk about the incident that caused you to flee the U.S. to begin with. You killed a man during a mountain search."

"What about it?"

Declan took his time reviewing a report he had nearly memorized. Pacing this interview was important to get at the story behind the facts. "As a sheriff, using lethal force in self-defense or in the defense of others is not criminal when done as a direct result of authorized police action and is rarely questioned. You saved Jessica's life. You could have stopped those stories easily."

Declan's neck grew hot as he recalled Jessica's reaction to his questions about the search as he was about to leave Electra's farm.

On impulse, she had lifted her shirttail. The white skin along her ribcage was crisscrossed with scars from wounds received from Magnus' operative. "You're working on cleaning up the mess surrounding the mountain search? Well, clean up these." Her blue eyes flashed with a mix of anger, fear, and challenge. He remembered how her words hung on the air as she spun on her heels and strode to the barn. He remembered how her legs flowed up to her hips.

Declan could almost hear Michael's wheels turning, and pressed harder. "I simply want to understand why your first reaction was to cover up the death."

"The search was a smoke screen set up by my father to test my loyalty to the Charity. Jessica had identified him as a murderer. Being indicted destroyed everything my father had built. I was to kill Jessica to prove my loyalty and exact revenge."

"That's quite a statement," Declan said, careful to pace the conversation. "It must have pissed him off you failed. Jessica survived the mountain search. Magnus' key henchman didn't because you shot him."

A pause on the line said he'd hit his mark. He waited.

"My father was in ill health and died shortly after the search," Michael replied in a careful tone that said each word was weighed carefully. "I'm not sure what he knew at the time of his death."

"If Magnus' ability to lead was in question even before he died, wasn't it your uncle who encouraged you to run the Charity?"

"Initially, I resisted being heir to the Charity. As soon as I took over, I hired you to begin to dismantle it."

The response was too quick and tried to push him into being defensive without answering the question. He let it slide. "All along, Jessica was aware of the Charity and your connection to it?"

"Yes, er, well, mostly."

"And you convinced her to flee the country with you when word of your cover-up of the death of Magnus' operative threatened to break by telling her any involvement in the hoax search could jeopardize her recently won freedom?" He waited a few seconds before he prodded again. "Must have scared the crap out of her."

"These questions aren't helpful," Michael growled. "We were falling in love and wanted to be together. The Charity is dead. Whose side are you on?"

"Yours, of course," Declan said with a voice of dark honey. "You've never been exposed to any legal issues stemming from the search, a fact Jessica found surprising. Like most people, she believed what she read in the papers." He paused, waiting for his next sentence to gather power. "You could easily have put her fears to rest."

"People believe what they want to believe."

"I don't have to tell you that Jessica's involvement and subsequent departure with you makes her look wholly complicit in some kind of scheme."

"Rotten luck. I can't do enough to help her."

Alone in his office, Declan placed a hand over his brow and rubbed his eyes.

"Jax reported some agents stopped by Electra's home," said Michael, changing the subject. "Why didn't you mention them?"

"Because you inquired if anyone spoke with Jessica. They didn't. I made sure of that. You didn't ask about Electra."

"Fine. If you feel you handled it, that's enough for me." Michael's voice deepened, directing the conversation. Was he making it clear that further insolence would not be tolerated? "How'd your conversation go with Jessica?"

"You were right about her. She didn't give up her father. Facts in public records will lead to her mother so she'll talk about Bridget's details, but only if forced."

"What about the bishop?"

"She didn't even mention him. I never would have guessed another alternative existed to explain her father's identity. She'll stick to the story that Gus Adams was her biological father. Most people would assume as much, given his relationship with Bridget, and the family here in the States and won't probe deeper. Did you consider you were taking a risk in telling me about Bishop Hughes?"

"Not at all. If coming from good stock wasn't enough, violating attorney-client privilege and the threat of being disbarred was."

The jibe and threat were clear. Declan remained unperturbed. "How important is it that the bishop remain unnamed?"

"Very."

Did his inflection rise at the end of the word? "To you or to him?"

A noise, like something heavy being thrown, thudded across the line. Michael's voice lowered, the effort of controlling his temper poorly concealed. "Exactly what are you questioning?" Burrowed inside his tone was the command to be obedient.

"The bishop is the glue holding together factions within the IRA," Declan said.

"A group that calls themselves the Provisional IRA is threatening additional bombings. If the bishop is discredited or made impotent by scandal, the coalitions he built will unravel. My companies will be the ones to pick up the pieces. What's your assessment of how vulnerable he is to being discovered as Jessica's father?"

Declan knew what he had to say and what information he needed. Michael was already edgy, demanding compliance without question. But Declan knew that navigating through turbulent facts needed clarity. He continued, cautiously, knowing his questions would trigger Michael to hide facts from him. Open communication and having all pertinent facts shared was the only way he could be of any use. "U.S. and U.K. authorities are combing through every document Jessica ever touched or was mentioned in. The Stormont investigation is being pushed by First Deputy Minister Reginald Bragdon. You know him?"

"Yes," Michael said.

The transatlantic line hissed as Declan waited for more information. A minute passed. "I need details," he said.

"Bragdon hired 2100's companies to build the wall in Belfast separating the nationalists from the unionists during his terms as city councilman." Michael's tone telegraphed impatience at having to explain background. "You've seen pictures of it. The twelve-foot high reinforced concrete structure is topped by razor wire. Impossible to scale and it's bombproof. People here call it the Peace Line. He's tried to get more information on 2100's holding companies, but the paper trail led him to blind alleys and away from MMC's enterprises. He has no idea he's done business with any Connaught corporations. If he becomes a problem, keeping that fact from becoming public will neutralize him."

"Did he receive kickbacks?"

Another hesitation. "You know I won't answer a direct question like that. Even to you."

"Then I will assume you're comfortable in being able to, er, encourage him to act reasonably if matters get out of hand."

"Of course. My people are very good."

The information fit into what Declan already knew. Bragdon was a crooked politician with ambition. Boston was full of them and Declan was no stranger to how manage them. "It's clear Jessica's affiliation with you fueled the scrutiny that led to the discovery of the passport issues. As yet, Bragdon has no firm evidence that Bridget was her mother, but discovering she and Margaret Wyeth were sisters is an easy enough task, and no doubt he's learned that already. I don't know how many clues he has to Kavan. I do know Bragdon has been a frequent visitor to the bishop's flat and is reported to have a precarious working relationship with him. Any more insights on your end?"

"No. I've nothing to add."

"If he can confirm Bridget's maternity, he'll work hard to find the father. Bragdon is highly motivated to discredit Kavan, but confirming Kavan's paternity will be difficult barring a sworn statement from a credible source or physical evidence. My bet is there's a document showing Gus Adams as her father. Most likely, it will be a baptismal certificate or other church record. I've hired an investigator to search Boston area church archives. Jessica must know such a document exists, or hinting at it was a guess like mine."

"There's more?"

"As you said, she's good at keeping secrets, and I sensed a fierce urge to protect her biological parents' legacy. She'll keep up the façade of being a Wyeth as long as she can, but the uncle could be a problem."

"Uncle? In the States? She never mentioned one."

"Jim's brother, William, is a Wyeth family black sheep. He's coat-tailing on her fame for his own benefit."

Declan could almost feel Michael's shrug of the shoulders in a *so what?* gesture. "Let him think what he wants."

Michael's disinterest was clear. Declan pressed. "The more exposure her story receives, the more likely it is that someone will say or uncover something that will lead to the truth."

"Again, rotten luck. That's why we have to keep her sequestered."

Luck implied strings unintentionally pulled, but levers moving nonetheless. From Declan's point of view, luck, rotten or otherwise, had nothing to do with Jessica's problems. He kept Michael focused on Bragdon. "It seems counterintuitive, but you and Bragdon share the same interests."

"I don't know what you're talking about."

"Having the peace talks dissolve would ignite violent reactions. Bombings, murders, and riots would destroy lives and property. The economic opportunity for the Charity, er, I mean to say *2100*, is unprecedented."

"I'm not interested in blood money. My focus is on MMC, 2100, and their affiliates. I'm not sure what the new entity will be named."

"Of course, of course. But it is ironic, isn't it? The U.K. and Bragdon would be happy to have the issues surrounding Northern Ireland put to rest by stopping any hope of reunification, and your company would enjoy robust revenues. And everything hinges on whether Jessica is able to protect the bishop."

"And your assessment is she'll do anything to protect him?"

Declan paused, allowing what he heard to sink in. "Yes," he answered. "I can't help thinking if she hadn't left the country with you after the mountain search, or at least had waited a year before she did, the worries she's being radicalized—and the question of her paternity—would have never been raised."

He could hear a chair squeak over the line. Not a cheap metal squeak that could have been made by the chair in Declan's old office, but the scrunch of richly padded leather. "Lousy timing."

"And she's wanted for questioning about ordering some two-bit thug to be beat up. There's a police report about how she attacked him."

"I can only assume that report, combined with her recent travels and exposure of her parentage, would keep the authorities busy for quite a while."

Declan tapped a staccato beat with his pen. His stomach clenched against the reality sharpened by Michael's words. Bombs fell on schools and hospitals. Women and children died. Paying the price of war created a moral debt. How big the debt became was tied to the value of winning. The world of war and organized crime accepted innocents as collateral damage.

And was Jessica such an innocent? Time would tell.

Declan wouldn't allow himself to be distracted by such thoughts. He cradled the phone between his ear and shoulder, and grabbed a paper showing a list of dates. "I'm glad you mentioned timing and her travels. You brought her back with you on your second trip to Ireland? Or was it your third? I'm talking about March and April of this year."

"I made two trips." The chair scrunched again.

Declan pulled more papers from a file. "Take your time. Are you sure?"

The phone line hollowed in the void. He envisioned the cavernous study with a solitary lamp switched on, light pooling on a carved desk. He heard the nervous patter of fingers or a pencil eraser tapping on the desktop. "Hmm. Right. I remember now. I made two trips to Northern Ireland in March. One to Ireland in April."

"Right. That makes sense. Dates show one trip before your father died and two after. My condolences, again, on your loss. These past months must have been very difficult for you."

"I need no condolences. My father's death was no loss." The words hissed.

"Forgive me. Social habit. Anger only makes people suspicious, so please, get a hold of yourself. As I said, the estate will take more time to settle. Your signatures on the paperwork I'm sending will keep the process of releasing property and transferring ownership to you moving along. Gaining title to real estate and accounts both in the States and abroad takes longer than anyone imagines." Having the deceased indicted for murder and suspected of being a kingpin in organized crime complicated matters further, but he kept those thoughts to himself. "Are you in need of any cash to tide you over until then?"

Michael stifled a chortle. "No. I'm good."

Alone and unobserved, Declan allowed himself to smile. "I didn't think so. I was under responsibility to ask." He put one file away and brought out another.

He could hear Michael take two deep breaths and settle back into his chair as he spoke. "It has been a rough few months," Michael said. "I hired you because you're the best at the corporate and financial work. And loyal. I need to knit my enterprises together. MMC's charitable focus presents a strong and favorable public image. By merging my father's business dealings with 2100, potential conflicts are daunting. The sooner the corporations come under my leadership and leave everything to do with Magnus behind, the better." He paused. "The line is sealed?"

Why ask again? Declan straightened in his chair. "Yes."

"You are the best at identifying potential causes of action against me personally for inheriting my father's mess."

He understood. "And identifying criminal charges that may come of such. The more transparent you are in assuming control, the easier it will be to extricate you from issues created by your father."

"I'm focused on the criminal charges. I trust you're finding all of the documents needed to make sense of my concerns."

"Yes. I drafted the syndication agreements for Lavielle and Jessica to sign. You understand that if Jessica signs them, the fact that they're back-dated would further implicate her in the Manchester bombing."

"That would be for the courts to decide. I'm working on the money trail on my end. The documents must be signed before the Olympics."

"Why? What's your hurry?"

Michael paused. "The gathering of international teams is a perfect opportunity for Jessica to be seen as forging her own international relationships."

"Understood. Is that's why you're going to Geneva now?"

"That and other matters. Have you gotten all of the documents out of my father's home?"

"Most. I have at least one more trip to make sure."

"And?"

"Any criminal actions I've identified so far died with your father." He heard a sigh. Of relief?

"Good."

"Are there any other places your father would have kept records? Any other hiding places in the home or people he would have entrusted documents with?"

"I can't think of any. Let me know immediately if you find anything." There was another pause as he spoke with someone in the room. A trill of feminine laughter stopped as quickly as it started. "Look. Gotta go. Do what you have to do."

Declan put the phone down in its cradle, holding it there as if he could stop the words that flowed from it from entering his world. The weight of his head pulled him forward. He waited a full minute before his temples stopped their relentless pulsing. His stomach churned.

Michael was too smart to overtly order him to destroy any incriminating evidence or to falsify documents to exonerate him. The lack of clear and transparent migration from Magnus' illegal enterprises to Michael's alleged charitable ones bothered him. Every document from Magnus' dealings showed corporate fraud, forgery, and tax evasion—the tools of white-collar organized crime.

But Michael did not take clear and convincing steps to extricate himself from tainted dealings.

Declan had thought his struggle of being a good Irish Catholic boy from Southie, to being a good and loyal soldier to the Connaughts, was behind him. The trappings of his new job worked to seduce him into being comfortable, but he was aware how his future was tied to Michael being who he said he was—an upright and decent businessman trying to make an honest living.

In the world of law, facts can be viewed through different prisms. A smoking gun in the hand of a person could be evidence of intentional homicide or self-defense. The judgment lay in the surrounding details.

Was Michael inept in disengaging himself from his father's illicit enterprises, or was he asking Declan to carefully construct an alibi with Jessica as his smoking gun?

When it came to attorneys and clients, the client was always right.

War, whether waged with guns or money, was a filthy business.

Declan shrugged on his suit jacket and tugged at his cuffs. If Michael was on his way to Switzerland, it meant he was tending to international business. He wondered if the recent sectarian violence in Bosnia was done with equipment that bore the 2100, Ltd. logo.

He was confident it did.

The office was silent as he shut off the lights.

Another day at the office done.

ELECTRA SAT AT her massive roll-top desk, a prized heirloom from her father's days as a newspaper editor. She liked to retreat to her office when the heat of the day made gentlewomen wilt and men excuse themselves for naps. The dark green walls imparted a feeling of being deep within a cool forest and the location at the back of her manse ensured she would neither wilt nor nap when working.

"I knew I would find the captain at the Bridge."

Electra looked up to see Brooks Carter, her dapper corporate attorney, standing in the doorway. Today's outfit included crisp white linen pants, a mint green shirt, and yellow tie. A navy blazer with gold buttons was draped over his arm.

Electra's desk was specially built to have a sliding extension that jutted from the side of the desk to allow guests a surface to lean on while writing and not be blocked from view by the towering roll. Brooks joked that the desk, with its array of drawers and cubbies, was her personal mahogany control center. In a fit of laughter, she called it the Bridge, a reference to Brooks' beloved *Star Trek* series. The name stuck.

"Thanks for coming on such short notice, Brooks," Electra said, motioning him to sit beside her.

Brooks air-kissed her cheeks in greeting before he sat and placed his briefcase on his knees and opened the latches with a satisfying click. His comfort in his surroundings was evident and in contrast to what most people felt when summoned to appear.

A benefit Electra enjoyed about the Bridge was its intimidation factor. People unaccustomed to wealth, often froze at the sight of it—hat in hand and slack-jawed—unable to progress into her office. Whether she interviewed new grooms and trainers—with skin burnished from the sun, wearing clean jeans—or neighbors and townsfolk, they entered her office and scuffed their feet from side to side until invited to sit. The longer she took to offer the invitation, the more uncomfortable her visitors became.

Brooks seemed to relish her summons and she suspected he even dressed for the occasion.

"How's Robert? I've not seen him in ages," she asked with affection.

"He's well, thank you. Busy," Brooks said, smiling.

"Pass along my regards, will you? I'll have you both out for dinner after all of this craziness subsides."

"From the sounds of things, that could be a while."

"By God, I hope you're wrong," she said, smoothing the skirt of her peach colored dress. Having a home office did not stop her from donning professional attire as her workday demanded. "I wanted to manage this myself, but I think I'm getting in over my head."

"Are you more concerned about your house guest or your business partner?"

Electra fingered the pearls at her neck. "That's just it. Right now? Both." She told him of the FBI agents' visit.

"And you're worried that Miss Wyeth has a darker side you haven't seen."

Electra nodded. "Hmm. My gut says no, but I need to be smart. That's why I wanted to go over things with you."

"Okay. Start me from the beginning."

"Jessica bought the old Smythe farm a year ago last spring. I met her after one horse she trained, Gapman, won my Harvest Hunter Pace event."

"I remember how that win shocked everyone. People were abuzz that a young woman no one had ever heard of won a coveted event!"

"Right. The Wyeths made their fortune racing thoroughbreds. She thought by staying away from the track, she wouldn't call attention to herself and could still use her talent to train horses in other disciplines. We became friends. I never suspected she was using an alias to hide from a murder charge!"

"False pretenses bothered you and others in town. I understand most folks are still keeping their distance."

"Honestly? I think they're more rattled that our own Sheriff Co-nant deceived them, too. One day he's our beloved sheriff helping to run a school for the disabled and the next he's Michael Connaught, heir to . . . to . . . " Her voice faded as words failed her.

He raised his hand to stop her from saying more. "I can't say I blame them. His lie could be far worse than hers. She was running for her life. And him?" He stopped and reassessed his tact.

Electra chewed her bottom lip. "Exactly! What about him? I'm worried."

"He'd been working as Harlan County's sheriff for a few years be-fore Jessica came along and everyone thought highly of him. Includ-ing you. When did you say they met?"

"Last fall. October. At my Harvest Ball," she said referring to the annual event considered the pinnacle of Southern society.

Brooks closed his eyes. "No one throws a party like you do, my dear. I was there when they met! You could see the air around them shimmer with heat. He pursued her harder than a horny stud on a brood mare farm."

Electra whooped with laughter. "He was smitten with Perc's beau-tiful newcomer and asked me to introduce them."

"I remember what happened next. All hell broke loose for her. Then it was March when he rescued her from that mountain search." He fell silent. "When did she leave with him for Ireland?"

"April."

"Five months after his father was indicted for the murder she had been framed for and only a week or two after his old man died." He spoke more to himself than her. He paused, head cocked in thought. "If his father was still alive, would they have gone?"

"I . . . I have no idea how to answer that. He swept her off her feet and offered her love and acceptance, both things she sorely lacked for many years. She had a pretty tough reentry to the world when she shed her alias."

"But you stood by her even when the locals turned against her. You said you saw something in her that connected you."

The hot tears that sprang to Electra's eyes startled her. She blinked them away. "For a woman in my position who always has people asking her for one favor or another, she only asked for friend-ship from me. Nothing more. That counted for a lot. She was so strong and tough to the outside world, but in those quiet moments, she opened her heart to me. I never had anyone open up to me like that. I wasn't surprised she sparked toward Michael or that she left the country with him. I know she was hoping her story would die out of the press while she was gone."

"But a trip to Ireland made sense from the standpoint of the businesses you and Michael had entered."

"Yes. I benefitted from his talent for making money. Our real estate deals were very successful."

"And I scrutinized the contracts making sure everything was legal and transparent."

"Yes! With your blessing I didn't hesitate to form syndicates with him to own horses. Jessica was involved only as a trainer."

"Why?"

Electra shrugged. "It's what Michael wanted and it was the beginning of me seeing his protection of her as controlling. He made every arrangement for the businesses and for her travel. Flights. Where she stayed. What they did."

"Who they met?"

She nodded slowly. "Yes, she said she mostly kept to herself training and was happy enough to be out of the media spotlight. His keeping her secluded bothered me more than it bothered her."

Brooks tilted his head back and stared at the ceiling in thought. "Each decision he made for both of you brought more and more scrutiny." His eyes remained fixed. "How much time did you say she spent with him?"

"Not a lot. She was at a training facility in a small town in the northwest of Ireland and he was tending to business matters with his uncle in Northern Ireland."

"And he showered her with attention?"

"Well, if material goods and grooms trained in the martial arts count, then yes. Otherwise, no."

He nodded his head slowly showing he was taking in all the details—said and unsaid. "You're torn about what to think about him. Was Michael a son trying to carve a life separate and apart from his father or was he biding his time until he could take over his father's enterprise?"

Electra closed her eyes, trying to will away the fear Brooks triggered.

Brooks filled the silence. "What do you know about his businesses now?"

She drew back her head in surprise. These questions were leading somewhere, looking for something, but she couldn't figure out what it was. She heard Declan ask the same questions of Jessica. Was Michael in jeopardy if she answered wrong? More importantly, was *she* in jeopardy?

"I know only what Michael told me about MMC's or 2100's enterprises," she admitted, embarrassed.

"Isn't there an uncle? Where does he fit in with all of this?"

Electra shifted uncomfortably. "His uncle felt Jessica was a distraction that kept Michael away from more important matters. What are you getting at? What are your thoughts?"

"Well now, darling. You know darned well I've dined with Sheriff Conant here, in your home, at a few of your splendid dinner parties."

"And?" she asked, glad for the connection and perspective.

"I'm only saying this since you're asking for my unvarnished opinion and not as a guest in your home, so I'll give it to you straight. I didn't like the guy."

"Oh! You hide your disdain well!" she joked, uncomfortable in its hollow feel.

"He could charm the rattle off a snake, but I remember your daddy saying it takes one to know one, and I'm not talking about the rattle. I'm the one who pushed you to talking with that Boston reporter to keep your name out of any article associated with him."

"Brooks," Electra said, jutting her chin forward to show she could accept any answer, "what have I gotten myself into?"

He leaned over and clasped Electra's hands in his own, looking into her face as he spoke. "I don't think you're in over your head. I think *both* you and Jessica are. But she's not reaching out to him either, right? I'm wondering if she knows something. Worse, what if he knows something about her or is setting her up? Or both?"

Electra bristled. "He loves her!" she said, hoping for something she lacked in her own life. "All of this makes sense if he's in love. He's done everything for her. He adores her."

"Oh, honey. I know what a man in love looks like, and he ain't it," he said, exaggerating his drawl.

"If you have something to say, you should say it to my face."

Electra turned to see Jessica standing at the door. The afternoon's heat didn't dissuade her from wearing tall black boots with buff colored breeches. A strand of blond hair had freed itself from her ponytail and floated on each puff of her breath.

"Jessica! I didn't see you. Come in! This is my corporate counsel, Brooks Carter. Brooks, this is Jessica," Electra said, hoping a genteel introduction would right a sinking ship.

Jessica's glare burned into Electra then focused on Brooks. "Pleasure," she said, voice reflecting anything but. "Why were you talking about me?"

Brooks shifted, trying to adjust his ruffled feathers. "Darlin' girl. Miss Electra was just bringing me up to speed on all that's happened in your life since we first met," he said, looking for acknowledgement. Receiving none, he continued. "At the Harvest Ball? Last October?"

Electra watched Jessica's eyes travel the length of Brooks' arms and legs, taking her time as she took Brooks' measure.

"I remember, but I still don't know why that gives you the right to dissect my relationships."

Electra's heart wilted as Jessica turned water-filled eyes to her. "We were doing no such thing," she said, trying to mollify. "We were only observing that Michael has provided you everything except ... except..."

"Him," Brooks finished her sentence. "Pardon my intrusion here, Miss Wyeth, but from where I sit, Mr. Conant—"

"Connaught," Jessica corrected.

"Connaught," Brooks continued without skipping a beat, "is everywhere but here. I'm concerned for you."

"My relationship with Michael Connaught is just that. *My* relationship. I don't recall inviting you into it."

Electra watched, horrified by the edges she saw fraying.

Brooks changed course, his body morphed from stiff interviewer to relaxed acquaintance, a contrivance to make his words sound like small talk. He adjusted his shirt cuffs then rubbed his knuckles along his cheeks, changing his physical demeanor along with his tone. Was he trying to show Jessica the techniques the agents would use during her interview? Electra waited to see what he was going to say.

"How well do you know Michael?"

Jessica exploded. "What the hell do you care? What difference does it make when we met or how? We met. Became lovers. Now you want me to believe he's tipping the authorities with lies to make them come after me. Who the hell cares how well I know him!" Her chest heaved with her words.

In cool control, Brooks didn't flinch, but pulled one shoulder up and let it drop. Nonchalant. "I care about what kind of facts they could try to link to your travels. Besides, I'm curious."

"Curious? You're *curious*?"

Electra could see the past weeks of poor sleep and stress dissolve her friend. The usually tight controls on Jessica's emotions stretched to the point of breaking. Without words, Electra could see the evidence that in the middle of Michael's protective fortress, Jessica felt entrapped in a prison rather than protected.

Brooks dusted invisible lint from his sleeve. "It's a simple question. You don't have to answer if you're too upset."

"I'm not upset," Jessica yelled. "I'm not worried about Michael or why he hasn't contacted me since I've been in the states. I'm not in the least upset he hasn't tried to see me. He's given me anything I could have hoped for." Electra's heart skipped a beat as Jessica fixed her gaze on her. "You've helped. You've provided him with ways to help me."

"That's why I've called Brooks here. I wanted an objective opinion on what he thinks is going on."

Jessica started to leave and stopped. "I'll tell you what's going on here. Michael loves me. He's the first man to ever love *me*—as tainted and wrecked as I am. Michael wants me, but he doesn't know how to get us together in a way that we can live our lives in peace."

Electra rose and opened her arms to hug Jessica, but Jessica shrank away. "But do you know who he is, who he really is?" she asked, voice heavy.

"Who was he before he came to Perc? Who is he now?" Brooks turned in his seat to face them. "That's as important as who he pretended to be when you met him. I'd argue it's even more important."

Jessica set her jaw in anger. "What are you saying?"

Electra placed a hand on Jessica's shoulder. "We know the forces pulling on him would test the strongest of men. How he treats you is a large clue for who he really is."

"He's surrounded me with everything I could possibly want." Jessica looked out the window where the Pine River wound its way along the valley floor. "Everything."

"Except him," Brooks said.

"Except him," Electra echoed.

Jessica stifled a sob and left.

Wednesday, July 17, 1996
Pride's Crossing, Massachusetts

DECLAN DROVE THROUGH the massive iron gates onto the late Magnus Connaught's estate in the wealthy community of Pride's Crossing. Nestled behind a massive stone wall and a wooded hillside, the grounds consisted of acres of rolling lawn, formal gardens, and an Italian Renaissance revival mansion. The main house—built in the style made popular by The Breakers, the Vanderbilt summer home in Newport, Rhode Island—rose three stories and was built of pink granite. A gatehouse and gardener's cottage, both scaled-down versions of the main building, sat empty with shades drawn.

Gravel ground under the tires as he drove to the front door. He punched in the security code, taking care to look directly into the camera. While he waited for security to confirm his identity, he noted that the grounds had been freshly tended. The air carried the smell of cut grass, and flowers bent under the weight of the day's watering. Purple orchids, red and pink roses, and yellow zinnias bobbed in the afternoon breeze. The metallic click of the doors unlocking told him all was well. He feigned doffing a hat to the faceless crew of the security service seated somewhere in Boston and pushed open the heavy door.

The air inside was a perfect seventy-two degrees with modest humidity, settings chosen to maintain the home's museum quality furnishings. Boxes of every shape and bolts of bubble wrap lined the walls. A central staircase dominated the entry hall. Banisters carved from dark mahogany flanked black marble steps. Paneled walls and a vaulted ceiling ensured any visitor would feel imposed upon by a pervasive darkness no amount of light could brighten. An oriental carpet in hues of red and gold failed to warm the inlaid stone floor, but kept his footsteps from echoing.

His mouth twitched in irritation. The rug should have been rolled up and removed. Teams of appraisers had crawled through the house, cataloging and photographing all items in each room with explicit instructions to not disturb the office and master bedroom. A curved brass chandelier of four tiers of candle-shaped lights glowed above. Declan looked up at the second floor and down the two hallways, confirming the usual lights remained on. The undisturbed thin veil of dust assured him no one had been there since his last visit a few days before.

He had been to Magnus' home several times. At first, he was the reluctant junior member of the legal team Magnus used to help manage his sprawling enterprise. Reluctant because his freshly minted status as a member of the Massachusetts Bar meant he felt too inexperienced to carry his workload without a senior attorney acting as his oversight. Declan was the document reviewer and fact checker—the low man on the totem pole used to verify facts, figures, dates, and names of parties involved in contracts before they could be signed. He was also the man designated to catch term breaches early to mitigate possible damages. His lack of enthusiasm for his job increased when he learned the position he filled had become vacant due to the sudden death of his predecessor. Boating accident. Such a shame. Left behind a wife and baby, too.

The partners of his law firm, Boston's heavyweight Cabot, Dillon, Shreve, and Mahr, scrutinized his work. Early assignments consisted of reviewing contracts for modest manufacturing enterprises in Chelsea or creating holding companies for produce suppliers in Everett. Sleep was easy in the weeks when he worked on a contract he or his firm drafted, but eluded him the weeks when the other party drafted. Kill or be killed. The devil lived in the details, and he examined each word as if his life depended on it. Crafting terms was easy. Verifying the identities of parties involved required following the lineage of subsidiaries and holding companies, and knowing who the majority shareholders were. The mind-numbing work made most first-year associates sloppy, a lament against his predecessor Mr. Cabot let slip over a pint at the Black Rose.

Declan slept on his office couch and kept his mouth shut. His pay increased shortly after he identified Resource, Incorporated as the majority stockholder of a downstream subsidiary—a minor party to

SleepzzzWell, a mattress manufacturing company in the bowels of East Boston Magnus was intent on purchasing for a bargain basement price. On the books, SleepzzzWell was drowning in debt. Off the books, the cash fundamentals were an excellent fit within Magnus' acquisition profile—meaning the company was a perfect cover for laundering vast sums of cash. Diverting cash from illegal sources to enable legal access—and vice versa—was to be SleepzzzWell's primary use and well-kept secret. Without comment, Declan brought Resource, Incorporated to the attention of Mr. Cabot along with a list of Resource's executives, board of directors, and financial backers.

"What's your recommendation on this purchase?" Cabot's eyes had not strayed from the list of names.

It was the first time anyone had asked for Declan's opinion on any of Magnus' business matters. He had expected as much.

"I recommend against it."

Cabot's eyebrows ticked upward, but he said nothing more. During that evening's rounds at the Black Rose, Cabot was surprisingly warm and chatty with Declan.

"You've got a fool's nerve to suggest Magnus shouldn't buy a company he has his heart set on." Cabot, red-faced, beamed an admiring smile. Other associates pretended not to notice, and hid their jealousy behind yards of ale.

"It's only my opinion. I've expressed it to you, and you only." Declan finished his stout and placed the glass on the bar. Tan foam slipped down its sides. He wiped his mouth with his knuckle.

"He doesn't like to be told no. If I go with your recommendation, what should I say I've based it on?" Cabot's expression was a mask of concern and puzzlement. His demeanor begged for explanation and guidance.

Any other junior associate would have leapt at the chance to impress a senior partner with a tale of brilliant research and analysis, leaving no detail unturned. Discovery of two sets of books would be enough to send them into a froth, imploring the firm to advise the presumably law-abiding Magnus to turn tail and run away from SleepzzzWell's acquisition.

Declan had waited for this opportunity for longer than he cared to admit. With one sentence, he sealed his future.

"Resource's shareholders are not ones Magnus wants up his ass."

Declan's research revealed that Resource, Incorporated was a shell corporation used by the FBI, a tactic the Bureau favored to gain inside knowledge of companies suspected of being linked with organized crime and used to launder money. The attractive acquisition was proof the FBI was getting desperate to find evidence against Magnus Connaught and all of his ventures. The FBI created Resource, and invested in SleepzzzWell as bait, a fact Cabot would have seen easily had he done the due diligence himself. The footprint of a shell is unmistakable to a trained eye like Declan's.

"And if he decides to move forward anyway?"

"Then we hire priests, nuns, and choirboys for all positions and make mattress manufacturing a model of corporate ethics."

Cabot again ticked an eyebrow upward, this time in approval. They spoke no more, but the look they shared meant the gateway to another world had opened and Declan had walked through without hesitation.

Magnus died before Declan's acceptance into the innermost circle was complete. Combined with Declan's Southie lineage, the fact that Michael perceived Declan as being fluent in—and not yet calloused by—all things Magnus, ensured Declan's loyalty to Michael. Declan became Michael's first and only choice to be his stateside counsel. Michael's employment offer tripled his salary. Saying no was not an option.

Settling the details of Magnus' estate was one of the many tasks assigned to Declan, and getting the mansion ready for sale was more time-consuming than he would have liked. Magnus' widow, a lovely but vapid woman Magnus married shortly after the death of his first wife, was dealt a tidy sum and their Florida home in accordance with the terms of their ironclad prenuptial drafted under the loving eye of Mr. Cabot himself. With hardly a glance in her heated and self-adjusting rearview mirror, she drove her Rolls-Royce Silver Spirit to her home in Palm Beach.

Select art and antique experts had been invited to appraise the contents in preparation for private sales and auction. Declan needed to complete the inventory, verify the work begun by Magnus' remaining house staff, and pack the remaining items. He gave particular care to everything in the home's office.

Being alone in a thirty-five room mansion was no big deal. He just wanted to make sure he was. Keeping to the balls of his feet, he moved down the hall, slipping his body sideways past stacks of boxes. He walked through the kitchen, servant areas, and living rooms, pausing occasionally to listen to the sounds of the home. He circled back to the main entrance and turned toward the double doors leading to the office. Before reaching for the handles, he examined the doorframe. Thin slices of transparent tape, barely a quarter of its regular width, remained secured in place. One was placed in the obviously clever location of straddling the seam where both doors met, higher than eye level, to be slightly out of sight. The others were placed along the top, bottom, and sides of the doors and jamb, betting that if the obvious piece was found, the search for more would cease and entry would be made. The tape itself was Declan's favorite—a super-sticky brand that gripped pieces of aging varnish with particular gusto, guaranteeing detection of dislodged flecks if the tape was hastily replaced by someone not versed in the intricacies of low-budget intruder detection.

He grabbed a bundle of flattened cardboard boxes and packing tape, and entered.

Magnus' office was a well-executed expression of power. The top of the massive desk, made of intricately carved ebony, held only a red leather blotter, green-shaded brass lamp, two phones, a computer monitor, and a framed picture of his second wife. The leather chair, throne-like in size, rolled on silent casters. Brass nail heads dotted the soft black leather. The walls were lined with shelves of books and artifacts from a life lived on the world stage. Pictures of statesmen and natural wonders punctuated spaces with their importance.

Declan sat at the desk and opened each drawer. After placing the contents in a box, labeling and inventorying the items, he closed his eyes to block out distractions and felt with his hand inside the space, using his fingertips to detect a depression or loose slat. Most of the desk's contents had been subpoenaed and removed by the Attorney General's office in response to Magnus' indictment. Remaining files were reread, then packed. Drawers were pulled out and tipped over. He ran his hand along each inner desk surface, looking for a button, lever, or seam that would lead to the answers he sought or questions he dreaded. He placed the lamp on the floor, using its light to search for unusual wear patterns or scratches. When he was certain the desk held no more secrets, he catalogued it as well.

He started the same meticulous process on the bookcases and began with the cabinet behind the desk. Opened, he found three canisters. Each narrow tube was as tall as the length of his forearm and marked with a red cross and "O2." One had yards of clear plastic tubing attached to a nozzle. A yellowed "U" of plastic nasal cannula and more tubing sat in a tangled heap on top. Plagued by heart ailments, Magnus' health had been declining in the weeks before his death and bottled oxygen provided some relief. Declan estimated the length of the tubing to be long enough that Magnus could walk inside his office relatively freely without lugging an oxygen tank behind him. The nasal prongs were kept in place by what looked like a pair of eyeglass temples, with a strap that fit around his head, leaving his hands free but ensuring a generous volume of air.

He spent the next hours handling each book, fanning their pages for loose notes tucked away or forgotten, and packing them away. He then explored the newly emptied shelves for anything unusual. Magnus loved his office and coveted his library. His rare book collection was his pride, and he forbade anyone from touching it. The amount of dust and motes clustered on top and behind many volumes evidenced not even trusted household staff were welcome to touch them. Declan was not surprised when, behind a leather clad and gilt-edged tome of Shelley's poems, he found a lever that allowed the bookcase to swing open on its hinges to reveal a small room outfitted for surveillance.

One of Michael's first actions was to order Declan to hire a security firm that could remotely monitor the estate's grounds, making this room obsolete. The new firm installed state of the art video and surveillance equipment focused on the grounds and the exteriors of the buildings, not the interior of the home. He flicked a few switches. Nothing happened. Power had been cut, probably during the upgrade. Paperwork confirmed the room had not been inventoried. If anyone else knew it existed, no one had mentioned it or been inside.

Enough light flowed from the open door to allow him to see inside the cramped space. Monitors stared blindly at empty chairs pushed away at haphazard angles as if the occupants had left hastily and not returned. A control panel with rows of lights and buttons mirrored the property by buildings and rooms. The largest panel was for the main house, showing alarm systems and audio and visual surveillance gear. Shelves of video tapes lined one wall, labels indicating records dating back several years. He ran his finger along the tapes, then along the top of the case. Consistent dust patterns told him nothing had been moved. The dates ran sequentially in weekly periods, ending the week before Magnus died. He made a note to himself to double-check whether the new security company knew about the room. Being the discoverer could give him certain flexibilities. He wanted to be certain how much latitude he had.

The tedious work bored him and he knew enough to change his task before his attention wandered, opening the possibility for mistakes. He closed the room, affixed new strips of tape, and loped up the grand staircase, two steps at a time. The master suite was strewn with boxes readied for Goodwill.

Magnus' bedside table was untouched and displayed the artifacts of the private life of a busy and ailing man—two phones, pads of paper, vials of medicine, tissues, and oxygen canister. This time, a full mask, the kind that covered the nose and mouth, was at the end of the tubing. Another picture of his wife. A picture of his late son Liam and another of Michael sat side by side.

Declan was tired. He had been in the house for six hours, looking for something, anything. A thought buzzed around his head, but he couldn't stop it long enough to examine it.

The room. Why didn't Michael mention the room? If Magnus' and Michael's relationship was estranged, why would Magnus have Michael's picture beside his bed?

Declan pushed aside the folded comforters and sat on the bare mattress. The bed groaned under the unaccustomed weight. Even stopping for a moment coaxed his body to yearn for sleep. He resisted the urge to lie down and steal a few minutes of rest. Discipline kept him upright and his brain ticking through checklists. What records did Magnus have? What does Michael need evidence of or protection from? What exposure does Michael have because of Magnus' activities? Did that risk change after Magnus died? Who benefitted from Magnus' death? Declan felt the answers were close if he only could figure out what questions to ask.

He thought about making a pot of coffee, and quickly dismissed the idea, as the kitchen had been emptied of food and inventoried. He inhaled and exhaled rapidly, forcing more oxygen into his system to clear his head. It wasn't enough.

Impulsively, he grabbed the oxygen mask and placed it against his face. He turned on the flow, but quickly realized the nozzle had not been completely turned off and the tank was empty. He walked down the massive staircase to the office and reached for the tanks behind Magnus' desk. He turned on the tank and placed the cannula under his nose. Air hissed through the tubing and he felt the cool breeze of gas against his nostrils. He inhaled deeply. Rather than feeling refreshed, he felt more sluggish and slow. Maybe he was more fatigued than he thought. He cupped his hands over his face and sucked the air into his lungs. His vision closed and he yearned for sleep. He hoisted the canister and compared its weight to others in the cabinet. The weights were nearly identical telling him both canisters were full. Curious, he attached the tubing to the toggle post valve of a different canister, opened the flow, and sniffed the air escaping through the cannula. Fresh. He felt the immediate boost of clarity only pure oxygen could provide.

He cupped his hand over his nose and mouth and each breath washed away his fatigue.

He ticked through another mental list. The intensity of his concentration stilled him. His heart beat more slowly. His breathing deepened. Even though his eyes were open and unblinking, he saw nothing but what was in his mind's eye.

Magnus died at his desk.

Alone.

No one was seen entering or leaving his office in the hours surrounding his death.

Standard autopsy required at all unattended deaths revealed no abnormal results.

Toxicology clear. No poisons. Blood chemistry within normal ranges.

Physiology clear. No trauma. No indication of suffocation.

No indication of foul play.

His death ceased all actions against him.

No examination of motive behind Gus Adams' murder.

No criminal trial.

No discovery process into his business dealings or family connections.

Widow happy with prenup settlement.

Only heir was estranged son with no contact over several years until one last failed attempt at reconciliation in the months before Magnus died. Last will and testament never changed to disinherit son.

Son became instant billionaire.

Michael.

Michael claimed he didn't want his father's money or his organization. Michael gave every outward appearance of being a reluctant heir, making the best out of a bad situation. Magnus' death created a vacuum at the top of the multinational behemoth. Uncle Liam was too old to take on management. Plenty of men coveted the role. Only a younger man, comfortable with numbers and with the ability to see beyond spreadsheets and goods shipments, could take on the leadership of a multinational, billion dollar Medusa.

Yet, days before Magnus' death, Michael had failed to prove his loyalty by not killing Jessica as Magnus had ordered.

In the ways of the Charity, you either did as you were told or you were killed.

Kill or be killed.

Declan reattached the tubing to the first canister and inhaled. Within a few breaths, his thinking clouded and fatigue resettled. He didn't struggle for air. He did not feel like he was suffocating. No panic triggered.

He cursed himself for touching the metal with his fingers. He stripped off his necktie and lifted the canister from the cabinet.

The markings were identical to the others.

He placed the canister on the desk and looked at the bookcases. At the top of the bookcase on the opposite wall, a book's spine was halved by the Cyclops eye of a camera.

Sunlight streamed through the windows at an evening's angle. Entering the control room again, he pulled the last recorded tape off the shelf with his tie. The date ended the week before Magnus' death. Where was the tape showing the week he died?

He pushed the button on the recorder. Nothing. Without power, the machine could not eject. He jammed his fingers into the flapped opening, wedging them down and under as he jimmied a cassette out of the machine.

He placed the two videocassettes aside, replacing them with new ones. After listing and packing the remaining items, he secured each box with a telltale strapping of tape. Carefully, he tucked the air canister and videocassettes under his jacket and walked to his car, mustering as much calm as he could as he nodded toward the outside camera.

Thursday, July 18, 1996
Pine Mountains
Perc, Kentucky

LEEANNE WAS CAREFUL to leave the security of Electra's farm during the shift change after she was done with her night feeding and turnout. Agreeing to stay in Electra's guest house was a way to get people to stop fussing over her. She was right under everyone's noses, right? She was safe and being obedient, right? But she was desperate to see if Rudie was alright. Being away from him, even for a few days, was hard, even if she was living more luxuriously than she ever had.

The side of the road was thick with brambles, but she found the old logging trail easily enough with the light of the half-moon. Or rather Ginger did. She followed the dog's shape along the black smudge of road as it wound through woods and stream beds to the dilapidated hunting shack all the kids from Perc used. How the adults were ignorant of its existence was a mystery to her. Beer cans, half-burned logs, and graffiti littered the inside of the dirt floor building. She walked as quietly as she could, worried any one of Perc's less than honor-student teens could be humping their best friend's drunk sister inside. The only sounds she heard were the rush of wind in the trees, the whine of mosquitoes, and the buzz of cicadas. The air was heavy with the scents of pine and earthen rot. Surprising. She was expecting whiffs of pot and dollar-store cologne.

She stayed in the brush and emerged only after she saw the red glow of Rudie's cigarette as he leaned against his pick-up. When he saw her, he ran up to her, burying his face in her hair and murmuring how much he missed her. The words seeped into her like balm. Her body relaxed into his. In no time, his hands were under her shirt, sliding her bra up over her breasts, pinching her nipples until she yelped.

"What took you so long? I've been here waiting for three nights." He kissed her neck and worked his way down to her breasts.

"Missus Lavielle's been checking on me night and day. 'Do you need anything, dahlin'?'" she said in a mocking falsetto. "I couldn't get away 'til folks relaxed some. They're convinced you're gonna do something bad to me."

"I'm sorry, Babe. I'm so, so sorry."

She found his mouth and kissed him hard, tongue sliding between his lips and teeth. "I knew you'd be sorry, Rudie." She smoothed her hands over his head and grabbed his face. "I knew you didn't mean to push her." She could feel his breathing quicken and urgency build.

"Like hell I didn't. She's lucky I didn't throttle her for trying to get between us."

His mouth pressed so hard on hers she couldn't respond. She twisted her head away, mouth cupping for air.

"Fuckin' A, Rudie. You serious? Why'd'ya go after her? I told you she had men around her." She put her arms on his shoulders and pushed as hard as she could. His arms stayed locked around her waist. "I mean it. Now she an' Missus Lavielle are drillin' down into my shit like they's some kind of savior. I don't need anybody in my face."

"No, Babe. You've got me." He thrust his hands inside her pants and squeezed her ass. He pulled her hips up and pushed his face between her breasts, biting and kissing as he ground her body against his.

She squirmed to get free. "C'mon, man. I'm serious. You've never been that stupid before. Does this have anything to do with those people from Boston?"

Rudie dropped her to the ground. "What do you know about them?"

Her upper arms stung from his grip. She could feel her skin redden. "Remember? We was picking up more feed and hay at the Aggie Co-op when that bitchy looking woman and wimpy guy walked over and asked if you knew her. They knew she had a farm around here and was trying to find her. I was in the truck and heard you play an angle to get paid for what you knew. I heard enough to know they're from Boston and looking for Jessica."

"So?" he said, voice sharp.

"So, just before Jax's men decked you, you said someone was coming looking for her and I guess it must be them." The back of Rudie's truck held three toolboxes. Big. Very new. "I figured either you got paid or ripped them off. Which is it?"

He moved his hand to the front of her jeans and worked the button free. "They got what they wanted." He shoved his hand down, pushing her jeans past her hip. "I need you, Babe. When you comin' home?"

She tried to turn away from him. "No. That was stupid, Rudie. You almost cost me my job. Ow! Knock it off." His stubble raked against her face.

Ginger, ears back and tail tucked under her butt, tried to nuzzle her body between them. Annoyed, Rudie grabbed her collar and yanked with one hand while he raised the other in threat.

"Don't hurt her!" LeeAnne begged.

Rudie lowered his raised hand and hoisted the dog into the truck, slamming the door shut. Ginger barked once, but stopped when Rudie turned and yelled, "NO!" Ginger sank down. "See that? That dog's a mess because of you."

The woods closed around her. This was all too familiar. The needing. The anger. The blame.

"I miss you, LeeAnne. You know you're the only one who can keep me out of trouble." He pulled his shirt free from his pants and opened his belt. He pushed her hand down on his groin. "C'mon. You know how I get when you're not around." He mashed his face against hers. "You know you've missed me."

"I just want to know what you've got goin' on with those Boston people. You're up to something, Rudie, and I want to know what it is so I can stay away from it. It's bad for my esteem."

Her words ignited him. "Esteem? You never used that word before in your life. That Electra woman's been getting' in your head. I don't hear you talkin', I hear her." He threw her on the ground, pinning her arms above her head with one hand, and fumbling with her pants with the other. "I want my LeeAnne, not some overripe, past her prime grandmother." He grew more determined the more she struggled. "You came here to see me. Alone. Don't say you don't want it."

"Not like this," she said, voice pinched with control. "You're hurting me."

"What's changed? Your *esteem* turning you off?"

"You just ... I don't ..."

"*You* don't? You don't what? Why are you here? You come here wearing my favorite shirt and smelling like roses and you tell me you don't want this?" In one final move, he peeled her pants off and cast them aside. He pushed his pants to his knees.

He used his legs to spread hers and thrust inside her with such force her back skidded along the ground. "Go 'head. Tell me. Why you're. Here."

"I. Don't. Know." He beat each word out with every thrust.

"Tell. Me."

He drilled her harder, forcing her hands over her head, and finding her mouth with his own. She tried to speak, but he didn't want her answers.

"Say. It." His pelvis rammed against hers, demanding a response. He held back at the height of his pleasure, forcing her to look at him. "Say. IT."

Tears streaked down her flushed cheeks. "I ... love ... you, Rudie."

He collapsed on top of her with a groan, chest heaving and out of breath. His seed burned. He jerked once more, then scrabbled over to a cooler in the truck bed and popped open a beer. He raised the can in salute.

"When you leave here, you'll never forget why you're here or what you're going to do for me." He tossed her a can.

She caught it with one hand and wiped her nose with the other. "Fuckin' asshole, Rudie." She rolled over and reached for her pants.

In one motion, he kicked them farther away. "I'm not done."

LeeAnne waited until after Jax and his men finished the morning feeding to walk back, the route taking longer than she thought. Rudie left her a Mountain Dew and half-eaten bag of Doritos when he drove away sometime before dawn. Ginger ate each chip from her shaking hands and licked the bag clean. She stopped at a stream to wash the greasy orange seasonings off her fingers as best as she could while Ginger waded belly deep and lapped water, desperate to rid her mouth of spice. LeeAnne stripped down and scrubbed her body and clothes with cold water. The morning summer sun was hot enough to dry her clothes quickly, and she lay on a rock, feeling what a snake must feel when it suns itself. Her heart hurt. Her body hurt. Her soul hurt. The past hours felt like days.

She nodded at the security guy seated in a jeep at the base of Electra's drive. He looked up, checked a clipboard in front of him, and gave her a two-finger salute acknowledging her name was on the list.

The guard would not be the one to question her night out on the town. The long way around to the guest house was clear, and she slipped inside and locked the door behind her. She needed a nap and a scalding shower before she went to work.

She woke from a dreamless sleep when the sun had passed its peak, and she crawled into the shower. Within minutes, her skin had turned bright pink, and after scrubbing herself, she sank down into the tub, knees hugged to her chest. Why had she let Rudie get to her again? All she wanted was to make sure he was okay, to let him know she was still his.

She nudged the water up, hotter and hotter. Steam clouded the air, making it hard to breathe and her lungs pushed against her ribs trying to suck air in. The familiar panic started in her gut and forced its way up. She stopped it somewhere mid-chest. The water no longer felt hot against her upturned face. She no longer felt.

Electra's guest house was the perfect sanctuary and LeeAnne felt safe from prying eyes. A small refrigerator held an assortment of juice and soda. A coffee maker reminded her of a hotel she once stayed at when her mother took her and ran away from her father, just that once, so many years ago. A bowl on the small table contained fruit and crackers, enough food to tie someone over until dinner would be served in the big house. Even a bag of dry dog food sat discreetly in the corner. The bathroom had a large wicker basket that contained rolled white towels, the thickest LeeAnne had ever felt. A series of glass jars on the vanity held cotton balls, Q-tips, lotions, and soaps. She found what she needed in the drawer, next to a badger-hair shave brush, marble bowl, and shaving cream.

With assured motions and a mind clear from worry, she cracked the razor, extricated a blade, and drew a precise line down the white skin of her arm.

She watched her fingers as if watching a movie. Detached. Disembodied. The relief was instant. Anxiety and fear mixed in the swirling red tide and disappeared down the drain. Only after the water ran cold did she get up and towel herself off, taking care not to leave bloodstains behind.

Of course, Electra was hostess enough to foresee that a guest might need a bandage. A first aid kit sat in the second drawer down. It was as if Electra could look inside each guest and know what she would need.

But it was Jessica who looked inside of LeeAnne with an expression that said she saw everything—every doubt, every thought that maybe LeeAnne caused her own life's problems—but she never judged. Jessica instantly saw LeeAnne's relationship with Rudie for what it was—a man hiding his own worthlessness behind the abuse of a woman. It was Jessica who talked about esteem and regaining personal power by shunning the control Rudie demanded. More importantly, Jessica never accepted how LeeAnne felt about herself. Jessica saw how good LeeAnne was with horses and encouraged her to do more, even encouraging her to ride the more hot-tempered horses. There was something behind Jessica's eyes that said she understood being with horses was more balm than chore. Jessica never looked at LeeAnne with blame or pity . . . only promise.

She pulled on fresh jeans, T-shirt, and boots and prepared for her shift, happy to know the horses waited for her. She smiled as she anticipated their whickers of welcome.

Her life used to be so simple. Rudie. Work. Rudie. Work. Now, she just had work, but her life felt more complicated.

How could she ever forgive herself for being so stupid? Worse, how could anyone look her in the eye for what she had allowed to happen?

Electra. Jessica. Why did their lives have to be so damned perfect?

Saturday, July 20, 1996
Brandywine Farm
Perc, Kentucky

ELECTRA FINISHED BRUSHING her bay gelding, Wino, and reached for the saddle and pad while murmuring the equestrian's version of love talk.

"Easy child. Gentle ride tonight. Listen to the katydids? There you go." She hoisted the saddle and pads forward as one unit on Wino's withers then slid them back, ensuring no mane or hide would be pulled to cause the horse discomfort. The heat of the day had passed and the air freshened with the coming dark. Aside from cocktails on the veranda, Electra could think of no better way to spend the end of her day. Most often, riding won and cocktails were relegated to star gazing when the night had fully bloomed.

As involved as she was in the community and in managing her businesses, living a simple life was what kept her sane. Sure, she knew everything there was to know about the families and people of Perc and Lexington. You can't have four generations of family living in a thimble and *not* know a thing or two about your neighbors. Knowing all didn't mean she had to *be* all. Riding her horses, living alone, and socializing when she wanted to—which was frequently, but always on her terms—was her idea of a perfect life.

But she was the last of her line. If she could have filled her home with a brood of children, she would have happily cut back her professional life. An only child, she basked in her daddy's light and determined to be the son he never had. Bracebridge never lamented not having more children or a son, but Electra vowed he'd never have a reason to by throwing herself into every activity her father had an interest in. Luckily for him, she had more energy and smarts than mere mortals. She managed his newspapers, encouraged him to get into radio and cable news, facilitated the adoption of streamlined production and electronic syndication of news, and now headed a media empire that rivaled Rupert Murdoch's. No girl ever made her daddy more proud.

But after his death, she realized her devotion came at a cost—being alone while surrounded by people.

Maybe it was her uncanny ability to spot a dolt, a loser, or a liar, or maybe she never learned to soften her demands when it came to friendship, but Electra Lavielle had very few people she could call a friend, and Jessica crept into her heart in a way that surprised her.

She had chosen wonderful people to run her companies. Trust was the keystone of her networks. She benefited from their talents and rewarded them accordingly. She paid out hefty bonuses rivaling a full year's pay to those employees who embodied the best skills and ethics. In the often dog-eat-dog world of headline-grabbing news, she rewarded balance, integrity, and honesty. Sure her news outlets may have lost a scoop or didn't break a headline because fact-checking kept the presses still, but she could sleep at night. So could her employees. Were they her friends? No. But they were loyal to one another nonetheless.

Loyalty to her instincts was unquestioned, as was her habit to give millions to charity.

It was these two traits that tied her fate to Michael Connaught.

And she was afraid it was evidence her ability to spot a liar had let her down.

The time arrived for what her daddy would call her come-to-Jesus moment. Her jaw stiffened at the thought as she slid the bridle up Wino's face, using her thumb in the corner of his mouth to open his jaw for the snaffle bit. She secured the noseband and throatlatch, checking to make sure the keepers were snug.

Before mounting, she led Wino in a series of tight circles, using only her body position with as little physical contact as possible, a trick she learned from Jessica to warm up the horse. Wino had earned his name for the lazy stride he adopted when trying to discourage unskilled riders. Encouraging the animal to yield to a leader forced the horse to attention and made it more alert. Groundwork, like walking beside the horse in random patterns, was Electra's signal of dominance in the herd. Wino accepted her.

Usually an ornery cuss, who in recent years had developed the habit of nipping at everyone except Electra, Wino pricked his ears forward at the sound of Jessica's voice. Jessica accepted nothing less than full cooperation from human or horse, and Wino responded to the coaching Jessica provided Electra.

"Okay, girl. Spill it." Electra said as she tightened the girth and pulled down the stirrups.

She watched as Jessica unhitched Breezy from the crossties and walked the Thoroughbred, a chestnut with four white socks, to stand beside the mounting block. After checking the girth, Jessica placed her left foot in the iron and swung up in one easy motion. The leather tack creaked as she situated herself. She leaned down and patted the burnished neck.

"Breezy looks great, Electra. So does Wino. I'm glad you're still riding as much as you used to."

"I swear these beasts look forward to our evening rides as much as I do, but you're changing the subject." Electra waited for Wino to settle before mounting. She climbed the mounting block's three wooden steps, hoisted her right leg over Wino's back and settled in the saddle with a little groan. "My body might be slowing down, but don't think for one second my mind is. I said spill it and I mean spill it."

Since their last conversation, Electra felt Jessica avoiding her. Seeing her young guest was rattled to the point of becoming mute, she let matters rest for a couple of days until the vertical furrows between Jessica's brows softened and the haunted look faded. Still, looked like a wilted rose. Their paths converged only because Electra strode up from the paddocks with the horses and handed Breezy's lead to Jessica with a terse, "Tack up," command.

Dark circles or no, it was Jessica's come-to-Jesus moment, too.

They warmed the horses up slowly, enjoying the rhythmic plod of hooves on firm sod and the sounds of the farm quieting for the night. Horses nickered to one another and a few galloped in their paddocks expending their last energy before being retired to their stalls. Even in silence, Electra enjoyed the comfort of Jessica's presence. They both drew their peace from these moments and needed no words to bind them together.

After a few minutes, Electra clucked and tapped Wino's sides with her booted legs. The horse set off at a trot toward the trails around the farm's perimeter. Jessica and Breezy tore off along the cross-country course, taking a few of the smaller jumps. Jessica's ponytail streamed behind her helmeted head. Her arms and upper body relaxed, she held her legs steady and strong against the horse's side. Electra could see in that moment Jessica had forgotten her worries and rode suspended by the gossamer threads that bound horse and human. Above the katydids and crickets, she heard the peal of her laughter. The pair looped around the course and exited on the far side to a knoll that gave a view of the Pine River and mountains beyond. The fact Jessica often rode to the same spot didn't surprise Electra, as it was her favorite place as well. After a few minutes, she pulled Wino up beside Breezy.

The glow of the ride was still on Jessica's face. Electra let the moment linger before she began to talk, knowing what she was about to say would wick away the joy. They headed down a wooded path.

"It's been impossible to talk to you. Either someone is hovering about or you're as tight-lipped as a lemon-sucking nun. The time's come for you to dish."

Only the sound of hooves thudding on the dirt path filled the air. Electra waited.

"I'm not sure you should know everything."

"You've been silent about Michael. If you're not going to talk, then you're going to listen. You have my promise that all of this is off the record. I'm not trying to pick your brain for some inside scoop. I know enough to know that Michael inherited his father's problems along with his business. From where I sit, nothing has changed since he brought you to Ireland. In fact, I think you're in a worse situation. No more disguises, remember? No more lies, yet it seems like that's what he forces you to do if you want autonomy. Are you staying under his wing because you love him or because he knows something about you that you don't want known?"

The question hit its intended mark. Jessica straightened in the saddle. "Being with him at Ballyronan was amazing. Walking where he walked as a child allowed me to know him at a deeper level. Our time was magical. We explored the lake and woods and never left each other's side. He's like me in so many ways."

"You're telling me nothing new and nothing important." Impatience creased her words. "Do you think he loves you?" She watched Jessica closely for any signs that her answers were calculated, signaling that she was deciding what information to give and what to hold back. Stress, sleeplessness, isolation, and fear ripened the interview to fruition. Declan's visit and Brooks' inquiries were the final straws. Jessica was ready.

"He says he does. He's put himself at risk to protect me so I don't doubt him. At night, wrapped in his arms, his home seemed safe, almost cozy, even though Ballyronan makes your place look like a duffer's cottage."

Electra chuckled. "I had no idea he came from such means. I was charmed by him from the start, but now I'm not so sure. You talk about the risk he's taking ... All this business about his father ... " Her voice trailed off.

"You and Michael had business dealings together."

"That was well before I knew anything about his father. Remember? Michael seemed the perfect partner for many of my charities. He had means, certainly, and entered our community in a position as a respected leader, so trusting him was easy." She paused, careful to probe for answers in a way that wouldn't shut Jessica down.

Electra continued. "There are pieces that don't fit with someone trying to live a law-abiding life. What concerns me is his paranoid stance on security. I don't question that he desires to protect you, but I think he only buys the illusion of security. I feel like he's hiding behind a wall and trying to keep you under his thumb. As for him loving you? I'm not buying it."

Jessica tried to hide her shock by clearing her throat. "How can you say that?"

"Brooks is right. He's not calling you every five minutes like a man besotted with love. What's stopping him from being here? How much time did you spend with him in Ireland anyway?"

"We didn't spend as much time together as I thought we would. He was taking over his father's enterprises and settling the estate. He was," she paused to find the right word, "overwhelmed."

"And those grooms! They spend more time watching people coming and going on my farm than they do the horses. You're not fooling me. They're some kind of bodyguard. Why?"

"He wants to make sure someone is always near me."

"*Why?*" Needing to ask the question unsettled her. Even as they rode, she knew Jax was in the barn, watchful and wary.

"Because Michael said there are people in his organization that hate me for triggering Magnus' indictment. They've tried to kill me because of it. Because someone might use harming me to manipulate Michael into doing something he doesn't want to do. Because–"

"Because he needs to keep an eye on you to make sure you continue to be the marionette on his strings?"

Jessica adjusted the length of her stirrup leathers. She didn't answer.

"You listen to me. You owe Michael nothing."

"This isn't about owing anyone anything," Jessica snapped. "Besides, you're the one who played matchmaker. Remember? Or has your senility crept up on you and you've forgotten your shameless maneuverings?"

Rather than being affronted, Electra smiled. Jessica's irreverence was one of the things Electra adored about her. Very few people could call Electra senile and get away with it. Most people were nervous as a cat in Electra's presence, always feeling watched and judged, knowing nothing escaped her notice. She had heard people say that talking with her felt like being wired to a human polygraph.

"I forget nothing!" Electra said, wagging her crop in the air like an admonishing finger. "Mixing two ingredients together does not mean you've made a soufflé. All I'm saying is if it's right, you'll know it. You're hot for each other. Fine. I get it. But, from where I sit, the score's even. A balance sheet isn't worth fighting for, especially if it's not yours." She lowered her voice and cooed, trying to lighten the mood, "Besides, you're a young woman without a ring on her finger."

Jessica hit the heel of her hand against her forehead in a gesture of mock disbelief. "What is it about being in the South that makes me feel like I've gone back in time?"

Electra's expression must have betrayed her mirth, as Jessica's eyes gleamed. Flouting Southern manners both maddened and amused Electra, but she'd never admit how much she enjoyed wondering which ladylike conventions were going to be disrespected by Jessica. Breaking rules worked only if a person knew the rules to begin with. A well-bred Yankee knew damned well how to rattle a Southern belle's cage. Electra loved Jessica all the more for it.

Jessica continued talking. "Being married is the last thing on my mind, trust me. He's doing everything he can to create a life for me within his world."

"That's not love, Jessica. That's control." Wino lowered his head on a loose rein. "What about you? Do you love him?"

"I . . . I'm not going to answer that. I don't want to talk about Michael and me in a way that says we are an 'us.'"

"It's kinda late for that, don't cha think?" Electra barbed her words and tone to push her point across. "Either you're together with him or you're not. Right now, you are as tied together in the public consciousness as any celebrity couple. Why do you feel a need to wait for him to get his act together? You might be covered in dust and cobwebs by the time he gets himself untangled from his own legal mess."

"You said it yourself. He and I are a lot alike."

"It's true. Both of you are beholden to your pasts. He's still running from his father's connections. I know he says he's making over his father's enterprise—what did he call it? Oh, right, the Charity—into something of his own. But I can't see . . . I just don't know how he can take something so tainted and clean it up."

"Electra," Jessica's voice lowered with a combination of worry and warning. "What do you know about all that? *Why* do you want to know?"

"Michael is sending Declan to secure other investors and to see about the possibility of forming a second syndicate. Michael's channeling more of his assets into horses and has said your advice will be essential."

Jessica ventured cautiously, slowing her words. "I'm not sure how much I want to be involved with Michael's businesses."

"You keep saying you don't want to talk about him, but there are things that have to be brought out into the open by us. He and I are partners in one syndicate. He's pressing me to join him in others, but I'm holding off until I know more about how he's going to extricate himself from his father's mess. I don't want my name tainted by rumors of money laundering. I know the cost to your family. They had to die to get out from under that weight. I'm concerned that Michael's business practices are not all that different from Magnus'. You were in Ireland with him. What's changed?"

Jessica's mouth twisted with unspoken worry. Electra strained to hear her response. "I don't know."

"I'm worried that all of this security he has built around you is for his benefit, not yours. Your every waking hour is under his watch and he has you as scared as a rabbit about any stranger lurking about. Why?"

"Because . . . b-because he said rogue men in his organization would try to harm me to manipulate him." Jessica brushed her hand across her ribs in an unconscious gesture that hinted at unspoken fears. "Because I-I've been targeted before and he's afraid it will happen again."

Electra sniffed. "Who said they were rogues? Michael? For all his efforts, you're telling me exactly the opposite of what he wants you to say. I never would have agreed to invest in owning Kilkea, Planxty, and Bealltainn if it weren't for knowing my involvement was only going to help you. I'm not comfortable getting more involved on the business side. But what about you?

"I've trained the horses, and that's as far as I want to go. I'm not sure I even want to go to the Olympics if it means implying I'm okay with participating at a deeper level, even with something as innocuous as scouting for new horses."

Electra rested her hands on Wino's withers and took a deep breath. "I overheard what Declan told you in my garden. If Michael is truly in love with you, he's not setting you up and is using this time to clear the way for the two of you to be together. And, if he truly does love you, then he'll respect you want out of his shadow and will leave you alone. But if he loves himself, his money, or his power more than you, you're in trouble. And if you're in trouble, I am too. I need to know if I'm . . . you . . . *we* are making a mistake being involved with Michael."

Jessica shook her head as if trying to rattle together pieces of a puzzle. "I . . . I know too much."

"Ooooh." The word exhaled out of her as her head and shoulders dropped forward. "Do you think he's afraid of what would happen if you talked? Fear is a bigger motivator than love."

Seeing Jessica's struggle for an answer flicker beneath the surface of her face made Electra's stomach clench.

"I don't know how he couldn't be afraid," Jessica said. "I saw how his organization operates. I saw how his uncle pressured him until he agreed to step into the leadership role and I saw how he began to change when he realized the scope of what he commanded. I didn't want his wealth; I just wanted to be left alone with my horses. But he arranged the sale of everything I owned, even my farm, and purchased steeplechase horses in the syndicate for me. I resisted all of it until I knew *you* were involved. Ironic, eh?" She managed a weak smile.

"Not ironic. Manipulated. He used both of us to do his bidding."

Jessica shrugged.

"Don't think I'm free from this shadow. Those agents came to *my* house to question *my* guest. It won't be long before we can't dodge their interview requests any longer by employing—what does Declan call it? Oh, right, *scheduling difficulties*. This is bad for both of us. What do you think will happen if you try to leave?"

More silence.

Electra pressed. "Don't be a mute fool. I'll tell you what happens. No one leaves Connaught organizations alive." She sucked her lips together after Jessica gave a faint nod of her head.

For the first time in her life, regardless of the political scandals her news teams had reported or the crimes her investigative reporters had uncovered, Electra Lavielle was afraid of the truth.

She continued. "You called me from the airport panicked that Michael was arranging to have you leave the country again. I agreed that if you had left then, guilt would have torpedoed your reputation. I think your being here and staying tied to his world," she said with a sweep of her hand to barns where Jax's men waited, "was to keep the bad dog with you until you could figure out how to tame it."

The carefully cultivated defiance started to crumble. Jessica's lower lip began to tremble. "I . . . I don't know!" Jessica braced her palms against her temple. "I . . . don't know what I should do. I'd feel safer if I knew no one could find me."

"Nonsense" The word hurled from Electra's mouth. "You've spent too much of your life under lies of all colors. You need to live a life . . . *your* life."

Jessica choked back a sob. "My life? I don't know what that is anymore! Michael came to me when I needed someone who understood the insanity of what I had been though. He . . . he made me feel like I could belong to someone again. Then . . . then when I thought I was getting a grip the world turned upside down again. I need to live a life? *What* life? *Whose* life?" The wailed words scattered birds from the bushes.

It is a truth of life that mothers feel the pain of their children more acutely than their own pain. Seeing Jessica struggle opened a wound of longing Electra had thought died long ago. The instinct to provide for and protect Jessica galvanized her. "You work on figuring out what to do with your life. I'll help you figure out what to do about Michael."

She urged Wino to a canter and they rode in silence to the end of the wooded path and up a small incline, jumping over fallen trees and across streams. Once back in the pastures, they rode up the double rows of fencing that separated the fields into paddocks. The gap prevented ill-mannered horses from reaching and biting one another if turned out next to a grumpy neighbor and created a shortcut to connect woods and barns. The insect chorus grew louder as they rode, lulling Electra as it always did. Brandywine was her heart and soul, and she loved every blade of grass, stone, grub, and critter on it.

Once up on the rise, she had a view of her home in the distance and the cross-country course with its log jumps, water challenges, and combination flights. The course was designed by the same firm that built the Rolex competition area. Electra gave strict instructions to make sure her course was the hardest around. Any horse that trained on her farm would be trained on the best course by the best trainers to be the best in the world. She would settle for nothing less.

The ride had worked its magic on both of them. Jessica again looked like a young woman in full bloom of life with her worries and cares stripped away.

"Okay then. I may have to make a deal with the devil himself to help you get out of this mess, but I'm willing to put my life on the line and try if you are. But I have to know we're together on this. That your heart is with me."

"My heart?" Worry worked Jessica's mouth. "What do you mean?"

"Leaving Michael's world means leaving his business *and* him behind. I can't have you second-guessing my actions when things get tough, and I have a feeling things could get pretty damned ugly. I need to know you're through with him."

Asking a woman to give up on a man she had already given so much to was hard. Jessica was a stand-by-your-man gal and would fight to the last for him. It was one thing to end a relationship with a "It's not you. It's me," and "We can still be friends" lie, but this was different. Making a clean break and moving forward on a path that could ultimately destroy a man she shared a bed with was asking more than most mortals could give.

"It's not like you haven't been having doubts about Michael."

"T-true."

"What do you need to know to be sure Michael is either the man he claims and is truly in love with you, or is using you as Brooks suggests?"

They walked on. The ride's silent magic worked on unlocking truths. The night air freshened as the sun slid toward the horizon. The same humidity Electra cursed during the day rewarded her by layering the hills in hues of blues and purples. If it was possible to bottle the perfection of a moment and dip into it when times got tough, this would be the moment. She was content to wait for Jessica's answer.

"I've thought a lot about this. If I found any shred of proof that he has taken an action in direct disregard of my wishes."

"And if he did?"

"Then I'll know what you've said is true—that he loves his power and money more than me. If … if he intentionally hurt me or used me for some scheme, I'll find a way to expose everything I know about him, his father, and his organization."

"If you do, he'll spread lies about you and your family in retaliation, or worse, violate your confidence by exposing something you don't want exposed." Electra fixed Jessica with a knowing glare. Jessica squirmed, but remained silent. Electra continued. "Listening to Declan question you, I agree with Brooks that Michael is trying to set you up." She raised her hand to stop Jessica's protest and took a deep breath. "And you'll find out if those attempts on your life for harming the Charity were real. It could get ugly."

"You know something."

"I know that calling a posse of reporters to meet you at the airport caused a hornet's nest of problems for you."

Jessica gasped. "Yes. He knows I *hate* reporters and the lies they've printed about me. If that hadn't happened, I could have slipped back into the States as a regular citizen. My story would have faded from memory soon enough."

Electra puckered her mouth, working against words she knew must be spoken but not knowing how.

Jessica leaned over, grabbed Wino's reins, and pulled the horses to a stop. "Out with it. What are you trying to say?"

"There's a reporter in Boston who has been on the Connaught trail for a while. Only my intervention stopped her from writing some really explosive articles about both Magnus and Michael that—at the time—sounded like a lot of conjecture. I know how lies can stick once published, so I needed today's conversation to know if I was wrong to stop her. It's hard for me to admit it, but I was. You need to know the details of your arrival in Kentucky were provided directly to her in a phone call after you left Belfast."

"How do you know that? How can that be true?"

Electra's heart ached to watch the sorrow and hurt of betrayal erupt. Jessica buried her eyes in the crook of her elbow to hide her sob.

She waited a long moment to let the reality of the loss of love harden. "I'm so sorry Jessica. I didn't want to say anything until I had it confirmed through my sources at the Feds. The reporter, Colleen Shaunessy-Carillo, received a call from Northern Ireland while your flight was en route. She was the one who alerted the rest of the press."

"How do you know it was Michael?"

"Who else would call from his estate? Who else knew the whats, whens, and wheres of your flight? Don't be a fool."

"He loves me! He wouldn't do anything to hurt me!" The words rose up from a well of darkness Electra could only imagine.

The sun dipped behind the distant hills, setting the clouds on fire with blazes of orange and red. Electra cut across a field and headed toward the barns, letting Jessica and Breezy follow behind at their own pace. In time, Jessica trotted up beside her.

"You think Michael is using the threat of media coverage as a way to control me," Jessica said, "I'll prove he loves me by neutralizing the tool, by embracing it, and using it as my own."

Electra wanted to shout, *It's about damned time*, but restrained herself, fearing too much whoop and holler could hamper a fragile breakthrough. She ventured a cautious, "And?"

"And, if he's trying to frame me, then I have to make sure I have the facts I need to clear my name."

A smile flirted at the edges of Electra's mouth. "*And?*" she pressed.

"And it's time I tell you about my rebel Irish mom. You've got some stories you need to write."

Electra couldn't stop the sigh of relief she heaved. "What about Gus? You want me to write about your dad too, right?"

Another wave darkened Jessica's brow. "How much wine do you have back at the house? There's a lot you don't know."

Thursday, July 25, 1996
Brandywine Farm

THE DAYS PASSED in a blur. Jessica poured her heart out to Electra, then rode like a banshee across the countryside, caring for her horses and her soul. The connection between two strong women, which had initially formed on gut feelings and intuition, firmed to an unbreakable bond. Jessica never felt pressed for more than she was able to share, and rewarded Electra for her patience by unfolding her story, petal by petal, until the truth of her complex life bloomed. She cried herself raw, held tight against Electra's bosom. Searing pain softened to confusion, and confusion morphed to acceptance. Most importantly for Jessica, the isolation developed by a life of fear began to soften and the seeds of trust were sewn.

Electra's sense of urgency to get out ahead of any damning information and undo the damage to Jessica's reputation drove her to begin researching the articles on Bridget's life. They spent hours huddled at Electra's kitchen table, tape recorder and team of writers present. Other times, only the two of them sat, hands clasped around goblets of chardonnay or mugs of tea as Jessica poured out her story, fears, and sorrows. Electra pushed for immediate publication, but Jessica would have none of it, preferring to wait until after the Olympics.

"But why?"

"Because the Games are going to suck up the dominant share of media attention and because I'm Bealltainn's trainer. I want my focus to be on the horses. There'll be time enough afterward to put my story out there and cope with all the upheaval it will generate. Deal?"

Electra's pride in how well Jessica was beginning to understand the machinations of public relations showed when Electra smiled and said "Deal." Jessica began to feel hopeful. Knowing the force the two women would create, Jessica ventured, "And that goes for any strategy we put together to get me out from under Michael's thumb."

Neither hid their fear, but only nodded in unison, heads lowered and shoulders slumped.

Electra tore up little bits of napkin as she spoke. "I've been thinking about this. I've already met with my legal and financial teams and instructed them to make sure my companies have not already been infiltrated with any schemes that could benefit an illegal enterprise—including charities."

The swift action worried her. "So soon?"

"If I haven't been infiltrated and if my companies have not yet been used by Michael in any nefarious way, I believe I'll be safe from retribution."

Jessica nodded. "I see your point. Brooks said if you haven't been privy to any illegal dealings, Michael won't be concerned that you could provide harmful evidence against him. By confirming your minimal exposure, you further ensure your safety."

"I don't like being at risk on a personal or professional basis. I trust my corporate counsel and he'll make sure all of my affairs are in order and begin unraveling connections from all of Michael's affairs."

"He'll question *why* you're doing all this."

Electra touched her fingertips to her lips. "I've been wanting to do something here at the farm for a long time, and you and LeeAnne helped me firm up my goal."

"Me? LeeAnne? I don't follow."

"Brandywine needs to have a purpose more than just training a horse to jump higher and faster. I want to focus on the people as much as the horses—you know, as a safe haven of sorts." She waved away the thought. "This is an old woman's fancy, but will help explain why I'm divesting assets. Brooks suggested I begin selling my shares under the guise of a corporate restructuring."

"Restructuring? To what?"

Electra reached over and took Jessica's hands in her own. "To create a non-profit that focuses on abused women and women who are in toxic relationships."

Jessica pulled her head back, affronted. "I am not abused!"

Electra spoke softly. "I didn't say you were." She waited until the realization of her denial sunk in. When Jessica finally nodded her head, she said, "You and LeeAnne showed me the need to create such a place. Will you help me?"

Jessica's eyes glistened.

"I figure I can untangle from Michael's web without him questioning me or working against us. Imagine how poorly it would reflect on his new image if he did! Having a different vision for Brandywine with you as an important part of it will explain why I'm changing things around now."

Jessica began to wring her hands. "Go slow, Electra. Don't tip him off until we know what we're doing and that you're in the clear. The logical next step is to sell the horses you and he purchased and dissolve the syndicates you are partners in."

"So, let's get ourselves to the Olympics and see if we can find a buyer for Bealltainn. I'll make sure the market knows Kilkea and Planxty are ready for sale, too. I'd rather do private sales than auctions right now just to keep buzz and idle chitchat to a minimum."

"The Olympics are the best place to find a concentration of buyers for horses of that caliber. Okay then. What's our plan?" Jessica asked, hopeful for a change in topic.

"I have dear friends there who would love to have us as guests while we are in Atlanta. Friday is the cross-country portion of eventing for teams and individuals. Saturday is team dressage. Being there does not mean you're agreeing to be more involved. You're simply scouting talent for Brandywine's future entries into Rolex. It's business. Pure and simple."

"I wasn't planning to see the Olympics. My going is not without its problems."

Electra shrugged. "True enough, but you can't *not* go. Jax and his men will be with us. If that's not good enough to keep Michael happy, then tough luck."

"We keep looking like we're going along with him, then shut him out when we're safe to do so."

Electra smiled. "I'm glad you're finally going to get out and start living your life. We've been invited to watch the eventing in the VIP tent with the trainers. You can talk all the shop you want and we can finally see that horse of ours in action."

"I heard Bealltainn was just the ticket for that Irish rider. The cross-country course is a rough one, and once that man conquered the four-hoofed rocket he felt more confident."

"For the life of me, I can't understand why on earth that poor man wanted to ride that hellion?"

"The answer is important for you to know as you move forward with your new vision to compete at Rolex," Jessica said. "Like the

Olympics, equestrians at Rolex can compete in one or all of three main events—dressage, stadium jumping, and cross-country. Bealltainn's training in steeplechase meant he was well-suited to train over a cross-country course with various jumps and water hazards. He needed to be controlled for speed and ridden for technically precise jump approaches, the exact skills the Irish team member needed to hone. Using Bealltainn rather than one of the team's horses allowed the rider additional training without fatiguing a horse the team may need for competition."

"Won't Michael question us selling those horses if they are so well suited for one event?"

"Maybe, but the fact is the horses have to be adept at dressage, too. Getting Bealltainn to do a side pass in a dressage ring would be like getting a linebacker to do a ballet adagio."

Electra chuckled. "Placing Bealltainn for sale at the Olympics will expose him to more prospective buyers who could see his potential in the one discipline he can do well. Excellent. We can do what we need to do without raising more questions. Striking deals there will be exactly what the syndicate needs to help make a profit. No one questions profits."

They clinked their mugs together, eyes shimmering with love and fear.

The activity surrounding their departure hummed. As much as she tried not to look inexperienced in the ways of the super-rich, Jessica couldn't help but be awed by the ease that came with money. Growing up in Hamilton, Massachusetts, she was no stranger to wealth, but New England's old-money ways were different from the ways of international new money. Where her childhood friends' parents' frayed Oxford button-down shirts and ancient Volvos belied generations of wealth from descendants of original settlers, the resources on display at Brandywine flabbergasted her.

With one call, Electra set in motion everything they would need. Electra's personal assistant laid out clothes and assembled outfits for the various events. If Jessica found nothing suitable in Electra's overstuffed closets, armloads of new clothes were delivered for her choosing. Temporary horse handlers checked in with Jessica for training schedules and routines. Whether Jax was suspicious of the sudden activity or not, he never left Jessica's side.

The burden of indecision had lifted from her shoulders, and he noticed a difference.

"Aye, Miss Jessica. Good to see you in fine spirits and happier. Nice to see you're going to the Olympics. Why the change of heart?"

How could she answer him? Fear and uncertainty had hobbled her ability to see Michael clearly. The bubble had burst and she realized the only way she could lead a normal life was to break away from Michael, even at the threat to her life.

She wanted to answer Jax truthfully, but not tip her hand, knowing that whatever she said would be reported back to Michael. "I want to see Bealltainn's progress and get feedback on his performance from the other trainers. It's best to see everything first hand."

"Maybe you'll find another horse or two to add to your roster? You'll be in demand and folks'll be wanting to have you train their beasts. Better yet, use that keen eye of yours to buy a few. Train 'em up and sell 'em at a profit."

She gave Jax her best enigmatic smile. "We'll see. I'm not in a hurry."

An eight-seat helicopter arrived the next morning. Jessica was surprised to see Declan step off and lope toward her, head down, and arms cradling a sheaf of papers.

His manner provided no warmth even though his greeting tried to. "Electra. Jax. Jessica," he said with a nod to each, "Michael's seen to our transport."

"Why are you here?" Jessica crossed her arms and shrank away from him.

Electra placed her hand on Jessica's arm. "I suggested we didn't want to bother anyone with our plans, but once Jax told Michael of our intent to go to the Olympics, Michael insisted on providing our transportation. It would have been rude to refuse." A cloud of fear darted behind her eyes. "Silly of me to think Michael wouldn't want to be involved and send his very best men to be with us." She flashed a smile and oozed Southern warmth. "Right, Mr. Cleary?"

"I'm here at the pleasure of Michael Connaught. He's spared nothing in ensuring your comfort and safety. I suggest you relax for a change." He acknowledged Jax with a steady gaze. Declan's curt nod seemed more of an afterthought than greeting.

Declan didn't look Jessica in the eye, but spoke to a spot somewhere over her head. "I've documents for both of you to sign."

"Documents? For what?" A pit formed in her stomach, a physical warning of what her instinct told her. Don't sign anything. Play for time. Delay.

The white papers looked innocent enough. Red sticky tabs protruded from the sides, indicating where she should sign. Each page was embossed with *MMC, Ltd., Boston.* "Is this about deportation proceedings? Or Gus?"

"Neither. Michael wants to make you an equal partner in other companies he's forming."

Jessica tried to hide her surprise behind disappointment. "Oh. I was hoping to get more information on how much trouble I'm in or not. We still have to meet with those FBI agents, remember?" she said, voice sharp. "Forming companies might be his priority, but it's not mine." She took the papers and gave them a cursory glance. The documents were backdated to March. Electra's name appeared on some pages. "I've not heard of any of this. Why sign me as a partner in syndicates that are already established?" She looked over at Electra, busy with last minute details to her staff. "Does Electra know?"

"Mrs. Lavielle and Mr. Connaught have had conversations. I cannot attest to what she knows or doesn't know."

His lawyerly answer angered her. "Why have it look like I had a role in the business for the past few months? I was a trainer. I wasn't involved in any kind of business management like transport decisions or money flow." She regretted her snipe as soon as she had uttered it. *Down girl. Play for time.*

Jax interjected. "I'm sure Michael simply wants to clarify your position with MMC's companies."

"I didn't ask for your opinion," she snapped. "Can you give me a little space?"

Declan remained silent, but his look was steady and lethal. Jax stepped away.

The hairs on the back of her neck stood up. "But doing so makes it look like I had access to more information or had more power to make decisions than I did. No. I'm not signing these."

Electra stood at Jessica's side, tops of their arms touching as if forming a human wall could strengthen them. She shoved her shoulder against Jessica, a signal to redirect their conversation. When Declan's head was turned, she stole a look at Jessica and raised her eyebrows. "Whatever it is you need signed," she shouted, over the whine of the engines, "no person in their right mind would sign a document without reading and getting her own counsel's advice. Wouldn't you agree?"

Declan flashed his teeth in a grin. His oily answer, "Certainly. Miss Wyeth can review the papers in her own time," grated Jessica's nerves.

Electra motioned with her head toward Jax. "You can tell Michael his security measures have been greatly appreciated, but some of my help finds them intrusive and oppressive." She craned her neck around Declan to see a man seated next to the pilot. Both men wore uniforms with MMC embroidered on the pocket. Rifles stood upright, strapped in a rack by the open door. "What we see is only the tip of the iceberg. It's stifling."

"I'll tell him to be more discreet. We should get going. Shall we?" Declan opened his arm and directed them to the helicopter.

Jessica weighed everything she said and did through a filter of fear. One misstep or poorly phrased statement could pique Declan's suspicions. She wanted to remain on the outskirts of his interest, if that was possible.

Declan looked at Jax with an unspoken command. Jax grabbed the last of the suitcases and climbed into the craft.

Within an hour, the ease that came with wealth delivered them to the grounds of a private home on the outskirts of Atlanta. Getting to the Olympic venues proved to be just as easy when limousines brought them to private entrances away from the main crowds. Michael's insistence on security bothered her, but Declan's presence concerned her more.

She needn't have worried.

"I'm staying at a hotel in town. I'll meet up with you later."

She wasn't going to argue with him not being around.

July 26-27, 1996
Atlanta, Georgia

ATLANTA AND THE United States scored a coup when they won the bid for the one-hundredth anniversary of the Olympic Games. Spread out over a large section of the state of Georgia, twenty-nine venues held competitions. No expense was spared in creating the primary focus locale. Centennial Park was hailed as visionary in addressing the immediate needs of the major international event as well as the practical needs of urban living after the Games. Georgia citizens paid for infrastructure as any American city would, through taxes, but Georgia alleviated much of its financial burden through a heavy reliance on corporate sponsorships. In return for corporate support, the Olympic Committee gave exclusive rights to goods and services and allowed banners emblazoned with corporate logos to be draped from every conceivable surface. The proliferation of advertisements raised a few eyebrows and drew criticism of over-commercializing the Games. Banners for MMC, Ltd. hung beside logos for Coca-Cola, MacDonald's, Panasonic, and Visa.

Security at the Olympics was a different story. The U.S. government covered the cost and most dollars were spent away from public view. Control rooms, walls lined with monitors, dotted remote corners of the city and state. Visible measures were seen with the first time use of metal scanners, giving the additional benefit of imparting a sense of safety among the spectators. Long lines inched their way forward as people queued up to enter through security scanners. Uniformed guards, stifling yawns of boredom and fatigue, searched purses and coolers with sloppy gestures. Once inside, people with bags and backpacks strolled up walkways dotted with benches and garbage cans. Uniformed and plain-clothes officers—obvious with curled wire earpieces—were occasionally seen walking the perimeter. More security was present, but better concealed.

News reports on the tight security surrounding the Olympic Village and venues dominated the nightly news. Memories of the massacre at Munich were still raw. Despite vocal concerns of security raised by Israel prior to the 1972 Games, the Palestinian group, Black September, broke into the Israeli athletes' apartments. At the end of the twenty-one hour siege, eleven Israeli athletes were dead along with five terrorists.

Drills for a powerful response to any threat were thorough and public in the days leading up to the games. Security prepared for the terror of hostage taking or the overt disruption of specific events. Intelligence scoured communications looking for organized groups and planned attacks. Threat assessments modeled after the Munich experience ascribed the greatest risk to political groups looking to orchestrate attacks against athletes as proxies for their home countries. Communications were examined for coordinated attacks. Lone wolves posed an unlikely threat.

The athletes and their villages enjoyed the best security the U.S. government could provide. Cameras pointed to every conceivable access point. Images of parking lots, public transportation, and spectator entry points were transmitted to security centers. Goods, service people, and vehicles were monitored as they delivered everything from T-shirts to food, and removed truckloads of garbage. Millions had been spent on protecting the people and the structures. Security was efficient and professional despite rumors that bags were checked more to find contraband Pepsi products in a Coke town than knives or guns. At no point were Jessica's three guards less than twenty feet away, leaving her wondering if she was better protected than the venue.

Regardless, the atmosphere was festive. Banners of the Olympic torch proclaiming "100 Years" hung from lampposts. The official mascot, Izzy—a six-foot tall blue cartoon character with huge eyes—posed with children and families. Vendors sold pecan pies and peach ice cream by the truckload. Hats, T-shirts, pins, and bandanas with five interlocking rings, torches, or any number of international flags adorned the crowd. At no point was a patron allowed to forget the importance of the Games. Impressions of athletic prowess, strength through diversity, and international cooperation and peace saturated the atmosphere.

A chauffeured electric golf cart with seats for six wove through service alleys and avoided the major thoroughfares. Tassels bobbed from the brightly-colored surrey roof as it hushed to a halt in front of the VIP tent overlooking the cross-country course. The course was immense and strewn with obstacles of different heights, widths, and demonically complex approaches. To combat Georgia's torrid heat, mesh hung over unshaded portions of the course. Competitions began in the early morning and ceased during the peak heat of the day. Huge fans and misting stations for horse and human dotted the grounds.

For those of a certain status, Southern tradition demanded women and men dress appropriately. Men wore jackets despite the heat and women's hats added to the festive air. Jessica wore a dress of off-white lace and a wide-brimmed hat, one she hoped would provide some cover from inquisitive eyes. As the effect of her presence rolled through the crowd, she clenched her jaws and dipped her head to use the hat as a shield. Before long, her discomfort at her Electra-mandated attire faded as she began speaking with the other trainers, but her anxiety of being in a crowd did not. She sat with her thumbs clenched inside her fists while her eyes never ceased drifting over the multitude of faces. Twice Electra had to place a steadying hand on her arm when sudden noises made her jump. One glance at Jax told her worry was wasted. He was quick to intercept any curious onlooker with an implied threat that ensured no one would approach her, and she was kept well out of earshot.

They had a perfect spot to view all entrants in both the team and individual eventing. Jessica was to be the trainer for several horses in the three-day trials at Rolex in less than a year, and she listened to the coaching tactics of the trainers carefully. When the day's events concluded, her group took a tour of the grounds and training facilities. Michael seemed omnipresent as MMC banners, hung at sporadic intervals, flapped in sudden breezes and demanded her attention. Eventually, they were brought to see Bealltainn.

The stables at the Olympics were a microcosm of the Olympic Village where the human athletes lived. Barns and blocks of stalls were festooned with flags and symbols of the different countries. Shared lounge areas and break rooms had platters of regional foods from the U.S. as well as international favorites intended to stave off homesickness of the riders, trainers, grooms, vets, and officials from the many teams. Nationalities mixed easily in the corridors, love of the horse bonding all in a common language.

Bealltainn was even more magnificent than she remembered. He stood seventeen-plus hands tall, almost six feet high at his withers, and his inky coat rippled with energy. He assessed the humans surrounding him coolly, as if measuring their motives and strengths. At the sound of Jessica's voice, his ears pricked forward and he took a step closer. She let herself into his stall and stood still, talking in a calm voice and waiting for him to decide if he wanted to come closer. While working with him in the U.K., she had learned that he was not a horse to be trained, but an animal to be partnered with—if he accepted you. A few minutes of sniffing the air with flared nostrils was all he needed to be assured. She kept her hands by her sides, palms out to let him approach at his own pace. Eventually, he placed his muzzle into her open hand. Only then did she reached up to rub his withers in greeting.

"He looks terrific. I have to say I'm pleased he's so relaxed. He's almost a different horse than I rode at Aintree in June."

A ripple went through the group. One trainer remarked, "It *was* you! I heard about that ride. Damn glad you bested those feckin' West Brits. Had it comin' to them! How'd a lass like you stay atop him?"

Jessica warmed. "I was worried. I confess to being barely in control on the last stretch," she said, editing out the fact that someone had shot her with a high-powered rifle over the last jump. She would have been dead if Michael hadn't insisted she wear one of 2100's bulletproof vests. The memory quickened her heart and she pushed the thoughts aside. "He ran the last of that race without my help. He has a mind of his own and isn't afraid to use it."

"Och, that he does, for certain." Another man, man clad in loose trousers and an open-necked shirt, stepped forward and leaned against the stall door. "I'm Ian," he said, extending his hand to her. "I've been riding this beast for the better part of four weeks."

"Hi Ian. I'm glad to finally meet you and to get a chance to see you ride. I hope our phone calls helped."

"Took your advice, I did, and started off slow. Tossed me the first day, but I'm a better man for it." He held her hand a moment longer. "I've got to say, I expected Connaught's woman to be more done-up than you. I guess in America I was expecting more of a tart."

Electra stepped forward, fuming. "She's not 'Connaught's woman,' as you say. She's her own person."

Ian motioned with his head to Jax and his men. Unlike the owners who wore seersucker suits, open-necked shirts, and loafers, Jax wore the Belfast version of inconspicuous security garb—loose fitting sweatpants, short-sleeved knit polo and trainers. "So, you'd be telling me all you Yanks have dofts with earpieces trailing you. I doubt that."

Jessica stammered. "This is . . . this is just temporary until . . . until . . ."

"Until what? One of you is dead? No. You're a nice girl and your troubles reach as far as your man." He made a show of looking around the barn. His gaze settled on the MMC banners. "The only thing I've seen of him is his money. If you'd be asking me, you're too fine a lass to be wasting your time with him. The tabloids are interested in you, for certain, but they'd leave you be if it weren't for him."

Jax reached out and placed his hand on Ian's shoulder. The motion not entirely friendly. "I'd watch yourself. You know nothing of what you're talkin' about."

"Don't I? Whose voice do you have chirping in your ears?"

"It's none of your damned business, but if you need to know, we're patched in to the main dispatch feed. If some troubles kick up, we'd be among the first to know. But, you wouldn't know that from the rag sheets you read." Jax's eyes narrowed and the distance between him and his men closed with a shift of bodies. The challenge was clear.

"I'm only saying what I've read," Ian said, jerking his arm away from Jax's grasp. "You forget, the Irelands are a small town and folks have their opinions. Her family was killed because they threatened to expose Magnus Connaught and his crimes. The tangles she's in are due solely because of her closeness to the Connaught clan."

Should she run or laugh? Where did the greatest threat lie? Ian spoke her truth. She tried hard not to react to his words, fearing Jax would read her mind.

Jax moved Jessica aside. "I won't have a bugger like yourself questioning why blokes want to believe the shite they do. Michael Connaught is doing his best to make matters right. Like our lady here, he didn't ask for what he's gotten. I'd suggest you take a good look around and see whose banners are waving for the good of all." The words were spoken with barely concealed glower.

Electra pushed Jessica aside and stood in front of Ian, drawing herself up to her full height. Barely reaching his chin, she commanded the attention of a giant. "You're underestimating the situation. Yes, she's famous. But fame can't ride a black rocket named Bealltainn."

Laughter was easy among the new friends and the tension broke.

Electra busied herself in getting to know the horse's owners from the various countries, asking about their plans for acquiring new stock. As a stallion, Bealltainn's stud fees promised to be astronomical, and it was clear the owners of the other horses were impressed enough to pay any price to acquire him. After a brief conversation with the head trainer for the U.S. Olympic team, Electra produced a folded paper from inside her purse, numbers were entered, and a deal was made. Information on Kilkea and Planxty was given as well with a promise to have the horses ready for viewing when a representative arrived after the games.

Jessica caught Electra's eyes glittering at seeing her surrounded with genuine admirers, not merely fame mongers. Electra's maternal demeanor showed approval that Jessica proved herself to be adept not only at managing animals, but men as well.

The Olympic Games created a bubble in which the impossible could happen. Citizens of warring nations sat side-by-side and cheered together. Jessica began to allow herself to interact with others easily, not looking at each person as a threat or a nuisance. She felt good, secure in the knowledge she and Electra made a great team.

When she first arrived, the open stares of total strangers unnerved her. Jessica did not follow the stories about her, intentionally keeping herself sane by not learning of published lies. She gauged the impact of her coverage by the manner in which she was treated by anyone who recognized her. Many were bold enough to greet her with a "Hey Jessica!" More gave her a thumbs-up sign or asked if she had met with her uncle yet. A few said, "Welcome back," whether a tribute to being back from the dead or Ireland unclear. Jessica watched Electra take in every reaction, knowing each emotional thread would be strengthened and woven into the upcoming stories.

After a few interactions, Electra hugged Jessica with joy, and spoke quietly into her ear. "This is wonderful, Jessica. I can feel the people are with you."

A few encounters were unpleasant, with people forcing themselves to get too close or to ask for an autograph. She allowed herself to enjoy the bright side of Michael's care. Jax never left her side, telegraphing without words that she was under his watchful gaze. The day progressed, and Jessica encouraged him to move away so she could interact with others freely, but he remained close, dampening opportunities for contact and conversation.

As evening approached, Electra pulled Jessica to the side. "I've checked in with the office and my bones are done wore through! As I suspected, though, Ian and others have invited us to the concert tonight. I've told them I'm simply exhausted from all this walking!" she said with an exaggerated yawn. "You all can drop me off at the house and continue on to Centennial Park. Besides, I don't think the music of *Jack Mack and the Heart Attack* will be my style."

Jessica hesitated. "I'm not so sure they're mine either, but there's no way you're leaving me. I haven't been to a rock concert since, geez, who knows when, but you're *staying*."

The steely reserve softened, replaced by gentility. "You sweet thing! It's been *years* since I had the pleasure of dancing on my seat, but I hear all you have to do is jump up and down, wave your arms, and scream. Seems like something these Irish boys would love to help you with."

Electra was right. Holing herself away from people was a habit built upon years of hiding. Michael's protection served to heighten feelings of danger rather than security. Living a full life meant doing so in the open. If she didn't reach outside of her bubble, she'd forever be locked away in a prison of her own making.

"Well, it has been a while," she ventured.

Electra looked up as Jax stood to her side. "Getting out and enjoying a night will be good for you. Right, Jax?" Her smile squared and showed her teeth, the stainless steel spine of the Southern belle on full display.

He frowned. "You're a hard one to argue with, Missus Lavielle. I agreed we could all do with a good titter and giggle, but *not* if it opens the door to more risk."

Electra pulled back her shoulders. "There is not one person here who didn't go through some kind of security clearance to get in here. Enough already."

Jax scanned the heads of their small group. Two other grooms from Brandywine, trainers and grooms from Ireland's equestrian team, and members of Electra's syndicate stood in clusters of twos and threes. Pieces of overheard conversation pointed to everyone looking forward to the evening. "Me and my men are here to keep this woman safe," Jax said.

"But not dictate her life," snapped Electra.

"I be not dictating anyone's life. You want clear of that? I suggest you to talk to him," Jax said, yanking his thumb in Declan's direction.

The fissure between Jax and Electra visibly widened and Jessica felt the tug of power. Jax wanted Jessica under his thumb. Electra wanted her out from under undue control. Jessica didn't know whether to strangle her friend for challenging Michael's authority so openly or hug her for it. What was clear was that Electra offered her something Jax and Declan didn't. She linked her arm through Electra's and pulled her to the side.

"Please don't leave."

Ian walked over to them and addressed Electra. "You're joining us, then, right? We're to grab a spot of dinner before the show. We've seats for you." He looked expectantly at Electra, but his body inclined toward Jessica, hinting her answer was more important to him.

"I am flattered you'd want an old bag like me to tag along. All right. I'll get my second wind. Sounds like a go!" Electra smiled at Ian, "I know we'll all be in good hands."

Ian shifted slightly under Electra's direct gaze, keeping his eyes averted from Jessica. "It would be good of Miss Jessica to join us." As nonchalant as he tried to sound, his flushed cheeks betrayed his hopes.

The concert was better than she expected. MMC's sponsorship afforded them front row seats with plenty of room to dance. The international crowd was electrified by the mix of Southern rock and blues—American music at its homegrown best. Each face showed unified enjoyment in their country's unique expression. From broad toothy grins to restrained joy, red-faced glee, or stoic happiness, Americans' open exuberance blended into one common experience of fun.

One face caught her by surprise. LeeAnne was walking with a group of friends, mostly young women about her age. They each wore a variation of each other's outfits as friends sometimes do. Oversized shirts opened to show bandeau and tube tops. Ripped jeans. Doc Martens. Black lips. Crimped hair, some swept back with scrunchies, some wild and loose. Tattoo choker necklaces. Slap bracelets. The others chattered away, trying hard not to notice the people who noticed them. LeeAnne walked on, one stride behind, head inclined forward to listen but far enough away not to be forced into the mix. Two of the girls stopped and checked their ticket stubs and led the group to the upper seats. LeeAnne hesitated, looked up at the retreating backs of her friends, and behind her. An older woman in the group, perhaps in her early forties, stopped, hands clasped behind her back, and said something to her. After a minute, LeeAnne nodded and trotted up after her friends.

Jessica nudged Electra. "What's LeeAnne doing here?"

Electra hugged Jessica's arm as they walked in a conspiring 'hey, girlfriend' way. "I found one of LeeAnne's neighbors. Wonderful woman. Heart of gold. Anyway, I gave her money to bring LeeAnne and a few friends to see the Games. I told her not to mention my name."

"That's wonderful, but why?"

A frown touched Electra's brow. "Timing seemed right. I think she's done with Rudie! I'm hoping she sees that there's a whole world out there without him clouding it."

Jessica gave Electra's cheek a light kiss. "Thank you for making my night event better!"

Regardless of her initial worry of being out in public, the evening wasn't akin to being boiled in hot oil as she had expected. Even Declan's incessant glowering at her did nothing to dampen her fun. The group lost themselves in the joy of the music. Ian was able company, if a bit spastic when dancing. Jessica was surprised that not only did her feet hurt from the shoes Electra made her wear, but her cheeks did, too. From smiling. Electra was right. A night out with nothing but fun on the agenda was soul healing.

The crowd slowly filed out after the concert, as if reluctant to have the evening end. Declan took control of the group as they exited the venue. He spoke a few directions to Jax to clear their way to the limousine. Jax resisted Declan's authority, but Declan's black eyes bore through, and Jax departed, casting a cold look at Declan as the lawyer stepped in beside Jessica. The suffocating heat of the Georgia day had mellowed to a balmy night, encouraging the crowd to linger. It may have been after one o'clock in the morning for those accustomed to Eastern Daylight Time, but for many, their inner rhythms began to wake. Jackets shed, lovers nuzzled, troubles forgotten. People sat beside the reflecting pool or along benches, engrossed in conversations or taking in the sights.

Leaving the music stage, Jessica and her group walked toward their waiting cars parked on the opposite side of Centennial Park. Light illuminating the fountain of five rings changed to all the colors of the Olympic symbol, its water hopping and stilling in synchronized spurts. Waterfalls and a park-like settings surrounded square brick areas created to form a quilt of different people, places, events, and history important to the games. Planned events for the evening were completed, but the crowd was reluctant to leave. Flashes of light popped as pictures were taken in front of anything Olympic. Flag, fountain, flowers, or each other. It didn't matter. They were in the middle of a world event and each moment needed to be immortalized.

The crowd's celebratory mood seeped into Jessica. Her laughter spilled more easily than it had in weeks and her shoulders relaxed. Electra hugged her arm as they walked. They talked about what friends talk about—observations of the day's events, the concert, and the spectacle of the Olympics.

Ian paused in front of a fountain. Dozens of coins glittered under the water. Pennies, dimes, and quarters mingled with pence and kroner. "Do Yanks make wishes?" he asked digging through his pockets. "It's bad luck to pass up a chance."

"I've a quarter or two." Electra stepped up and placed coins in his hand, offering more to others in the group. "Keep your wishes to yourselves! I don't want to hear anything that isn't for world peace!" She walked ahead, face alight with laughter.

Declan held up a penny. "I heard this penny has a direct line to the Big Guy. All wishes granted." The penny's side glistened with a burnished glow, offering a challenge.

Jessica snapped it out of his hand, closed her eyes, and made a show of pressing her hand to her forehead, concentrating on a wish. Then she tossed it over her shoulder into the fountain where the water swallowed it with a gulp. She opened her eyes slowly, using the moment to look Declan up and down. With one eyebrow cocked, she shrugged. "You're still here," she chided. "I wonder what else you're wrong about."

He surprised her with an easy laugh. "Me? Wrong?" he said, with what could have been a genuine smile. "Time will tell."

Leaving the fountain area, they approached an outdoor café, white umbrellas open wide to welcome passersby at an hour when other establishments in Atlanta were closed. Temporary white structures of tents and pavilions loomed on either side of the walkway. One tower, standing as high as a two-story building, was constructed of scaffolding sheathed in a large plastic-like tarp and used by the media. Open window areas gave it a layered appearance. The top level cantilevered out to provide protection from wind and rain. Cameras, technicians, and journalists peered down on the crowd. Sound trucks idled nearby with thick cables snaking across the ground. Benches lined its base. A metal fence, looking more like a bicycle rack than a security feature, surrounded three sides.

The group approached Tribute, a fan-shaped bronze sculpture, and marveled at the detail of its three athletes. Closer, Jessica could see how the figures progressed through a leap in a similar way they progressed through time. The leap's arc started with a man near nude in the ancient Greek tradition of displaying human perfection, then progressed upward to a male figure wearing clothes suitable for competition in the 1920's—rumpled knee-length shorts, slim shoes for running, and a thick T-shirt. Lastly, the leap was completed by a woman wearing the modern clothes of a twenty-first century athlete, long hair flowing freely behind her.

Engrossed in the detail, she didn't notice the sudden activity. Uniformed and plainclothes officers materialized, gathering near one corner of the sound tower. As one, they began to push back the crowds. Their actions were slow. Deliberate. Urgent.

"Clear the area!"

More officers joined them.

"What's that they say now? Time for the park to close?" Ian responded to his friend with a comment tossed over his shoulder. "I thought the Yanks would at least give us a last call."

Laughter rippled easily.

"Damned Yanks don't know how to treat a punter right," Ian shouted to others, broad smile on his face.

In the distance, Jessica saw Jax running toward them, hand cupped over his ear, face closed with the effort to listen. His attention was on the officers and their no-nonsense expressions, not the group. Tribute's fan shape blocked her view of the sound tower and the commotion at its base.

Jax shouted something to Alfie and Sean.

"What is it?" Jax's urgency contrasted to what Jessica saw around her. The night was too beautiful, too perfect to be marred by the park closing down early. In a cascade of different languages, partners asked each other if they were ready to return to their hotels. All were reluctant to leave. What was to fear? They had entered the park through metal scanners and had their bags searched. Security was visible. They were safe. In the too-common mirage that happens in the shimmering heat of tragedy, smiling and relaxed faces pulled her into the oasis of calm.

No one sensed danger.

Later, Jessica couldn't believe how stupid she had been.

Jax added his commands to the orders of the uniformed police. His men motioned to the group, directing them toward the exit.

Declan steered them in a wide path around the officers. His eyes scanned side to side, looking for the obvious threat as he moved his body between Jessica and the group. He hurried them in the direction of the limousine, and continued forward.

Jessica felt panic rise despite knowing Centennial Park was a city within a city, and each Olympic event was held in secured venues. Why should she be concerned? Yet, small details pelted her. Jax radiated urgency. Uniformed men appeared and shouted instructions. Heads snapped upward in the instinctual way of small animals hearing a twig snap on the savannah.

Declan moved with a big cat's stealth, assessing angles of attack with more expertise than she expected from a book-learned lawyer. His black eyes swept over people, walkways, buildings, and structures. Subtle shifts in his body registered threats, calculating each and moving to the next. His investment of effort narrowed to protecting her. His right hand slipped under his left arm, inside his jacket. He paused long enough to offer his left hand to Electra, who hurried, flushed and hobbling, toward them. In the fading delusion of safety, Jessica allowed herself to anger by wondering if he was merely protecting more of Michael's assets.

Lost in the details, Jessica became aware of a bright flash of light.

More pictures? She stopped, stunned. The flash grew into the maw of an explosion.

An instant after the sound concussed her ears, small objects sprayed the air around her.

A wall of air pushed against her, snapping her head back and throwing members of the group to the ground. Synapses fired at once, projecting memories on top of current sensory. She had no time to process that the objects whistling past her were not pieces of wood or branches from an exploding tavern

They were nails and metal shards.

The force of the blast whirled her around and her body jerked as metal ripped into her. Pavement chipped and pocked as shrapnel forced its way into it. As quickly as it started, the commotion ceased. Quiet descended as nails and shards tinked to the ground.

It is a trick of the mind to register a myriad of details in less time than it takes a heart to beat. A rotten egg smell of smoke mixed with the stench of burned skin and blood. She saw only black, but knew she was commanding her eyes to be wide open. The force of the blast that had lifted her with invisible hands slammed her to the ground. Smells of tar and rubber mixed with leather from footfalls of thousands of shoes. The urge to run overtook her but stopped somewhere below her neck. More flashes, but not of light. Searing pain. A vague sense of dread.

Like water escaping from a sink, she felt her body drain through her toes.

Then, nothing.

The sound wasn't anything Declan would have expected from an explosion, more of a *whomph* and *pop* of fireworks than the proper *kaboom* of a bomb. The shock of air had pushed him off his feet and he stumbled, unbalanced, onto the bricks, his easy smile of seconds ago frozen before it fell as well. The most distinctive sound was the tinny *chink! chink! chink!* of nails as they rained to earth. Stunned silence settled over the area before the moans of the injured and screams of others fleeing filled the air. Americans drifted, shocked and disbelieving. Others from war-ravaged nations bolted, fearing more explosions would come. Experience made Declan scan the area, looking for a sniper's scope.

He drew his body up on one knee using the knuckles of his left hand to steady himself and his right hand to dust grit from his face and head. Only after he felt something wet and sticky on his palm did he begin to feel the pain of the laceration.

"Jaysus! What in the bloody hell was that?" Ian stood over him, hand outstretched to help him to his feet. "Hold on there, my sham. You've got yourself a decent bonk." He fished around in his pocket and produced a handkerchief. Declan pressed it to his head as he surveyed the scene.

Jax gripped his shoulders and shook him alert. "I've seen worse on Shankill Road, but I've not expected this." He glanced coolly to the side as uniformed men ran toward them. Declan could see they held no interest for Jax. This was not his battle.

"Where's Jessica?"

Sirens wailed. More personnel flooded the area.

"Get back! Get back!" Men wearing black jackets with "Georgia FBI" printed in white letters used their arms to shepherd people away from the tower. A cloud of smoke rose from the corner. The tower leaned at an angle it hadn't only seconds before.

The explosion had ripped out a section of the lower left corner of the sound tower. Strips of plastic sheathing flapped around a gaping hole. The extent of the damage was unclear, but the threat of the tower collapsing was obvious.

Declan looked around at their group, desperate to find Jessica. He could hear Jax call, "Have you seen Miss Jessica? I thought she was right behind–" Declan's heart froze as Jax stopped, midsentence.

His chest crushed as he processed what he saw.

Electra lay on the ground, her matronly figure sheathed in a swath of fuchsia linen. A sea of dark red grew around her. As the puddle grew, her color drained to white. He stifled a gag as he realized a piece of her neck was missing.

In the seconds it took for the smoke to clear, soft moans and cries for help continued to build. That's when he saw her.

Her blond hair was splayed in a fan shape as if to mock Tribute. Patches of dark red splotched her white lace dress. The longer he stared, the larger the stain grew and expanded.

In one stride, he was beside her. "Jessica? Jessica!"

Her eyes were wide but unseeing. Her mouth formed the beginning of a scream or a warning that she never uttered.

He folded his hands over hers, careful to only offer comfort and not trigger pain in a person broken in places he could not see.

No muscle twitched in recognition of his presence. The cold of her hands absorbed the warmth of his.

May 1977
Hamilton, Massachusetts

TO WAKE THE dead in the Irish way is to drink, sing, and cele-
brate life without reservation. Tears of joy and sorrow flow like
whiskey, and voices rise in song and keening. In the netherworld between life and death, time and physics have no meaning. The living
yearn to talk with the dead. The dead yearn to touch the living.

Ten-year-old Jessica Wyeth sat hunched and numb in a throne-
like chair. Adults milled around the parlor of the funeral home, placing an awkward hand on her shoulder or casting a pained look before
they flinched away. Those who wore gabardine with patrician airs
talked with hushed voices. Others with ruddy skin and nubby tweeds
sang stray bars of ballads to warm their vocal cords for the evening's
song.

The light blue casket held Margaret Heinchon Wyeth. Grained oak
with burnished brass handles held James Kent Wyeth. A corner of
pink velvet dangled between the cap and frame of the hastily closed
shell of a small white coffin that cradled their youngest daughter
Erin. Custom would have dictated the tops remain opened, but the
car accident that took their lives demanded otherwise. Some may
have chosen cremation, but young Jessica was too bewildered to
know she had any choices when it came to burying her family.

The late May day hinted at the coming sweltering New England
summer. The verdant colors of the leaves and grass were fresh and

lush, and the pinks, yellows, and blues of tulips, daffodils, and hydrangea filled the beds along Hamilton, Massachusetts' streets. Black shutters flanked the windows of immaculate white colonial homes. Parents dragged reluctant children forward, unsure themselves of how to handle the stark reality of death. Couples walked slowly on the brick walks, some stiff with shoulders pulled back and heads raised, others hunched chin-to-chest with grief. All greeted one another solemnly, but took care to be acknowledged. A wake was no time not to be seen.

Cars parked along Bay Road as far as the eye could see. Lights flashed on the two police cruisers detailed to manage traffic. Jessica was too numb to learn the lesson that nothing pulls a community together, or draws a crowd, like tragedy.

Cool fingers brushed a strand of hair behind her ear. She felt a kiss on the back of her neck in that special spot that usually made her shoulders shiver in delight. Today, her head dropped forward. Bridget Heinchon cupped her fingers around Jessica's chin and lifted.

Bridget's expression was a mask of grief and anger. "How you holdin' up?" A brogue lilted her words.

Jessica managed to shrug and tugged at the lace of her hanky. Words stuck, unformed, in her throat. She looked up at her Aunt Bridget in a fog of confusion and fear. From anyone who cared to see, her rounded eyes implored for direction and comfort. *I don't know what I'm supposed to do*, they said. Her voice seized from non-use, mute since the morning of the accident. Guilt drained the last bit of color from her face. Her mouth worked for sounds that remained locked away. *I was supposed to be in the car, too.*

Bridget pressed her lips together. A simple black dress hung off her once lithe frame. A strand of pearls and an amethyst and gold brooch were her only adornment. Her beauty was unmistakable, if faded by the ravages of poor health. "You're doing fine, my child. No need to trouble yourself to make small talk if you're not up for it. Folks here are comin' to pay their respects to you and your family. Tomorrow is the burial."

Two pools of watery blue begged. *And then?*

"And then life will go on." A spate of coughs rumbled from deep inside Bridget's chest. She curled her arms around herself to brace against the pain.

"There now, Bridgie. Be easy on yourself." Gus Adams reached out and supported Bridget by the elbow. "D'ye need to sit?"

Jessica wanted to tease the manager of Wyeth's Whirlwind Farms for looking uncomfortable in a black suit with his curly hair slicked back with goo. Where were his tattered trousers and crusty boots? His suit was out-of-date and smelled faintly of dust and mothballs, togs of formality shunned unless forced into service. She wanted to tease him, but couldn't muster the strength. Gus had been the one to keep her home, saying he needed her help in breezing out several horses. He had said that visiting Aunt Bridget could wait. Gus and Jim almost came to blows, but in the end, Jim relented and left Jessica home.

And then their car careened off the road when it took a turn far, far too fast. Very little was left of the car. Even less was left of her family.

Jessica wanted Gus back in his dusty pants and cotton shirt. She wanted him to look at her with amusement and awe the way he did when she flattened herself against the back of a horse and rode at full gallop across a field with nothing more than a handful of mane to guide her. She wanted him to curse at her for leaving lights on in the barn or not properly cooling a horse. She wanted anything but to see him in his funeral best with a look of resignation and sympathy in his eyes. Another look, one that tightened just behind his temples, betrayed the fear and desperation she knew swirled around his heart.

"Our girl has just asked what will happen next and I've told her life goes on."

Gus rounded his eyes with approval. "She's been talkin' then? Ah, now. Glad to hear it. Glad to hear it." His eyes glistened.

Bridget hesitated. "No words, just feelin's, but it's a start."

A child's intuition told her more wanted to be spoken, but she wasn't to overhear. Conversations about her filled the room. Only Bridget spoke directly to her. To most, she was a traumatized child to be handled with care, not treated as a person—a bone china bird with fragile, outstretched wings that would fracture from the force of an ill-phrased wish. When other adults did draw near, they hugged Bridget and murmured condolences on her sister's family's deaths. Words failed them when they looked at the child left behind.

A white-haired priest, wearing a floor-length black cassock, shuffled toward them. Stooped with age, sweat soaked his stiff Roman collar. His piercing blue eyes settled on each person as he passed a tray of glasses filled with amber liquid. Some of the glasses had cubes of ice. Others served the whiskey neat. "For your pain," he said with a respectful bow of his head.

Gus took two glasses and handed the one without ice to Bridget. "*Sláinte.*" To health.

"*Sláinte,*" she replied. She took a sip and wrinkled her nose.

"I'll get you a Scotch later," he said under his breath.

The look they shared was layered with love and loss, and maybe something more, but Jessica couldn't bear to witness any more of it and rose up from her chair. A path cleared as people parted in the overcrowded room to let her pass. The *tsks* and *such a shames* floated around her. Other words swirled, too. *Inheritance. Heiress. Millions. Guardian. Custody. Battle.*

She kept her eyes downcast as she made her way to the door. She hated the attention of people she considered strangers and especially hated their sympathy. The few days since the accident felt like months. Nothing made sense. She woke each morning in her own bed. The light was the same. Smells too. But the sounds were different. She could still hear the stablehands' voices as they joked with one another or shouted a command. The horses snorted and squealed their displeasure at one another. Gravel crunched under hooves and tires as men turned out horses and ran their errands.

The house ticked. It never ticked before. She had never heard the grandfather clock—tucked near the front door in the downstairs hallway—all the way up in her room. How could that be? As she lay in bed, she strained to hear the sounds of Margaret's morning ritual of waking and dressing Erin. Margaret's soft voice soothed Erin and caressed Jessica. It wasn't until Jessica had walked downstairs to the kitchen that she found Gus and a pot of tea instead of Jim and a pot of coffee. Gus jumped up to offer Jessica boiled eggs and sliced ham. Margaret would have given her Lucky Charms and a warm smile. Gus greeted her with small talk about his day's training. Jessica looked at him with lifeless eyes and couldn't reattach her thoughts to her body. When her Aunt Bridget arrived and enveloped her in a hug, she felt her load lift enough to let in a flicker of light. Bridget brought comfort and the possibility that she would be okay.

Would she be? She felt in the middle of a tug of war. Normalcy and keeping her on the farm pulled one way, and she knew Bridget and Gus pulled the hardest. Change would pull her off the farm, but she couldn't see who supplied the force.

A feeling grew inside telling her she needed to be aware. She needed to know who stood next to whom and which smiles were real and which were fake. The flowers smelled too sweet and the air was too hot. Her grief kept her aware the outside world was only as far away as her skin.

If she had cared to look up, she would have seen the priest pull his cuffs and fill his chest. With chin raised, he began to sing.

The first few bars of *Danny Boy*, the traditional Irish song of mourning, were sung in a clear, unwavering tenor. Something unseen shifted in the room. The people parted and clotted along invisible lines. Women clustered together. Men stood along the wall. The voice was joined by other singers, the heart and harmony growing with the bond of loss and love.

A few voices changed the words from "Oh, Danny boy" to "Our, Bonny lass." A few heads turned and nodded their approval. Jessica felt sweat trickle down her scalp and over her cheeks.

A fife was produced from inside a coat pocket. Its high-pitched notes blended with the voices. The song grew. Lyrics of a parent searching for a child's resting place tugged at hearts and minds.

The crowd began to pull apart even more. New groups formed. Irish faces flushed with heat and whiskey gathered, bent to hear the nuance of their neighbor's harmony. Men in pressed suits, striped shirts, and French-knotted ties scanned the crowd for their wives, mouths closed against any song. Women with dry eyes and tight chignons fingered pearls at their necks and took frequent sips of their chardonnay. Other women, with shades of auburn hair and sensible shoes, fanned themselves with prayer cards, dabbed their faces with tissues, and filled their chests with verse. Glasses of stout and whiskey sat half full within easy reach.

Voices rose in harmony, acknowledging how death reunites lost souls with their loved ones.

The ballad ended, its purpose served. The crowd shifted in the burdened silence. Feet began to shuffle in slow rhythm. Hands patted against linen-clad chests. A rhythm formed. Another song birthed. The lively tune animated the tweeds and froze the gabardines.

Jessica inched her way to the door. The songs meant nothing to her except to show how the adults were affected. The air felt too tight around her, made tighter by the stiffened backs and stifled gasps when the singing began.

God damned Irish think they own the place.

Did she hear that? It didn't matter. Nothing stayed inside her. Not even words. The only thing real to her was her physical self. Her stomach lurched upward. She swallowed to lock the contents down.

Jim's father never spoke to him again after they married.

Why didn't her mother tell these people to go home? Margaret hated being around people, so why were they here? Jessica's knees weakened as she remembered.

There's rumors it wasn't an accident.

The long sleeves of the only demure dress she owned began to cling to her arms. Her feet, suddenly concrete blocks, were too heavy to lift and she dragged them along the carpeted floor.

Jim would never drive like that and jeopardize his family.

Humid air and sweat pasted the cotton to her back. The edges of her vision narrowed.

The brakes failed.

So many people. Too many people. Jessica felt the walls close in. Faces bobbed and weaved around her like a handful of balloons in the hands of a carnival's hawker.

Jim wanted out.

Words rambled, disembodied from lips, yet somehow echoed in her head. The voices jumbled into a buzz. She felt the words more than heard them.

The vibration settled on two figures. One old, the other a year or two older than she, hovered at the back of the crowd. They were distinct from all others with their thatch of unruly hair, prominent chins, and strong brows over impossibly blue eyes. A father and a son paying their final respects, but having a proprietor's air that raised them above the others. The father raised a cigarette to his lips and lit it with a silver lighter. The engraving of a shamrock ripped down the middle by a dagger clear against its polished sides. Where had she seen that symbol before?

No one leaves the Charity alive.

A filament of memory became incandescent. Margaret and Jim. Planning their escape. Hopeless even as they plotted. Cursing themselves for not seeing how they were used.

She locked eyes with the son and felt some acknowledgement flicker before the air heated and shrank around her like plastic in an oven.

"There she is. The last one standing." Her vision tunneled to a gray circle. A blob hovered somewhere over her. The smell was familiar. Like Jim. A flash of a green bottle with a metal cap in the shape of a crown was forgotten as quickly as it surfaced. Royal Lyme, only it wasn't her father. Her parents were dead. Those people were in that room because her family was dead. Her head became too heavy to hold up. Weakness overpowered her.

She was aware of a hand gripping her arm and of being pulled out the door. She was half pushed, half carried to a wicker chair in the shaded corner of the porch. The slight cool breeze revived her. Gus and Bridget stood between her and a growing group of women. The women clucked and wrung their hands with concern.

A man strode through the crowd and pushed his way past Gus and Bridget. His hands were hot and moist and he drew up Jessica's into his own. "She looked about ready to pass out." Lime scent clung to him.

"Aye. 'Tis too much." Bridget pressed the back of her fingers against Jessica's cheek. "She's not said a word and is like a corpse herself the past few days. It's time I take *my niece* home." She turned to Gus. "Can you bring the car around?"

The man pressed on. "There are people who haven't seen her in many years. They'll be sorely disappointed. Let her stay on the porch." Jessica tugged her hands. He wouldn't let go.

Gus faced him, brows one bar of anger. "She's going to be in the same home in ten minutes that she's been at for ten years. If folks wanted to see her, they could figure out a better time." In the moments needed to take a centering breath, Gus straightened himself up to his full height and made it clear he was not to be questioned. He was a scrappy Irishman, and a betting man wouldn't bet against him.

"But now *is* the time, isn't it? Families pull together in times like this. Wouldn't you agree, *Mrs. Harvey*?"

Why say her name like that? Jessica pulled her hands free. Bridget stiffened.

Bridget took a step forward. "Right you are, William. That's why I'm here to care for my *niece*." Funny how Bridget talked about her, like someone who didn't know who she was.

"You forget yourself," William said, adjusting the tie at his neck. Gold cufflinks engraved with three interlocking "W's" flashed on starched white cuffs. He smoothed the front of his jacket with his hand and peered down his nose. He was a head taller than Gus, but Bridget could look him squarely in the eye. His sand-colored hair receded at the temples, but the cut of the suit evidenced a *bon vivant* nature where nothing but the finest would suffice. In the full light of day, the resemblance to England's Prince Phillip was uncanny, if completely coincidental, but was one he played up when a free drink was in order.

"She's my blood, too," he said.

Bridget wheezed and her chest pulsed with the effort of holding back a spate. "Blood is something she can't escape, but it's familiarity and comfort she be needing now," she managed to reply.

William cupped his own cheek with an open palm in a gesture of profound concern. "I couldn't agree more. Our niece needs to be surrounded by family and you need not burden yourself with caring for a child in your weakened state. That's why I plan to step up as her guardian."

"And you'll do no such thing," Gus said. Did Gus close his fist and cock his arm back? Is that why Bridget reached down to hold his hand? "You Wyeths made your disdain of this family quite clear. Jim and Margaret took the hint and provided for their daughters independent of any involvement from the likes of you. She won't be needin' your support or your money-grubbing presence."

"I take offense at that, sir." William raised his nose and dropped his shoulders in a display of unadulterated hurt.

Gus' face reddened to deep purple. "Jim had enough pressures in his life without dolin' you out of your debts. Never came 'round the house, you did, unless you needed a check. Latching on to this lass is your last attempt to get at what you've lost because your own father, may he rest in peace, didn't trust you with a wooden nickel. I saw your disappointment when I stopped by your home to give you the news of your brother's death and you learned Jess was still alive. Havin' her dead would've meant it all would've gone to you."

"Gus. Now is not the time," Bridget cautioned.

But Gus was not to be deterred. "You think gaining control of your niece means gaining control of the money that will be hers. One visit a year and a Christmas card isn't enough to entitle you to anything more than a line in their obituaries. Jim feared this day, and you used his fear to wrangle an insurance policy on his life with you as the beneficiary. He wanted you out of his life and the life of his women, but you are to money like flies are to honey." He paused, gathering himself to finish his tirade. He glowered. "You make one move to inject yourself into her life and I'll make sure the police investigate your finances with an eye on how you benefit from their deaths."

Bridget gasped, and then doubled over as coughs wracked her body. "Enough you say! I won't hear of this!" She darted a panicked looked over the crowd.

The words. The meaning. A memory of her parents' car the night before the crash. Jessica remembered something but was too frightened to draw it into daylight. Faces turned in her direction. Then one face crystallized, not in front of her in a mourner's flesh and blood, but in the strobe-like images of memory from a traumatized child. Her family was killed, but not by William. A man, with a tattoo of a shamrock sliced by a dagger, tampered with their car. She knew, but couldn't speak, as her brain repressed the images until she'd be old enough to deal with their meaning. The knowledge that people in the world were intent on harming her solidified, even though she didn't completely understand why.

William did not cause her family's death, but a child's sense to fear him grew.

The chemicals of fear and grief combined with the cloying smell of Royal Lyme. Her stomach pitched itself upward.

With arms clenched to her stomach, Jessica spewed on William's brightly buffed and tasseled loafers.

August 1996
Ballyronan, Northern Ireland
United Kingdom

ALONE IN HIS study, Michael bellowed with pain and frustration. His thatch of black hair accentuated the dark circles under his eyes. The lower half of his face was covered in stubble, the upper half was puffy with exhaustion. The last days had been hell. His entire being yearned to be with Jessica. Gravity pulled him to be beside the woman he loved. She needed him now more than ever and his heart told him to go. He teetered with indecision.

For all of the resources he surrounded her with, for all of the shelter he could buy, he had failed to protect her.

A new knowledge flirted with the edges of his heart; he had failed to protect himself.

News of the explosion came to him minutes after it occurred. Was it a shift in fate's wind before the phone call that made him unusually anxious that night, tossing and turning in the same bed he had made love to her? He felt Jessica's presence as keenly as his own skin. The air filled with her scent and his skin heated as if from her touch. He felt his fingers coil in her hair as he pulled her mouth toward his, but pushed her away when frigid air stung his lips instead of warm breath.

Moments of sleep were fitful and filled with images of her. In some, she was blue and frozen on a mountaintop. In others, she was trussed up inside a box. In all, she looked at him with the flat stare of a shark's eyes. He would reach for her, only to have his hand pass through, her image dissipating in the mists of a dream. Giving up on sleep, he had lain awake, staring at the ceiling. Then, his phones had sprung to life.

Foreboding filled him. He walked down to his study, acutely aware of the hollow sound his footsteps made in his empty manse. A cold breath over his shoulder made him jump and peer into dark corners. Was it the absence of sleep that haunted or a presence he couldn't see?

The moments after the bombing triggered a dizzying array of actions. He tried desperately to reach the detail of his men surrounding Jessica. Unsuccessful, he activated every computer and TV screen with live video feeds and cable news. What he saw sank his heart. Fused in the public's mind, with the images of bleeding people and Olympic flags ripped and burned, were MMC's banners and their promise of safety.

Michael spent the days after the bombing wracked with conflict. Images of the closing ceremonies flickered on the TV screen. A somber-faced president of the International Olympic Committee appeared in newscasts to urge the public to stay focused on the hopes the Games presented. Man-on-the-street interviews showed people of all colors and nations with raw emotions for the three dead and one hundred and eleven wounded by the blast. The Israeli athletes who had died in Munich twenty-four years before were acknowledged in stories about violence at the Olympics. Grief renewed in the hearts of all.

He channeled his resources into learning as much as he could. A security guard had spotted a green canvas military-issue carry-all abandoned under a bench at the corner of the sound tower. Upon inspection, metal pipes with protruding wires were discovered. Law enforcement immediately began to push back the crowd. Not everyone heeded the warnings.

The bomb was meant to inflict as much bodily damage in as wide an area as possible. The explosion was also intended to inspire terror. Several officers were wounded by the nails and shrapnel packed inside the pipes. One woman died when a nail pierced her skull. A Turkish cameraman covering the games died from a heart attack during the ensuing chaos. Electra Lavielle, Michael's essential connection to U.S. businesses, and to Jessica, was mowed down as metal fragments tore through her body. The woman who defied the laws of nature by being more alive than anyone he knew, bled out in Centennial Park.

The carnage didn't stop there. Injuries ranged from minor lacerations to gaping wounds to shrapnel lodged in organs. Jessica was one of five who remained in critical condition.

The carry-all, with all of its lethal cargo of explosives and metal projectiles, passed undetected onto the grounds of Centennial Park, right under the noses of the very manpower and equipment Michael paid so dearly for.

If only he had the gift of foresight.

Michael snapped off the TV as the closing ceremonies transitioned away from somber reflection to the planned entertainment. The last thing he could stomach was a trumped-up version of a Southern hoedown.

"Any word?"

Hearing his butler's voice startled him. The portly man, clad in a simple black cardigan, white shirt, and gray trousers—Murray's preferred uniform—set down a tray holding a silver tea service and china cups.

"No, Murray. Nothing. Early reports of the bombing indicate the guy was a lone wolf without ties to a larger political group or country. Injuries would have been much worse if a call to emergency services hadn't set in motion a search of the area."

Murray clasped his hands in front of him as he cleared his throat. "I was referring to Miss Jessica."

"Oh, right. She's still unconscious." The horror of what she experienced haunted him. As well as having a fractured skull and being badly concussed from the shockwave of the blast, metal fragments had torn through her body. Some sliced cleanly through her, hacking bits of muscle. Others shattered bone, and fragments had lodged near arteries and nerves.

"I've no doubt every resource you can bring to bear for her you will." Murray's cheeks had paled under the strain of his concern. Days of stress wore him down.

"I want her to be in Boston."

Murray sucked in his lips. "Master Declan assures us that the care she's receiving is excellent. A lengthy transport would be difficult in her fragile state."

"The hospital in Atlanta is good, but it's not at the forefront of medical science as are the hospitals in Massachusetts. As soon as Jessica is stable enough to fly, I've demanded Declan arrange her transportation to Boston."

"If it's a risk for her to travel, why push? There are frenzied forces at play in the universe."

Michael looked Murray in the eye trying to understand his resistance. He tried to find a reason Murray would accept. "A search went out for next of kin of the victims."

"Aye. I heard the States' news has been filled with praise for the uncle who wishes to be reunited with his niece. I've no doubt doing so would erase years of estrangement. Most blokes believe having the comfort of family helps the sick and injured recover."

"That man is no more a blood uncle than I am," Michael seethed. "William Wyeth is no relative. He's a leech, and a bankrupt one at that."

"Then why move her closer to him?"

Michael's eyes darted around the room. "Because it's where I'm comfortable having her and," he faltered, "it would look like the uncle wanted her to be closer to family."

"How are you going to handle him?"

"He's bankrupt so he'll be easy to manipulate with a few well timed, er, *donations*. He might be useful later on, but I don't want to get involved with him now. I've enough to deal with." He jabbed his fingers at the keyboard and opened the most recent email from Declan. Declan called with updates on Jessica's condition, but followed up with written reports Michael could read through again and again to assuage his bottomless need for information.

"You're still here." Liam Connaught wheeled himself over to the tea service and poured himself a cup. Liam's shock of white hair and bushy eyebrows seemed to hover independent of earthly supports, shadowing the rest of his face. Murray helped him into a leather club chair and placed the cup within his reach on a marble-topped side table.

"Will there be anything more?" Murray inquired.

"No. Thank you. Make sure the grounds are secure for the night. I'm not expecting anyone else," Michael said as he tucked a blanket around Liam's legs. He waited until Murray's footsteps could no longer be heard before he spoke.

Michael grimaced. "There is a mountain of subpoenas piled on Declan's desk in Boston. The political climate may push the U.S. to extradite me. If that happens, our contacts in Stormont will grind the process down to a halt. Whether I'm dragged to the U.S. by a marshal or arrive on a sight-seeing trip, the racketeering unit of the FBI promises to greet me at the airport."

"With glee, I'd imagine." The china cup held in Liam's gnarled and arthritic hands rattled on the saucer. "You could always kill them with kindness and agree to a meeting with copious protective measures to ensure your free travel. They would find your willingness to meet a testament to innocence."

"Regardless of how quickly Declan works to negate the underlying allegations, the gears of the legal system grind slowly. As you've warned many times, once on U.S. soil I'll be questioned under oath about my father's dealings."

"Questions are just words. No need to run from that."

"Being questioned I have few qualms with. Being arrested I do. With it would come withering scrutiny inside my organization. The bad press would do years of harm to our PR efforts."

"That counsel you've hired. Isn't he good enough to get you in and out of the country without notice?"

"Yes, but getting me on U.S. soil without being discovered is one thing. Getting me to Jessica is another. Declan presented me with options, but overall I agree with your analysis. It's best I stay in Northern Ireland and away from her. If I appear at her side, attention would shift away from her and inquiries and investigations would focus on me. You've never varied from that assessment."

Liam flicked his hand in a dismissive way. "Besides, that woman of yours is unconscious and wouldn't know if you were there or not."

Vacillating somewhere between rage and helplessness, Michael agreed, hoping Declan would do him justice as his proxy by Jessica's side.

"Your stocks have plummeted," Liam said as he dropped a lump of sugar into his cup.

"I'm not worried about a lasting decline."

Liam sipped his tea, slurping in air to cool it. His eyes moved over the walls as he spoke. "These walls have heard more than their share of Connaught's enterprises tales of woe and wonder. The past week is no different."

Michael reviewed the ephemera of three generations. Family photographs occupied every inch of wall space not filled with bookcases. Here, sitting by his father as Magnus sipped tea or whiskey, Michael absorbed the importance of presenting a positive image to the world regardless of the private truth. The pictures and artifacts of lofty achievements had been culled through and curated. Awards of excellence and appreciation, dulled with dust and tarnish, retained the power to impress. Presidents and heads of state shook the hands of his father, uncle, and grandfather. CEOs and celebrities beamed in his family's presence as they held oversized scissors poised over wide ribbons. Bishops and cardinals blessed.

If the pictures told the full story, he would be holding the woman he loved in his arms and not wandering around alone in a cavernous home. He turned his head toward the corner of the study where his uncle sat as if the other half of his legacy could be glimpsed in those shadowed recesses.

Liam's recent stroke was not enough to dull his mind. Michael weighed his uncle's words with increasing appreciation for his wisdom. He prodded Liam. "You're wrong when you say *my* stocks. Your brother and father built money-minting corporations. You're a part of this, too."

"It's your name and initials on the masthead. Not mine. The stock crash reflects on you, not me."

Michael shrugged. "You're the one who taught me that when Connaught's Charity enters a war, we know no losing side."

Liam chuckled. "You come from a long line of astute businessmen, not clairvoyants. We plan for our future without being able to see it. War? Peace? There are opportunities in being the suppliers of war-related goods as well as selling the detection and defense equipment of those same goods."

"But it was you who divided the corporations into two distinct categories," Michael said with admiration, referring to the war-related businesses branded under the 2100, Ltd. title. "You expertly worked public relations. I admit you have a certain genius in the art of manipulation."

Liam sipped his tea and hid his smile behind his cup like a teacher intent upon pulling the best performance out of an already stellar student. "The public face of MMC, Ltd. is cherubic and generous, but the Charity's relationships with terrorist groups bring too much unwanted attention."

"You're referring to the IRA as a terrorist group?" He rounded his eyes in mock horror. "I thought your preferred term was *freedom fighters.*"

Liam sniffed. "I was only trying to make you feel like I've heard your complaints. 'Groups that bomb public places are terrorist organizations.' Right?" he said in a mocking falsetto. He flicked his hand in the air, dismissing the concept. "But what about this Olympic mess? How big an organization pulled that off?"

Michael sat down, stunned at how he had to answer. "No organization. One man. A lone, rabid wolf." Those words coated his mouth with a hatred that threatened to propel him to exact revenge in any way he could.

"Under the watchful eye of millions of dollars' worth of MMC equipment. The incident-free Games were to have been your segue into new markets."

Behind the scenes, 2100 supplied scaled-up weapons directly to U.S. government contractors with the official mission of supplementing security at the Olympics. It was one of the last sales brokered by brothers Magnus and Liam Connaught. Magnus died only months after penning the deal. A pit formed in Michael's stomach as he wondered how connected the Charity—the criminal organization that joined both sides of their businesses—was to the carnage he saw.

MMC received the public benefit that bolstered its brand, while 2100 stayed in the shadows. With promises of discretion, together both sides of Connaught's ventures supplied the Olympic venues with the metal detectors, surveillance equipment, and weaponry needed for detection and deterrence.

"You failed," Liam pressed. "What's your excuse?"

Michael's chest crushed with the reality. "I don't have one."

"Perhaps not, but you do have an out."

"What? I'm not following."

"Yes, you are."

A month ago, Michael had declared to Jessica that the Charity was dead. The organization that had killed her family and loomed as an ever-present danger in her life would be no more. As the outwardly reluctant heir to his father's enterprises, Michael inherited the Medusa's head of managing multinational corporations as well as the debts and layers of organized crime. As much as he yearned to leave the baggage of the Charity by the wayside, the reality was he was the primary shareholder and CEO. Responsibility for whatever crimes the corporations had done in the past landed at his feet with a sandbagged thud. Jessica was both a victim of his father's crimes and a target because of them.

Once again, his father and his organization were at the epicenter of a catastrophic event.

Once again, Jessica was caught in the maelstrom.

"You need to finish the job."

"How?"

"First, you need to get yourself clear from the suspicions that the Manchester bombing was something the Charity had a hand in. You need an airtight way to shift the focus for that bombing and others away from us and on to another viable network. The response to this bombing confirms our strategy."

"I know that. I've taken the first steps." He pushed rising bile down with a forceful swallow.

Over the past days he had been able to make sense of the reports that had trickled in from the States. Whoever pulled off the Olympic bombing acted alone. Under intense pressure, authorities identified a suspect within four days, the same person who had alerted police to the presence of the bomb. Michael scoured every resource he had for information on the suspect.

He knew in his gut they were targeting the wrong man.

The authorities must have known that, too, because the individual was not formally named as a 'person of interest,' nor were charges brought against him. The only thing the suspect had done wrong was to see something alarming and to notify the authorities. Instead of hailing him as a hero, he became the easy target for rumors and conspiracy theories.

All the suspect had done wrong was to be at the wrong place at the wrong time.

Just as Jessica had been with the Manchester bombing.

In the quest and thirst for the Next Big Story in follow-up to the Olympic bombing, the press had descended upon the man's home and camped out at FBI headquarters. The nightly news unwittingly served the authorities' intent to propagate the impression that all was well and that security was established.

"It's time to use Jessica. Her hospitalization does not help you. You need to do more. Immediately." Liam tried to place the teacup down on the table. The tea sloshed from his shaking hands.

Michael's stomach clenched as he bent down and used a hanky to blot up the spilled liquid. The stroke had weakened Liam's left side but left unscathed the portions of his brain responsible for reasoning and linear thinking. Rather than finding fault with the old man's ways, he practiced forgiveness.

"Wouldn't take much to set her up," Liam said. "The authorities are already skittish about her. You have all the contacts and everything else you need. Just a few phone calls and you'd be set." He motioned for Michael to help him back into his wheelchair. "Work faster. The teams will be leaving Atlanta soon. The opportunity to question and search will be lost." The rubber wheels did not make a sound as he rolled out of the room.

Michael raked his hands over his head, then vigorously rubbed his face, hoping to snap himself alert. He opened the ornate wood box on his desk and pulled out a phone. "Get me the bishop."

Grundy Hospital
Atlanta, Georgia

THE FACT THAT lights in Atlanta's Grundy Memorial Hospital's ICU never shut off irritated Declan to no end. At best, they would be dimmed slightly for the late night and early morning hours to encourage patients to rest even if sleep was more hope than reality. When most Atlantans were rolling over in their beds to slam alarms silent, Grundy's hallways were in full blaze. The constant bustle of medical staff and the never-ceasing rattle of med carts added to Declan's annoyance.

The first hours after the bombing had passed in a fog of confusion and fear. The frenzied chaos at Centennial Park migrated to the halls and trauma bays of emergency rooms throughout Atlanta. Flesh opened from nails and metal fragments spilled copious amounts of blood from the multitude of victims. Atlanta's supplies ran low. A call went out for donors.

Patients needing emergency care are provided immediate measures to preserve life and limb. Barring explicit directives or evidence to the contrary, no consent is needed to provide medical treatment. This is especially true when the patient is a young woman in the full bloom of life. Triage placed Jessica on the critical list. From the moment she was wheeled into Grundy, nurses, doctors, and interns never left her side and the hospital's chaplain never left Declan's.

Chaplain Carlton, a round man with ebony skin, provided help and support to others, and frequently appeared at Declan's side with a bottle of water or cup of coffee. Even tending to those in inconsolable grief, inner peace encompassed him with a glow. "I'm sorry about the death of your friend."

Declan pinched the bridge of his nose. "She was an incredible woman. I only wish . . . I wish . . . " His voice thickened.

"She was close to you?"

Declan hesitated. What was it he saw in the relationship between Electra and Jessica that pricked under his skin? His typically steely resolve to see people as pieces on a game board had begun to soften since his discovery at Magnus' home. He wanted to keep speculation about Jessica and her relationship to Electra to a minimum in an instinctive urge to control the message. He grieved for Electra, but also for the loss of her savvy.

He wrapped himself in the cloak of professionalism and provided only the raw essentials of information—something Electra was supremely gifted at.

"I didn't know her long."

Chaplain Carlton nodded as if acknowledging that ties between humans are complex and unexplainable in any worldly sense. "She was alone in this world except for the young woman. Surely someone who knew them both will step forward on the news of her death."

"I know they both valued their privacy."

"How is the young woman?"

"I need to do everything I can for her. I'm," he struggled to find the right words, "I'm as close to family as she has."

Keeping Jessica's name out of the press was essential to ensure any family member—a.k.a. William Wyeth—would have limited information. Declan positioned himself as Jessica's watchdog, if not her guardian, forcing his way to be privy to every decision and demanding to be involved in every minute of her around-the-clock care. For all of the might and strength of Michael's wealth, neither he nor Declan held the passcode to be her kin.

From the moment the EMT's ran to her to stem the flow of blood from her wounds, Declan remained by Jessica's side. The surgeries done, the glacial business of recovery began. "She needs someone to advocate for her best interests," he said. Alternating between demands for additional attention to razor-edged barbs if his requests were not immediately addressed, Declan had marshaled the staff to do his bidding.

"You've been at her side from the first," Chaplain Carlton said. "You obviously have a deep connection to her."

"I only want what's best for her."

"You've been granted all the access any family could want. I'm impressed with your resolve and resourcefulness."

Declan hid his satisfaction. A mix of cloying Southern warmth and icy dictates proved effective, but it was the prompt payment of expenses, and a deposit for future care, that helped secure the attention Declan wanted for her; a private room in the intensive care unit.

Chaplain Carlton put his hand on Declan's arm. "What can a person do when there's nothing more to do?" he asked, watching the hive of activity through the narrow windows of the closed doors.

"Pray," Declan responded, surprising himself with the answer.

Jessica's room was large by hospital standards. An oversized chair doubled as Declan's guest bed at night and office by day. He left her side only to badger doctors or to give updates to Michael. Nurses encouraged him to hold her hand or stroke her forehead and arms, explaining that stimulating her unconscious mind could coax her back to consciousness. He did, reluctantly at first, feeling like an imposter, and worrying about being caught in his trespass.

Agents Baxter and Sanford had arrived at Jessica's room sometime after midnight the first day, surprised to see Declan encamped beside her. In the dance of cat and mouse—predator and prey—they kept their visit short and their message clear. Even as they spoke, authorities were combing through video surveillance from all Olympic venues. The fact that the bomb could have arrived days earlier, perhaps in gear belonging to an athlete or vendor, was their prime concern. To Baxter, Jessica and anyone affiliated with her, were suspects in the Centennial Park bombing investigation and he expressed his frustration that the investigation might be focused elsewhere. He leaned over Jessica, nose almost touching hers. He remained there for minutes before he grunted with satisfaction and left, Sanford close on his heels.

Declan dozed by her bedside, not sure if his hope for healing fooled him into observing changes that were not there. Digital numbers marked her progress along with a jagged green line that bounced across a screen. Each hour felt like a day, but hints appeared that she was rising up from the depths of a slumber. He held her hand, rubbed her arms, and surprised himself by placing a cool cloth on her head when she seemed to fret.

The sound of his voice calmed her. At first, he felt uncomfortable endlessly repeating where she was or what had happened, but eventually he settled on what he wished he could tell her. About himself.

Or Michael. In the hours spent at her side, he told her motionless body things he had never told a soul. He never spoke of Electra, preferring to hope Jessica would become strong enough emotionally to recover from the news.

He wasn't sure how many days or nights had passed before she called out for Bridget and Kavan. His heart clenched when she called out for Electra, but beat more slowly as he realized she was recalling recent memories. The possibility that her brain was intact took hold. He clung to the hope even as he tested her ability to think.

He dug through her stupor, picking at information to determine what she knew or what kind of threat she posed.

He sat, pen poised.

Declan remained by her side. Television off. Newspapers unread. Despite his daily and thorough updates, conversations with Michael became tense. The fallout from the failure to get Jessica's signature on the syndicate contracts fell at Declan's feet. A letter from Electra's counsel apprised Michael of her divestiture of all shares from several businesses they shared and that a full audit was underway.

Suddenly abandoned, Michael raged at being blindsided.

Caring about profits was reasonable, but Declan expected more from him. Grief being one.

As he knew it would, news leaked that the Murdering Heiress was injured in the blast. The rubbernecking of people in the hallway told him that once again Jessica was in the news.

Nurses entered, bustled, adjusted, then left. The head nurse, a buxom woman with chocolate skin said, "You'll be relieved to know her uncle is on his way. You've been a wonderful friend to her, but this is a time for family." Her message was clear and delivered. Firmly. He was to step aside and let kin take over.

Declan wanted to kill the myth that William Wyeth was in any way connected with Jessica and chafed at the urge to tell him the truth. William's puffed face appeared in newspapers and his dramatic pleas for calm and prayers—in numerous interviews—exposed the fact that the desired reunion was more for William's own aggrandizement than for the love of his family. Cleaving to Jessica was William Wendell Wyeth's last hope for redemption—or solvency. Declan almost pitied him. Almost.

"Oh, my God! My God! It's my niece!"

Declan didn't need introductions, but he rose and presented his hand anyway. "William Wyeth? Declan Cleary." He stood a head taller than William. Even wracked by fatigue and in need of a shave and a shower, his presence was crisp and authoritative. Declan tried not to smirk in satisfaction when William shrank away.

"What? Oh, right. Hi." William peered around Declan at the bed. "Christ almighty! Look at all of this! She's still listed in critical condition, right? That means she could die any minute, right?" His eyes shone in the bright light.

"Jessica is out of immediate danger and has been upgraded to serious." Declan bit his tongue before he could utter, *Disappointed?*

"Oh, serious. Good. Good." William took another step into the room, hesitated, and then took a step toward the window. Declan's suit jacket was thrown on the only chair in the room. William looked at the chair and the bed, face clouded as he debated where to perch. He moved to prop himself up on the window sill, a deep shelf-like area designed for air vents that doubled as extra seating.

Declan watched him with amusement. This was William's big moment; one he had been waiting for and milking attention for even weeks before the bombing. The long-awaited reunion was finally happening and William didn't have one clue how to handle himself.

The last thing Declan was going to do was make it easy on him.

William shifted on the sill, crossed and uncrossed his legs, and fiddled with the knobs on the ventilation. Cold air blasted. "Beastly hot out there. Not like Boston. Air's as thick as soup. Been out?"

Declan waited a full minute before he spoke. "No."

William's skin shimmered. "Oh, um, how about Boston? Been there?"

Another minute. "Yes."

William suddenly brightened, his manner upbeat as a thought struck him. "I'm thinking, um, I'm thinking of having her transported to Boston as soon as she's stable. You know, bring her back home!" His most recent interviews had said as much. The familiar topic animated him.

Declan was well aware of William's plans. The fact that they agreed with Michael's plans caused him consternation. Both men wanted to give Jessica the best possible care, and that fact alone proved they *could* care—even if it was more about their own images than about another human life.

The question of whether Jessica considered Boston "home" itched around his head. He refrained. "She's not well enough to be moved."

"She'll be transported to Silvern Rehabilitation as soon as she's able."

He hid his displeasure. "Oh?"

William nearly glowed with victory. "Yes! Isn't that great!"

"Getting her the best care is my main concern and the care here has been excellent. I see no reason to put her through that stress."

William sucked on his teeth. "Christ! Silvern! That's world class! How can I not push for the best for my niece?"

"The best comes at a price. Who's paying?" He wanted to ask more, but to do so would show his hand.

"Not me! I can't afford that!" He blurted the words and the look on his face said he wished he could take them back. "Well, er, all this, um, attention we've gotten, I mean *she's* gotten, has flushed a few heavyweight donors out of the brush. Arrangements have been made."

"Arrangements have been made," Declan repeated, keeping his black eyes on William, unblinking.

"It will be great to bring her back home! It's been years since I've seen her. Years. I remember one time, gosh, she must have been eight or nine years old, Margaret, Jim and their youngest daughter, Erin and I all went to Crane Beach in Ipswich. You know it? Beautiful stretch of white sand. You'd never know you were only thirty-five miles from Boston. Anyway, we had a grand time! The girls played in the surf, and Jim and I brought our lacrosse sticks and tossed a ball around for a while."

Declan didn't move his eyes off William. The pressure and stony silence made William talk faster and faster, blabbering on about nothing. It was the first amusement Declan had had in days, but boredom with William's preppy drivel threatened. Declan moved to sit next to Jessica.

"Then, on another Christmas, Margaret made the best dinner. Surprised the hell out of me to learn an Irish woman could cook. I thought they boiled everything, but my God, the lamb stew she made was delicious! Jessica was always happy to see me. I was her favorite uncle, you know."

Declan didn't react. It's easy to call yourself the favorite when there were no competitors. He remained impassive as he listened and let his mind drift.

Jessica's eyes opened, translucent blue lids pulled up from bloodshot eyes.

A wave of relief washed over Declan. Instinct and compassion made him reach over the rails of the bed and pull her hand into his own, careful not to disturb the tubes or needles anchored in her skin with bands of white tape.

Her eyes seemed to float in their own orbits before finally working in unison. They focused on parts of the room, settling on one detail for several seconds as if waiting for her brain to catch up in deciphering one object after another. They swam over objects, rehearsing for the complicated task of decoding a face.

William prattled on, unaware. Several minutes passed as Declan watched and waited. His skin heated, evidence of his body's visceral reaction recharging her to life. She was conscious. Aware. Thinking? He hoped to God she was.

Aquamarine eyes surrounded by squiggles of red meandered over his face. His heart caught. Did he feel her hand move?

Her chest rose and face worked as she struggled to speak.

"Eh . . ." she said, barely more than a whisper. "Eh . . . lec . . . tra?"

"What? She's awake? She's speaking?" William shoved Declan aside, grabbing her hand. Tubes and drip bags swayed. "Jessica! Jessie baby! It's your Uncle William." He turned to Declan. "What did she say? Did she ask for someone? Me? Did she ask for me?"

Declan put his hands up, palms out. "William, you should take things slowly. For her sake." The beeps increased their tempo. Her eyes moved faster, looking from William to Declan and back. The unmistakable hallmarks of panic tugged at the corners of her lids.

"She asked for . . . for . . ." William's brows furrowed as he tried to piece together what he heard. "Electra! She asked for Electra!" His cheeks glowed with the thrill of discovery then sank with realization. "She asked for Electra Lavielle. My God, she doesn't know!"

"William. Don't. Please. Think of her." Declan begged, but knew his words fell on deaf ears.

Declan fought his own rising panic as he watched the scene unfold. Nothing in his life prepared him for this. Instinct urged him to wrap his hands around William's neck and squeeze, but he knew this was neither the time nor the place to kill. Powerless, he watched William usurp, then botch, the biggest role of his life—as family, as a concerned and loving uncle.

"Jessie, oh Jessie baby. Electra's dead. It's just you and me now."

If eyes could bleed with sorrow, Jessica's would have. Declan watched in horror as a year of seconds passed while the news of Electra's death created connections in Jessica's damaged brain. Evidence of a target hit, her eyes filled and threatened to overflow.

An alarm chimed down the hall. The room began to fill with nurses and machines wheeled in on carts.

Before her lids closed, spilling the pool of tears, she looked at Declan.

Please help me.

He cocked his head. He heard her voice as clearly as if she spoke aloud. "You want Michael?" he asked.

The tiny muscles surrounding her eyes tensed, creating circles of terror.

Not Michael. Not William.

William jumped to his feet. "What? She asked for Michael? Isn't that the creep who–"

Declan shoved him aside and gripped her hand to his chest. Was he imagining her voice? For the hours he had spent at her side, forcing a connection, no, *needing* one, was now the time he learned she had forged one of her own? "How? *Who?*"

You.

That was the last connection he had before she closed her eyes and slipped away.

Brandywine Farm
Perc, Kentucky

AUGUST IN THE foothills of the Pine Mountains proved to be a study in contrasts. Rain-parched fields stretched out in swaths of brown with patches of green while the air hung heavy in moisture-drenched sheets. The occasional soaking rain would bring back Kentucky blue grass to its lush and blue-green fame, followed by days of cloudless sky that made a Kentuckian's heart soar. The syncopated rhythms of humans and horse would blend into one as creatures lived side by side. Pine pitch and the sweet tang of horse drifted on the thick breeze. Water trucks, round tanks ballooning over make-shift trailers, bounced and rolled over pastures, replenishing troughs and giving the turf just enough water not to die completely.

The days at Brandywine feigned acceptance of their new normal. Horses continued to be exercised in the dew-dappled mornings, and evenings filled with cicada song. Stable and house help parked their Ford F-150s behind the equipment shed and nodded greetings to the changing shifts. Flowers bloomed in brilliant patches and bougain-villea draped in deep purple swags over walls and trellises. Bereave-ment smudged the beauty of normal life to ragged edges of blurred and faded colors.

If the horses missed Electra's nightly treats and neck rubs, they could not say, but evening hours saw ears cocked to gates and heads hung over stall doors waiting for a woman who no longer came. Buds opened to blooms. Only a discerning eye would see weeds where there once were none. Chrystal vases sat empty on polished tables.

The looming manse ticked its emptiness, and the trees and grasses sighed their sorrows.

Grief didn't stop Brooks Carter from being the best damned corporate counsel there was. Protecting Electra's professional interests was the formal aspect of his job, protecting her personally was a natural extension. Passion to deliver on his promise to further Electra's interests did not diminish with her death. In fact, it increased. Her unquestioned and early support of gay rights fostered a fierce loyalty in him and he was determined to keep her legacy alive as long as he could in as many ways as he could.

Electra Lavielle was not a woman Brooks would trifle with. When she wanted something done, those who worked for her knew that yesterday wasn't fast enough. If she demanded speed from her employees, she expected nothing less from herself. After listening to Jessica pour her heart out, it took her one night's fitful sleep to firm her direction and make her plans. Her directives had already been set into motion, so when the news of her death hit, shock and heartache did not slow the players into inaction.

As is often the case, the last conversations with the deceased are replayed over and over in the living's mind—a way to anchor a spirit to the present even if the body is gone. Brooks was dogged by such memories.

"Do you understand all that I've said?" Electra's voice rang clear and loud.

He replied to her that he understood.

"You know my life depends on this."

The panic that fringed those words would ring in his ears forever.

He had cautioned her about any involvement with Michael Connaught, urging restraint until enough time had passed that the true colors of the man would show. Actions prevail over crafted words, and he advised Electra to audit her business prospects on their deeds as well as checkbooks. She steadfastly obeyed each of his directives, but challenged his protections with decisions made from her huge heart. Emotion clouded her normally clear thinking whenever the safety of a vulnerable friend was at stake. She opened her home to naïve starlets, runaways, and at-risk youth. It came as no surprise when she made it clear that whatever opportunity could benefit Jessica Wyeth, Brooks was to make it happen, even if it meant doing business with a scumbag.

Electra's success came, in part, from seeing an opportunity and grabbing it, but it also came from a keen sense of planning for what she called the "What ifs."

What if a business partner went bankrupt?
What if a source lied?
What if a business partner is a scumbag?
What if I die tomorrow?

For all of her worrying, never once did she ask, *What if I'm the victim of a terrorist's bomb?*

She was the last of her line and the mold had been broken. There would never be another Electra. Maybe she felt some foreshadowing, for she looked around her and determined ways to shape the world to do her bidding even after her death. At her written request, Brooks set up his temporary office in the Bridge to act as her proxy to accept condolences and to guide helpless grief into action. Donations poured in to her favorite Thoroughbred rescue charities, churches, women's shelters and other causes.

From the Bridge, he directed Electra's last gifts. He clasped a check into Father Steeves' hands and insisted the amount was to the penny of what Electra wanted to give. The personal note thanked Perc's local priest for keeping families informed of estranged members, near and far. Brooks didn't understand her message or question Electra's word, but made sure Father Steeves did not reject the donation.

Electra's home filled with flowers, mementos, photographs, and people. After the hours spent watching Perc's citizens file through and listening to their memories, he bid a good night to the last of the stragglers, pressed his shoulder against her front doors, secured the bolt from the inside, and sank to the floor to sob.

At the end of each visitor-filled day, he had a good, purging cry, and then got to work following Electra's directives to a T, admonishing himself there would be time for a pity party later.

Brooks didn't question Electra's first and most emphatic request: Make sure Jax and his men leave Brandywine, and sell all interests in the syndicates that owned Kilkea, Planxty, and Bealltainn. A shiver of realization of what Electra feared rippled through Brooks when Jax said, "Suit yourself for us to be gone, but it wasn't Electra who paid us."

Following through on Electra's other adamant request proved to be more difficult. Again, her forethought unnerved him. Electra demanded Brooks monitor and insure Jessica's protection and well-being no matter what her needs may be. He would have done so even without a direct mandate from Electra because he had a sense that events revolved around Jessica like pawns and knights around a chessboard's queen. At every parry, he was thwarted by that damned Boston attorney. He took his own advice and channeled his grief into dogged action. No man would better him.

Declan Cleary had damned well better watch his back.

When he tired of one task, he moved to another and reviewed the checklist he and Electra created. God! Did they write it one day before she was killed or two? He shook his head in disbelief at the foresight her fear fostered. Several items of the multiple-page list had been checked off before shrapnel ripped her carotid. Once the fog of shocked grief cleared, he followed through on other items to ensure all would be completed as quickly as possible. Progress was steady but slower than he wanted.

No matter how many times he began to work, he had to breathe in his sorrow when he sat down at Electra's desk.

After going through the process, he could see Electra's wisdom in having him take control at the Bridge. He could oversee the workings of the farm more easily. Notes, phone numbers, past correspondence, and more were at his fingertips.

After he made each phone call and sent all the emails possible, he ran his hand along the surface of the desk, absorbing the feel of the silky wood. Lemon oil and memories mixed and made him weepy again. He wanted to do Electra's bidding even better than she would have expected, but he was stymied by her world. Her world of media and public relations revolved around personal connections and trust, two commodities he lacked with people he had never met. When he called and shared with them Electra's request, he could feel them weigh their choice—believe someone sight unseen and risk their reputation, or play it safe until someone else stuck their neck out.

He wanted to go top-tier, and refused to settle for second best. He had never questioned her drive for personal connections, now he understood how much he had underestimated their worth. After a handful of conversations, he knew he needed something more and only a first-person source would do. Reluctantly, he admitted it would take weeks more time to get to the level Electra wanted, and she would haunt him for his error.

At least he'd be close to her.

He took out the notes of Jessica's interviews and combed through the details. When he hit a wall, he stopped, napped, and began again on a fresh tack. Something swirled in the background of Jessica's life, not a shadow, but a force. He needed a way to remove the eclipse.

With one last blown kiss to the empty house, he shut off the lights and made his way out.

Grundy Hospital
Atlanta, Georgia

DOSES OF PAIN meds decreased. Lucidity dawned. Lights on. Lights off. The walls remained the same color grey. She couldn't escape.

She couldn't move.

The hours slid by. Into days?

Piecemeal images. The hospital chaplain hovered over her bed, dabbing holy water on her forehead and incanting prayers. Silver cross on black shirt. His words muddled and morphed and disappeared into the sounds of the hospital. *Your father, who art in Belfast, Kavan be thy name . . .*

Was he here? Who was there? People in. People out. She lay there as the nation grieved and wrapped its collective head around the reality that a bomb had been planted to harm innocent people and gain attention for a cause no one had yet claimed.

Another day or the same day? Her nurse moved around the room soundlessly. Pillows fluffed. Curtains drawn if opened, opened if drawn. Shades up. Shades down.

Jessica wanted to scream.

But she wouldn't.

She allowed her eyes to settle on the rectangular bar pinned on the nurse's uniform.

N-O-E-L-L-E.

Sleep. Awake. Her ears and eyes followed Noelle's movements. It would have taken more energy than she had to stop tracking her. Noelle leaned over and used her hip to brace one of Jessica's arms, keeping it straight. Then she used her hand to flex Jessica fingers upward. Jessica felt the pain of the stretch up to her elbow. Twenty seconds. Twenty times. Then her other arm, but no pain of stretch accompanied the movement. Her legs and feet required more positions held for longer periods. Knee straight. Ankle flexed. Knee bent. Ankle straight. When the workout was over, Noelle fastened a bag of grey goo to a long pole and fiddled with the tubing.

She could hear what went on around her. Making sense of the sounds was laborious.

Noelle's voice. "That'll do you, Darlin'. I'll be back again tomorrow. Sherry's here for the evening. That girl packs the most delicious dinners. Tonight's some chicken fritters with collard greens. Smelled it as soon as she walked in. Open a restaurant, I tell 'er. You'll be up and eatin' her cookin' soon enough and you'll see what I've been talking about. Now then, be good!" After that, sounds of movement fussed around the room. A closet door swished open. A hanger rattled. The door swished closed.

The muffled sounds of the hospital sharpened as another door opened.

"G'night officers. See you in the morning?" Noelle's voice gratingly perky.

"Afternoon shift for me. Any changes in her condition?"

"You know I can't say anything. Now stop trying to work me up with those doe eyes of yours! I don't know what you think you're going to learn from me and I sure don't understand why it takes two of you to guard a woman who's not going anywhere fast."

"We only do what we're told."

"Well, that makes two of us, but I'm going to ask you one more time. You boys donate blood yet?"

"Yes, ma'am. Did at the first call a few days back. Line around the block."

"You must have gone when that uncle of hers made it a state event to give blood. I've never seen so many reporters!"

Laughter. "Rotten timing, but yeah, he was there. We made sure to shame some of those reporters into donating, too!"

"Well, good for you! I went earlier in the week and tried to avoid standing on a line any longer than I needed. Like right now. My feet and back are telling me to leave, and that's just what I'm gonna do. She's bein' transported up to that fancy hospital in Boston soon enough. I sure will miss your pretty faces." Male and female voices chuckled. "'Night now!"

The door clicked shut. Sounds muffled. Rubber-soled footfalls retreated down the hall.

The shadows slid across the floor and the sunlight gradually changed from yellow to pink to soft blues. The only sound was the clock on the wall and her breathing. Five ticks. Inhale. Six tocks. Exhale.

Flowers. Too many flowers. The smell made her sick. Every surface flat enough for a basket or a vase held two.

Nurses swooped around her. Doctors stood with crossed arms, hands covering mouths as they muttered to one another. Some came back alone, speaking to her in low tones, faux concern dripping off their worried brows. A chirpy woman with a riot of white hair and a penchant for chunky necklaces sat with her for hours on end holding charts and pictures up and moving them left to right. Right to left. Up. Down.

Question after question after question.

"Great job following the picture! Now try moving your eyes to the upper right corner while I hold the picture still. Can you do that?"

Jessica stared straight ahead.

"Try again. I know you can hear me, now show me you can understand. Move your eyes to the upper right corner of the picture to say yes." Minutes passed. "Let's try blinking. Close your eyes once for yes."

She remained still.

A tall man with impossibly dark eyes dressed in sharp suits never left the side of her bed. Did she know him?

Should she know him?

He showed her pictures, read her stories from the newspapers, and updates on training progress of horses. He massaged lotion into her hands and rubbed balm on her lips. Peppermint and eucalyptus filled the air.

"Jessica? It's Declan. I'm here to help you." He repeated the same phrase to her a zillion times already.

Enough, she wanted to scream. But she wouldn't.

Get out!

"Jessica. I'm here to help you."

No. No you're not. You're here to hurt me.

"The doctors say you're healing well. You're conscious. They tell me you can hear me."

No. I can't hear you. I stopped listening to you when you told me Electra died. It was you, right? Too many people in and out. All that matters is I stopped caring. I stopped healing.

Electra died. Electra died. Electra died because I wanted her to stay with me.

Why wasn't it me?

He moved his face in front of her, forcing her to turn her head if she wanted to escape him. She lay still.

His relentless questioning of her as she moaned in pain dominated memories of her first hours of awareness. She imagined her contempt for him shining through in blue laser hate. *Why are you here? Go away!* Once, he rocked back on his heels when he saw her expression.

"I'm here to help and I won't go away," he answered.

He reached under the covers to pull out her leg, and repeated the stretches Noelle had taught him, holding them longer, pushing her further. With her leg dangling over one arm, he used his other hand to rap the soft spot under her knee. Her foot jumped in mutiny to her resolve of not giving the satisfaction of movement. She closed her eyes and retreated.

He massaged her hands. The lotion he rubbed on her legs and arms was cool and fresh, so different from stale hospital air. His touch was gentle, yet direct. Fingers pressed into muscles, kneading knots and urging blood flow. He pressed his thumbs into her palms and milked her fingers, pressing each fingertip. He laced his fingers in hers, stretching her hand back. Her body awakened more and more with each day's massage. When he started to let go, she tightened her grip before she remembered to give him nothing.

Layers of medical protection provided a cocoon. Drugs. Hushed voices. Routine. Wait-and-see. Inside the spun and dark interior, sounds deadened and the world couldn't intrude. She was alone again and having isolation be her choice, rather than the pain reality forced upon her, was easier. She didn't have to answer questions. She didn't have to face Electra's death or William Wyeth's presence. She didn't have to feel Michael's absence—or his betrayal.

Inevitably, time healed some of her wounds.

In tandem with physical healing was the ratcheting back of drugs. The drug-induced veil lifted. Her pain ebbed. Her awareness flowed.

Two guards twenty-four, seven. Nurses. Doctors.

Declan.

Her heart thudded and she was glad not to be hooked up to a machine that would tattle.

He was at her side day and night. At first, she hated him and all he represented.

Then she began to wait for his touch.

People passed in and out of her room. Sometimes another man, familiar to her in some far-off way and smelling like limes, joined Declan.

Sounds sharpened. A rustle of curtains. The room dimmed. Evening? Footsteps.

"Mr. Cleary, I should have expected you to be here." The chirpy woman's voice pressed with tension. "Hello Jessica! It's Doctor Bosworth. How are you doing today?" Warm hands gripped her own.

"I was disappointed Doctor Seehaus was not available" Declan said. "I'd heard she was the best trauma physician around."

"Jessica? I'm going to talk with Mr. Cleary for a few minutes and then we can get to work today." She felt a pat on her arm as the warm hands left her. "Dr. Seehaus assigned Jessica to me. I specialize in PTSD and catatonic states brought on by physiological and psychological trauma." Papers fluttered. "Has she given any intentional or purposeful movements or utterances?"

"No."

"What about eye contact? Many patients' first methods of communicating after a head injury are with their eyes. Following movement, looking away, or blinking can all be signs of emerging consciousness."

"No. Nothing."

"Are you sure? She was tracking movement with me during my last visit."

"Nothing."

Silence. A scratching sound as a pen scribbled across paper. Jessica resisted the urge to pucker her eyes with disgust. *Don't probe me*, she wanted to warn, *don't pretend to know more than you do*.

With each upward level of consciousness came a firm resolve. To say nothing was easy—at least until she figured out his game. She yearned to feel nothing.

"Unusual. Night nurses reported spontaneous utterances. They distinctly heard her cry out." A pen clicked.

"Jessica cried out?" Heavy footfalls moved around the room. "Why? What happened?"

"It's not unusual for the protections of a conscious mind to be turned off when unconscious, as in during sleep."

"What did she say? Did they write it down?"

"Let's see." A pause. "One name was Electra. I assume Electra Lavielle is who she called for. Pity. Her death is such a waste. She called for her mother, too, but she seemed confused."

"Confused? How?"

"She called for her mother, then, let's see . . ." Pages turned. "Then she called for Aunt Bridget? Then she became agitated, almost like she was in a feverish delirium. She called for her mom in a way like she was confused what to call her. Was her mom's name Bridget?"

A long pause. "Bridget? Name is familiar. Did she say anything more?"

"For Jessica to have endured all that she has," her voiced trailed as she sifted for the right words, "it shows me how some people are just born strong. It makes me wonder about that whole nature or nurture issue."

"What do you mean?"

A pen scratched across a surface. "Well, you wouldn't think a Boston blueblood would have the kind of grit needed to persevere. Jessica is so different from her uncle. You'd never guess they came from the same family tree. He's so, er, well, so *mealy*." She cleared her throat. "Remarkable."

A chuff and a short pause. "Yes. Remarkable."

"Her injuries give us a constellation of issues to address. She had a fractured skull and was severely concussed. Each TBI is different and we're just learning the best ways of treatment."

"TBI? I don't follow."

"Traumatic Brain Injury. The damage to her skull triggered massive inflammation. The cranial swelling is diffuse, meaning it's not focused on one location. Areas impacted are language and movement, but we're not sure about comprehension and memory. She's lucky, but we don't know yet how lucky. We are worried about the piece of shrapnel removed from her neck. A bone fragment abraded the nerves, but didn't sever them. Still, combined with a TBI, we're not sure about her mobility. Have you seen any movement at all? Twitching? Muscle clenching?"

"Yes. Some reflex. Maybe a spontaneous hand movement, but nothing I could call purposeful. Are there still concerns about paralysis?"

"At this early stage of recovery, even small movements are a good sign. Lots of healing to go before we know more."

"How long before we see improvement?"

"There's no magic schedule. Skin can heal and bones can mend within weeks, but it can be months before the inflammation subsides well enough to stop impacting nerves or brain function. Three months would be one milestone we use as a direction for therapeutic interventions. Two years is when we consider all inflammation to be medically resolved."

"Three months?"

"It's just a benchmark we use to know what kind of therapy will be most efficacious."

Heavier footsteps. Door closing. Declan's voice moved to be closer to Bosworth's. "When will she be cleared to move out of ICU?"

"It's hard to say. As soon as her medical needs are not acute and she is stable. Days? Weeks? We don't know, but, again, she's making good progress. Physical healing is visible and linear. A gash scabs, then once the skin knits together, the wound doesn't open. Brain injuries, like Jessica sustained from the bomb's concussive blast as well as being slammed to the pavement, are much harder to heal from. Not only is the brain's physical circuitry infinitely more complex, but we just don't know if severed connections mend, or, if they do, if the mending process doesn't tip something else off balance, like cognitive abilities and emotions. Amazing how the body and mind heal in phases."

"I don't follow."

Window blinds adjusted. Jessica felt sunlight on her face. "The week after her injury, she scored well on perturbational complexity index. That's where we measured the brain with a magnetic field using a non-invasive technique called transcranial magnetic stimulation."

Doctor Bosworth's voice warmed as she spoke a puree of words, each blending into the next with no individual form. Jessica let the words flow through her—face muscles slack, eyes hooded, breathing steady.

The doctor continued talking. "Oh, um, you know, we hooked her up, looked at her brainwaves, and recorded the complexity of the response with EEG. The science is emerging, but it's a pretty good indicator of the depth of someone's unconsciousness." Papers rustled. "According to her chart, you reported she regained consciousness, and then it was almost like she suffered another injury, like a shock."

The clock on the wall ticked. The chime of an elevator door opening mixed with voices from the nurses' station.

"I believe news of her friend's death caused the setback." Declan snarled the words.

"Hmm. That fits. An emotional trauma can be just as devastating as a physical one and more difficult to heal from. Tell me more."

They talked. Jessica screamed inside her head to not hear them.

"Her care here has been excellent. I'm not an advocate of moving her."

"We appreciate your support. But her uncle was quite clear in his wishes."

A pause. Feet shuffled. "So, she'll be transferred to Boston in a couple of weeks?"

"Or sooner."

Or sooner. Jessica pressed her eyelids shut millimeter by millimeter, relieved that they obeyed her. Commands to move a finger or toe produced only terror. Was this real? What happened? A deep, dreamless sleep welcomed her.

Patterns of bright and dark. Night and day. Was it two days? A week? More? The only reality was the sameness of her room. Sometimes her eyelids glowed red in the brightly lit room. Sometimes blue-black.

A flurry of activity. Several nurses flocked around her. Items plunked into plastic containers. Her legs almost twitched as they placed something alongside them.

"Good news! You're moving back to Boston today!"

Bustle. A metal clang as the bed's brakes were unlocked. A silent whoosh as the rubber wheels rolled on highly polished floors. Rectangular lights strobed by overhead. Elevator doors dinged open. Closed. Her bed glided down a hall. Bright.

A face dropped close to hers. LeeAnne. Black tracks of mascara ran down her cheeks.

"Jessica. It's me. LeeAnne. You just got to come home. I can't stand it without you there. I . . . I'm sorry for bein' such a bitch to you. The horses and me, well, we miss you." She reached over the rails and gripped Jessica's arm. Calloused palms scraped up her forearm. "I call every day to talk to you and heard you were leaving today. I figured this was the only way to see you. I've been treatin' the horses good, but they need you around. Ginger and I have been holding down the fort, but with Missus Lavielle gone, I'm afraid the place is going to get shut down an' all the horses are gonna get sold to anybody."

Jessica let her eyes drift over LeeAnne's face. A crescent of purple and yellow sat in the hollow of her eye.

"I been doing good, keeping things running. Jax and his men are gone and there's new help there. All women. I'm glad about that. Keeps me calm." The gurney bucked as it maneuvered around a corner. "You'd be surprised at what I done. The new folks're good horse people, but I helped them with details on the farm. We make a good team. Without you and Electra there, it all feels so hollow. Rudie and me are done. He ain't never gettin' near me again. Folks been good about keeping him away, but–" She faltered, looking up and down the hall for something or someone. "That man from Boston noses around once in a while. Says he's your uncle."

Her forearm burned and she could feel her skin redden from the fervor of LeeAnne's rubbing.

"You gotta get better. I need you."

"Hey! Who the hell are you?" Declan's voice. Feet clad in expensive dress shoes clicked nearer. "Who is she? How did she get in here?"

A flurry of commands and stifled sobs. "Excuse me. You need to leave here this instant!" Noelle's voice a model of nursely authority.

LeeAnne's voice. "The only way to see her was to come when I heard she was being moved! I drove all night to say my good-byes!" The sound of bodies moving and feet scuffling came just before she felt the bed yank as someone gripped its rails. "Jessica. You need to know. You an' Electra helped me. Ow! Let go of me!" The bed shimmied. "Thank you, Jessica. You helped."

"You must go." Noelle's voice. Softer this time.

"Alright. I'm goin'."

Footsteps retreated down the hall.

Noelle's face appeared, upside down in front of Jessica's head. "Jessica? I'm sorry about that!" Noelle tucked Jessica's arm back under the covers.

Her bed accelerated down the corridor and around another corner. A different room. Bright. The whine of a helicopter's engine grew louder.

"There now! All set and dandy." Noelle rolled a long pole with a fresh bag of grey goo hanging from it. "Just in time for lunch!"

Jessica studied Noelle's profile as she fussed with the cannula at the end of the clear tube attached to an oxygen canister. Next, she reached for the stent in Jessica's chest.

Jessica opened her mouth, jaw sticking with the effort, voice croaking from lack of use.

"Don't . . . touch . . . me."

~

203

~

Colleen Shaunessy-Carillo tossed her voice recorder from hand to hand, wishing she could turn it on to document the circus she suddenly found herself at its middle. The sound of an approaching helicopter grew louder, adding to the lunacy of each word spoken by Franklin Post, Grundy Hospital's chief administrator. A portly man with a dot of gray hair on the crown of his head, Franklin juggled an armful of papers with one hand and jabbed at highlighted paragraphs with the other.

"Yes, Ms. Carillo. I agree that our policies are quite clear on allowing family access to patients in ICU. An emergency like the Centennial Park bombing was quite chaotic and many well-intentioned people rushed to the bedsides of loved ones. Miss Wyeth has had the benefit of her lawyer being with her from the moment of her injury. Quite devoted he has been, indeed. You should be thankful for Mr. Cleary's care."

"We're not here to talk about Mr. Cleary," Colleen sputtered and craned her neck in the direction of the engines. "His devotion is not the point and Mr. Wyeth needs to be on that helicopter to accompany his niece to Boston." She didn't reveal that battalion of photographers gathered, waiting for the money shot of the dedicated uncle accompanying his niece to bring her home to Boston. She had it planned out in her head. William would be holding the gurney rail in one hand and a saline pouch in the other, head down, jogging slightly beside his niece, a look of divine concern on his face.

"And Mr. Wyeth here," Franklin said, ignoring her urgency and prodding her back to the present, "enjoyed the benefit of those policies and had access to Miss Wyeth based upon that policy."

"We, um, *he* demands to get on that flight."

Franklin frowned. "It's not our habit to speak with reporters about any private matter. I'm not comfortable with you involved in this conversation." He looked at William. "You being present and allowing this questioning to happen by a reporter is tantamount to giving your permission to have private health matters discussed."

William shrugged.

"*All* health matters," Franklin emphasized.

William ducked behind Colleen. "Yeah, um, yes. You can talk in front of her."

Colleen's face reddened as she spoke. The technique of the indignant bluster worked by intimidating even the steeliest resolve to soften. Few people could withstand an interrogation by a reporter, but a blustering one was even harder to ignore. She wasn't getting what she wanted and turned up the heat of the attack a few degrees. "Mr. William Wyeth is livid at the limitations forced on him by Mr. Cleary. Visitation constraints, limited access to personal information and treatment options–"

Franklin cut her off. "We've been over this. Mr. Cleary made a compelling case to limit Mr. Wyeth's access to Miss Wyeth after establishing that Mr. Wyeth's presence caused her undue stress resulting in her unfortunate setback."

Colleen continued, rant unbroken. "Mr. Wyeth has dealt with each obstacle with the utmost restraint, but shutting him out of making decisions for her ongoing care and not permitting him to accompany her during her transfer from this hospital is heartless."

"I can assure you, we are not heartless, and our policies are clear," Franklin said. He began to blink, eyelids fluttering with a nervous twitch. "Very well then," he said, turning to Colleen, "I'm sorry, Miss Carillo, but your friend is not a relative."

Colleen rejected his statement. "There must be some mistake! This is Jessica's *uncle*, William Wyeth. He has done everything you've asked of him to prove his identity."

"And then some. And it's because of that we know conclusively that he cannot be a blood relative."

Colleen and William stood motionless in the wake of the news. Colleen was first to talk. "DNA? You ran a DNA test on him?" She punctuated each question with a wave and flick of her hands. "Who gave you permission to do that? Who knows about this?" Crimson bloomed from her neck to her scalp.

"I'm sorry. I'm not at liberty to discuss matters more."

"Who knows about this?" she demanded.

"Only the people who need to know. We have strict policies on confidentiality."

"Run the tests again!" She turned to William. "Go on! Tell them to run the tests again!"

William tugged at his cuffs and searched the floor for something to examine. He said nothing.

Colleen tried to check her anger. "Then stop the fricking transfer! You don't have permission to move her to Boston! She should stay here." Droplets of spittle, propelled by the force of her words, flew through the air and landed on Franklin's lapel.

His face closed. "I'm sorry. You can be assured we've followed all regulations and procedures to the letter. After a rigorous review, we have determined you both should leave. I'm afraid the hospital can't vary from the policies set in place. Family dynamics aside, I cannot argue with blood ties and the laws which support them." His rubber-soled shoes squeaked on the linoleum floors as he turned and walked away.

She glared at William. "What the hell is this about?"

As he spoke, she whiffed his gin-soaked breath. "I saw the report. We don't share an ancestor. There is no way we are related."

Colleen erupted with anger. "You *knew* this! You knew you were dragging me on a wild goose chase all along!"

"I swear to you I didn't . . . I couldn't . . ."

She leapt at him, slapped her palms against his shoulders, and scrambled forward each time he took a stunned step back. Her face contorted with anger. And fear. The crusted and healing wound on her back itched from nervous sweat. "You used me to help you get access to her. What's your game, Wyeth?" she demanded, forcing him backward down the hall. Her mind raced. How could she have missed the clues? The series of articles coming out on Jessica hadn't hit the mainstream press yet, just tabloid and entertainment sites. Colleen dismissed them only until she could verify their truth.

Is this somehow connected to the warning she received to stay away? She hated to admit it, but a knife in her back had a chilling effect on her usual drive to get to the bottom of things. Rather than tearing through each shred of information and hounding each source, she made a half-hearted attempt to confirm or refute rumors. Would anyone really blame her if sat back on her heels while she caught her breath?

As much as she thought she knew the game, she'd been played as a sacrificial pawn in Connaught's gambit. The truth of Jessica's lineage would come out without him lifting a finger. Eventually. The longer it took, the better, as the timing of this bombshell would only make the feeding frenzy of speculation all that more insane. *Shit! Shit! Shit!* She should never have gotten involved, but now she was in. Deep. "What are you trying to do?"

He drew his shoulder up between them to thwart the onslaught, holding his hands up for protection in a motion of surrender. "I—I don't know what to make of this."

"I staked my *reputation* on you! I helped you tell your story."

"I . . . It's . . . " William stammered, making his way to a bench. "I can't believe this is happening." He felt behind him for the seat and fell into it with a thump.

"Well, believe it. Holy Christ, this sucks." She sat beside him.

They stared in silence, the traffic in the hallways not registering. Orderlies pushed the business of the hospital with shuffled steps. Some gurneys were flat and empty, with sheets folded neatly. Others were lumped with bodies. Lunchtime approached, and tiered stainless steel carts loaded with meals rolled soundlessly, mixing aromas of food with disinfectants and medicines. Colleen's stomach lurched.

William shook his head with disbelief. "All this time, the stories you've written focused on Jessica as my estranged niece and me as the stalwart and loyal uncle who is trying to rekindle contact with her." His voice caught as he repeated, "stalwart and loyal."

"Yeah, so?" Colleen spat. William's self-pity nauseated her. No way she was going to make the conversation easy. She turned her back to him.

She started to dig through her messenger bag for a tissue, averting her face. Giving him the satisfaction of seeing her cry wasn't going to happen.

A loud sniff startled her.

William sat, shoulders hunched, fist pressed to his nose with eyes screwed shut. His cheeks distended before giving a loud *pff pff*. Seconds later, a tear rolled down his skin.

Colleen shoved her wadded tissue into his hand. "Get a hold of yourself."

The muffled sound of a helicopter lifting off battered the hallway and was joined by his soft blubbering sounds. People slowed and stole quick glances, no doubt thinking they were looking at a man who had received devastating medical news on a family member. Cancer? Surgery? Terminal?

Nope, she mused. *Just a gravy train leaving the station without him.*

He popped his head up and looked around, eyes blinking in bewilderment. "I . . . I have to get back to Boston."

The corners of Colleen's mouth puckered with irritation. "Yeah. No rush."

Boston, Massachusetts

THE FUSS AND gear of hospitals intimidated Declan. Stand in the wrong place and a person risked being plowed over by anything from a doctor responding to a *stat!* page or a janitor, mop and bucket in hand, rushing to eliminate whatever a body had just eliminated. Not knowing what each part of the whole would do at any point in time unnerved him. He liked knowing. He liked planning based on that knowledge. He liked being right.

He hated surprises.

The medical staff of Grundy and Silvern executed Jessica's transfer to Boston flawlessly. The helicopter lifted off from Atlanta in blue skies and settled in cloudy, but the staff made every effort to be sunny. Their good humor irritated him.

Wind from the chopper's blades buffeted nurses and orderlies as they rushed beneath them, heads down, and grabbed the railings of Jessica's gurney. Plastic bags swung from IV poles. Oxygen canisters stood at the ready, plastic tubing and cannulas in place. Declan stood to the side, watching. He catalogued each face and examined body language for any hesitation that would belie nerves or a role poorly executed.

Jessica was back in the land of the Charity and now was not the time to let his guard down. Her life depended on it.

And his.

The oxygen tanks held his interest the most. Similar to the ones he found at Magnus' home, they were the last items to be unloaded and received the least amount of attention. Jessica didn't need help breathing, but they were part of the protocol and readiness for transporting a patient. Nurses with clipboards scanned equipment and checked off items on a list. The canisters barely received more than a glance.

Two orderlies in white scrubs wheeled Jessica across the landing pad and through the double doors, the equipment and attendants trailing in a parade for the sick and ailing. The nurse with the clipboard took one last look at the area and followed, her hair bouncing in time to her quick steps.

Declan joined her. "Everything in order?"

She smiled. "Yes. Perfect. You must be Mr. Cleary. Nice to meet you. I'm Tracy Ridley, transport coordinator."

He walked with her through the hall, letting his senses track Jessica's progress. "There's a lot to keep track of." He infused his eyes with warmth.

"There is. I make sure all the personnel and equipment are prepared for any emergency in flight, medical or otherwise. Our first concern is for the patient, but we consider everything from the crew to the craft. The Grundy team did an excellent job. I want you to know she's in great hands. I know you had some concerns bringing her here."

"Just being cautious. My concerns had nothing to do with the care she'll receive with your team, but only for her welfare. I was concerned about the stress she would feel during the move." He motioned to the canisters. "Seems like a lot of oxygen for one person."

"Not just for her. We have to consider the attendants, too. An oxygen canister is standard equipment on any kind of commercial flight, but an obvious need on medical transports. And it's not just oxygen we carry. There are other gases on board."

"Other gases?" He stepped closer to her, intentionally entering her personal space, and smiled. He tried to make his interest be about Tracy and not the topic.

She gave a little shudder. "The med flight crew has to be prepared for all types of emergencies. Because a medical or mechanical issue may cause us to land outside of an airport facility, we carry nitrogen gas, too, to ensure the tires are inflated to the proper pressure. The tires on the helicopter are filled with nitrogen because it's less susceptible to temperature changes and isn't a fire hazard like oxygen in case of a crash."

"Fascinating." He rounded his eyes and shook his head in amazement at her knowledge. "Must be pretty important not to confuse the two. You know, filling tires with pure oxygen or patients with nitrogen."

Tracy fiddled with papers on her clipboard in a poor effort to feign disinterest. "Oh no! That would never happen. Nitrogen is all around us. It's in our food and the air we breathe, so having detectable amounts in our systems is normal. Prolonged inhalation of pure nitrogen is fatal and virtually undetectable in autopsy. A nitrogen gas-induced death looks like a death from natural causes. A death from carbon monoxide poisoning causes tissues to turn cherry red. With nitrogen, there are no physical clues that a poisoning or adverse event occurred."

"Oh?" He let his eyes sweep over her. No ring. Blouse open one button too low. Toned. He moved an inch closer. She wanted to be noticed. He wanted her to talk.

She obliged, moistening her lips before spoke. "Each gas is odorless and a mistake would be hard to discover until it's too late. Inhale carbon monoxide, from say, vehicle exhaust, and you'll feel sick, like a flu coming on. When a person inhales carbon *di*oxide, they feel starved for air. You know, like they're suffocating. People breathing nitrogen gas feel no such symptoms."

"Phew," he said, blowing a thin stream of air through his lips, impressed. "There's so much to know!"

Tracy's cheeks bloomed. "The feeling of suffocation comes from the buildup of carbon dioxide, but nitrogen slowly shuts body functions down without that panicky 'I need air' feeling."

Declan rocked back on his heels. "The person doesn't feel anything? They think everything's normal?"

Tracy's patter of words increased. "Many accidental deaths occur from nitrogen suffocation each year from industrial workers using the gas for different operations. But you'd never have to worry about any mistakes like that happening here. We keep the vendors who supply medical and industrial use gases separate, as well as storing them in difference locations on the craft. Also, the hookups are unique. A medical use delivery tube uses a very different connection to an oxygen canister than tubing to a nitrogen canister."

"Wow," he said, hanging on her every word, "I'll bet you have to get the gases from vendors located far away and have to have a lot of permits to get it."

"Not at all! Boston is a hub of pharmaceutical research, development, and manufacturing and it's very easy to secure any amount of gas. There's no need for any kind of permits or licenses to get gases and we have our pick of vendors here."

Declan didn't respond as he absorbed the information.

They approached the elevator bank just as the doors closed with Jessica inside. Her face was void of all color. White. Drawn. One orderly turned and stared at Declan. With a motion that looked like an innocent scratch of his back, the orderly stretched out his arm and showed his forearm. The tattoo of the shamrock sliced by a dagger, the symbol of the Charity, was clear. But another mark bloomed next to the image. A red rose with a thorny stem encircled the shamrock, and the two symbols blended together in a way to show evolution and growth. The orderly smiled and thrust his chin toward Declan with a "Don't worry, she's home now" message clear in his greeting.

Declan's stomach clenched.

Tracy followed his eyes. "You really don't have to worry about her, Mr. Cleary. She's pretty lucky to have someone as dedicated to her as you are. A lot of patients here can go for days without a visitor. I understand you've requested a convertible easy chair to stay with her."

"I don't want her to feel alone."

"Well, Silvern is a twenty-four, seven, three sixty-five place. It's a luxury to be alone here."

"Thanks. I'll keep that in mind."

She looked at his briefcase. "You're traveling pretty light for someone who's intending to camp out indefinitely."

"I'll be coming and going at odd times."

"Let me know when you're here. I'll stop by to say hello."

"No need." He shut down his charm as quickly as he had turned it on.

The worry ignited from his last visit to Magnus' house had triggered him to have the canister he removed analyzed. The report had arrived that morning. The canister, clearly marked as oxygen and having all of the appropriate safeguards in place, contained with pure nitrogen. The error was not accidental. The canister, with all of the hookups and nozzles in place for facemasks or cannulas for human use, was intentionally filled with a gas known to be lethal when inhaled on a prolonged basis.

If Declan had any doubts how Magnus died, they evaporated.

Magnus was murdered.

Declan wished to God he was wrong.

He had reviewed the tapes retrieved from Magnus' secret room frame by frame. He cross-referenced dates with travel itineraries and triple-checked everything against conversations, letters, and all other documents depicting Michael Connaught's whereabouts.

At first, what he had seen on the tapes confused him. Date-stamped days before Magnus' death, their grainy images showed Michael entering his father's office. Without audio, Declan couldn't be sure what they talked about, but the allegedly estranged father and son were anything but. The men shared a Scotch, bodies relaxed and open, the friendship clear in the first meeting. Then the tone changed, and Magnus rose from his chair, holding the desk for support, jabbing a bony finger in the air toward Michael's nose. Michael stood up and shoved Magnus; the old man stumbled backward into his chair, face contorted with shock and rage. Michael leaned over the desk and gripped Magnus' shirt collar in his hand, pulling the old man forward. Words were exchanged. The next minutes showed Magnus' office being flooded with men, and Michael was roughed up and dragged out.

Then, according to the date time-stamped on the tape, the day before Magnus died, at two o'clock in the morning, a man entered Magnus' office, hunched over something tucked under his arm. Most of the lights were off and only dim shadows and outlines were visible. The man opened the cabinet behind the desk and stayed there, crouched. Without the benefit of context, Declan assumed the man was rifling through files, looking for a document or even a bottle of fine Scotch. The man stayed less than two minutes. Declan had sent the tape to be enhanced and reviewed it carefully. When the man turned to survey the office, Declan froze the image. Michael's face, with the strong Connaught brow and set jaw, was unmistakable.

Could an image digitally manipulated and enhanced persuade him into seeing something that wasn't true? Declan wanted more than anything to be wrong.

With Tracy's words ringing in his ears, he knew the man in the tape had remained at the cabinet long enough to switch out tanks and attach nozzles and cannula to a tank filled with pure nitrogen.

Magnus Connaught died because he breathed in nitrogen gas thinking he was breathing oxygen. He didn't gasp for air. He didn't feel sick. He just slipped away peacefully. Michael Connaught had found the perfect murder weapon and had executed what he thought was the perfect murder.

Even Magnus' autopsy results supported natural causes. Magnus' death was unattended. He was found slumped over his desk and no witnesses saw him die. An autopsy is standard procedure for all such deaths, especially if the stiff was the head of an organized crime syndicate. For an elderly man known to be in poor health, the exam would not be thorough unless someone had a reason to be suspicious. Finding evidence of nitrogen poisoning is difficult—even if the coroner knows to look for it. Without evidence of physical trauma and with the standard toxicology screens being negative, the inquiries stopped not long after Magnus' heart did.

Too bad for Michael that Declan had uncontestable proof of motive, opportunity, and intent. Oh, and he had the smoking gun in the form of a videotape Michael didn't know existed.

But what if it wasn't Michael? What if he was wrong?

What had Electra called these times? Right. This was Declan's come-to-Jesus moment.

He had no intention of meeting The Man himself until he was damned good and ready. And old.

Whether it was Michael in that tape or not did not matter. What Declan had done was an act of treason. He investigated a death that had no suspicions surrounding it. Magnus' death escaped any additional investigation. A sick and ailing man died from an extreme amount of stress resulting from a murder indictment. No questions swarmed around the corpse. The dog lay sleeping.

Declan had kicked the dog awake and now questions bred like flies.

Magnus had killed men for less. If disloyalty was even suspected, a family would be without a father in the blink of an eye.

If Michael could set up the perfect murder, what else—or *who* else—could he set up? If someone else killed Magnus, an assassin was on the loose and it was only a matter of time before his skills would be used to target Michael. Declan's job was to protect his boyhood friend at all costs.

A thick film formed in his stomach. The odds were overwhelming that Magnus' assassin was sitting in a sprawling mansion in Northern Ireland.

Declan knew better than anyone how the Charity operated and he knew that as strongly as Michael insisted the Charity was dead, the machine chugged on. A rose by any other name is still a rose and the orderly's tattoo signaled Michael's embracing of all things Magnus.

He had been careful in getting his information, but it was only a matter of time before another Charity operative, working alone on an unrelated issue, would stumble across a clue that would lead to the room. Once the room was exposed, Michael would know he was surveilled and that a tape existed. Michael would not bother asking why Declan didn't bring those facts to his attention immediately.

Even if the existence of the room was unintentionally withheld from Michael, he would know immediately that his perfect murder had been discovered.

Charity justice was unquestioning and quick. He could only guess how much more efficient justice by 2100 and MMC, Ltd., Michael's Rose, would be.

COLLEEN WATCHED AS Agent Baxter held the plastic bag containing the dagger up to the light, turning it to different angles. Two blazes of color crept up his cheeks as he squinted with concentration.

"Cheap tourist crap. Must be a *million* of these out there." Baxter turned and looked at Colleen. "You sure you're alright, Miss?"

Colleen fought the urge to roll her eyes. "Yes. Fine. I must've said that a *million* times," cringing inwardly as her fatigue and irritation crept to the surface. "Look. I'm sorry to be snippy, but you called me in here to talk about some of the articles I've written, and all you're doing is staring at a knife in a bag."

She put her coffee cup down on the long wooden table. The room was one of the 'friendly' interrogation rooms at FBI headquarters. Along with the mirrored wall—behind which she knew was a camera and other agents scrutinizing her every move—she had a window. Lucky her. Maybe the agents felt that giving her a view of the grey and monolithic Government Center building in downtown Boston would soften her up.

They needn't have worried about getting her to open up to them. Amanda Boch, Colleen's best friend since grade school and her inside source at the FBI, had set the meeting up. Amanda was a fireplug of a woman with a cap of black curly hair. The bond between friends was strong—partly because it was never tested and partly because they were made from the same stock. They were buddies from Southie. When Amanda said agents from Louisville, Kentucky needed help, Colleen immediately said yes. She wanted to help as much as she could. After all, doing so would not only help their investigation, but would strengthen relationships with her sources. Right?

"Great work getting close to the uncle. Gotta hand it to you, you know how to cultivate your sources." Baxter offered Colleen a stick of gum. Big Red cinnamon. Her favorite. Amanda must have prepped him.

She declined with a wave of her hand. "What do you mean?"

"Well, getting him to open up about Jessica as a little girl and implying that he was the source that tipped you about her return to the States was brilliant."

Colleen busied herself with a pad and pen. The humiliation she felt at being duped into believing William was a blood relation to Jessica was too fresh to see beyond her hurt. She had spent the past days avoiding the newsroom until late at night when she was sure no one was there—a reporter's version of putting her tail between her legs. Her editor had browbeat her, but kept her on the story. For that, she was grateful, but the stony gaze she received told her to tread carefully. And now she was in an FBI interrogation room being asked about William Wyeth. They knew something and pinning the tip on William was a way to keep her off-balance. She responded with a measured, "It was a great tip, all right."

"Problem is, it wasn't William Wyeth who told you. How *did* you know Miss Wyeth's jet was going to land in Louisville?"

Colleen darted a *what the fah?* look at Amanda. The interview was off to a hell of a bad start. "I don't divulge my sources. Sorry."

Baxter smiled. "You not being forthright with us on the simple questions isn't going to make the rest of our conversation run smoothly. We don't have a lot of time here, but Electra Lavielle asked our office to confirm a phone call had been made from Northern Ireland to you during the time the jet was en route to the U.S. Our sources indicate the call originated from Michael Connaught's estate."

"Information on Jessica's return was given to Mrs. Lavielle as a professional courtesy. You know. One journalist to another. She must have guessed the source and used your office to confirm," she sputtered. "It's outrageous you know this!"

"Well, I'd say, take it up with her, but you can't very well sue a dead woman, can you?"

At the mention of Electra, Colleen's bravado seeped out of her like air from a balloon. She mourned Electra's death with a sharpness reserved only for people close to her heart either by friendship or professional admiration. Although they had been on opposite sides of an issue more than once, Electra was a woman Colleen respected and admired.

Her wilting was also due to her source, and it wasn't a raspy voice on the end of the line with a date, time, and place. From the moment Colleen received the tip that Jessica was kicked out of Northern Ireland, she'd become part of a larger game she struggled to understand.

"Calling Electra after learning Jessica was on her way back to the States made sense," she said, trying to keep a defensive edge out of her voice. "Louisville is practically Electra's backyard and everyone in the business knows Electra was the engine and the fuel behind major news outlets. So what if I hoped to better position myself with one of the most powerful media moguls I knew by giving a heads up on Jessica's arrival? I thought doing so would put my name on the top of the list to be on the inside of another one of Electra's scoops in the future." The chair felt hard under her butt. She shifted. "Get a tip. Give a tip. Big deal."

"Yeah. Sure," Baxter said, sucking on the inside of his mouth. "Too bad for you she didn't leap at the opportunity to be in on the tip of the year. My hunch is she declined to help you for a reason. Maybe she was too much of a friend to Miss Wyeth to rally the troops."

Colleen managed to mold her face into an indignant glare to hide the truth. It wasn't out of loyalty to Jessica that Electra declined. She wanted to believe Electra was trying to protect her own ass, but wondered if she had missed something. She remembered their last conversation too keenly.

"All news from the U.K. shows Michael as a benevolent philanthropist who is madly in love with Jessica," Colleen had said to Electra in one of their last phone conversations, "and that he wants what's best for her."

"Be leery of a wolf in sheep's clothing, child. That could be a spawn of the devil you're working with," Electra had warned.

"You could be right. He probably is. But if I'm being asked to do something that's completely legal and logical, why not use the tip? I want to see where this goes."

Colleen remembered the long pause on the other line before Electra spoke. "I have a hard time believing that a man in love would do something his beloved would abhor. My daddy used to say, 'When in doubt, don't.' If you do his bidding and rally the reporters now, you're going to be asked to do more. Even if you're not asked directly, the seed of bias in giving you a tip of this size will soften your opinion of Connaught enterprises. They offered you a carrot and you nibbled, encouraging you to view their actions through a rose-colored prism.

If you hesitate doing your job of investigation, you give that snake pit the benefit of the doubt. The Connaughts are seeding your thoughts that staying on the good side of them will mean getting the inside scoop on other major stories. If you decide to play this game, all I'm saying is be careful. If their carrots don't work, a stick is next. Keep your eyes open and your back covered. Don't let your naked ambition get you killed."

Recalling their conversation made Colleen's back itch. She looked at the dagger Baxter had placed on the table and shivered. She'd already experienced a chilling effect on her usual abilities to do her job. Was that what was happening?

She kept the conversation on what the agents knew and didn't confess her own fears. "Fine. So I got a big tip. A jet landed at an airport in broad daylight. It's not like I exposed some big conspiracy."

"Not at all. You did good."

Baxter's disingenuous smile made Colleen's skin crawl.

Nervous energy flowed through her arms to her fingers, making them drum the table's top. "I don't want to do well by them," she snarled.

"Then what do you want?"

"I'm a careful journalist. I don't write anything I don't have corroboration on. I keep my sources safe and my facts straight. Everything points to Michael Connaught wanting us to believe he has forfeited his father's criminal ties and has taken up an honest living. I got that tip on Jessica because . . ." She faltered.

She hated to admit the truth. Months before, Electra had stood in the way of Colleen breaking the story of her career that would have exposed all of the Connaughts' dirty deals and put her in the running for a Pulitzer. The thought that her action to squelch the story was misinterpreted as allegiance to Connaught's political efforts nauseated her. Was that why she was on the inside track now? She took the tip to prove her worth as a reporter to Electra despite her warning. Colleen wanted to prove that Jessica Wyeth was a terrorist, funded and trained by Connaught. She wanted to break that story wide open whether she had help from the FBI or not.

She finished with a weak, "The focus of the publicity on her will, er, will," she stammered.

Baxter placed his palms on the table and leaned toward her. She could smell the remnants of falafel on his breath. "Forget it. I don't care why Connaught called you. He did, so he feels some kind of connection with you. That's all we care about." He looked over his shoulder at Amanda. "Michael is stepping into his father's shoes. We all agree you'd be dead if he didn't have another use for you."

"Or turning over a new leaf," Amanda said.

"Excuse me?" Baxter crimped his mouth, irritated.

"You said it before. Michael could be trying to cultivate a new life. If so, he wouldn't order a prime connection stabbed." Amanda didn't blink or turn away when she spoke, holding her ground. Colleen liked that. "You said keep judgments to a minimum until the evidence is in. I'm making sure we can see things for what they are."

Relief that Amanda had her back, and fear that events unfolded too quickly to progress carefully, combined as Colleen drew in an unsteady breath. "What about the old guy? Magnus' brother?"

"Intel says he's suffered a stroke. He never stepped up after Magnus died. Anything that happens from now on will point to the son," said Baxter.

"I know," Colleen said. "I need to find out what he's up to."

Baxter continued. "The younger Connaught is complex. Amanda has a point. Michael is pushing for a major image rehabilitation. Publicly, he's shunning his father's businesses. Privately, money is flowing. He wants to make a big splash and firm up his image as the new kid on the billionaire's block. His trips to Switzerland and the Middle East are supposed to be low-key affairs, but nothing travels faster than a secret."

Amanda placed photos on the table. Her navy blue jacket opened slightly revealing a shoulder holster strapped over her pink blouse. Her badge and ID hung from a leather case clipped to her waistband. "We received these from the INTERPOL office in Manchester, England. We learned about them from a reporter you had contact with." She waited as Colleen had a moment to familiarize herself with them.

The photographs showed scenes of a private airport terminal outside of Manchester and captured Jessica Wyeth unloading crates and other gear from a private jet with MMC on the tail. Colleen knew the reporter, Dally Thorpe, was a shoddy writer for a crappy tabloid in the U.K. Any information that came from Dally would be questionable at best and an outright lie at worst.

She looked up. "You need to fast forward through the *verifiable* facts. I'm not interested in spin or conjecture."

Amanda spoke, animated. "The pictures provide evidence that Jessica Wyeth traveled with a large quantity of goods and arrived days prior to the massive bombing at the Manchester shopping mall."

"I'd heard Wyeth was the mule for the explosives. All you have here are pictures of her that confirm rumors, except for one important point," Colleen said as her eyes narrowed as she leaned forward. "You're missing the piece that documents what is *in* the crates. Horse gear? Plastique? Gelignite? Lingerie? Saddle blankets? Pretty different picture depending upon what kind of proof you have."

"Wyeth isn't some sweet young innocent. Before the Olympics, she ordered a guy beat up by her thugs and even landed a few blows herself. As for the bombing? We got the proof." Baxter picked up a file and moved to the window. Sunlight through the grimy glass was bright enough to turn the stubble on his shaved head to a halo—the look incongruous. He reached into the file and threw down an envelope.

Colleen's eyes widened. "That's addressed to me. What are you doing with it?"

Baxter shot a look at Amanda.

"The envelope arrived around the same time we received the pictures. We busted up a gunrunning ring out of Gloucester," Amanda said, taking the cue. "We'd been watching a small fishing outfit for a while. Two boat operation. Under the radar. One boat leaves with a hold full of ice and guns and returns with fish and cash. We tracked them to the Irish Sea. Kinda far if you logged George's Bank as your fishing ground. Fast boats. Very nimble. When they docked, we arrested them. A search found a bundle of letters to be hand-delivered to different people in the Boston area. Interesting stuff that exposed networks we didn't know about. Anyway, this envelope, addressed to you, was part of the haul. No return address. Guys in forensics had it swabbed and dusted. Clean. No markings as to who it's from, but we have an idea."

Colleen's heart beat hard in her chest as she put the pieces together. "These were supposed to have been delivered to me anonymously. I was supposed to dig further." She slipped a paper out of the sleeve. "It looks like a sworn statement of some kind. An affidavit."

"We had the name on the document confirmed. The alleged affiant is a suspect in the Manchester bombing. Seems the guy isn't too swift," Baxter said, tapping his temple, "but he states he swore out this affidavit in return for leniency."

She read in silence. "Holy shit! This guy, this . . . this," she looked at the name, "This Timothy guy says he loaded the boxes full of explosives in front of Jessica. That she knew about the bombing and willingly participated."

"Right. Exactly," said Amanda.

"So, what are you going to do with this information?" Colleen slipped the paper back into the envelope. She placed it back on the table but didn't take her hand off it. If it was true, this paper was the holy grail she was looking for, and it was supposed to have gotten to her through an anonymous source. Events were unfolding in a way that put her on alert.

If she spilled her theories on Jessica, that she was a ready and willing participant in the Manchester bombing and could easily be the key player in a domestic terrorist campaign, she risked too much. Divulging a theory based upon conversations with William Wyeth and the facts she'd uncovered by herself, she was afraid she would be forced to turn over all of her notes. Expose the DNA findings before she had a chance to break the news in a headline? Not a chance. If she brought the FBI in before she published, she'd risk losing control of her own story line.

Sure she owed Amanda a bite or two, but the whole enchilada? No way. It was Jessica's rotten luck that brought her into contact with Michael Connaught just when she was most vulnerable, but she had little backbone to resist his steady pressure to corrupt her in the same manner Patty Hearst had been. And the DNA finding on the heels of the Olympic bombing? That tidbit was hers to publish when she damned well pleased, but this meeting might result in her pushing up her timeline a bit.

Her case kept getting stronger. A woman without an identity or a family is protected and cultivated by an international crime syndicate. By getting the woman, she'd hook the network. She was the one to make it happen.

Gloating would have to wait. First, she had to figure out what the FBI wanted from her.

"What are you going to do?" she pressed.

"That depends on what you would have done if this had gotten to you directly," said Baxter.

Colleen looked at Amanda, then Baxter, and back, confused. "Aren't you under some kind of code to act on this information as soon as it's received? Aren't you supposed to be running off to arrest her or something?"

Baxter cleared his throat. "That Centennial Park bombing was one of those bad things that yielded some good results. She's not going anywhere."

Colleen felt her skin heat. "*Good results*? Are you serious? What kind of callous ass are you?" The words spilled out before she could bite them back. "Some nut with a grudge planted a satchel full of nails in the middle of the Olympics and she was unlucky enough to be there. She was a millimeter away from being a lifelong veggie and you're saying that's *good*?"

"If our information on her is correct, it wasn't just some 'nut with a grudge.' She got what she had planned for someone else, so sympathy is not something she's gonna get from me. She's bedridden and not a flight risk. All of her communications, from visitors to doctor visits to phone calls, are mined for information. From my perspective, her rotten luck makes my job easier and anything that makes my job easier is a good thing," he barked back. "And to answer your question, no, we don't have to take action unless we are convinced that doing so is in the best interests of the public or the investigation. For the time being, we can marshal our facts together without tipping our hand." He tilted his head toward the envelope. "So, if this had gone directly to you, what would you have done?"

"First, I'd verify its authenticity. I'd use my network. If that didn't yield results, I'd ask for help from . . . from," she hesitated and looked at Amanda.

"Go ahead. You can say you'd ask me. We're all on the same team here." Amanda smiled in that lopsided way that put Colleen on edge. They had known each other too long not to know one another's clues. Amanda was nervous, but about what? Was it about exposing Amanda as the "off the record" source for many of Colleen's leads? Or was Amanda sensing that Colleen had more to hide and was giving her a graceful out?

Colleen smiled at Baxter, treading carefully. "I'd ask for help from Amanda. She's one of the best agents I know. By the book all the way."

"Good enough," replied Baxter, his jowl color receding to normal limits. "I want you to follow the leads exactly as you would normally do. No variations."

Amanda drew in a sharp breath. "You have a tail on her! You're trying to see exactly who she contacts, when, and where. I'm the lead contact in Boston on this matter. You're supposed to check actions through with me. Why wasn't I informed of this?"

Baxter sniffed. "You're being informed now. Calm down, already. It's not like we didn't know the two of you might help each other out once in a while."

Amanda started to say more, straightened her shoulders, and leaned her hip on the table. "That wasn't what we discussed."

"No? When a terrorist threat is leveled at the United States, or when a suspected terrorist is attempting to organize a hostile event, we can and will dog anyone involved. Your friend here was contacted directly by the very organization we initially thought was behind these bombings and was requested to notify her colleagues to cover Wyeth's return to the States. For all we know, her response could have been a signal for this network to spring into action. We will monitor both of you for your safety as well as for our investigation."

"So, Connaught is the focus of your investigation?" Colleen watched the tension build between the agents and smiled to herself. She was back on the trail of something mammoth. Connaught and Wyeth planning a terrorist attack together? The possible headlines were beyond her wildest dreams.

Amanda cut Baxter off from replying. "No," she said, waving her open palms in front of her in an 'absolutely not' gesture. Baxter stepped back. "We're focused on Wyeth and her network. Those articles on her mother," Amanda sifted through papers and pointed to a name, "Bridget Heinchon Harvey, are a concern to us. The mother was expelled from Northern Ireland as a terrorist. We believe she radicalized her daughter to continue fighting for expulsion of the United Kingdom from Northern Ireland. From the faked family to recent travels, Wyeth is the one who has our full attention."

"You're not following up on Connaught at all?" Colleen said, incredulous.

"Until Connaught does something overtly connected to a crime, we cannot assume the pattern established by his father will continue."

Baxter moved his mouth close to Amanda's ear. Colleen thought he was making a show of trying to keep the disagreement between them. "I thought we agreed."

"I've been working this family's Boston's connections for years," Amanda whispered. "You need to listen to me."

Amanda bent her body around Baxter and spoke to Colleen. "That tip helped us identify Wyeth and her network. Our hunch is our investigation is being aided by supplying you with information like these pictures and affidavit. We appreciate the insights."

Baxter stepped back and looked from Amanda to Colleen as if deciding who to back. He clenched his jaw and raised his head in a prideful motion that turned Colleen's stomach. "We're interviewing more contacts in the States, but we're confident in our direction."

Colleen stood up abruptly. "Are you saying you think Connaught's one of the *good* guys? You just called *me* out for complying with one of his requests, and now you're dropping him down in priority?" She placed her hands on her hips and stood as tall as she could. Even so, she had to tilt her head back to look at them.

Amanda smiled, lips parting to show one half of her mouth. "Our eyes are wide open, but first things first."

"And that knife in my back, you think Wyeth is responsible for that?" Colleen's face reddened with anger. Amanda, her closest friend and ally, donned the magic cloak of 'agent' and had disappeared.

"Anything is possible," Amanda said.

Colleen was too stunned to speak as they walked to the elevators. Their shoes squeaked on the linoleum floors, filling the silence. Her reporter's sixth sense began to tingle. The pieces were falling into place and everything fit together neatly. It was so right, but very wrong in a way she couldn't put her finger on. Evidence swarmed around Jessica like sharks in chum-filled waters. Colleen had trouble swallowing the bait.

The elevator chimed and doors slid open. A group of people stepped out. Colleen was too engrossed in her thoughts to be aware of everyone around her. She shook hands with Baxter and Amanda, turned, and walked into someone. The solidity of his chest felt like she hit a wall.

Shouldering her way onto the crowded elevator, Colleen looked up just as the doors closed. She shuddered as she looked into two unblinking black eyes.

Beacon Hill
Boston, Massachusetts

LACK OF IDEAS was not one of William Wyeth's weaknesses. So, when he sat in his living room and drummed his fingers on the marble-top side table, narrowing his focus was difficult.

First, his mind scoured every conversation Margaret and Jim had had with him about their marriage and her first pregnancy or, rather, her alleged pregnancy. Then he examined every facial expression Jessica had and matched it against his own family tree. He grew angry when he realized her beauty and intelligence were not Wyeth-given—something he had taken pride in, thinking no Irishman could ever produce such child, and that the favorable and dominant Wyeth genes had triumphed over weaker and defective Irish ones.

When his memory finally settled on the family's wake, pieces started to fall into place. Playing the fool was not something he would tolerate.

The damned Irish took over as if the Wyeths had no say in how to treat a dead Englishman. It hardly mattered to William that Jim had long forsaken the family's blood and politics. Remembering the song and whiskey of that day made William's blood boil. No doubt Margaret's ailing sister and that stall mucker Gus Adams were Jessica's real parents. He had suspected as much. Margaret claiming her unmarried sister's illegitimate child as her own was an age-old ploy of Irish Catholics. Sometimes, a mother saw a daughter's need. Other times a sibling stepped up. Inevitably, someone would claim a budding bastard as their own to save a reputation and family name.

The ruse worked well enough for polite circles, but desperation made him dig into Bridget's past and search for adoption records.

Getting information from either Ireland was impossible, and he found nothing on Bridget since she entered the States. The solid wall of family kept him from learning the truth years ago. He admonished himself as a fool for believing them. So much so, he even dismissed recent revelations as a publicity-mongering ploy.

He read every article and listened to every entertainment news segment on Jessica and Bridget. Enmeshed in the details of bringing Jessica back to Boston, he remained ignorant of any peril. He promised Colleen sole and exclusive access to him. She set up his interviews and he had no reason to doubt her competence or judgment. Colleen didn't pay much attention to rumors of Jessica's rebel mother. She didn't pepper him with questions about the aunt, so he felt comfortable ignoring calls and pleas from other reporters who wanted details. Besides, it was so much easier just to sit back and watch.

While memories loaded and ricocheted around his liquor-rotted brain, self-righteous entitlement filled the gap where feelings of shock and anger once flowed. Recollections freshened of the indignities he had experienced for being the lesser Wyeth. Jim was the handsome one, the smart one, and the one who got out from under their father's overbearing control. Everything Jim touched minted money. William cursed one failed opportunity after another. Jim bailed him out of a series of jams. Not without a price. Jim made William beg, hat in hand, for each measly check. Jim should have been happy to lend his brother whatever was asked.

He could almost hear Jim's voice say, *Lend*?

William smirked. Didn't all family gifts start off with, "You know I'll pay you back as soon as I can," and end with, "Payment schedule? I thought this was a gift!"

So what if William fell behind on some of his loans? Families were supposed to support one another.

The sound of keys jangling and being fumbled into a lock rang in his ears moments before Connor Battington stumbled across the threshold.

"Happy hour at Top of the Hub?" William didn't bother to hide his disdain.

Connor stopped midstride, blinking his eyes to adjust to the sudden dark. "I thought you'd be busy playing Spurned Uncle Willie." He swayed and braced a hand on the table.

"I'm not her uncle and I'm devastated at the revelation." He placed his open palm over his heart and lowered his head.

Connor snorted. "I can't be the only one who isn't surprised. Not one thing about her reminded me of you. Guess you're gonna rent out more rooms now, huh?"

William turned his head toward a rectangular silhouette on the wall. The faded wallpaper and grimy outline marked where a painting had hung, untouched, for decades. "Not right away. Skinner Auctioneers finally got their hands on my Dwight Blaney oil. They say the auction price might break records. That will keep me for a while."

Connor wove his way into the living room and sat down in a wingback chair. A cloud of dust rose around his butt. "Seems a bit premature to be selling Daddy's favorites, don't you think?"

"Hardly." He cocked his head. "Premature?"

"Well, my buddies at the Hub and I were talking. You fought a long battle, but the only reason you're in this mess is because probate finally decreed your brother's estate to go to his sole surviving heir, right?"

William sat up straighter. "Right."

"You spent a good chunk of that life insurance payoff to try to get it, but she resurfaced just in time. Pulled that rug right out from under you." Even sloshed, his words and meaning were crisp.

"You don't need to remind me."

"Well, the way my buddies and I see it is like this. If she's no Wyeth and your investigation didn't show up any adoption records or anything like that, seems like that inheritance should have gone to you."

Pieces of the puzzle fell into place. "Well, you say *I'm* the victim?" William rotated his shoulders to turn to him.

"Victim? You? Mr. Blueblood is a victim? Hardly. No one's gonna fall for any 'Poor me. I didn't get my inheritance' crap."

"No?"

"You were a target. A victim of a fraud of this magnitude means two things." Connor waved his index finger in the air. "One. Victims deserve to be paid damages."

William raised his eyebrows. "And two?"

Connor wagged two fingers. "And two? This makes for one hell of a story."

Was it possible? Once again, when he thought the moment was at its most bleak, hope bloomed.

"You mean, Jessica Wyeth stole my inheritance and I have to get it back?"

"Damn straight," Connor said, pushing himself to his feet. "You should call that reporter pal of yours and tell her to get on this."

William peered at Connor. Did that little shit know the story of Jessica's lineage blew up in Colleen's face? Was Connor being facetious or goading him? "I think it's best to leave Ms. Shaunessy-Carillo out of the equation."

Connor paused. "What? No way. You owe it to her. I don't know what you have to say to her, but my take is she'll forgive and forget as soon as you kiss and tell. I gotta tell ya, this story is going to put you over the top. Turn the Jessica Wyeth story on its head. She was bad from the start and never one of us."

The news angles were too delicious not to savor. William's mouth almost watered.

Connor looked at the wall where the Blaney once hung. "I'd stop that sale if I were you. My buddies are adamant you can really make a stink about this." He wove his way to the door and paused. "Oh, right," he said, patting his chest and hips, searching through his pockets. "They wanted me to give you this."

He tossed a flattened and rumpled red rose on the table.

West Roxbury, Massachusetts

COLLEEN DIDN'T LIKE having a secret admirer.

She didn't like feeling stalked and she sure as shit didn't like roses.

She wished the asshole who sent her bouquets would stop. It was bad enough that the red monstrosities filled her tiny cubicle at the *Globe*. After a while, even the secretaries she had tried to pawn the roses off to didn't want them, as they insisted interfering with Colleen's love life would bring bad luck to their own fledgling romances. Colleen was coming off a horrific divorce and they didn't want to jinx progress. It was almost beyond horrible that her colleagues at the newsdesk jammed their elbows into each other's ribs and joked about her "getting some" and "who's the lucky guy."

The worst was arriving home and finding a dozen long-stemmed red roses with baby's breath and feather ferns waiting on her doorstep. Her landlady stood at her screen door with arms crossed, waiting to get the first scoop on Colleen's new suitor.

"Sorry to disappoint you, Rhonda," Colleen said as she picked up the vase. "It's the guys at the office having a fun wager at my expense."

Rhonda, a short, round woman with blunt cut bangs, would not be put off the scent of a new relationship. "I'm not buyin' that fish story for a second. These roses've set some poor jerk back a good fifty bucks. Those guys you work with can't even cough up a fiver for a draught during happy hour. No way. Somebody's serious on you."

"The only thing they're serious about is seeing who I'll pin it on. If I start mooning over somebody, they'll get to thinking I'm secretly wishing it was true. They get a good laugh and I'll want to crawl under a rock. Here," she said, handing Rhonda the vase, "take these and enjoy. I can't stand the look of them."

Rhonda gripped the vase with two hands. The roses towered over her. She looked at Colleen from between the stems. "I'll bet it's that guy I've seen parked across the street. Handsome fella."

Colleen's movements slowed as she retrieved her mail from the brass box on the porch wall and thumbed through the envelopes, trying hard not to look up. "Oh? Did he have blond hair?"

Rhonda hooted. "Ha! Don't go pulling that sneaky reporter thing on me. You know damned well that kid had a head of wild red hair. Couldn't miss him in a crowd."

"Heavy?"

"Stop that! He's that wiry red-haired urchin who plays the pipes at Flannery's Hall. First time crushes are the worst. He musta gone sweet on you."

"I know that kid and no way he's gone sweet. I got to know him years ago when I turned him in for underage drinking and possession of fake IDs. I can't count the number of times I did that. If anything, he hates me." She turned her head. "Are you sure it was him?"

Colleen's stomach churned as Rhonda nodded her head. Seamus Finn was a punk, an opportunist, and a thug in the making, if he wasn't one already. With a rap sheet as long as her arm, Finnie, as he was known to his pals, had obviously decided a life of school, church, and honest labor was boring at best and at worst would put him on the same road his poverty-stricken mother followed. Finnie used his youth to his advantage, knowing the courts went easy on juvenile offenders if they expressed enough remorse. He'd do anything for a quick buck and became the go-to boy for any nefarious job deemed beneath the major players of crime rings. Whether he was the courier for drugs or guns, or the lone point on a stakeout, he accepted cash with sealed lips and eyes on a career path that would lead him to a waterfront condo or jail. Most likely both.

Finnie had been Magnus' favorite tail. The fact he was so quickly back in business after Magnus' death worried Colleen. Finnie's presence at her home meant that not only were the people of Magnus' network thriving, but working in a coordinated effort. Coordinated efforts happened with good leadership.

Michael was proving to be a star student.

Amanda could think what she wanted about Jessica acting independently. Colleen was not going to be put off the mark. First she'd nail Wyeth and keep Amanda happy. Then she'd explode the Connaught clan, with or without Amanda's help.

If Jessica Wyeth's head was on the chopping block first, so be it.

Colleen gave her good evenings to Rhonda and entered her apartment. Finnie's presence coming with the appearance of the roses unsettled her. Everything looked untouched. No doors or drawers looked like they had been opened nor papers moved, but Colleen couldn't shake the feeling of being violated. She grabbed a beer, popped off the cap and collapsed into her easy chair.

She looked around her living room. A lamp illuminated a pile of unread books. Did she leave that light on? She couldn't remember. Pillows on her sofa looked askew. Did she do that?

Animated with nervous energy, she stormed through her rooms. Everything looked in place, but she was too creeped out to stay put. She grabbed her satchel, stuffed a few more beers in it and went back to the office.

Max greeted her at the door holding a paper cup filled with black sludge. "Get you a coffee?" he offered. He took a swig and wrinkled his face in disgust.

"No way I'm drinking that shit. Here." She tossed him a beer. "I need to bounce some ideas off you."

Max held the beer in his hand, looked at the label, and then looked at Colleen. "Sam Adams? Seriously? I had you pegged for a Miller Lite kind of girl."

Colleen scoffed. "Sam packs more alcohol. We're gonna need it."

Max cocked his head. "It's against policy. No booze in the office."

"Fuck policy. We've got work to do." She pushed past him to his office, swept papers to the side of his desk with her arm, and placed the brown paper bag holding the beer down with a defiant thunk.

"What's this about?" Max's face crimped with concern. "The roses?"

"I got a delivery at my home. Landlady ID'd one of Magnus' contacts as the delivery boy."

Max sat in his chair and motioned for Colleen to pull another up to the desk. He rerolled his shirtsleeves up to his elbows. She used the time to settle herself down. Max's unflappable calm was exactly what she needed right now. She was getting too close to the story and needed a dose of objectivity.

She gulped a few mouthfuls of beer and nodded she was ready.

"What were you doing just before the roses started to arrive?" he asked, fingers tented in front of his nose.

She lined up dates and times in her head and compared them with the timeline of events every reporter carves into their brain when figuring out who knew a fact and when did they know it.

A pattern emerged.

"My articles on Jessica's arrival to the States earned me a knife in my back at the T-stop." A chill crept up her spine at the memory. "Since she had arrived in one of his jets, I referenced Michael Connaught's associations with his father's organized crime activities as part of that article. I guess he didn't like the publicity."

Max nodded. "Mentioning Connaught negatively brought negative consequences." He paused. "Then?"

"I focused the next series of articles on William Wyeth. They were puff pieces. Nothing hard-hitting in them. I didn't notice anything."

"Next?"

"I wrote about Jessica's injury from the Centennial Park bombing, and rose petals littered my car parked at the same T-stop I was stabbed at. A little over three weeks ago I broke the news on William's DNA test and received a single red rose placed on the hood of my car."

She could see Max's wheels turning. As a result of massive interest in the current dramas, William Wyeth had granted her exclusive access to the details behind the lawsuits he wanted to file to recoup his brother's inheritance from Jessica. That's when the roses started to appear on her desk at the *Globe*.

"A bouquet arrived each day one of your articles on the Wyeth family debacle ran," Max said. "Roses started arriving here with the story entitled *Jessica Wyeth, A Woman Without a Claim*. It was some of the best writing you've ever done, so I didn't question a bouquet from an admirer."

Colleen could feel herself blush. Praise from Max didn't come often and she wished she had time to savor it. Instead, she plowed on. "The pieces of the puzzle of Jessica Wyeth's life slipped into place like a glass slipper on a dainty foot. Everything came together—from William's DNA test to revelations pointing to Bridget as Jessica's mother."

"You started to craft the perfect picture of a disenfranchised, confused, and errant woman. Your narrative was quite clear. At the most vulnerable time of her life, Wyeth came under the control of an international crime family known for building its wealth from the commerce of conflict. Those facts, when combined with your research on behavior modification, created a personality profile on Jessica Wyeth that fit the formation of a radicalized belief system perfectly. You didn't mention Connaught and you received roses." He stared at her. "You're building up to something. What are you withholding?"

"Nothing," she said, voice involuntarily rising at the end of the word.

Max shook his head. "Out with it."

She told him about her meeting with Amanda and Baxter and the affidavit. "They gave me the affidavit, so I'm not withholding evidence or interfering with an investigation. I'm just not ready to drop the proverbial bombshell on the United States' most freshly minted terrorist by exposing it. Like the agents said, Wyeth isn't going anywhere and that fact gives me time to flesh out the story."

They examined each building block of her story with the concentration of structural engineers.

"What's holding you back from publishing one of the biggest scoops of your career?" Max teetered his chair backward, staring at her.

She felt as if truth serum had been injected into her veins. "If you had asked me weeks ago whether or not Jessica was a terrorist, I would have given an impassioned, 'Hell yes!' and not questioned myself. The affidavit was intended to be the irrefutable evidence that supported my theory. It was the key that unlocked her story and it fell into my lap."

"And that's a bad thing?"

She chewed her lower lip. "I'm feeling played. The tip she was coming back to the States and the affidavit?" She shook her head. "Too easy. Connaught certainly wants this narrative to be at the forefront of the public's mind."

"So, you're pushing against what you think he's approving of?"

"I don't want to be his tool."

"But truth is truth. Are you questioning your terrorist theory?"

"I don't want to be seduced by a sexy story even if the facts line up." She drained her beer and popped the cap of another. Max's bottle was still half full.

She began to talk about her research, alcohol fueling her ramble. "William Wyeth is on the warpath to reclaim his rightful inheritance and from the way his court documents read, I surmised he is hell bent on getting every last cent—plus interest and damages. An exhaustive search of records revealed nothing that would have solidified Jessica's status as a Wyeth heir. With irrefutable evidence no blood ties her to the Wyeth fortune, adoption records would be essential. No adoption proceedings were ever completed—or initiated—in any forum. I don't know inheritance law, but I can understand why William had an extra spring in his step lately."

She took another swig. "The only document I unearthed was a baptismal certificate showing Gilchrist "Gus" Adams as Jessica's father. I missed it earlier because it had fallen under a file cabinet and was only discovered by happenstance around the time of the bombing. It is all too neat, too tidy. But its mere existence points me in a different direction."

The stories may have zinged with fact, but Colleen's senses fell flat.

"Okay. Tell me about the birth mother."

Colleen burped. "Bridget Heinchon wasn't the first Irish Catholic girl to hide an illegitimate child in the marriage of a family member. But why did she go to such lengths to hide her pregnancy?"

"Tell me more."

"Typically, illegitimate children of a wayward mother are adopted by the claiming family. I grew up in one of the most Irish Catholic neighborhoods in all of Boston," she said with a dramatic wave of her arm. "I'm familiar with the ways of the well-intentioned. Hushed meetings with a priest would lead to an introduction to a sympathetic lawyer during coffee hour after Sunday mass. A few quiet gatherings around a kitchen table, and properly executed and notarized documents would be filed without fanfare or undue notice. That got me thinking. Why wasn't Jessica formally adopted? I can only guess that no one wanted to draw attention to Jessica as a baby. Why? Part of the answer could have been that Bridget was in prison in the U.K. as a terrorist, and drawing attention to an unsavory branch of the family tree was not in keeping with preserving the Wyeth family name."

"Could that have been the reason?"

Colleen shook her head. "Jim Wyeth, unlike William, did not give a flying fuck about proper appearances or reputation. I think he would have loved poking his finger in his family's eye. Nope. There's got to be another reason."

Max sipped his beer. "You've been focused on the Wyeths. The articles published via Electra Lavielle's outlets focused on Bridget Heinchon."

"Shit," Colleen waved her bottle in the air. "She did one damned good job on those stories. Musta had them lined up and ready to go before she ... before that bomb ..." Her chin started to quiver as booze-fueled emotions flowed to the surface. She swallowed and got herself in check. "Bridget's name and face are known to everyone thanks to Electra. Civil rights activist. A modern woman in an unmodern time. Imprisoned for years without formal charges being filed. A hero."

"Or a terrorist."

Colleen tipped her open hand from side to side in a balancing gesture. "Or a hero. I gotta say, I kinda like her."

"Electra is dead and Jessica can't talk. We've got a pretty good picture of the biological mother, but what about her father? Gus Adams seems barely an afterthought in everything we've learned and was never mentioned as Jessica's father except as conjecture." He held up his hand to stop Colleen's protest. "That conveniently discovered baptismal certificate raises more questions than it answers. I'd never let you go to press with a statement of paternity with something as flimsy as that." He leaned forward over his desk. "The clear direction of your stories lays the foundation to bridge the gap from hapless victim to intentionally nurtured terrorist. Your stories, combined with those published through Lavielle's outlets, build the framework in the readers' minds that Jessica was the product of a rebel and had been acculturated to radicalism. Her entire life pointed to a clever and devious plan, but you're still sitting on that affidavit that completes the portrait. Why?"

Colleen pulled out a file of photos, selecting a picture of three people. A fresh-faced Bridget, barely into her twenties, stood with her arms slung around the shoulders of two men. Colleen pointed to one with a mass of black curls surrounding a round, smiling face. He seemed shorter in stature than the other two people. "This man is Gus Adams."

"And the other?"

She pulled out a second photo of Jessica and compared the faces. The resemblance between mother and daughter was clear. Both had an aloof, almost regal bearing and their eyes glowed with intelligence and wit. Colleen searched the faces for structural clues that would have shown Gus' blood tie.

Max studied the pictures. "I'm not seeing the Gus-Adams-as-father smoking gun. Your answer to why did the Heinchon sisters go to such lengths to protect the father might be right here." He tapped his finger on the first photo. "This guy, the one wearing a Roman collar and cassock."

"The priest?"

"He looks one hell of a lot like Jessica."

Colleen's intuition revved. "Even in a private adoption, the birth parents have to be listed. Avoiding a formal adoption proceeding avoided divulging who the father was."

"I agree, but he wouldn't be the first priest to have a secret family."

She looked out Max's door at the empty newsroom. A vase of wilting roses sat at the receptionist's desk. "And each time I write about the lack of blood tie to the Wyeth's, I get roses. The fact that the roses are being delivered to my home is them letting me know I'm safe as long as I play along."

Max placed his elbows on his desk and squeezed his head between his hands. "Connaught makes money on war. Northern Ireland is a powder keg. I've heard the factions are held together by the strength of a personality. You know, a true leader of men. So, if this priest is a somebody in the struggle, then outing him as the father would be hugely destabilizing. I wonder if it's the identity of the priest that Connaught wants you to find out."

"This agrees with the direction my source at the FBI wants me to take, too. Investigate Wyeth. Leave Connaught out of it."

Max rolled his head up to look at her from under his brow. Hands pressed against his temples. "Whoa. What? They said hands off Connaught?"

Colleen nodded.

"But he's in it as deep as he can be." Max drained his beer. Colleen tossed him another. "We'll figure that one out as we move forward."

They clinked their bottles together.

"The truth is the truth," Max shrugged. "And you gotta go with the truth."

"Even if I feel that somehow I'm being used?"

"First, figure out who this priest is. Is he the father? Who is he in the church? Important? Is the guy still alive? What's he doing now?"

Colleen grabbed a pad of paper and a pen and began writing. "Right. And why now? I feel like there's something brewing that I'm supposed to find this out sooner rather than later."

Max drained his beer. "Right. Why now?"

MICHAEL STOOD OUTSIDE Kavan's apartment looking up and down the deserted street. Stormont glowed in the distance, flooded by yellow spotlights, in an image meant to convey power as much to intimidate. Kavan liked his proximity to Stormont for the same reasons. His apartment building was five stories tall and made of washed white marble. Small terraces with wrought iron balustrades graced each floor. Flowers, fragrant and damp from a recent rain, hung from baskets forming brilliant formations. Soft hues of purple and blue contrasted with deep greens of lush leaves. Impeccably manicured hedges guided foot traffic to a secured area where residents could key themselves in and visitors could be surveyed and verified, then buzzed in. Camera lenses eyed different directions and Michael recognized night vision lenses as well as infrared, surprising him that the bishop and other residents of the stately building regarded their security as important as the government offices of Stormont. Of course, he chided himself, many government officials lived here as well and would spare no expense in protecting themselves against the villainous threats of the IRA.

The fact that he was standing there as an invited guest twitched the corner of his mouth up in a satisfied smirk.

He had barely raised his finger to press the call button before the door chimed and the metallic sound of a geared lock whirred. The door swung open.

"Down the hall. Take the lift to five. The bishop will greet you on the landing." The puffy-eyed security guard jabbed a bony finger on a series of buttons. The khaki uniform was huge on his reed-like body. No weapon bulged from hip or holster, but two HK-417s, Heckler and Koch's gold standard assault rifle, sat racked and ready within easy reach. Retrofitted with an extra-capacity magazine, the weapon could mow down multiple assailants. Shoot first, ask questions later. A green garden hose with a pistol grip nozzle sat coiled and ready for watering the plants—or clean-up.

In the few seconds it took to ascend, Michael drew in a deep breath, rolled his shoulders back, and felt the reassuring tug of the holster against his chest.

He kept his muscles relaxed as the elevator settled to a stop, bouncing once on its cables. The doors slid open. The reception vestibule glowed pink from a combination of soft lighting, textured wallpaper, and two enormous vases of cut flowers. Gilt-framed oil paintings of rugged oceanside cliffs hung on the walls. The bishop shifted his weight from foot to foot, ill-at-ease. A black robe with purple buttons looked as if it had been hastily withdrawn from the bottom of a hamper. Its deep creases crisscrossed the towering figure did nothing to diminish the bishop's height or presence. The trappings of a priest did not hide the power of the man. Sweat prickled Michael's scalp.

"Mr. Connaught. You're the spitting image of your father when he was your age."

The urge to narrow his eyes was strong, but he kept them round and neutral. "Bishop Hughes. You're a hard man to reach."

"Only when I want to be." Kavan swept his hand toward an open door. "And you can be very persistent."

Michael allowed himself to be ushered into the living room. Habit and nature drove a quick inventory of sights and sounds. Combined with measuring the bishop's body language, he assured himself they were alone, as had been promised.

Stacked boxes, sides rounded to fullness, sat beside the ash-filled hearth. A faint smell of crisped paper stung his nostrils. White sheets draped over chairs. Rugs laid rolled and tied. One lone chair sat away from the dining table, a lamp illuminated papers scattered across its surface.

"I cannot be at my daughter's side." Pain tucked in the corners of Kavan's mouth. A grey pallor floated just beneath his ruddy skin.

The declaration came as no surprise to Michael. Impatient operatives within the IRA had begun to agitate. The ceasefire Kavan struggled so hard to broker hung by less than a whispered promise, and

Kavan was that promise. Only Kavan's word knit the truce. Michael watched as Kavan's impossible choice drained the life from him.

"*Can*not or *will* not?" Michael swallowed against the lump in his throat as he spoke the words.

Kavan's eyes narrowed. "Who are you to ask me such a thing?"

Michael could feel the hairs of his neck stand on end at the sound of the challenge. He opted to be conciliatory. "I am the same as you. We love her but have other matters that keep us from her."

"Are we the same? Do you love her with an intensity to risk every-thing to be with her? Is every waking moment spent figuring ways to make her life better or to be by her side? What of you? Why can't you go to her? Or, why *won't* you?"

"I, er, *we* have obligations."

"'Obligations'?" Kavan needled. "Our obligations are a wall that stands between us and our goal. We can take down that wall brick by brick or fortify it through our actions. Which do you do?"

Once spoken, the words were like a curtain drawn away from a window. He hesitated to see what they revealed. "She needs you."

Kavan pressed on. The air around him heated with his anger. "You expect me to go to her bedside and think I won't be questioned as to why I am there? You wish to use me to fortify your wall."

Michael had stood on this precipice before. He drew himself up, centering between duty and desire. Existing on a razor's edge proved to be too narrow an existence. He needed to thrive. He had felt the power of making decisions and living in a world he could control. The curtain was drawn back, but he chose not to see. "She's your blood."

"And the blood of your father runs through you and you now feel the pull of that destiny."

"We decide our own destinies."

"Do we? But you want to decide her destiny and mine."

"That's not true."

"Isn't it? You want to use everything her mother and I sacrificed our lives for as mortar for your plans. You dismiss her as one life while I am the shepherd for thousands. *You* are not to decide if *or* when my paternity is to be discovered."

"Are you concerned that your ascension to Archbishop would van-ish?"

Kavan rolled his shoulders back as he exhaled, a move Michael sensed was only feigning defeat. Kavan spoke, eyes focused on a point in the distance, beyond the confines of the room. "My concern lies with the violent who would no longer be kept in check without guidance."

"You are not the first priest to cheat on God. He knows you won't be the last."

Michael was trained in the art of killing as well as skilled in detecting those who could. The black panels of the cassock did not fool his eye nor his senses. He tensed as Kavan's body flinched as if hit with a bat. He kept his shoulders back and knees loose, reflexively readying to defend. Kavan was a man in full and he was threatened. Lives were taken for much less.

Instead of a physical response, Kavan modulated his voice to cajoling notes. "I've not a fairy's wish that ascending to Archbishop could do more than I ever dreamed. Access to peacemakers is one thing. Having the ear of the powerful is another. You may fault me as being worldly, but the influence I wish for is to save the lives of the humble."

Michael sensed an opening, a common ground where self-centered motivations could be exploited. "So you see there is something more you crave."

Kavan's enigmatic smile chilled him. "Ah, I've been discovered," he derided. "In fact, you are one of the souls I crave to influence. If we combined our efforts, men would stop fighting. Your father sent men to their deaths and you've not called off the flow of volunteers. I stem the flow of good men with a raw conscience to those ranks. You must stem the flow of the evil men without a moral code."

"I've nothing to do with the men who wish to die for freedom."

"Don't you? If someone wishes to kill, but they have no means to do so, soon the passions fade and they go on about their lives. If they are hungry in peace but satiated in war, which do you think they will chose? Work with me, Michael."

Michael felt as if a hand had grabbed his throat and tightened. What if he worked with Kavan? He knew all too well what that would lead to. He was not about to give up his future. "People give their lives for freedom every day. The world is filled with them."

"I've heard the confessions of men tormented by their decisions to kill and the plans of the men determined to have their voices heard in the roar of an explosion. When the weak fight, they strike at the heart the mighty. The Manchester bombing was only an opening foray. The IRA is desperate for representation at the bargaining table during the peace negotiations. They are impatient with words. I'm afraid of what will be next."

"Are you afraid being by your daughter's side will hint that the IRA was to blame for the Olympics bombing?"

Kavan sneered. "Only the foolish could think our tweed-clad lads could reach across the pond. Your father's businesses reach every corner of the globe, whereas our troubles end at our border." A rueful smile crossed the bishop's lips. "But yours are another matter. I'm sure business is booming for the Connaughts' companies."

"That's not your concern."

"Isn't it though? Your father and grandfather built their wealth for the pursuit of freedom. Don't think I don't know how Magnus fueled the hatred of the British with the passion to reunite the Irelands. Your choice is here. Now."

Michael could feel Kavan's eyes look beyond his skin and into his heart. Kavan's eyes, no, *Jessica's* eyes implored him to make the right decision. He teetered in a trick of time that let seconds slow to years. "We share the vision to unify our country. You and my father worked toward that same goal."

"We shared a *desire*, but not a method. Magnus wanted our emerald isle to be one country again and not divided. We shared that passion. I wanted to marry the hearts of men to the desire of peace. Magnus wanted them to be bedded in war. The tools and destruction of war filled his pockets. We both spoke of peace. I lived for it. He hated it. And you care only if you profit by it."

The prickle of sweat at Michael's scalp bloomed to rivulets that tracked down his neck and between his shoulder blades. He didn't want this meeting, knowing speaking with Kavan was like walking into an X-ray machine calibrated to bring the shadow of his thoughts to light. He had come too far for his soul to be changed now. His goal was clear and he would not waver. He needed Kavan to go to Jessica's bedside. He needed Kavan to be the model father.

Michael's his voice lowered to a dried husk. "Be careful what you say." The words were all he could risk in response, fearing more would tip his trembling hand. Instinct coiled his muscles as it firmed his resolve.

A flicker of recognition gleamed in Kavan's eye. Kavan spoke as if sensing the fading moment to turn a soul to good. "I've listened to deathbed confessions of your father's henchmen and the desperate cries of men imprisoned for your father's crimes. I marveled at how he was able to turn the hearts of the good into fodder for the bad. The Connaughts turned more than one man bent on honoring family by honest labor and faith into a killing machine by stripping him of livelihood and self. With cunning calculation, a man would be built up by being paid for leaving a heavy parcel on a train or in a garbage can, only to learn later that its heft was gelignite. I listened to the tormented pleas of souls afraid of damnation because they helped a massacre yet they fed their family for months from the payment for it. Was such an act pure evil if they were able to pay for medicines or tithe the church? Was there good in war? When their arms were blown free from shoulders because they were not adequately trained, was it God's will they would never again cradle their babes or embrace their mothers? These are the questions I was forced to answer for them. These are the questions your father forced me to face."

"I am not my father." He stepped forward bringing his eyes level with Kavan's.

Kavan drew in a breath. His face was alight with hope as he locked his eyes on Michael's. "You have the power of free will to make your life your own. Work with me, man. And you can have the woman you love."

The invisible hand that gripped Michael grew cold. Could he have all that he wished for? He spoke, voice faint, as he reached for his good. "I pay for schools and charities that repair the men and families impacted by this game of power. My men stand beside your priests in dank slums handing out food and rent vouchers and are blessed by your brethren for their efforts."

"As I stood side by side with your father and blessed him for his charity. I stopped when he used those missions more for recruitment than for charity." Kavan leaned into Michael's space. "Your father lured desperate men. His death cleared the way for you to lure desperate countries."

A vision of what his future could hold appeared. In that moment, Michael looked ahead to see who could stand beside him. His balance shifted. He blinked and shook his head as if coming out of a trance. "You don't know what you're talking about." He refused to yield. Standing his ground forced Kavan to his limits.

"Don't I?" Kavan answered, his words thorned with anger. "Don't come here with hat in hand and wish me to visit the bedside of the woman in whose shadow you need to function. Doing so only furthers your game. You play the world media game too well not to know the attention from such a revelation would suck the air from any suspicions of you. I would be destroyed and all the compromises and peace talks would dissolve like a lump of sugar in hot tea. You know better than I the violence that would start because of it."

"I know nothing. You accuse me of profiting from war—"

"—as your father did."

"And of knowingly creating the rifts that men race to fill with bombs."

"The rifts existed before you came along. The bombs no doubt bear the 2100 logo." Kavan dropped the guise of civility. "No. You are not your father. You are worse. Your father was man enough to stand on his own two feet in the broad daylight. You have to hide behind the skirt of a woman."

Like the spring in a watch that has been wound too tightly, Michael broke, uncoiling in lethal flash. Cold enveloped him in a veil of drunken rage.

The sharp crack of ribs breaking sounded as the two men collided in midair. A blade flashed joined by the soft hiss of skin sliced open. The metallic smell of blood mixed with the acrid taint of fear. Boxes toppled and chairs fell as they wrestled, each trying to best the other and emerge alive. Michael trapped the corner of the cassock beneath his knee and a split second later the rigid bones of Kavan's neck bent with the force of his grip. The thirst to kill begged to be slaked.

Michael's vision reddened to blinding rage. He tried to hang on, to stop Kavan's breath from flowing. He forced all his strength into his fingers and was shocked when his arms were thrust open and a slice of pain in his upper arm joined the other in his back. The room swirled and turned. In a second he went from staring down at Kavan's bulging eyes to looking up at the molded ceiling. He gasped for air as his own larynx flattened under the bone of Kavan's forearm.

Kavan caught his breath as he straddled Michael, torn cassock bunching around his hips, exposing a sheath strapped to his lower leg. His left arm pressed against Michael's throat. His right hand pointed a dagger at his nose, the intertwining Celtic pattern along the quillion and hilt unmistakable. "There is mutiny in your ranks and you are losing control of your men. You know it. You will not use her to be your alibi or your shield."

Sharp pain radiated from Michael's cracked ribs and he could feel his shirt pucker with the spread of blood from his wounds. "You should know what it feels like to hide behind *skirts*. You let her mother rot in jail so you could convince those around you that you had no interest in Bridget except as another soul to save."

The dagger's blade inched closer.

"You think killing me will be cleansing that part in yourself that lurks in all men," Michael croaked. "The hate is in you. The desire to kill is there. Don't fool yourself into thinking your hands are clean when you hear the confessions of men who are simply *between* killings if do nothing to stop them. You lie to yourself and feel it's truth when good men believe you."

"The difference between you and me is you believe the lies of men who wish to curry favor. I struggle to be ruled by a higher power, but you are your own God." The tip of the dagger made hatch-like designs in the air. "You need me more than I need you. You're not the only seller of arms, just the most convenient one." Kavan shifted his weight forward, increasing the pressure on Michael's throat. The smile on his face said he was rewarded with a deepening hue of crimson. "Your father's business was failing. Coalitions were breaking apart. What a stroke of good fortune that a man as well-versed in business as you was so ready to step up and take over when he, um, *died*."

Michael's throat ached with the effort to keep his trachea from collapsing. "I only stepped into my father's role to stop the violence. His companies needed a strong leader to direct the mission away from terrorist strikes and into peaceful enterprises."

Kavan gave a wry chuckle. "Don't think I don't know your companies' weapons are in demand by governments and rogue states. You profit from destruction. Magnus told me of his desire to have you take over all of his organizations, but cringed at the thought of where you would lead them. His death cleared the way to his limitless coffers. When he died, any barrier to power did too. He watched you as a boy master the skills needed for power. Vision. Financial acumen. Charm." His voice lowered. "Manipulation. If what you told my daughter was true, you would have washed your hands of Magnus' taint and divested yourself of his frock, placing it into the hands of men you could trust to steer to the good. Instead, you let her believe you were trapped as you used her."

"That's not true."

"Isn't it? How long have you been planning these events?"

"I shunned my father and only stepped in after his death."

Kavan laughed. "Your stealthy approach speaks to a soul corrupt at birth. You were one document away from letting her take the fall for the Manchester bombing," he growled as he leaned more weight on his forearm. "Once the authorities saw evidence pointing to her *knowingly* transporting materials used at Manchester, her life would have been over and the resulting investigation would no doubt lead far away from you."

"'Once they saw?'" Michael's brow furrowed in an effort to think. The shock of the attack, the incongruity of being on the receiving end of the bishop's dagger clouded his thinking. Did Kavan know about the affidavit? How? "Are you saying the investigation hasn't progressed? How do you know this?"

Kavan ignored his questions. "You set yourself up as the innocent son of a criminal mastermind, all the while setting the chess board to your favor. It all would have worked out so perfectly to have the love child of a revolutionary and a bishop's bastard prove nature over nurture."

The shores of Michael's vision darkened and streaks of light swam in the pool. He coughed and struggled as he moved his head from side to side. "Not . . . true," he croaked.

In an instant, the pressure on his throat vanished. Blood rushed to his head and air to his lungs, re-inflating him to life. Kavan stood up and offered his hand. Michael refused and struggled to his feet, clutching his blood-soaked shirt to his arm. He wove, stumbling to regain his balance, and looked at Kavan with blurring vision.

"I . . . I only came here because she needs you."

"You came here to destroy me." Kavan walked to a cupboard. With a shaking hand, he poured a half tumbler of Scotch. He knocked back the amber liquid with a toss of his head. "You're no fool. These streets have more cameras hidden in the greenery than a boulevard in your Hollywood. You were relentless in demanding an invitation here knowing damned well one sighting of you entering this building would threaten my credibility to the point of implosion."

"But you *did* invite me," Michael croaked, working his neck in circles to mitigate the pain.

"I had hoped our visit would have been seen by you as one last chance to work with me to stop the violence. You tried to use my daughter to get me to do your bidding. Don't think I cannot see your planned moves in your game of chess. You forget the long range abilities of a certain game piece." He poured another shot, finished it, and wiped the back of his hand across his mouth.

Michael's bowels dropped as a slow smile spread up the bishop's face as he raised the empty glass in a toast.

"Checkmate."

Silvern Rehabilitation Hospital
Boston, Massachusetts

NORTH STATION SPREAD its tentacle tracks along twenty acres of Boston's West End. Waves of commuters ebbed and flowed along grimy walks. The heat of the summer gone, cooler temperatures encouraged sweaters to be clutched at necks and walk tempos to increase. The change of seasons inevitable, incremental progression toward winter undeniable.

The incremental process of recovery continued as well.

Jessica sat in the bright solarium positioned to give her the best view of the Charles River. A prime seat, but no one would shoo her aside to claim dibs on the bentwood and wicker rocker that groaned any time nurses came to shift her position. Her wheelchair sat beside her, only temporarily at rest.

She allowed the creaks and moans of the rocker to be her voice. What good would crying do? Tears never brought anyone back from the dead or changed a fact, and she saved herself the effort of dabbing her eyes and blowing her nose. The hanky sat dry and wadded in her fist, and a nagging itch on the back of her neck remained unsoothed. Her silent mourning was a comfort to her but unnerving to anyone who saw her. Like a scratched vinyl record, her thoughts skipped and looped with visions of Bridget, Margaret, and Electra. For hours and days on end, Jessica sat motionless, looking over Cambridge's grey skyline, quietly yearning for fields, horses, and family from a past that never existed.

A little beyond her sight was the Boston Common and the swan boats she delighted in as a young girl. What was the point of childhood memories when they evidenced a lie? The place in the world she thought she occupied warped and rotted away with each revelation. The only truth that existed in her life was that she was alive. Thinking and feeling were the prices she had to pay.

She had wrapped herself in a cloak of silence, the messy work of grief buried behind frozen muscles and dry eyes. Too many losses, too many deaths occurred because of *her*. Her very existence triggered a series of events no one could have foreseen. Yet, somehow, she couldn't shake the feeling that she could have changed everything if she had only known. The responsibility crushed her.

As each day passed, she became more able to face the cost, but her injured brain thwarted her ability to pull out one piece of information, deal with it, and file it away for future use. Thoughts cascaded and crashed around her skull without rhyme or reason. Her days passed in simple routine.

Jessica closed her eyes as she listened to the sounds of the hospital echo around her. Nurses spoke in hushed tones and the occasional chime of a patient's call-alert triggered soft-soled shoes to pad with hurried steps down the hall. No breathing. No creak of a chair or shifting of a body searching for a comfortable position revealed someone near. Someone? Usually Declan was by her side, but today was one of the few times he was gone. Only when she was sure she was alone did she allow herself to become aware.

Turning her head away from the window caused flash of pain. Her arms and legs felt like they were on fire and she began to sweat. She almost cried out.

Almost.

Doing so would blow her cover.

She'd have to do better if she wanted to stay alive.

A funny thing happens to a body when one sense is taken away. The blind often say their hearing sharpens to compensate for a loss of sight, or smells become important clues to the unseen world around them. The deaf see words formed and emotions not spoken. For Jessica, the ability to see beyond a person's façade honed to a fine point. Bridget said she was *fe*, an Irish word meaning her intuition was evolved to be as strong as a sense. *Fe* enabled her to see thoughts ripple below the skin and behind brows. Smell clued her to hidden nervousness. Her skin absorbed life force through the touch of another.

People patronize the paralyzed. None questioned her failure to flinch away her stare or demanded attention to their conversation. She could observe, and with that observation came something she had long lost—the ability to simply be in someone's presence without channeling effort to support her own artifice. With no expectation of a reaction, people revealed themselves in the safety of someone who could not judge. The innately generous sat beside her, rubbing her arm, telling her the day's gossip or a funny cat story. The timid moved soundlessly, greeting her with a near whisper and bidding quiet goodbyes. Not all people at Silvern were generous or kind, and brusque words, hard movements, and callous touches exposed them. Jessica committed their faces to memory and planned for the day she would get her revenge.

When Declan was near, she watched him with an intensity gifted to the infirm and the narrow focus of a brain struggling to filter input.

Something had changed in Declan since arriving in Boston. He had hovered over her in Atlanta, but there he imparted more a feeling he protected her as a lion would covet a recent kill—snarling at anyone who got near. He thrived on keeping people away. As the days wore on in Boston, he began to fill them by talking *with* her, not *to* her as most did. He began engaging in a one-sided conversations much as a confessant would when looking to relieve their soul of burden.

As the fog of her injury lifted, she would listen to him with eyes closed. Demands of living in Southie as a hardscrabble youth challenged his budding morality. Iron-fisted father and opportunistic brothers flourished in a world where playing by the rules meant breaking most of them. In a true Irishman's way, Declan cultivated stories that bloomed with humor and pathos. Even with the primitive functioning of her injured brain, a chuckle would erupt from her slumber and cough out to the world.

As relieved as she was not to have to react, he seemed relieved to break his disciplined silence of the day to talk to someone who could not act against him. With the artifice of social norms stripped away, she felt his yearning to connect and allowed him the space to find his way how.

"There now. Time for bed." A nurse appeared at her side and locked the brakes of her chair to prepare for transfer. The nurse was large, artificially orange hair covered her head with coiffed perfection. Her scrubs were dotted with images of schoolbooks and chalk to acknowledge the time of year. "Come on now, reach your hand around," she said as she grabbed Jessica's wrist and limp arm, draping them around her own neck. The nurse scooted her other hand under Jessica's thighs and lifted Jessica's limp body with ease. The wicker groaned and the wheel chair creaked as they accomplished resettlement. The scents of flowers and antibacterial soap floated around them as they moved through the hallways.

Activity passed by Jessica in a blur. Her thoughts remained on Declan.

If she had been able to factor the complexities of her plight, she might have expected his interest in her to lessen once they arrived in Boston. Instead, he made it clear he would do everything possible for her comfort.

"Oh! No visitors today? Such a shame," the nurse commented as they entered the private room Declan had arranged for her.

Nurses flocked around, but Jessica wasn't convinced the attention was all for her. Declan's appeal was strong and nurses lingered long enough to message their interest and to gauge his.

On the nights he didn't sleep in the oversized Naugahyde-covered easy chair in the corner of her room, he arrived at her side the next morning, briefcase filled with papers. His first moments didn't vary. He greeted her first, then checked her comfort, and spent a quiet moment holding her hand. Next, he would get updates from the staff. She watched every conversation and each interaction for any duplicity.

He didn't disappoint her. His performance was flawless as he crossed his arms and tilted his head, listening to one nurse after another talk about family, or weekend plans, or cats. He didn't deceive, but cultivated them to care for Jessica as a way to get close to him. He looked into their hearts with dark eyes that could turn to molten chocolate. The nurses scurried to fluff her pillows. Perfect. His body softened and warmed to nurses Jessica had grown to like and his eyes chilled to black ice when speaking with someone he mistrusted. The only curious thing he did was to remove each delivery of roses by placing them on the nurse's station. He never read the card. He never acknowledged who they were from.

His routine would then turn to the papers in his briefcase. Sometimes he would spend hours reading or writing, only looking up to check on her or to adjust her covers. If he made a phone call, he took care to keep his voice low, a fact Jessica interpreted as not wanting to disturb her rather than trying to conceal the content of the conversation.

He kept her informed of the legal storm swirling around her. Some of what he said stuck, other information slipped through the crevasses of memory. He no longer spoke of syndicates and Michael's wishes, but of blocking William Wyeth at every money-grabbing turn, and ensuring no deportation proceedings would ever spark against her. When he spoke the name of Timothy and mentioned an affidavit had been uncovered that proved her participation in the Manchester bombing, he stroked her arm and held her hand, letting silence envelop them.

Within those moments of quiet, she pushed aside the certain knowledge that Michael put the pieces in place to have her indicted on international terrorism charges. She had loved a man who cared for her with a selfishness she couldn't understand. Even as her broken thoughts floated in untethered blocks, she knew she could survive. Within her body stilled by stealth, a resolve to rejoin the world ignited.

The orderly with the shamrock tattoo fueled it.

After dinner had been served and the trays cleared away, the nurse left, marking the part of the day Jessica dreaded the most. All she could do was wait.

Without Declan there, she knew it was only a matter of time before the orderly would arrive. His was one of the faces she had committed to memory long before she saw the tattoo.

Something in the way Declan had moved around Brendan made her pay more attention, so she was already on her guard before Brendan slipped his hand under her top and squeezed her breast until she wanted to scream. As the days slipped by, Jessica noticed Declan was by her side during Brendan's shifts. Brendan must have noticed it too, for he started to come at odd hours.

She could not avoid him. When it was time for physical therapy, it was Brendan who wheeled her to her sessions. Time in the solarium was another opportunity for Brendan to push her through the halls. He was a pillar of orderly decorum in public, but waited for private to expose his true self. In the moments when he and Declan crossed paths, Declan morphed from benefactor to beast in the invisible way she had come to recognize. Brendan had waited until Declan was gone to show her his tattoo and delighted in its meaning.

"Michael is here for you," he said, smiling to reveal a broken tooth.

She wanted to scream and scratch his eyes out, but broken synapses shot only blanks and her arms and legs remained limp. Brendan's presence meant Michael was nowhere and everywhere at the same time, and confirmed her feeling a fool for not seeing Michael for who he was. She never needed anyone in her life more than she did since her injury, and Michael had abandoned her for his own convenience. Worse than that, she knew she was disposable to him because he allowed a man like Brendan to be near her. He did not value her life as much as his own, and she sensed she still lived because the opportunity to use her one final time had not ripened.

Her injured brain knew that as long as Michael and law enforcement considered her helpless and incapacitated, her body, mind, and soul had time to heal. So, she lay still while her body and spirit mended.

But it became increasingly difficult to hide in a body that wanted to move. As muscles regained function, her heart remained gashed. Her grief would never leave her, but it would change. Her life was her own to live.

Unless Michael's Rose decided to take it.

She hated the smell of Brendan as he leaned over her bed. His one broken tooth was surrounded by a mouthful of yellow and crusted teeth and his breath stank with a mixture of last night's booze and decay. Her muscles heated to flee, but weak connections sputtered and failed. He delighted in his perversion of power as his hands ran over her skin. She kept her eyes fixed on a point on the wall.

"Won't be long now," he said, eyes darting to the hallway. "Boys at the harbor say the Feds got what they need."

She breathed slowly, pushing her belly upward to keep her shoulders still.

"They got the pictures of you with the crates and one of our guys is making it easy to figure out what was in them." He looked pleased with himself, like a small boy snitching a cookie from a jar when he thinks he's unseen.

She weighed the risk of speech against the safety of silence and knew odds were against her living either way.

"W-why?"

Brendan's head snapped back in surprise. "You're talking?" He stuck his head out of her door and looked up and down the hallway. She remembered how he looked as a sly grin spread along his face. Before he left, he turned to her and said, "Because one country is more important than one person."

Days passed as she considered his words. Could it be true that one person's life could be destroyed for the sake of a country? What about the countless lives taken by bombs or bullets for a cause that started as a political compromise to avoid a loss of life?

The blood of her mother and father coursed through her veins, bringing the energy of healing to her shattered bones, ripped muscles, and torn heart. The cause they fought for strengthened Jessica's desire to return to the land of the living.

She listened for footsteps in the hall and scrutinized the shadows of her room for movement. Only when she knew she was alone did she force her body to move. Many nights she stared at her toes, being rewarded with only a flicker of movement, but the memory of motion returned, fueled by the yearning to ride a horse again.

The rewiring of healing in the wake of injury is an alchemist's puzzle. What is the ingredient that caused the change? Jessica's physical injuries were severe, but paled next to the wounds her soul had received. Locked in her body through a combination of injury and will, she sifted through the silt of her life and picked through the flecks of fool's gold to find her own precious metal. Part of her wanted to run free, unencumbered by her injured past. The dominant part of her knew the code of survival and refused to telegraph messages of movement to her limbs. The battle within waged.

Be still or be strong. Her body twitched and jerked with indecision.

Sheets drenched with sweat as she clenched and released muscles with isometric will. She clawed her way to sit upright, and then fell back against the pillows, listening for clues her recovery might be discovered. Her bent knees rose and fell, slowly at first, but eventually with more strength and confidence. Stomach crunches started at five, then reached twenty. Then one hundred. She could feel the change in her body and her heart, but the terror of discovery and what that would mean to her freedom remained fresh and active.

As her body grew in strength, her new self emerged. She had been ignorant of her mother's cause and her parents' homeland's struggle for reunification. She could only blame herself for not being more aware of what Ireland needed to mend its soul. But hatred of the cowardice of placing a bomb in a trashcan to bring attention to an issue was as carved into her own soul as the rippled and red scars on her skin.

If anything proved to her the senselessness of violence in brokering peace, it was the loss of Electra's life and the scarring of her own. The Centennial Park bombing was connected to Northern Ireland's struggles only by an ignorant act, but it tempered her resolve into unbreakable steel to stop the cycle of violence.

The knowledge that MMC and 2100 profited from war and violence did more to drive Jessica away from Michael than his willful absence. She had struggled with the knowledge his father's identity and wondered if Michael could rise above his genes. Surrounding her with threats proved his culpability. She felt his absence less as a void and more as him lying in wait.

His businesses made profits through conflict. Weapons bore his initials. There was only one thing more clear to her than the violence of war . . . and that was the money that was made from it.

The innocence of not being actively engaged in the planning stages is irrelevant when a person takes informed, active, and intentional steps to cover up the crime afterwards. The Manchester bombing was planned and executed without Michael's knowledge, but he willfully covered it up, making him an accessory after the fact.

She stood in the way of Michael living a life free from criminal charges and her father stood in the way of his profits.

Moving the bed rail on outstretched forearms, she forced it upward and over slightly to unlock and lower it. Pushing herself upright with her arms was difficult as they obeyed her like stockings filled with sand. Balancing on flattened palms and stiffened arms, she swung her legs over the edge of the bed and let them dangle, heart pounding with effort. When her strength gathered, she set her feet on the floor and stood. Many nights, this was as far as she got before collapsing back on to the bed.

Tonight, and every night from this point on, was going to be different.

Balancing with hands on the bed, she slid her right foot forward and leaned her weight onto it. The left foot followed in sequence, body trembling with effort. A bead of sweat trickled down her face. Concentration blocked out everything but the commands of motion so she did not hear footsteps approaching until they stopped at her door.

Her body trembled and her muscles burned with the effort of standing.

She crumpled to the floor, shutting her eyes in hope that her fall would be attributed to something other than healing.

Someone knelt beside her, scooping their arms under her, and helping her to sit upright on the cold floor. She expected to be hurried back into bed. Strong arms and hands held her head against a masculine chest. His chin rested on her head.

Senses, intensified by the process of healing, began to flood with a stream of input. The essence of a recent shower and freshly pressed shirt mingled with his unmistakable musk. The cotton weave of his shirt, smooth against her cheek, rolled above his chest hairs. Her ear felt the pressure of his heart as it beat in time to hers.

Declan.

Her body, asleep with injury and desensitized by medicinal touch, awakened with a power and a yearning she was not ready for. Like eyes adjusting to bright sunlight after hours of dark, her senses overloaded. Hearing, seeing, and feeling became a cacophony of signals and her brain churned to process them. Taxed with the job of decoding the onslaught all at once, her brain systematically shut down one sense after another. A velvety silence engulfed her one moment before the light faded to shades of gray and black.

Declan kept her enfolded in his arms as if he, too, was absorbing something from the moment. She let her chest rise and fall with a sigh that filled her with his scent.

Her head fell backward, straining her neck and parting her lips. The heat of his body radiated through her thin pajamas. Circuitry for legs and arms overburdened and grew numb. He moved, bringing his face to hers. His breath fell on her neck and up to her cheek, and her lips warmed as they sensed his closeness. Movement left her and she went limp.

The full armor of catatonic self-preservation locked in place once more.

Fragments of reality cut through the veil. She was jostled and moved. Muttering and urgent voices buffed her ears.

In a possum's guise, she kept her consciousness hidden behind closed eyes.

October 1996
Silvern Rehabilitation Hospital
Boston, Massachusetts

COLLEEN SAT ON the bench by the nurses' station for longer than she thought humanly possible. Her butt hurt and her legs were falling asleep. Jessica was late returning to her room after her morning's therapy session. Colleen wanted to see for herself the extent of Jessica's recovery, or lack of it, as various sources claimed.

With arms crossed and foot tapping, an hour passed. Then two. Colleen glanced at her watch for the third time in less than a minute. As a reporter, she was accustomed to waiting for a source to appear, or remaining on a stakeout after receiving a tip that something was going to happen, or a person was going to be exactly where they said they weren't going to be. Such events were a reporter's reward for hours spent on cold streets or in crowded lobbies.

Today was different. Her source had given her exact times and locations. The fact she was in a hospital that ran on tight and predictable schedules increased her impatience. Some people love the feeling of being on the inside of a story, and more than one person had amplified a tip to get her attention. A group of youths at a playground could morph into a gang of thugs casing a business if the source felt doing so could somehow be glamorous. She had little precious time to waste and wondered if the point of this tip was to make someone feel important.

Feeling important she could handle as a motivation, but making sure she was at a certain place at a certain time, she couldn't. Complying with the anonymous demand made her an easy target. Her jaw clenched in fear. The knife in her back and bouquets of roses alerted her to the possibility that someone wanted her dead. She never would have taken the tip if the location and time put her in dark alley late at night. The fact that she was cooling her heels in the middle of a bustling hospital gave her a modicum of comfort.

But a modicum isn't a whole lot.

She was about to cross the source off her mental list and leave when she sensed the traffic in the hallway shift. There is something about celebrity that ripples through a crowd, and when Jessica approached her room, people slowed their pace and tried their hardest not to stare.

Colleen was rocked at what she saw. Her attention first went to Jessica. Her body had lost that wan and withered look she had when Colleen last saw her in Atlanta. A pallor remained, not just to her skin, but in the lackluster mask that inhabited her eyes. She was dressed in sweat pants and a T-shirt. Brightly colored sneakers, looking fresh out of the box, clad her feet.

The man pushing Jessica's wheelchair looked at Colleen. She recognized him immediately as Michael's attorney. A leather satchel hung crosswise over his chest and another small suitcase sat on Jessica's lap. His hands gripped the chair's handles, forcing him to slightly stoop, but his eyes cut straight through her. Whether the look was calculated to be repellant or not didn't matter, but she felt a shot of adrenalin course through her, her body's readiness to flee triggered by primitive instinct. He continued into Jessica's room, gaze never lifting. Two nurses entered after them.

Colleen hovered around the room and watched who entered. A few minutes passed and an orderly approached with a vase of roses. Declan placed himself at the center of the doorway and pointed for the roses to be placed at the nurses' station. The orderly, a burly hulk of a man with one broken tooth, smirked and tried to shove his way past.

The reason Colleen was summoned became apparent as she viewed the tattoo on the orderly's forearm. The message of the shamrock encircled by the rose was visible and its meaning clear. She recalled an Irish poem her mother would recite when times were tough, which was often. The sentiments in Mangan's *Roisin Dubh*, or *Dark Rosaleen*, were so anti-English they had to be disguised. The poem meant nothing to the English, but was full of symbolism inspiring to the Nationalists and evidence of treason to the Unionists. The rose became the symbol of Ireland and its image on the orderly's arm surrounding the symbol of the Charity proved Mi-

chael Connaught co-opted the meaning of the rose for his own purposes. She'd never look at a rose the same way again.

Her foot stopped tapping and her arms uncrossed. She watched
with increased fascination.

The two men froze as the standoff intensified, wills locked in an
invisible tug of war. Veins rippled beneath the orderly's tattoo as he
tried to force his way into the room. Declan grew more calm as the
struggle continued, seeming to draw strength from the orderly's panic. She strained to hear what they said, but their lips were pressed
into straight lines. Ten seconds passed. Then twenty.

The orderly was the first to break contact as he glanced down the
corridor. He straightened himself up and broke into cordial smile,
nodding his head in greeting.

A man stopped and chatted with both men in a familiar way, but
his manner toward Declan was especially warm and Declan's expression was one of open admiration. Colleen searched the man's face
and frowned when no recognition dawned. He was dressed in charcoal trousers and black suit jacket and his black hair ringed his head
like a modern-day Friar Tuck. It took a moment more before he
turned, and Colleen could see the collarless shirt with tabbed placket
denoting his priesthood. Declan gave the orderly a withering look,
almost as if forcing thoughts into the brute's head. It must have
worked, for the orderly gave the roses to the priest. The priest, with a
face rounded by the happiness of another act of God's will, continued
down the hall with an extra spring in his step and the vase of roses in
his arms, no doubt intending to brighten the day of another patient.

Colleen settled back on the bench, content to watch.

The nurses sat Jessica in a large easy chair by the window and left.
Declan seemed not to notice the open door and pulled a smaller chair
up by her side. The expression on Jessica's face remained unchanged,
but unmistakable awareness infused her eyes. Declan pulled out files
of papers and must have been reading them out loud, for Jessica occasionally nodded in response. The rapport between the two was
familiar and relaxed, but Jessica seemed guarded. He was trying to
charm. Was she trying not to be charmed?

The difference in Declan was most surprising. When Colleen had
first encountered him at Grundy, he carried himself with a thinly
veiled threat of violence. Any attempt at gaining access to Jessica was
met with his fierce opposition until he could fight it no longer. William was triumphant in seeing his niece again, but ham-handed and
insensitive in his interactions with her. Colleen had treaded carefully

in helping William gain access to Jessica as a close family member. Wielding the hospital's patients rights and privacy policies as leverage, she knew she was crossing a line when she helped develop William's story as an estranged uncle seeking reconciliation. Still, she took care not to become a part of the story. When DNA evidence barred his access, she was so livid at William she didn't question why Declan was able to remain.

Until now.

If the hospital denied William access to Jessica based upon the fact he was not a family member by birth or law, what did that say about Declan?

Her foot started to tap. Not out of frustration, but knowing she was on the brink of hitting on something. She cocked her head to the side, listening more carefully to her own thoughts.

She had missed something.

And now she sat on a bench in a hallway yards away from the year's hottest story. Someone had plunked her down and made sure she cleared her schedule to do nothing but sit.

And watch.

And think.

Someone had orchestrated this theater for her to observe and have time to mull things over.

Colleen used the time to review every shred of information she had read about Jessica's family, even allowing herself a moment of pity for Jessica. Bridget had stepped up and raised Jessica after Margaret and Jim died; but by all accounts, Jessica never knew Bridget was her mother. What would cause a mother to live with her daughter for ten years and never say the words, "I'm your mother"? The thought rocked Colleen.

Colleen thought of her own mother and the sacrifices made to give Colleen a secure roof over her head and a debt-free college education. Her mother was thin as a rail from meals skipped and double shifts worked. Colleen's mom wasn't the first mother to sacrifice her own happiness for the happiness of her children.

Would Bridget have been embarrassed by an out of wedlock child? Maybe, but she was certainly the kind of woman to own her mistakes and get on with life. She would not cower behind a lie.

No. The only plausible take was Bridget, with Gus Adams as an accomplice, had a secret.

Like the father.

She recalled the third man in the photograph. The man in the priest's collar.

The man who looked a heck of a lot like Jessica.

The priest Michael wanted Colleen to find.

She pinched the bridge of her nose in an effort to focus her energies and not jump out of her skin.

If the priest was still alive, he would know about his daughter's injury. The world press exploded with stories about the bombing and that Jessica was injured. There was no way he wouldn't have known what happened or where to reach her.

Hospitals serve the needs of the public through medical intervention and spiritual support. A formal network within a church could be supplemented with outreach to public services. Thanks to William, Colleen knew the hospital's privacy policies inside and out. The hospital would not divulge Jessica's secrets. Someone inside the hospital, like a chaplain or a priest, could have been the conduit to provide medical consent via confidential contacts and provided permissions as to who could be by his daughter's bed. If the next of kin was a priest, the network was hermetically sealed against outside discovery.

Colleen's head swam with possibilities.

She looked up to see Declan and Jessica, heads almost touching as they studied a letter. Why hadn't he closed the door?

Colleen felt the forces of change pull at her. She saw Michael's right-hand man at FBI headquarters and she witnessed him refuse the delivery of roses Colleen could only guess had come from Michael.

Was she a witness to a mutiny in the making? Doubtful. Most likely she was being played by whomever set up today's theater. Events don't happen in a vacuum. There was a reason things were playing out as they were. She had learned enough about Irish politics to know that the Irish Republican Army and its political ally, Sinn Fein, had not received their desired results from the Manchester bombing. Sinn Fein had not been invited by the British to have a seat at the negotiating table even though all other political parties and civic groups had representation. How could a country negotiate for peace when the group most impacted by the division did not have a voice in the process?

What had Baxter and Amanda said about another attack in the planning stages? Was Jessica recovered enough to be an active participant or was Michael's proxy playing her?

One piece of the puzzle was to learn the identity of the priest in the photo and her inquiries so far had yielded nothing.

As Colleen stood to leave, she stole one last look at Jessica. The last afternoon sunlight was streaming in through grimy windows illuminating Jessica's hair to a blond halo of light. Their eyes met. Jessica did not flinch away but looked at Colleen with a chin raised in challenge. A moment later, she cocked her head, almost asking why.

Colleen looked forward to seeing the expression in Jessica's eyes when Colleen exposed her as a terrorist.

Declan stood up and carefully rolled down his shirtsleeves, covering the white skin of his forearms. Next, he pulled a sweater on over his head. Colleen tried not to stare at his arms and broad back. He picked up the suitcases and walked toward the door.

He stopped, as if having a second thought.

He went back and kissed the top of Jessica's head.

Ballyronan
Northern Ireland

THE THREE GABLES of Ballyronan loomed above Declan as he wound his way up the tree-lined drive. Flawless green lawns swept down toward the waters of Lough Neagh that glinted in the late evening sunlight. Northern Ireland's temperate climate encouraged formal gardens to bloom with purple, yellow, and red of fall season flowers. He depressed the clutch and shifted down to fourth gear, then third, slowing the rented roadster to give him time to absorb the beauty. Too much time had passed since his last visit and he feared it would be too long again before he returned.

The air triggered a rush of chemicals that bathed his brain and triggered a sigh. Sweet flowers tinted the peat-like scent in the way that was unique to the northeast corner of the island of Ireland. He pulled his two-seater to a stop beside Michael's sleek BMW and took his time getting his luggage and briefcase from the boot, as the trunk was called in this part of the world. The only change to Ballyronan since his last visit years ago was a substantial improvement in its upkeep. The aromas of fresh paint mingled with recently cut grass. He couldn't see the web of security cameras, but could feel their one-eyed stares from every angle. In the distance, he could see the figures of armed guards walking the grounds, rifles held across their bodies, ready.

Murray emerged from the massive front door. "Master Declan! Top of the morning to you, sir!"

The smile on Murray's face whisked away much of the worry that had been building in Declan's gut during his travels. "Murray! I wouldn't recognize Ballyronan without you!" He pumped Murray's outstretched hand, a gesture the Irishman found amusing.

Murray looked at the briefcase and overnight bag. "Where are your things? Surely you've brought more than a change of knickers and a toothbrush! You're here as a man now. You need to give yourself time to rekindle your boyhood times."

Memories of careening on dirt bikes, chasing Michael and his brother along those same trails, surfaced. Spending a month at Ballyronan as a boy had opened Declan's eyes to a world that existed beyond the crowded triple-deckers of his childhood. What had started as a neighborhood outreach to less fortunate families—with a week's vacation at Ballyronan as the guest of the Connaught family—grew into a boyhood friendship with Michael that extended his stays by weeks. He and Michael started their friendship at eight years old—the age at which politics and passions were distant seconds to exploration and adventure.

Declan looked over the grounds. "I've been summoned on business, and pleasure isn't in the schedule. If time allows, I'll take a walk down to the lough," he said, using the local word to strengthen his bond with Murray. "Michael's at the helm now, so boyhood romps are out."

Like many boys before the emergence of their own power as men, Declan and Michael shared a fear and awe of Magnus, with Michael confiding his hatred while he hungered for his father's approval. Declan listened and said nothing. The childhood friendship grew into a summer tradition for years until the relationship between Michael and Magnus became so toxic that ceasing the summertime jaunts was one of Magnus' many power plays to mold his son as he willed. Declan, without the means to travel on his own, used to wonder why his trips stopped. Now, with the clarity of hindsight, he understood. Somewhere over the following years, Michael and Magnus made amends, and Declan wondered how much of his current employment was tied to those carefree summers. He allowed himself one moment of nostalgia before the night's work began.

Murray ushered Declan into Michael's office, and engaged him with a smattering of small talk concerning renovations completed and planned, with a look that hinged between friendship and pity. Declan had dressed for a social call by shunning his tailored suits for a pair of chinos, cotton shirt, and light sweater. He wondered if a Kevlar vest, issued by 2100 and designed to be undetectable when worn under clothes, would have been a smart addition. After the obligatory offering of tea or spirits, Murray left, pointing to the wet bar in the corner where Declan could help himself to the well-stocked bar and a platter of meats, cheeses, and breads.

Alone in the silence of the office, Declan shifted uncomfortably in his chair. The office was Magnus' private sanctum and was the room Declan and his Southie friends were forbidden to enter during their summertime stays. The feeling he was an intruder didn't leave him even as he looked at the pictures of a smiling Michael that lined the walls. Searching the pictures, he was surprised to find one of himself standing beside Michael, both mud encrusted and beaming over the handles of equally muddy dirt bikes. The closeness of their past friendship contrasted with the relationship's current gulf. His discomfort increased with the knowledge he had been summoned to meet Michael less than twenty-four hours before. Declan knew better than to refuse.

He didn't know how much time passed before the doors to the office opened and Michael strode in. He noted they were dressed alike, omission of a vest included.

"Declan! My God, man, having you here brings back memories," he said as he gripped Delcan's extended hand and used his left to give an embrace. Michael winced with the motion. "How long has it been since you were here?"

"A lifetime if a minute," Declan responded, keeping the tone of his greeting on par with Michael's. "Ballyronan has never looked so good. The place is thriving in your care."

Michael beamed with the compliment as he poured their drinks. "You noticed? Too many years went by where the only upkeep was a mowed lawn. Murray must have told you all I've done to bring the place back to life and to make it my own."

"I'm sure he left out a few details. I may have time to walk the grounds again before my flight tomorrow," he said as he took a long draw of Scotch, savoring its smoky smoothness. "If you'll join me."

"Oh. You saw the guards? Don't worry about them," Michael said with a dismissive wave of his hand. "They won't bother you. Thank you for coming on such short notice. I've had the feeling some of my dealings are reaching a critical juncture and meeting face to face will expedite things and make sure there are no misunderstandings." He moved to sit behind a massive mahogany desk, back stiff and upright as if concealing something. Pain? A weapon? The absence of a shoulder harness suggested Michael was nursing an injury. Why hadn't he mentioned it?

The similarity to Magnus' desk was unmistakable. Declan had to stop himself from looking for cabinets and oxygen canisters. Regardless of how wary his thoughts were, he kept his expression impassive. The Clearys were praised for keeping their friends close, their enemies closer, and their opinions blocked from detection. A Connaught clan trait was for emotions to flicker across their brows in marquee-like fashion. Keeping his thoughts to himself was one of his abilities the Connaughts marveled at during his summer stays and this was no time to falter. He had few advantages over Michael, and keeping his thoughts to himself was an advantage he needed.

Light from the green shaded desk lamp made the dark circles under Michael's eyes look like bruises. Were they? Stubble darkened the shadows across his face, making him look older than his thirty-one years. His movements, too, were not the movements of an athletic man, but jerked and tested as if under siege with pain or age. In total, the similarity to Magnus was remarkable.

"You're doing an excellent job on the corporate and financial matters," Michael said. "Consolidation of my father's enterprises under my name has gone more smoothly than I expected. Well done."

"Thank you." Declan waited for more. "You are not at risk of missing any deadlines for corporate filings or financial transactions." He spread documents along the desk. "You sounded urgent."

"All of my father's enterprises are now under my name. The Charity is dead." Michael spoke as if making a declaration.

"And the Rose has bloomed."

A brief smile tugged at Michael's mouth. "The speed at which the new organization firmed is gratifying. I have you to thank for that."

"Only for what exists on paper. The people needed a leader. You're proving to be quite adept."

"My uncle is well aware that I'm untested and he's urging me to make a bold move to establish my leadership."

At the mention of Liam, Declan interjected. "How is Liam? Recovering?"

"The stroke knocked the stuffing out of him, but he's fine." Michael brushed aside the inquiry. "You know as well as I do the tenuous relationships inside my ranks. Before I came to power, coalitions were forming that threatened my leadership. They're looking for a show of strength from me."

"You're moving money out of your non-profits to populist groups inside politically unstable countries. The charities have served their purpose and now you're funding destabilizing campaigns. You can't make a stronger statement than supporting political uprisings with money and arms."

"That's true enough, but men respond to action more than numbers moving on a balance sheet." The first light Declan had seen in Michael's eyes began to glow. "The people rely on me in a way I never envisioned. I started with the schools and changing lives by educating sons and daughters. I made a difference and it felt good, but it was their parents who have shown me how to create real change. Not just in one person or one family, but in entire communities. The money that I have," Michael paused, eyes focused on a point in the distance, "can change the shape of countries."

The crumbs of modest wealth no longer satisfied Michael. With full access to all Magnus had created, the urge to wield power was too strong. Reclaiming the six counties of Northern Ireland back into the fold of the Republic of Ireland was an opening foray into the world of global politics. Declan feared where the drive for total control would take his childhood friend.

Michael continued. "I've been worried the amounts of money I'm moving will come under scrutiny."

Declan searched Michael's face for the boy he knew. He looked for clues that the boy who loved building stick forts, and treated summer visitors as equals instead of pawns, still existed. The hatred of Magnus that once bound them had disappeared. Glimpses of the boy came in moments when Michael spoke of families fed or of medicines provided. The last sighting was months ago. Now he saw only a haunted man thrashing about in the deep end of life.

"You'll need to be careful to avoid drawing attention to yourself. Is that why I'm here?"

"Yes. I need to give the authorities something else to pursue. I'd hoped for that reporter to figure it out by now. I've provided as much direction as I could without exposing my involvement. I need a diversion now."

"Why the urgency?"

Michael evaded. He scanned his desk, gaze skipping from one item to the next, finally settling on a framed picture of Michael and Jessica taken at a formal event. "Oh, I need to hear about Jessica."

Declan didn't know what angered him more—the fact that Michael would pretend to care about her or that the pretension came as an afterthought. The real reason, he avoided. "I've kept you apprised of her progress. Physically, nerve damage is healing and she's regaining mobility."

"She's asked for me?"

Declan hedged. "I provide updates when asked."

"I should visit. I should have been at her side." Michael raked his fingers through his hair. "She knows why I couldn't be there, right? You explained it all to her, right?"

"I think she's quite clear on your limitations. By not visiting, you've helped keep her out of the public eye." Declan tried to keep the sarcasm out of his voice. He continued, hoping he sounded matter-of-fact. "The doctors have explained how her mental state impedes her recovery. She's no fool. Being perceived as incapable only works in her favor."

"How much longer will she be in the rehabilitation hospital?"

"It's unclear, but she's making enough progress to not be under medical surveillance anymore."

"Medical surveillance, what about . . ." Michael's voice trailed.

"Your crew is keeping a close eye on her. I'm sure they've confirmed she's made no attempts to expose you. That should count for something."

Michael shrugged. "I know her. It's only a matter of time before she makes her move." He scrubbed his hand over his face and head as if he could erase his worries.

Declan tried to hide his glower. "Is that why you're pushing to expose the bishop?"

Michael shifted his body to one side and winced, drawing his hand to his ribs. "I'm afraid my uncle was right. The bishop is an evil man and needs to be exposed, and Jessica is not loyal to me. If she was, she would have signed those papers, no questions asked. But she'd have done anything to protect her father."

"By having someone else expose the bishop, you get your diversion, but you lose your leverage over her. Is that wise?"

"She's biding her time until she can bring us down and guarantee her safety. And when she does, everything we've worked for will be dust." He jabbed his finger in the air toward Declan's nose. "I'm telling you right now, she's getting ready to bolt."

Declan pulled his head back. "She's not mobile on her own and not considered a flight risk. Plus, she's rattled by the affidavit and knows the authorities are watching her every move. That document had the impact you were hoping for."

"The affidavit did *not* have the impact I wanted. Nothing hit the news."

"Just because you didn't see her reaction or read about something in the news, doesn't mean the affidavit didn't have an impact. Authorities have focused on her and away from you. If they become aware of any overt actions taken for planning an attack, or if they feel she is a threat to others or a flight risk, they will move in. Otherwise, they are content to sit back and watch."

Michael began to pace. "The timing is all wrong. I have shipments leaving the States that have to make it to the Mideast. The profits I'm going to make are staggering."

"Shipments? I know nothing of this. Are you using horse transports as you initially hoped?"

"No, damn it. I had to change the operations to use coffins because she wouldn't go along. It's cyclone season and only a matter of time before a massive storm hits a place like Andhra Pradesh in India. Thousands will die. My agencies will use humanitarian aid as cover for getting arms out of the U.S. I'll use that cover until Jessica comes back into line. We have to be ready to move."

"Michael, you're overreaching," Declan warned.

"I need assurances that the diversion will be in place and that all available resources will be dedicated to monitoring an active terrorist investigation. If my operation is discovered, I'll need a scapegoat and building the evidence around Jessica as a terrorist will keep eyes off of me."

"If she doesn't go along with your plan?"

"Then her father will be exposed." Michael pounded his fist into his palm. "There's no other way for me to operate safely."

"There is. You can put off taking action." Declan waited until Michael's pace slowed. "My advice? You're moving too fast in an effort to look bold and in control. You've been in command for what now, six months? You accomplished the first thing you needed to, which was to assume command and prove yourself to be a leader. The threat of your organization imploding is gone. No one is pushing you to do more. Focus on Northern Ireland before you expand. The unification peace talks are on hold while decisions are made as to who will be involved in the negotiations. Sinn Fein needs to keep the lid on the IRA's violence or they will not get a seat at the bargaining table."

"You want time." The blue of Michael's eyes turned to ice. "I've told you what I needed and why, and you're playing for time. I need all the evidence in place that established Jessica as a terrorist. I need that now."

Declan watched as the panic that resided just behind Michael's brow seeped into his actions and words. "Why did you turn on her? She loved you."

"She turned on me first," Michael spat.

Memories of a summer night when they were teens sharpened. Michael, vying for the affections of a local girl and being rebuffed, suddenly turning on her and calling her a whore. Then, he stealthily eviscerated the girl's reputation through acts and words. Now? The drive for vengeance blinded him to the risks of doing the same to Jessica.

Michael's eye seemed to focus on something beyond the room. "Everything was in place. All she had to do was sign the syndicate papers."

"They were backdated. She was smart enough to see that and refuse to sign."

"You were supposed to get her signature and you failed! You should have used her father as leverage then!"

"There was no opportunity. And then the bombing happened."

"You failed," Michael repeated, fury building. "Couldn't you see when Electra and Jessica didn't agree to enter more syndicates with me that they were pulling out? Electra had me purged from her other companies, too. Did you have anything to do with that?" He spoke the words as if by rote. Was his manic behavior due to more than worry and desperation?

Declan adopted a soothing tone, like a parent calming the tantrum of a child. "Electra was wary of any involvement with you from the beginning. She became involved with your companies because she felt she was helping Jessica. When it was clear Jessica wanted out, Electra instructed her counsel to divest. He did so with great care and stealth. Brooks Carter was very skilled at not raising any alarms. I provided every safeguard that Jessica would remain under your protection and control. Neither Electra nor Jessica gave me any indication that they questioned your motives or plans. Electra had determined on her own that disengaging from your network was prudent. I believe she feared for her life if she became any more involved with you and terminated the relationship before MMC/2100 could co-opt cash flows."

"Electra's dead and I've had you spend day and night with Jessica for one reason and one reason only, and that was to get her signature on those papers as soon as she was capable. Jessica left me first," Michael seethed. "I could feel it. I could feel her doubt when she was here. She didn't let me decide things for her. I told her to stay, and she left. She never loved me the way I needed."

Declan's heart pounded. "She didn't trust you."

"I was protecting her! I'm the one who saved her on that mountaintop!"

"You were the reason she was bait."

"I brought her to Ireland so she could see what we could create together."

"You lied to her about the search and used her travels to set her up."

Michael ignored him, lost in his own thoughts. "If she refuses to help me, I'll expose the bishop. Once I do that, the coalitions he has built will disintegrate and I'll be able to step in and rebuild them to suit me."

Michael's expressions flashed from fear to confidence to ambition and back to fear within seconds. The brilliant corporate strategist flailed when politics and lives were added to the balance sheet. Liam was the genius political strategist and people manipulator, and Michael floundered in the vacuum created by Liam's stroke. As Declan watched the disintegration of rational thought, his stomach sank. A man who had the promise and the resources to affect peace for six counties fast-forwarded to delusions of world peace and centralized control.

The reason behind the manipulation, the paranoid practice of having spies watch spies, unsettled Declan to his core. Michael's threats evidenced his need for absolute control. When men have wealth and power beyond comprehension, boundaries of normal society no longer apply.

Declan glanced at his unpacked bags at the office entrance. "Once eyes are on Jessica, you believe no one will pay attention to you. Or me."

"Yes! Exactly!"

The gap between reality and fantasy grew.

"Time will only work in your favor," Declan responded. "The evidence against Jessica won't disappear and neither will she. As for the bishop? He'll be just another Vatican scandal within a week of the news hitting. You will stand a better likelihood of becoming a power broker if you work in the background with words and money. If you insist on pushing ahead with this plan, you won't need a diversion for your shipment if you follow the methods created by your father and uncle. Magnus took his time. He was careful. Most importantly, Liam made sure events happened without Magnus' direct involvement."

He stopped talking, knowing his words were unheard. What would it take to derail Michael's plan? He found himself in the middle of something he could not stop. This time, he cared about the outcome. The detachment he had cultivated from people and events to succeed as a cutthroat lawyer failed him.

Declan had committed the cardinal sin.

He cared what happened.

The days and weeks he had spent at Jessica's side had proven two things to him.

She was an innocent caught in a web beyond her comprehension and control.

And, he would kill to protect her.

He gave Michael his warmest smile even as the acid thought burned in his head. *You do not deserve her.*

"My father demanded absolute obedience from everyone. I ... I need to know I have that from you." In an instant, Michael changed, as if being inhabited by another person. A smile grew on half his mouth while his eyes began to gleam. "You're not doing all you can to follow my instructions. Why?"

"You hired me for my advice, not to be a puppet. A confident leader is one who knows how not to rush. Your people are not looking for action as much as they are looking for reassurance. There is plenty of time to prove yourself."

Not assuaged, Michael unrolled a diagram, using a phone, Scotch glass, and paperweights to hold down the corners. "I feel I've had plenty of time to work on my plan. Did you know? I had my father's home in the States surveyed."

Declan waited to swallow, noting his mouth had gone dry and the sides of his throat stuck together. The moisture that fled his mouth pricked at his scalp and under his arms as he spoke. "I'd mentioned to you how strong the real estate market is and how many developers are converting old mansions like your father's into condominiums. I'm glad you're considering maximizing your economic opportunity."

A survey. The room. The summoning to Michael's home was anything but formality. Michael had discovered the room and knew its purpose. With that discovery came the knowledge that Declan knew of the room and did not disclose it.

Declan's act of treason was exposed.

Beads of sweat mingled with the stubble on Michael's upper lip. "I took your advice. You had suggested diversifying my business interests. I thought trying my hand at real estate development would be an interesting addition. I've enjoyed bringing Ballyronan back to life. Developing my father's home would have proven to be a fun diversion." He pressed the curled edges of the paper down. "Funny the things the rich build into their homes."

Declan moved the lamp so its light would shine more brightly on the diagram, using the motion to direct it away from his face. "Most homes had servants' quarters with separate passages and staircases for them to move about the house without coming into contact with the family." He turned his head to the side, feigning interest. "What catches your eye?"

Michael had positioned himself behind the desk, leaving a clear path for Declan to reach the door. Was allowing an exit a fact of Michael's confidence or stupidity?

"The architect discovered a room off my father's office," Michael said, pointing to the schematic. "It took some doing, but he was able to find the latch and enter. I should have known it was there."

If Magnus had discovered his omission, Declan would have been a corpse at the bottom of the Quincy quarry within a day. He still had some hope, some way to explain.

"You didn't know about it?" Declan pressed. "I find that hard to believe. You roamed your father's home in the States as freely as you roamed Ballyronan."

Michael reacted as Declan hoped and pushed back, defensive. "He didn't ... I didn't ..." he sputtered, trying to sound in control, "I hadn't been there in years. I didn't know about this room."

"What else did the architect find?"

Michael raked a hand over his head. "Nothing. A table. Some chairs. Wires. That's it."

"Then what is your concern?"

Michael gave a look that was somewhere between torment and terror. The façade of the perfect murderer—cool under pressure, removed from suspicion—cracked open. Had Michael, a man who had killed in the line of duty, also killed his father in a planned, premeditated, cold-blooded way?

Declan was as sure of that as he was that he would be dead if he lied.

"I need to know what you know." Michael's hand moved to the lamp, gripping its base as if debating to lift it and crash it over Declan's head. "What was in that room?"

Declan smoothed the edges of concern as best as he could. "I found the security tapes. And the canister. I know about the nitrogen gas."

Michael blustered, then stilled. "Tapes? There are tapes? Of what? Over what time period?"

"Of the grounds and his office," Declan replied. "Up to and including the day he died." He waited while Michael absorbed the information. "Magnus was murdered."

Michael fidgeted, animated by a wave of nervous energy. He rearranged perfectly piled papers on his desk.

Declan's blood chilled as Michael spoke. "You're damned right Magnus was murdered. Liam killed him. I learned about Liam's plan and tried to save Magnus by swapping out the canister. He paused, body and expression morphing to warmth and admiration. "You were to inventory my father's home and someone discovered something I had hoped to keep inside the family. Who else knows?"

"No one. You're telling me your uncle killed your father and you don't want to take any action?"

"What would be the point of incarcerating an old man who has suffered a stroke? Why raise questions when the police aren't interested? I needed you to do a job, and you've done it perfectly. Do you have any questions?"

"None." Declan knew better than to ask questions of a liar.

"There's one last job."

"And what is that?"

"Destroy Jessica and the bishop. Make her a terrorist."

Silvern Rehabilitation Hospital
Boston, Massachusetts

CAMBRIDGE'S SKYLINE SHONE against lights reflecting off low-lying clouds. The morning commute had not begun and few cars traveled on Storrow Drive. Jessica let her mind's eye trace the roads up to the North Shore, through Beverly and into Hamilton. She wondered if she could ever again call the place of her childhood "home."

Declan opened the sliding doors leading from the lounge to the solarium. A blast of cold with a hint of musk stroked her cheeks. His scent mingled with train diesel and salt air, exposing his morning commute from the North Shore. Corners of papers from his open briefcase waved and flirted with the breeze. He balanced coffees with one hand and a phone in the other as he used his foot to pull the door closed behind him. He placed one cup beside her and the papers at his feet.

A minute passed in habitual silence. She was aware of him. Too aware.

"I ... don't ... want ... you ... here." Her voice was barely a whisper. Words were returning to her. Her brain conjured them slowly. Sometimes the word would linger behind smoke, its presence more felt than known, and not let itself be spoken. Other times, the right word would hover behind her eyes waiting for the commands of speech to trickle through nerve synapses and reward her with an utterance. When she finally spoke, sharp consonants would round and words would slur together. Most days, she just didn't give a damn whether she spoke or not.

"Yeah. I get that. I'm not exactly a fan of being in this place either." He danced a wooden stick in his cup, mixing white cream into the dark coffee. "I have a surprise for you."

She turned her eyes to look at him. "N-no. Hate them."

He brought his face close to hers. Was he smiling? "I'm not a fan of surprises either, but this I think you'll like." He shuffled through the stack of papers, chose one, and handed it to her. "The doctors say you're doing well with your physical therapy and are ready for the next step."

"No … more … therapy."

"No? Tough." He motioned with his hand. A moment later two nurses started fussing over her.

"Stop."

"No. I won't. I found a hippotherapy center north of Boston. You're getting on a horse. Today."

Hippotherapy. Physical therapy on horseback. Jessica didn't know whether to be thrilled or angered beyond reason. Regardless, she was terrified. Terrified at having the harsh facts of all she had lost become too clear. Buttoned away in her shell, she didn't have to face feelings or reality. She couldn't walk and she sure as shit couldn't ride. Riding a horse is all about the subtle cues and guides telegraphed through slight pressure on the reins or through a leg. If her body scrambled the signals, how was a horse to know what she wanted? And she couldn't be reduced to sitting on an animal as it was led around a pen like a child at a petting zoo. Cowboy hat and cap gun thrown in for no additional charge. Ride? No way.

She looked toward the door. A security guard walked the hallway, thumbs thrust in his belt. "Can't leave."

Declan followed her gaze. "Let me handle him. You're not a captive and leaving the grounds for additional therapy is encouraged. The physical and occupational therapists here think riding will help your recovery. They agreed to work with Windrush to devise and oversee a program for you. I've gotten all of the approvals from hospital admin. Besides, you're not exactly a flight risk, so don't worry about drawing the wrong kind of attention. Right now, the most important thing is to get you back on your feet."

The only thing that matched her resolve not to engage with the world was Declan's resolve to have her do just that. Within minutes, nurses dressed her in jeans, sweater, and boots—the first real clothes Jessica had worn in weeks. If she needed any evidence of the change in her body, her favorite Levis provided it. The faded denim hung off her hips when the nurses balanced her on her feet.

The day unfolded with precision. Declan drove over the Tobin Bridge and up Route 1. Jessica drank in the landmarks of her youth.

They passed the orange dinosaur at the mini-golf place and the huge neon cactus sign of the Hilltop Steakhouse. She screwed her eyes shut as she remembered family dinners and how Jim loved his steak rare and his fries dipped in steak sauce. The staff there always gave Erin an extra scoop of ice cream. Years later, Bridget and Gus would treat themselves and Jessica to teriyaki tips, unless grilled lamb was on special, a delicacy they reveled in. She remembered them jamming extra butter pats into the foil wrapped potatoes. Extra sour cream and chives mandatory.

She could remember. Like the little Dutch boy holding back the break in the dam with his finger, she let go. First, the memories started with a trickle. She could remember the angles of their faces, the sound of their laughter, and the scent of their clothes. Images of friends and favorite horses came next. Dinners at Myopia Hunt Club and too many horse shows to count poured out, details mingled with flashbacks of trips to Suffolk Downs holding Gus' hand. She remembered staying close to Jim's knee while touring the shed row stables. A breach in the dam and flood threatened. She struggled to keep her emotions from overwhelming her.

The memories sifted into place, but what they meant eluded her. The weeks spent in her own enforced isolation were essential for her to broker peace inside her warring heart. She was loved and lied to. Until she reconciled the stories of her family, she couldn't let go of her own bewilderment. She pressed her palm to the window as if pushing away the reasons why her life unfolded as it did. The pains of love and loss were too acute and stopped her healing.

She forgave them their lies and vowed not to add any more of her own. But forgiving herself? That was another matter.

She looked at Declan's profile as he concentrated on the ubiquitous Route 1 traffic that snaked slowly northward. How did he fit into the picture? Regardless of the fact he was Michael's key person in the States, she sensed a decency about him she hadn't sensed in Michael. This past week she felt an upheaval that shook Declan to his core. He had not left her side. Whether that was due to a direct order from Michael or not, she didn't know. What she did know was she felt a tremendous amount of gratitude for Declan.

Facts and questions floated, unmoored in the turbulent waters of her healing brain. What about Michael? If Declan had been ordered to watch her, was it out of Michael's desire to protect her by having a trusted aide never leave her side? Or was it as Electra had feared, that Michael provided body guards and a walled-off existence to maintain control? More than questioning Michael, Jessica blamed herself for falling under his control. She wanted what he offered. Security. Acceptance. Until she could forgive herself for being blind and weak, she didn't deserve to walk or talk.

Less than an hour later, they drove down a narrow road and turned into the graveled drive of Windrush Farm. Declan turned off the engine. They sat in comfortable silence as she took in all the details. The world of a hospital is a spectrum of whites and grays, antiseptics, and bustle. The world of horse is filled with a kaleidoscope of colors, smells, and sounds. A large red metal structure of an indoor arena sat to her left, yellow mums dotted the entrance. The forest was a shock of green trees and sugar maples bathed in the reds, golds, and oranges of fall. Beyond the parking area lay paddocks framed by split rails and white barns. A small pond with a duck house sat tucked behind a row of pine trees. Horses grazed in fields or stuck their heads over stall doors.

Immediately the tangy aroma of horse enveloped her. In spite of herself, the rush of endorphins warmed her. Her chest rose and fell with a deep breath.

A grey sedan with two men pulled in behind them. A few minutes later the white van of a news station pulled up on the shoulder of the road. The moment of peace passed. She balled her hands into fists.

Declan reached over and uncurled her hands. "You'll be inside the arena. No one will see you. You can do this."

"Can't."

"You can and you will. No more playing possum."

Before she could react, a wiry woman dressed in denim and a purple windbreaker strode up. "Jessica? I'm Mandy Hogan. We're so happy to see you." A slight drawl inflected her words. She looked over at Declan. "Mr. Cleary here has been telling us a lot about you. Do you want to see the stables or would you like to ride?"

Ride? Already? A woman led a compact chestnut gelding, fully tacked, to the arena. Jessica couldn't take her eyes off the pair. Resistance was futile. "R-ride."

Jessica was wheeled toward the arena as Mandy explained the process to Declan. "Not everyone knows how much benefit people with physical injuries or disabilities can receive from hippotherapy. Stroke, traumatic brain injury, cerebral palsy, and many more birth defects can impact a person's ability to stand or sit without assistance. Sitting astride a horse engages core muscles for balance deep inside the body, helping people stay upright. The gait of the horse mimics the human body's natural rhythm of walking. Riders receive the dual benefit of core strengthening and remapping the brain's signals to help regain independent mobility. A physical therapist will assist in our sessions, too."

Declan's brows furrowed. "What if she can't balance on her own?"

"We'll place this belt around her waist," Mandy said, holding up a white canvas belt, about six inches wide with two handles on either side. "This will give our sidewalkers something to grab onto to help keep her steady."

Jessica ignored the humans and focused on the horse. The small gelding's ears were pricked forward, not in an alarmed way, but relaxed, interested in the routine of mounting a new rider, not bored or threatened by it. Horses used for therapeutic purposes were different from the high-octane beasts she was accustomed to riding. Chosen for their even temperament, horses used for the disabled are trained to trust their handlers and to filter out many of the spastic cues a disabled rider may give.

Declan maneuvered Jessica over to the horse. Mandy placed the lead rope into Jessica's hands, but remained by the horse's head.

"This is Bojangles. Bo's been with our farm for six years."

Bo lowered his head, unafraid of her or the chair. The warm, pungent musk of horse filled her. She closed her eyes and felt Bo's breath move from her hands up her arms pausing to nibble at her shirt. Habit of horsemanship pushed the world away, allowing her to sense Bo's reactions and anticipate his next move. She could feel his calm. She could feel herself awaken and want to move. The realization empowered her.

Her heart quickened as she traced her body with her mind's eye. Cues between her brain and muscles logjammed, and her legs and arms remained limp and drained of energy. How could she ever ride again if she couldn't telegraph her thoughts through her body into the horse's actions?

She looked at Declan, eyes rounded with questions and worry.

"You can do this," was all he said as he wheeled her up the ramp to the mounting platform.

Mandy continued to speak in a languid way that hinted at Southern roots, rambling on about the training the horses and people undergo. She placed a riding helmet on Jessica's head and fastened the clasp under her chin. A lift whirred overhead and descended toward Jessica. Mandy placed two L-shaped braces under Jessica's armpits and pads under her thighs. A few seconds later, Jessica was lifted from her chair. An assistant reached over, grabbed Jessica's right leg and guided her into the saddle.

Muscles can remember even if a brain is unwilling. The creak of leather triggered a cascade of reactions Jessica could not control and the endorphin rush was better than any painkiller or drug. Warmth spread from her scalp through to her fingers and legs. Immediately her toes twitched in search of the iron stirrups. Her hands grasped the reins.

Mandy laughed. "Usually I have to explain what to do and how to hold the reins. For safety, we keep two sidewalkers beside the rider and one more horse handler at the horse's head. The rider has as much autonomy and control as they can physically and cognitively provide the horse. It's pretty obvious you don't need any coaching. How are you doing? Comfortable?"

Comfortable? Being on a horse again was like having a limb reattached. What brought her to this moment didn't matter. The only thing that mattered was that the first feelings of freedom and peace she had had since her injury flickered to life.

She didn't want to cry. She didn't want hot tears to roll down her cheeks. She only wanted to ride like the devil herself and leave this place in a cloud of dust.

But she couldn't. Not today, at least. Her muscles burned with fatigue by the end of the session, and her heart broke at being slugged with the reality of all she had lost. When Mandy asked if she was ready to dismount, Jessica surprised herself by nodding yes. Mandy suggested riding once a week. Jessica demanded more.

Mandy hesitated. "This is expensive. Hippotherapy sessions aren't covered by insurance."

"Book the session. The cost is covered," Declan said.

"N-no." Jessica turned in her chair to look at Declan. "No more help. I can pay."

Declan cocked an eyebrow upward and the corner of his mouth twitched. "Suit yourself." He turned to Mandy. "You heard the lady. Sessions three times a week," he said with a glance at Jessica for affirmation. Getting a nod, he finished, "Effective immediately."

He brought the car closer to the arena, and Mandy stood between Jessica and the cars gathered on the side of the road. Two news vans and three cars had arrived. A petite woman with short dark hair jumped up and shook a sleeping driver by the shoulder, pointing toward Jessica. The man reached into the back seat. Declan tensed as he pointed something in their direction. The rapid clicks of a camera shutter were heard over the clop of the horse's hooves. Declan hurried Jessica into the car and sped off.

They drove until they approached the turn off to take them back to Boston. Jessica put her hand on Declan's arm and uttered, "Hamilton." He drove on.

The present merged with the past in surreal images of her childhood home. Polo fields and hunting grounds were nestled between winding drives and mansions. Even the smaller, more modest homes were meticulous with clipped shrubs and cobblestone driveways. Expensive cars parked under mature trees.

He didn't ask what she wanted to see, but drove down the road that used to lead to Wyeth Worldwind Farms. The land had been sold and portioned into two-acre lots dotted with McMansions. They drove along Bay Road, past the funeral home and through the center of town. He slowed at the Wenham Tea House, inquiring.

"No. Too much," she said. Memories of Bridget and her together, sharing scones and a pot of Irish Breakfast tea, were vivid, but not painful. The flood threatened again. Her lower lip trembled and she turned her head away.

"Is there anything else you want to see?" Declan asked, concerned. She felt him tuning in to her mood like a ham radio operator trying to get the best signal.

"No. Saying good-bye." Whether she said good-bye to her childhood or to a person who would never exist again was unclear, but she felt progress. She could feel the momentum of her recovery and wondered how much of it she needed to hide.

Declan acknowledged a change in her and turned the car toward Boston.

They traveled on back roads and she used the time to sift through all of her experiences and conversations of the day. She waited until they were crossing back over the Tobin Bridge to speak. "Playing p-possum?" she challenged, drawing upon his earlier comment.

An uncharacteristic twitch tugged at his cheek. He fiddled with the radio station and eventually turned it off.

"Possums pretend to be dead hoping that a predator will pass them by. When they spring back to life, they are known for their fierce will to survive. They are one of nature's most vicious fighters."

She chuffed.

They drove the rest of the way in silence.

Rome, Italy

"I AM IN need of a confession," Kavan said as he sat on a wooden pew. The chapel glowed. Well-oiled wood reflected the light from thousands of candles, some in votives of red, most in creamy white. Stained glass windows punctuated the expanse of unadorned walls, giving the chapel a feeling of glory in the midst of humbleness. Set in a corner of the old city of Rome, the sounds of the street were a mix of vendors, carts, and barking dogs. A rosary, resplendent with onyx beads and gold links, interwove his fingers.

"My son, you've come here as Archbishop. Did you not use the time prior to your ascension to unburden your soul? What is so important that you have called me to meet you here?" Cardinal Kutu Balewa crossed his arms over his black simar. The red piping of the placket, sash, and close-fitting zucchetto cap offered a perfect complement to his ebony skin.

Hearing his new title burdened Kavan. Where had the time gone?

He smiled. "I'm honored to have received the Holy See's approval and appointment to Archbishop. I'm humbled by the respect I'm afforded, but I'm in conflict."

"The last time you summoned me with a troubled soul, we met at the tomb of Pope Julius II. The tomb remained unfinished to show displeasure at Julius' rejection of the oath of celibacy."

"The most generous epitaphs credit him with spreading the faith, but it was his seed that spread the virus of bastards," Kavan said. "And it was in the presence of Julius' remains I confessed my paternity to you."

Cardinal Balewa nodded slowly. "Your daughter is well?"

"She is on the long road of healing."

Balewa looked around the empty chapel. "This chapel, too, has great history. Its construction was commissioned by the Medici family. The family had humble beginnings, but the Medici bank they created became the most profitable bank in Europe during the Renaissance. The Medicis were patrons of the arts, and because of them we know Botticelli, Michelangelo, and Leonardo da Vinci."

"They are also known as the Godfathers of the Renaissance," Kavan said, his fondness for his African friend showing. "Is it any coincidence that the family helped the Church consolidate its power by forming a partnership with it?"

Balewa tented his fingers in front of his nose. "You did not bring me here to discuss Vatican history."

"No, but the Church is not ignorant of its role in shaping history. Even without a papal decree, individual clerics support men and women who fight oppression. That support is often enough to give a man the strength to stand in front of his peers and make the speech that galvanizes souls to action. You are famed as the priest who stood in the slums of Soweto and helped give voice to the wrongs of apartheid. You know the power of God worked through your words."

Balewa chuckled. "And now I'm in Rome. With you. Sitting in a Godfather's chapel."

Kavan did not hide the tickertape of thoughts that ran across his brow. The events of the past months had picked him up by the scruff of the neck and propelled him forward. Like a kitten in its mother's mouth, he was lifted from one den and deposited into another. The time had come for him to make sense of it all.

"When I first learned my peers considered me for Archbishop, I was stunned. My work in Belfast was the work of many. I tended births and deaths, weddings, and funerals as did so many other priests. I've done nothing more than they did to keep the embers of our religion strong."

"You have saved souls."

"And I have let souls burn." He masked his thickened voice with a cough. The weight of his truth pressed the air from his lungs and threatened to still his heart.

In a mad tumble of words, Kavan purged his burden. "It started with the simple act of listening. I listened to the fathers who failed to understand their sons. I listened to the politicians who lied about the bribes and voted against their hearts. I listened to women who sold their bodies to put food on the table for their children. I listened as I was taught to do and absolved them of their sins."

"We all are tormented by the sins we carry for others. This is the cost of our calling."

"As I listened, I learned. I learned which politicians were weak and why. I knew the spurned sons who wanted to make their fathers proud. I became the center of a web of information. I prayed to remain neutral, to open my heart so that I could love each as God intended."

"But inaction burned your conscience."

Kavan's head snapped up to look at his friend. "You understand!"

Balewa drew a heavy sigh. "I understand all too well, my friend. That is why I'm in Rome and not my home."

Kavan sputtered. "What? Why?"

"The eyes of the Church are the eyes of even the most humble person. I, too, was tormented by the injustices I witnessed. Yes, I tended the spiritual lives of my diocese, but I did not remain passive. Against a formal command, I actively participated in the planning and execution of civil unrest. Although my intention was pure, it placed the Church in jeopardy. The penance for my action was removal from Soweto. The reward for my intent was my appointment to Cardinal and Rome." Balewa sat in comfortable silence. "We come into this world as men first and become a man of God second. We share the support of the community when we wrestle with celibacy and what we give up to live as we do." When he could wait no longer, he asked, "Is this the reason for your confession?"

Kavan hesitated. The foundation had been laid for him to divulge all of his sins to his friend, compatriot, and confidant. All he had to do was inhale and form the words. "Your Eminence . . . "

"Kavan, we've been friends far too long for titles and solicitudes."

"Kutu," Kavan began, "you know of the Troubles in Northern Ireland."

"All too well."

"Once I found myself at the center of the web, I became the spider. Both sides confided in me. The politicians on Stormont told me of the Irish schools they planned to close or the marches they refused to permit. I was privy to the mechanisms of their oppression. Along the road to broker many compromises, I lost my neutrality. The soldiers of the IRA spoke to me of their plans for unrest. I used my knowledge to guide the hands of the rebels. The process to reunify Northern Ireland became stronger with my help."

"This is why you are in Rome with me. You are not to be an active participant in the machinations of war and death."

"I have used the time to extricate myself from the network. I had been the conduit between the political and the underground, but my ascension to Archbishop afforded me the reason to unravel the web that entangled me. I was able to do so without tipping tempers into violence and by keeping stability in the ranks."

"Politics is a filthy business and few are able to navigate its waters without drowning. You fear your paternity being discovered and have removed yourself in anticipation." Balewa's voice grew heavy.

Kavan squirmed. "The Church will survive the public outcry and I believe the seeds of my counsel will continue to bloom for peace."

"Well done, my friend. But this network you fostered is not the sole reason for your confession."

"Networks of war cannot exist without money."

Balewa lowered his head to his chest. "Ah, and that brings us back to why you chose to meet in the Medici's chapel."

"I know a family of great wealth who uses their riches for good only to mask their evil."

"Kavan," Balewa said, voice low with warning, "Good will win out. You cannot forsake your vows and use your position for ill."

"I cannot let the knowledge of their Achilles heel rot from disuse. I've spent the past months ensuring stability even if world events careen out of control. My stay in Rome is temporary and I am no longer needed in Belfast, but my influence there is stronger than it has ever been."

"My friend," Balewa said, gathering Kavan's hands in his own. The rosary dangled, unseen, from Kavan's little finger. "In your heart are the seeds of insurrection. You pledged your troth and married the Church. You cannot forsake her."

"I have heard the lament of murderers and given them absolution. I have heard the confessions of pedophiles and vomited after I bestowed God's forgiveness. I need to know if you will hear my confession when the time is right."

Balewa gripped Kavan's hands as he turned his face up to the altar. A crucifix, carved centuries before from rare wood, hung suspended in space and time. The light from a thousand candles glittered in the tears that rolled down his cheeks like stars in the night.

"I will always be here for you, my friend."

November 1996
Windrush, Farm
North Andover, Massachusetts

JESSICA STRAIGHTENED HERSELF in the saddle, stomach and thigh muscles screaming for relief. Her shirt was damp with sweat as she elbowed her sidewalkers' hands away from the belt. She wasn't going to ride like some sack of potatoes propped in a saddle.

"I . . . can . . . do . . . it," she panted. "Alone."

Kathy, her horse handler, looked at the two sidewalkers. "You heard the lady. Walk beside her with your hands up, ready to balance her, but don't touch her. I'll keep Bo on a loose lead so he'll listen to his rider and not me. Let's see what she can do."

Jessica willed her legs to press into Bo's sides, urging him forward. Bo's ears cocked back, listening for a cue. Muscles and nerves, mending after injury, scrambled the non-verbal language of riding into the tower of Babble. The more she willed her body to obey, the more her body jerked and stuttered its way to compliance. The tension from her emotions made her limbs stiffen even more.

The past sessions had been a mixture of promise and dashed hopes. She wanted to ride independently from the moment she mounted, but a lightning storm of emotions flashed through her, jolting to life muscles that had been accustomed to dormancy. She knew Bo would only interpret each degree of her own frustration or anger as a signal that the horse himself was in danger. Each session, a viscous circle of a rider's frustration and a horse's instinctive fear, set Jessica up for failure.

She forced herself to calm down, chastising herself for her own impatience. Improvement was happening, even if it was maddeningly slow and unpredictable. In the months since the bombing, flesh and bone had mended, but inflammation and nerve damage vexed progress. Complicating her recovery was the fear of what would happen to her after she was released from the cocoon of the medical world. She had always had a plan, always knew what her next sequence of steps or goals would be. Now? The tension that seized her body manifested both physical and psychological injury. She didn't know where the demarcation between the two started or ended.

Posters of empty wheelchairs, discarded crutches, and horses with smiling riders hung in the viewing area. For many people, sitting astride a horse and commanding it into motion was as close to independent mobility and freedom as they had ever experienced. For them, the power of confidence and the feeling of self-worth bloomed to replace dependence and hopelessness.

Doctors were unclear if she would walk again and she preferred to keep them guessing. The only progress she allowed them to see was her ability to ride. The rest of her healing would come in moments when four hooves flew across the earth, not touching the ground, suspended between life and breath.

Healing meant revealing her progress and facing facts she wasn't ready to face. What would happen when authorities found her well enough to navigate the world with little help? She needed a wheelchair, right? Flight risks don't use wheelchairs. Or do they? Riding at Windrush, away from the hospital, allowed her to explore her capabilities with a lessened fear of discovery. Doctors and nurses at Silvern, natural cheerleaders of the recovering, would be too thrilled with her progress to keep each improvement to themselves.

She could only trust a horse with her secret.

The knowledge that her horse only cared about the here and now comforted her. Would Bo decide to listen to the human at his head leading him, or the rider who swayed and tipped with each step? The simplest commands to have Bo yield to the pressure of her leg as he turned, morphed into a raised heel, a yanked rein, and an off balance body. Each week he had stood still, only moving when the horse handler and sidewalkers stood in their places. Each week Bo questioned if the tilt and jerk on his back was from fear.

I am not afraid of this horse. I only need a way to communicate with him.

Jessica closed her eyes and urged him forward with what she envisioned to be a gentle nudge with both heels. Her legs twitched and jerked at Bo's sides. For a moment, Bo stood confused, then took a hesitant step forward. Jessica willed her legs to work in unison, encouraging him until he engaged in a confident stride. Bo began slowly, one ear cocked to her, the other toward Kathy, asking who he should obey. Feeling the sway and rock of Bo's walk, Jessica relaxed.

Memories of Gus' lessons surfaced.

"Think past the jump," he would say. "Keep your mind three strides ahead. The horse will feel what you think better than your hands can communicate it. Convince the beast you are of one mind and you'll be through the tough patch before you know it."

She began to think past her injury to a time when she would become one with her animal again, refusing to acknowledge any barrier of scar or doubt. She had not tested herself beyond putting one foot in front of the other and could not conceive an impediment to riding existed. After two deep breaths, she envisioned pushing her weight through her leg to her heel and moved her hand out slightly, opening it with a command to turn. She could feel Bo yield as his back curved into a supple bend around a tight turn, and then another. For the first time in months, she determined which direction to travel, when to start, and when to stop.

After they had carved a graceful figure eight, she pulled him to a stop.

She reached down and patted his neck. Progress.

A pattering of applause came from ringside. A movement in the viewing lounge caught her eye. The priest from Silvern Rehab, Father Blanton, stood with Mandy and beamed.

"That was great!" Mandy strode out and patted Jessica's thigh. "Incredible! I've never seen anyone progress as quickly as you have." Mandy turned to the priest. "You were right. She needed to be around horses."

Father Blanton, a reed of a man with a shock of black hair rimming his head, walked up and stopped a respectful distance from the horse. He kept his arms crossed and positioned himself to keep Mandy between him and Bo. His eyebrows arched as he scanned the distance from hooves to withers, assessing the five foot height with poorly concealed trepidation.

Jessica shot him a look but said nothing. When did that priest become so involved with her care? Declan had pushed her to ride, and now Father Blanton stepped in seamlessly while Declan traveled. A hollow part of her heart remembered wishing Michael was there, encouraging her, supporting her. She pushed aside the feeling, knowing she was through making wishes based upon illusions.

"None of us had much of a choice," Father Blanton said. "If we cared about Jessica at all, it was pretty clear she needed to get on a horse as quickly as possible."

Mandy laughed. "No matter whose idea it was, Jessica is making great progress." She stepped forward and placed her hand on Jessica's knee. "Don't get frustrated and fall into the trap of thinking your life is over. Healing takes time. Your life will be different than it was before, but you're here, able to live it. Mold it into something that is *you.*"

Mandy led Bo and Jessica back to the dismounting ramp. The wheelchair was placed below the lift.

"No lift," Jessica said, steering Bo to a padded area instead of the ramp. She looked at Father Blanton. "Help me off."

"What? Me?" the priest blustered. "I'm not . . . I don't want . . . "

"It's easy," Mandy said, stepping beside Bo. "Watch." She reached her hands up to Jessica.

Jessica dropped her reins and reached her arms toward her and leaned to the side. Gravity did the rest as Mandy helped her slip to the ground with arms encircled around her waist, then guided her into the chair. Mandy smiled. "Baby steps. You'll find a way back."

Was Jessica finding her own way back? Riding again was more than a nudge, it was a kick in the pants. The indignant anger she wanted to harbor against the world for being injured didn't ignite. She didn't want to rely on anyone and she didn't want to be angry. Mostly, she didn't want to be vulnerable, as it softened her defenses. She didn't want to admit she missed Declan.

Returning to the car, Jessica looked out over the paddocks. Horses pulled at hay bulging through wooden mangers; others grazed peacefully on grass tufts that dotted the well-trod ground. Their shining coats and the contented calm that permeated the farm spoke to them being well cared for. Each was smaller than the animals she was accustomed to riding and their gentle personalities showed in the way they idly assessed the bustle around the barns. Brandywine's horses would have had their heads held up high, ears pricked forward, bodies ready to run. Windrush's horses sniffed the earth, one ear cocked for the sound of a grain bucket, the other toward the humans, ready to mosey over for an offered treat.

One horse trotted back and forth in its paddock, head held high, and tail flagged. The dappled dark grey coat mixed with the sunlight filtering through the trees. Jessica could not believe her eyes.

"Blue Jeep?" she asked.

Mandy smiled and nodded. "We've been waiting for a time to tell you."

"How? When?" Jessica looked from Father Blanton to Mandy, but settled on the horse.

"When Wyeth's Worldwind Farm was sold, most of the horses went to other breeding farms. Your family only had two horses they kept for their own riding. Blue Jeep was bought by a family in North Andover. He had a successful career with them as a hunter, but seven years is a long time to stay in competition condition. You're a hometown girl," Mandy said with a shrug, "so we followed your story and knew you had a horse in training at the Olympics." Her voice trailed off, leaving the unspeakable unspoken. "Declan reached out to us about helping with your rehabilitation. We've worked with people injured in many ways. Stroke. Veterans with PTSD. Women rehabilitating from human trafficking. Each person is so different, but one thing we knew. We had to find a horse to motivate you."

Blue Jeep. Jeeps. The horse Gus gave her on her sixteenth birthday. The horse she flung herself on and rode like wind across fields and over anything in her path. The horse she skipped school to ride. Panic at all she had yet to overcome threatened to overwhelm her.

The edges of her vision darkened and narrowed. She looked at Father Blanton, blinking her eyes dry. "Y-you knew about this?"

Father Blanton reached out and rubbed her arm. His expression clouded with uncertainty. "Only after the fact. The horse community is a small one. Declan had Mandy ask around if anyone knew anything about what happened to Worldwind's horses. Blue Jeep was easy to find because he didn't travel that far. The stable that bought him gave him a great life, but he's older now and can't be ridden as he used to be." They pushed her to Jeeps' paddock. Father Blanton knelt beside her and took her hands in his. "You need to have the faith that you can do this."

Damn them. Memories of Jeeps' mane in her fist as her thighs gripped his back, balancing over one jump after another . . . the feel of power as he surged forward, eyes watering as wind whipped her face . . . the way he responded to the smallest command, a shift of weight, a touch of her calf.

She pulled her eyes away from Jeeps. If she looked at him, she knew her heart would be lost to the horse and she feared where else it could be lost. Focusing on a distant tree, she repeated a silent mantra. *Declan is Michael's man. He's Michael's man. He's setting me up for heartbreak and failure.*

The pull of Jeeps was too strong.

Jeeps stood at the far side of the paddock, head raised and muscles coiled. He wasn't trained to the ways of Windrush and his life in a show barn had surrounded him with action and luxury. With ears pricked forward and nostrils flared, he listened and smelled for cues that would tell him friend or foe.

Mandy placed a peppermint in Jessica's hand. "We don't like to teach our horses that treats can be found our pockets. Many of our clients don't have the balance or the reflexes to stay safe when a horse is nosing around for food. Jeeps isn't in training to be a therapeutic horse, so we'll let him know you're his best pal." The sound of crinkling wrap and the smell of the candy was too tempting for Jeeps to ignore. He walked over and sniffed at Jessica.

It is a trick of humans to imprint emotions and memories on animals. What a person feels, they wish their animals to feel the same. Jessica felt Jeeps' breath on her face and hands and wondered if he knew the shriveled body on wheels in front of him was the girl who rode him bareback like hellfire. He took the peppermint and nudged her lap for more.

Jessica's chest burned with emotion. She wanted to scream, but knew that doing so would frighten the horse. The instincts of an equestrian overruled impulsive gestures. First impressions mattered. Any positive associations Jeeps had would turn to triggers of fear if she unleashed the wail of frustration and loss that swelled inside. Her breath hovered between worlds.

"No more. No more." Jessica could feel the hot upwelling of emotion and feared it would find a fissure in her crust.

Mandy squatted down at Jessica's knees and held her hands. "Don't get overwhelmed. Step by step. You don't have to make any decisions now. Just take in the information."

Father Blanton eased his shoulder forward, careful to stay well outside of Jeeps' biting range. "What would have happened to this horse if you didn't find him?"

Mandy stood and stroked Jeeps' neck. "The farm he was at was a good farm, but they're focused on high level competition. He's past his peak and upkeep is expensive. It's a sure bet he would have gone to a stable intent on wringing the last bit of performance out of him. Injuries and illness were next. After that? He's too hot-blooded for a school horse and too high strung for a family barn." She kicked a toe against a rock. "It's anyone's guess, but the odds don't favor a comfortable retirement.

"So, you're saying if Jessica doesn't take Jeeps under her wing, his future is uncertain?" Father Blanton pushed for more information.

Mandy handed one more peppermint to Jessica. "Well, um, uncertain is a nice way around what his future could be. Like I said, horses are expensive to keep up. Some people feel a merciful and expedient death is the most humane way to deal with the issues." She looked at her watch. "I've got another client coming in. Take as much time as you want to visit with Jeeps and the other horses." She turned on her heel and strode off toward the arena.

Father Blanton grabbed the handles of her wheelchair and pushed her up the hill to the barns. Five stalls lined each side of a broad concrete corridor. Horses munched quietly on hay or stuck their heads over stall doors to greet them. Stablehands prepped the evenings' feedings by lining buckets along the feed room's floor and glancing at instructions on a clipboard. Some of the stablehands were individuals with special needs. One was a woman with facial features signaling Down Syndrome. Another woman avoided eye contract and used sign language to communicate with the barn manager. A third man, wearing a U.S. Army baseball cap and a camouflage shirt, nodded a curt greeting and resumed grooming a stocky palomino.

A stab of grief shot through Jessica as she remembered Electra and her determination to use Brandywine as an oasis for LeeAnne. Each of the stablehands contributed to the animals and farm in their own way, and the horses accepted them as they were. No judgments. No recriminations. Jessica remembered how the hard edges of LeeAnne's face softened when a horse nudged pockets for a treat and how LeeAnne would heave a sigh of relief when she settled in a saddle.

Gaining confidence, Father Blanton stepped closer and rubbed the foreheads of few of the more curious horses. One large black horse with a white star, cross-tied in the corridor to be groomed, tugged his shirt asking for more attention while keeping a front leg cocked to bolt or to kick with a prey animal's instinct for survival. The priest hesitated, then obliged with a vigorous neck rub, and didn't notice the mint-laced slobber that darkened his sleeve. The horse relaxed and leaned forward, exploring with a nose shoved into his chest and stomach. For an instant, his guard dropped, enjoying the moment. He returned to Jessica's side and watched the routine of evening feedings unfold. Wagons of flaked hay lumbered behind stablehands en route to paddock mangers. The sounds of grain filling buckets made the horses whicker in anticipation.

Gravel crunched under Father Blanton's feet as they walked back to the cars.

When he bent down to remove her feet from the footrests to help her into the car, the scent of horse mixed with hair tonic and mouthwash. She remained silent until she could stand it no longer.

"Why? Why did you do that to me?" She turned to him. Her hands clamped into fists and pressed on her lap.

"I've spent many years helping people come to grips with a new life after a catastrophic injury. The life they knew vanished in the second it took a foot to slip off a ladder or a blood vessel to explode in their brain. What takes time to realize is that the person they were … the essence of who they *are* … still burns as brightly as it ever did."

She slapped the arms of her chair. "I … am … not *this*."

Father Blanton smiled. "No kidding. I saw you dismiss help today because you're determined to do whatever it is by yourself. Then I saw you nearly crumple because you couldn't do what you set your mind to do. You are not a cripple and you are not weak. In fact, I'll bet you can do more than we know." He raised his chin and looked at her from the corner of his eyes.

His expression made her stutter. "Wh-what? Then why f-force me?"

"Because you're content to wall yourself away from life. Because you've given up on your recovery fearing there's nothing more for you here. There is. You need to live and you need to start doing it now."

Her breaths came in shallow puffs. She placed her focus on the sound of hooves clopping toward the arena and the smells of hay and horse. Her breathing slowed and deepened. "I … I'm not ready."

A flicker of resignation shaded his brow. "I know. But no one can shield you from life forever. You've got to move forward."

Loss of the ability to move is one indignity of injury. Loss of control is another. It didn't take much to know Father Blanton was at Windrush for more than a pep talk. She wanted to hate him. "Th-there's more?"

He maneuvered her wheelchair over to a gazebo and picnic table. "You can't stay at Silvern forever. You've progressed to a point where you can live somewhere in an apartment with help. The hospital needs the bed and the doctors feel the time has come for your transition to outpatient." He worked his mouth, keeping his eyes averted from hers.

Her heart sank. Did he choose this moment knowing they'd be alone and not overheard? Living at Silvern gave her a feeling of security. People bustled around all hours of the day and she learned the ways of the staff. Each patient victory was celebrated as if it was their own. Words spoken or steps taken were broadcast as if a prodigy grandchild exposed another layer of genius in front of a proud grandparent. When the time came for a long-term rehabilitation patient to return home, the staff lined the hallway and cheered, balloons and flowers mandatory. Many days, she smiled at the tradition; most days it triggered anxiety. She had thought of the next steps, but her options were limited. Where would she go? No friends waited with open arms. She had no family to go to. The cold fact was she could not be on her own. Yet.

"No no no."

Father Blanton's mouth turned down at the corners and his eyes rounded. "I know you must be concerned with where you might go. The social worker at Silvern and I have been working on a solution."

Jessica sputtered. "Declan? Declan knows?"

"Not yet, because nothing has been decided and we're trying to generate ideas. We are only looking at ways to help. You understand that, right?" Father Blanton said as he brushed horse hair off his sleeve.

She chewed her lower lip and nodded.

"We have a few options." Father Blanton didn't wait for permission to speak before he rattled off his ideas. "People with handicaps can live alone, but we don't know when you'll be able to do so." He smiled at her, exhibiting the constant positive attitude and dangling hope that is ubiquitous in the rehabilitation world. "While you need assistance, you can live in one of our parishioner's homes. I've been made aware of two wonderful families."

"Aware?" she asked.

"Yes. Word's come through my parish of families who have had a rough patch in caring for disabled family members. Their homes are outfitted with ramps and broad doorways. You would have privacy, but skilled care if help is needed. Meals would be prepared for you and they are able to transport you to appointments. Everything a struggling body needs to function with help is there."

"I . . . I don't know . . ." Jessica tried to say she wanted a simple life, away from eyes that pried or oozed pity. The choice was hers. She knew the day was coming and wanted to be grateful to Father Blanton for stepping up with ideas. Instead, a slow boil of anger at her nose being rubbed in her loss of control began to heat. "Will Declan pick the home?"

"No. When we narrow down the suitable options, you'll have time to help with the final decision." He bent down and took her hands in his. "You don't have to make a decision now. You can see the homes and meet the people involved. You've a few weeks to make other arrangements. Let's take some time and look at your options," he said, urging her to consider his plans. He released the wheelchair's brakes, grabbing the handles.

He pushed her back to her car, leaving her wondering who was in command.

West Roxbury, Massachusetts

FATHER BLANTON DIDN'T want to ruin his chances of helping Jessica by being too pushy. He let Helen Grogan, the diminutive social worker at Silvern with a penchant for oversized jewelry that made her look like baubles on a stick, do the pushing. Helen worked hard to convince Declan to give Father Blanton a chance to find adequate housing for Jessica. A weeks-long campaign to get into Declan's good graces, with frequent visits cajoling the staff to look the other way as Jessica's riding lessons increased in duration, made little headway despite Helen's insistence that everything pointed to Jessica being well enough to take the next step in her recovery. When Jessica said she'd be willing to look at housing, Father Blanton did not waste a moment of Declan's absence. Rather than slowing the process with Declan's inevitable precautions of meticulous background research, Father Blanton relied instead on Helen's enthusiasm and Jessica's reluctant consent.

The Boston neighborhood of West Roxbury is the Irish-American's version of heaven. Neat, single-family homes dot leafy streets on perfectly square quarter-acre lots. Hedges, trimmed into perfect symmetry, sit in even rows beside brick front stoops. Regardless of the season, sidewalks reflect the care of the residents—swept clean of leaves and debris in spring and fall, filled with children on bikes in summer, and shoveled clear of snow regardless of the winter Boston suffered. Backyards hold not a speck of flapping laundry, for the people who move to West Roxbury leave behind a world of want and enter the land of plenty and clothes dryers.

A church is never out of walking distance and convenience stores fly the green, white and orange of the Irish flag next to the red, white and blue of the American. At some, the discerning eye would see the Irish flag flying a discreet inch or two higher than the Stars and

Stripes. Shelves of Fritos and Chef Boy-Ar-Dee share space with Flahavan's Porridge Oats, Chivers Marmalade, and coolers of Donnelly's Bangers. Lives revolve around Thursday confessions, Sunday coffee hours and evening socials. Faded flowers, tattered flags, and notes hang over bridges and walkways named after fallen heroes and community pillars. The life and breath of Ireland is never far from sight and lives in the people who call West Roxbury their home.

What would it mean to the people who lived here to have Jessica Wyeth live among them? Father Blanton pulled his car up in front of a home. A wooden ramp crisscrossed its way to the side door from the carport. Wrought iron railings, painted black, lined the carpeted deck. He walked to the curb, black robe flapping in the brisk fall wind. The schoolyard behind him was quiet and church bells pealed, calling all to Mass. He opened the trunk and pulled out a wheelchair, locking it in place by the passenger door. He helped Jessica into her wheelchair.

A tall man with graying hair held the house's door open. Jessica wheeled into a sunny and spotless kitchen. Yellow daisy wallpaper, orange cabinets, and green Formica countertops blinded her with cheer.

"I'm Thomas Sullivan. This is my wife, Mary," he said with a nod toward a round dumpling of a woman nodding feverishly in the doorway. "When a priest skips out on Mass, who hears the confession?" he chided, looking at Father Blanton from head to toe.

"I won't have to find out. I've celebrated two Masses this morning, so I'm in good graces." Father Blanton looked up and down the street. "But I see you live in a church-going neighborhood. Not a soul about. Residents must be at the nine o'clock service. Timing works for us. Keeps questions and gossip to a minimum."

Thomas addressed Jessica. "Father Blanton told us of your troubles and how you're making great progress." He beamed with a father's pride showing two rows of perfect white teeth. He carried himself with a patrician air that told of a different life before he came to the States. "My son was injured by a bomb as well. He lived with us until he was well enough to live on his own. We renovated the house to suit his needs and you're welcome to it if it suits you."

Father Blanton maneuvered Jessica through the door of the kitchen, specially widened to accommodate a wheelchair. The house was on two levels, with the center comprised of the kitchen and living room. The right hallway had a den, full bath, and master bedroom for Thomas and Mary. The left hallway held a second bedroom and large bath where he could see handrails and a lift to help with the care of their son. He could hear a TV downstairs where he imagined Thomas' den or office must be. The layout would afford Jessica as much privacy as she wanted and as much autonomy as she could handle.

"Thank you," Jessica replied as they followed behind Mary. "M-military?"

Father Blanton almost wheeled her into Mary's legs as the woman stopped and twisted around to look at her husband. "Military? You mean for the States?" Mary looked down at her feet, telegraphing she was mortified at having spoken out of turn. Her hands immediately set to work at fluffing and smoothing the skirt of her dress.

Thomas edged past them and put his hand on Mary's shoulder. The lines of his face softened. "Our son delivered a package." His eyes glistened and he lowered his head to look Jessica in the eye. "He had just turned his back when it detonated."

"P-package? Placed? Where?" Father Blanton could feel Jessica's grip on the rims of the wheels, as she tried to force the chair down the hall as she spoke. He struggled to keep the chair still. His Adam's apple bobbed as he swallowed his nerves.

Thomas put his chin down. "Yes. Barely four years ago now. He was in England when it happened. Warrington. Terrible thing."

The chair rocked in his grip as Jessica worked the wheels to turn it around.

"Warrington? Why was he there?" Father Blanton asked.

"It was the Provisional IRA behind those attacks," Thomas said with narrowed eyes.

Mary burst into motion and rushed in front of them to flick on the lights in the bedroom. She turned and tugged at the striped chenille bedspread then wiped her hands across the bureau, clapping them free of imagined dust. "No. No. He wasn't involved at all. Delivering a package on his route is all." She scurried to the window, pulled the shade down in one quick gesture, and let it settle an inch above where it had started. The curtains refused to open more despite her efforts. "Worked for the parcel service he did. Had no knowledge of what was in the package. Right, Thomas? Father? No knowledge. Lost the power in his legs and God saw to it that he came home to mend. Isn't that right, Father?" She looked at a picture on the shelf.

A round face with angry eyes stared back. The family resemblance clear. Their son sat beside a pond, handles of his wheelchair just visible. More startling was who pushed the wheelchair. Bishop Kavan Hughes'—no, wait, then *Father* Hughes'—smiling face rose above his tabbed collar. The son's shirt showed an outline of the island of Ireland colored with bands of green, white, and orange. The six counties in the northeast corner that comprised Northern Ireland were detached as if one last puzzle piece needed to be snapped into place to complete the image. Below the map was the equation, "26 + 6 = 1."

Sweet Jesus in Heaven. What have I brought this child into, Blanton thought as he scrambled for composure. The Sullivans enjoyed deep ties to the Church through their extended family and, through them, he learned of their son's injury, but not his involvement with the IRA. Blanton was an American priest and viewed the world through an American's eyes. Politics and policies of countries didn't matter when tending to the souls of his parishioners. He was beholden to the Church and all who cherished it, and his loyalties and the confidences he kept started and ended in the pages of the Gospel. He was no more involved in the Troubles than an emergency room doctor tending to the victims of a shooting. He was there to stitch hearts, mend souls, and to counsel better choices—not to undertake urban renewal to dam the flow of violence.

A pit formed in his gut as he realized his miscalculation. In honoring his promise to keep Jessica inside the Church's embrace, he had brought her to the edges of politics. He chastised himself for his ignorance in thinking religion and politics didn't mix in the States.

The wheelchair lurched forward under his hands with the sudden release of resistance.

He looked at the disgusted expression on Jessica's face and easily read her thoughts, *Well, I know a thing or two about that, don't I?* He let Jessica push herself into the room and stop beside Mary by the window. Jessica jammed the brakes on. With one deep breath, she put her hands on the arms of the wheelchair and shuffled her feet off the foot rests to the floor.

He had worked with patients at Silvern for over twenty years and had seen every imaginable injury at all stages of healing. Many stroke victims after weeks of therapy could only blink once for yes and twice for no. Patients with head injuries barely progressed for months, then went from bedridden to taking baby steps in a week. He could see when the body was fighting to stand or when the brain misfired commands. The desire to move and be free cannot be buried beneath useless muscles or blind eyes.

He knew of the spirits broken by horrors lived, and of the terror felt, when life changed in a flash. His career was dedicated to holding the hands of parishioners as they gathered confidence to face a life unimagined. He knew the miracles God granted and doctors performed.

What he saw in Jessica Wyeth made him question all of that.

Watching her ride horses prompted him to observe her more carefully. How she moved hinted at muscles mended and nerves knit. The jerks and spasms of her legs belied calculated thought intended to make her movements look infirm. Her comprehension of the world and her response to it betrayed her halting speech as a cover for a woman almost healed. Father Blanton recognized a soul fighting to be free. He also knew a terrified soul when he saw one.

No one spoke as they watched Jessica struggle to stand. Mary's eyes bulged with shock and fear and she gasped as Jessica toppled forward and braced herself against the windowsill.

With deliberate movements, Jessica pressed her face to the window and looked up and down the street. "S-school?" she asked, motioning to a brick building they had passed on the way in.

"Yes. An elementary school. Kids walk and ride their bikes. Nice family street," Mary said, content with her neighborhood.

Jessica sat back down in her chair and glared at Father Blanton. He could read her in a way he didn't think was possible. The contained world of the hospital forced a connection through familiarity where routine anticipated needs. Close relationships were unnecessary. With shock, he realized he could *feel* her thoughts as if she pushed them into his head.

Her eyes and touch told him more than he ever expected. Behind them was a desperation for him to know something.

She had agreed to tour homes today and not wait for Declan to return, knowing they would have time alone. She looked at him as if anticipating some revelation to spill from his lips. But what? The picture of the Sullivans' son animated her in a way that hinted more was in play than merely a confrontation of their politics.

He cleared his throat. "I don't believe Jessica wants to be by a school. Would that be right?" She sniffed and nodded her head. He continued. "She doesn't want kids staring at her as she learns to walk again."

Jessica exhaled one long breath of relief. *Thank you,* her eyes said.

"I'm sorry. You have a lovely home, but I'm afraid she really can't live here while she recovers. I hope you understand," he said. The school was a perfect cover for what he knew was the truth. He could only assume her reaction was that she did not want to live under a roof where violence was accepted and excused. Regardless of the Sullivans' politics, living within the membrane of an IRA soldier was too risky. A jolt shot through him as he read the expression in her eyes. She blamed him for placing her too close to a theater of war.

He wondered if something else bothered her.

Get me out of here.

He gave their thanks and goodbyes, wishing them well.

"There's another house?"

He was relieved to see a smile pass across her face as she motioned for him to push her out. He waited until he was helping her into the car before he spoke, keeping his voice low.

"I'm sorry. I didn't know about the son. I should have done my homework. The Sullivans are known in the parish as wonderful caregivers and generous people. They've helped others over the years looking for transitional housing, so they were the first to be put forth. I'm so sorry. I didn't know the son was injured by a bomb, or anything else. The next family is more, um, removed from Ireland's troubles," he said, collapsing her wheelchair and storing it in the trunk.

Mary's voice, high-pitched with shock, floated to them from the open door. "You told me they knew! You said you told Father Blanton everything!"

"There's nothing like lookin' in the eyes of a person when they learn your politics to know if they are one with you or not," Thomas said, voice audible over the sound of a broom being flicked frantically along the floor. "It's Father Gormley I be talkin' to. Blanton's from Southie. Besides, the girl's politics are good. The priest, too. You can see it in their eyes when they look at Richie's pictures."

Father Blanton drove out of West Roxbury and through Allston-Brighton. The street names and intersections became more familiar. Tremont Street. Melnea Cass Boulevard. Dorchester Avenue. Telegraph Hill. South Boston.

He could feel Jessica's eyes on him as they drove. He kept his eyes forward and made sure his worry did not crease his brow.

"Southie," she said as they drove past Thomas Park. "Your home."

He depressed the brake, surprising himself at stopping at an intersection when the light was still yellow instead of racing the red and gunning through, a Bostonian's driving habit that contributed to earning the nickname "Masshole" for all Massachusetts' drivers. Once stopped, he kept his eyes forward. "Yes. How'd you know?"

She raised and lowered a shoulder. "People talk. Small town." She kept her face turned to the window.

They pulled up beside a Victorian mansion that had been renovated into condominiums. A broad wooden porch wrapped around three sides. At the center, steps led from the street to two massive doors. A wheelchair ramp started at the back corner near a garage and rose gradually in a switchback pattern. A bay window was framed in wooden molding painted a deep green, complementing the gray clapboard sides. Layers of paint obscured details that had once been sharply carved.

Their visit was even shorter than with the Sullivans. The owners, José and Amarilla Ruiz, were rightly proud of their pristine home, renovated to care for José's mother before she passed. The home showed years of loving care and smelled of fresh bread and dinner, a point Amarilla took great pride in as she bragged about the average weight gain of past guests. No sooner were they in the home, than the phone started to ring. Focusing on their guests, they let the answering machine pick up.

"Rilla! I just heard about Jessica Wyeth! Tell me. How does she look? Did she say anything? You have to tell me everything when I see you at church."

"Amiga! Call me! Is she going to live with you? Did you bake bread as I said to make your home smell wonderful! Call! I can't wait to hear!"

The phone was still ringing as they returned to the car.

"This is just our first day. We'll find a suitable match. Don't worry," Father Blanton patted Jessica's hand as he pulled away from the curb.

"Why the Church?" She looked at him with a blue stare so intense it made the back of his head itch.

He peered through the windshield at the narrow street. "I was asked to find you and offer whatever assistance I could. I was told you were alone and needed the community of the Church for help."

"*Who*? Who told you that?"

The force of her question rattled him. "Well, er, I was asked to keep the contact a secret."

"That picture. The son and . . . and . . ."

"The bishop? Kavan Hughes?" He couldn't stop the chuckle from rumbling in his chest. "Lordy, no! I know he's held in high esteem by many here, but the Catholic Church is a huge organization. The Boston Diocese alone has over sixteen hundred priests. A local colleague asked me to check in on you. Most recently, I received referrals to families with a suitable home for you to live."

She balled her fists on her lap, a gesture that expressed her emotions physically when verbally they were thwarted. "William."

"Excuse me? Who?" Father Blanton asked, head turned to the side.

"William Wyeth."

"You're not serious!" he said, arms stiffening against the steering wheel. "I know he's offered for you to live with him many times, but ... but ... that was before–"

She cut him off. "Options? None. He's a ... a ..."

He placed his hand on her arm, stopping her from stuttering out the stream of expletives he knew would be next. He finished her sentence for her. "He's a snake."

"And d-desperate."

Beacon Hill
Boston, Massachusetts

ONE MUSCLE BELOW Declan's eye refused to stop twitching. Loud sounds and sudden movements made him slap his back up against the nearest wall or tree and reach for his gun, but walking in Boston Common didn't afford him much cover. The mist-filled night did little to help. He had to get a grip on himself. Better yet, he had to get a grip on events.

His meticulous attention to detail propelled him to success. It also damned him with an unyielding compulsion to make sure every "i" was dotted and "t" crossed. When it meant leaving no stone unturned, he knew talking to the worm in person was essential.

Jessica's decision to live with William Wyeth shocked him. No sooner had he returned from his travels than she and Father Blanton hit him with the news.

"You need to know your options before you make any decisions, okay?" Declan had implored as he adjusted her bedside table. He'd chosen midafternoon to talk. Silvern's hallways buzzed with activity in the mornings, but afternoons lulled with the expectation of visitors.

"I can't stay here."

He remembered how she pressed her fists into her lap and how she struggled to pronounce each word.

With Silvern encouraging her to move on, and Father Blanton beating the bushes for an acceptable home, he had few options. "You can rent your own apartment and have it staffed with people to help you."

She kept her eyes on her closed hands. "No. Beacon Hill. Close to rehab. I'll renovate."

"What about getting around?" he said as he offered her a blanket for her legs. "William doesn't strike me as the caring type."

She shrugged in an *I'll figure it out* way.

"We can help you hire assistants and whatever help you need."

"No."

Hiring people to surround her was exactly what Michael would want and Declan was trying everything he could to keep both Jessica and Michael happy—a balancing act he was becoming less adept at. If he could find bodyguards that doubled as stablehands, he knew damned well he could find a private nurse or two with hand-to-hand training. The kind of money Michael would pay could find anyone to do anything.

"I want. My life. Back," she said, eyes drilling into him.

"Of course, but first we–"

"No 'we.' *Me.*"

Renting a home and staffing it is easy enough, but William was an abhorrent choice. It was the only one she could make that was *hers*. Her aquamarine eyes bore through him with a physical wallop.

"I can't believe you're seriously considering living with that leech. You know he wants to sue you for fraud, right? He wants to grab everything he can from you. He rents rooms and sells art to keep himself in booze. You can't trust him."

The look she gave was repellant. In the short time he was away, that damned priest had emboldened her. He felt his control over her weaken.

"Fine," he said at last, voice flat. "If that's what you want. But I get to see the look on his face when he hears the news."

She was slipping through his fingers even as he held her as tightly as he could. His visit with Michael affirmed his resolve not to make any more mistakes. Michael's confidence in him depended on it, and letting Jessica out of the carefully constructed bubble was not going to happen without a fight. He strode past Frog Pond, its leaf-strewn surface reflecting streetlights with patched colors. His breath clouded in front of him. A few minutes later, he stood in front of a brick townhouse and jammed his finger on the doorbell. Nothing. He leaned on the button, finger bending with force, and listened. No bell chimed inside. The peeling paint and wobbly handrail evidenced needed maintenance. He drummed the brass knocker.

The satisfying thump of footsteps sounded. A curtain moved. Nothing.

He pounded the door. "William? It's Declan Cleary. We met in Atlanta."

He heard more thumps and the door finally opened. William stood in front of him, raking his fingers through his hair. Dark circles sat in puffs beneath bloodshot eyes. His trousers and shirt looked like they had been slept in—for days.

"It's hardly common to visit at this ungodly hour," William said. "Is everything quite right?"

"For you? I'd say yes," Declan said as he pushed his way in.

William's townhouse was exactly what he expected. Old money, mold-covered Yankee knickknacks. He assessed William. "Make a pot of coffee. You're going to need it."

The kitchen counter and floor were littered with restaurant to-go containers and pizza boxes. William fussed about, opening and closing cabinets, searching for coffee filters, rinsing a carafe, and cleaning mugs with a serious focus that protected him from engaging in conversation. Declan watched, entertained enough that the stench of fermenting garbage barely bothered him.

William turned to him. "Okay. Fine. You must have heard how angry I am at being wronged."

Declan smiled. This was going to be more fun than he thought.

"Yeah. Small world. Rotten luck she came back from the dead. I heard you were shopping around the case to see what lawyer would take it. Since you can't pay upfront, they'd get paid a contingency percentage of your judgment. Provided you win, of course."

William's faced screwed up with his version of mental anguish. "You have no idea how hurt and shocked I was to learn we don't share blood. Horrible. The millions she's taken from our family." His voice trailed off with Shakespearean sorrow.

"So you decided to sue her for, what, the fraud you say she committed?"

William placed his hand over his heart. "My pain counts for something."

Declan cleared his throat to cover his amusement. "Problem is, no lawyer's taken your case yet. Why? Because they know there's no way the court will decide in your favor. Even if in some warped reality you win in a lower court, any decision would be struck down on appeal."

"You don't know that! I spoke with a fellow today who'd be quite happy to take my case."

"Hmm. Right. Some lowlife ambulance chaser who shares an office with a sanitation crew in Dorchester. You think he's planning on a big payout? Not a chance. He's just hoping getting his name associated with yours will be enough to elevate him out of the trash bins. Your lawsuit is without merit."

"This is preposterous!"

Declan stood in front of William, intentionally invading his space. He drained all emotion from his eyes. Beads of sweat sprung up on William's upper lip, giving Declan a moment of satisfaction. Declan kept his voice infused with warmth as he spoke, knowing the mixed signals of friend and foe would confuse. "You're basing your claim of fraudulent inheritance on the fact that Jessica was never formally adopted."

"That's precisely right," William sputtered. "I've scoured every database and dusty cellar I could. If she's not the biological child of my brother nor was legally adopted, then everything Jim owned would be mine."

"Don't be a greedy pig, and a blind one at that," Declan snarled. "You're right about one thing. No document or proceeding happened which legalized Jessica's adoption."

Wary hope flickered in William's eyes. "So, I'm justified in pursuing this?"

"Not exactly. Let me help you understand your situation," Declan purred. "Greed may blind people, but the courts are clear-eyed. Courts look at the length of time a child lived with the adults and at what age the relationship started. In Jessica's case, she was under Margaret and Jim's care from infancy."

William pounced at the opening. "Right! That Bridget woman was a proven criminal. Her intent to deceive my poor brother was obvious from the start!"

"No," he said, delighting in wagging his finger in front of William's nose. "Another factor courts consider is who gave the child to them." He modified the cadence of his conversation, choosing his words carefully. "It is not contested that Jessica's biological parents willingly gave her over to them. Having Bridget and Margaret be sisters strengthens the argument this was an open and accepted relationship for both the recipient of the child and the givers. During the ten years Bridget lived with Jessica after Margaret's death, she never claimed Jessica as her own child. When courts see duration of the relationship and acceptance on the part of the birth parents, the laws of equitable adoption kick in."

"Meaning?"

"Meaning even though there is no formal adoption agreement, the courts will look at the family structure to decide legal rights."

At each fact, Declan raised a finger, delineating his points as simply as possible. "She's always gone under the Wyeth family name, Jim and Margaret provided and received a loving familial relationship from her, she was consistently represented as their biological child, so her status as their lawful child was never questioned." He shook his hand in the air. "I could go on, but there's not a court in the world that would question her status as their child."

William's slumped shoulders said he had heard as much from the other lawyers he had consulted. "But isn't their will invalid?"

"Your brother and his wife did not die intestate, meaning they did not die without a will. In fact, just the opposite is true. They had more trusts and safeguards in place on their wealth than most people." He winced at the thought. Jim and Margaret knew the cost of trying to outrun the reach of Magnus Connaught's Charity. They had been doing their best to address their fear that they were at risk of dying early. Trying to leave the Charity was their death sentence.

"They were killed. Their fears were well placed," William's face reddened with anger. "Jim wanted to protect his child. Since Erin perished in the accident as well, the estate would flow to me."

"Wrong. Jim and Margaret wanted to protect their *children*."

"Jessica is not Jim's daughter."

"Give it up. The law is clear. Jessica is considered to be Jim's and Margaret's child in every sense but biological. You've lost the argument, but you haven't lost your niece."

William's head raised an inch. "What? Does this ever f-fail?"

"With the facts as strong here? No. The only defense to equitable adoption is where a biological parent claims lack of knowledge of the adoptive relationship. He or she would then be required to put forth facts that show fraud or criminal intent to deceive. In that case, no adoptive relationship would be supported by the facts."

William came to life. "That's it then! Perfect! Bridget was a wanted criminal and Jim had no idea Jessica was not his child." He wheeled around, bumping his chest against Declan's. "My brother was deceived! He was lied to! He–"

William's sentence was cut short as Declan's forearm slammed his jaw shut and pushed his neck into the cabinet.

"Stop! Y-you're ch-choking me!"

"Give. It. Up," Declan growled. "You've got nothing on her. The more people you tell your tale of woe, the more people are going to see you for what you are—a bankrupt nobody without a retirement plan." He pressed on William's trachea until he heard the satisfying rasp of air forcing its way through a too-narrow passage. "Without her, you're nothing."

"*She's* nothing! She's the illegitimate daughter of a criminal and a barn rat!" William gasped and sucked in what air he could.

"What's it going to take for you to lay off?" Declan amused himself by watching the color of William's face redden and recede in tandem with the alternating pressure on his windpipe. Press. Release. Press. Release. William tried to scratch and claw Declan's arm away, but his efforts didn't register as more than an annoying insect buzzing. "I'll bet some money would help."

William's struggle lessened. "What?"

"She needs a place to live."

"*What!*"

"You're her only family and connection to her past. Your home will be repaired and outfitted with ramps, railings, and anything else she may need." He released William with a shove and stepped back. He peeled a sticky wrapper off his shoe. "She will hire and pay for any help you need to maintain your home and provide her care."

The prospect of attaining the goose and golden egg was tantalizing. "You're saying if she moves in, all my costs will be covered by her?"

"Yes." He added, "This is her idea. You can bet your ass it wasn't mine. She insists."

William began to snigger. "After all she's done to keep me away from her, now she's in a bind and needs old Uncle Willie? How grand! How very grand!"

Declan grabbed William by the collar and drew him up on the counter. Empty Chinese food containers scattered.

"Let me help you to understand," he said, bringing his nose to William's. "The only person in a bind is you. The only person who *needs* this situation is you. If for one second you subvert her desire to recover in the embrace of the only family she knows for your own sick purposes, you will not live long enough to regret your poor decision."

He dropped William to his feet, keeping a firm grip on his shirt. Last week's Pad Thai and an orange rind stuck to William's butt. The only thing missing was a tiny paper umbrella.

"Let's be clear," Declan began. "Your home will be cleaned, repaired, and outfitted for her needs. Your tenant will move out. She will pay a modest rent as well as all costs associated with her care. You will not utter her name in public nor will you divulge one detail of this agreement to anyone." He yawned from a combination of boredom and jet lag. "I will have documents to you in a day and crews will begin work the day after."

"That's all? Just a place to live?"

"I'll be a frequent visitor. Her happiness is your happiness."

William coughed. "Fine. Alright then. She can live here."

Declan released William and helped straighten his shirt. "I'll be in touch," he said and left.

He expected to have a lightness to his step after ensuring William's cooperation, but something William had said nagged at him.

Referring to Jessica's father as a barn rat meant William believed Gus Adams was Jessica's father.

Equitable adoption does a few things that the birth and adoptive parents may have known at the time. In formal adoption proceedings, termination of the birth parents' rights to the child is part of the process. The biggest factor that makes equitable adoption unique is that it does not negate the relationship between the birth parents and the child, meaning if Jim and Margaret were still alive, she'd be considered to belong to both Jim and Margaret, *and* Kavan and Bridget.

Declan popped his collar up against the cold and lowered his head in thought as he strode through the night air. Adoption and citizenship inhabit two different sets of laws, far outside the world of corporate law he inhabited. In a domestic adoption, citizenship is not an issue; A baby is born in the States and therefore is a citizen. Period. In an international adoption, a provision for citizenship is included in the legal documents that consummate the adoption. It's a diplomatic dance between countries which frequently ends in heartbreak where warring countries use such humanitarian issues to push their agendas. Denying visas and citizenships was just another form of war.

He pulled his coat around his face as he walked back across Boston Common. Mingled with the scent of warm cashmere was the unmistakable scent of fear.

The surface of Jessica's citizenship looked easy. Finding her baptismal certificate was enough to keep immigration off her tail by raising the evidentiary bar needed to prosecute her case. Birth documents get lost or destroyed. Baptismal certificates can be used in lieu of birth certificates, especially in proving paternity. Many times, the father is not present at the ceremony, leaving it to the mother and the mother's family to complete the documents. Baptismal certificates are used to prove paternity where a father is reluctant to step up. It's often the one time the mother can document the child's lineage.

Bridget and Margaret had knowingly used Jessica's baptism to implicate Gus as the father. Any search of records would show Gus had become a citizen prior to her birth. They used a document they knew to be false.

Bridget and Margaret did everything in their power to make sure Jessica belonged to both of them. Would the same be true for the countries touched by her birth?

What would happen if the connections to Kavan were exposed?

His strides lengthened in tandem with his growing concern. He didn't like surprises and he didn't like not knowing answers.

He had an Irishman's fe sense that time was running out.

South Boston, Massachusetts

"WHAT DID YOU find out?" Amanda dumped three sugar packets into her extra large dark roast and jabbed a wooden stick furiously at swirls of half-and-half. She took a sip, wrinkled her nose, and added two shots of cream.

Colleen surveyed the morning rush at the coffee shop. Amanda had chosen the farthest back corner of Norm's Doughnuts in a booth with a clear view of the door. The mirrored wall behind her revealed that even at the ungodly early hour of eight, Amanda still had time to run a comb through her mop of curls, making them spring from her head in some semblance of order. The tag from her blouse peaked over the collar of her jacket.

"Just rolling out of bed?" Colleen teased as she reached around and tucked the tag under Amanda's collar.

"What? Oh, nope. Been up for hours. Hoping to make it an early day so I can finally get some rest."

Colleen dragged a chair over and settled into it, heaving her messenger bag onto her feet and draping the strap over her knees in the way her mother taught her to do in public places to protect her purse from pickpockets. The patrons were the usual Boston mix of young professionals and students with a few crusty longshoremen thrown in for good measure. Located two blocks from the piers in South Boston, Norm's was famous for keeping fisherman's hours—open from one o'clock in the morning to one o'clock in the afternoon. Specialty coffees and double espressos were a nod at the neighborhood's encroaching gentrification. No one was caffeinated enough to notice them in the corner.

"Why the rush to see me?" Colleen asked as she peeled back the plastic tab on her coffee cup.

"You first," Amanda said.

"The Timothy guy who swore the affidavit is a close associate of Connaught's. Childhood buddy."

Amanda sat forward. "Does he still work for Connaught? Is there still a connection?"

"Nothing I could find. This guy worked with horses, so was a logical hire to prepare for that race in England Wyeth was involved in. His father worked for Connaught's father, but I couldn't find any recent connections. There's something about this guy that seems off, but everything else points to the document being legit."

Amanda peeled the paper wrap off her chocolate chip muffin, pinched off a bite, and popped it into her mouth. The muffins were a recent addition to the menu beside sausage, egg, and cheese bagels, and grilled steak breakfast bombs. "Good," she said, wiping crumbs off her chin, "so what's the holdup?"

"What do you mean?"

"Why haven't you written anything yet?"

Colleen shrugged. "I need a few more answers before I do. You aren't looking into Connaught anymore, so ..." Still smarting from their last meeting, she let the sentence hang, hoping for an apology.

None came.

And that pissed her off even more. "You gotta fill in some blanks for me here," Colleen began, shaking her head. "You and I worked together and compiled a damning file on Magnus Connaught, but you dropped the investigation into the son like a hot potato. What gives? That's not like you."

Amanda looked away, eyes drifting to the door. Colleen watched the reflection of a young couple tossing backpacks into a booth, the girl sitting and the boy heading to the counter to order. She waited for a response.

Amanda busied herself with licking chocolate from her fingers, then slid a picture across the table of a man in bishop's vestments holding a crozier. Colleen recognized the face as the other man with Bridget and Gus in the picture she and Max had discussed. The messenger bag with her stash of photos grew hot against her leg. Okay, so Bridget and Gus were friends with a priest. But a bishop? Things were getting interesting.

"Who's that?" Colleen asked, keeping the flash of recognition from her expression.

"Bishop Kavan Hughes. He's pretty popular in the Irish Catholic community. He has the reputation of having the ear of activists and leaders of the IRA. Frequent flyer in the halls of Stormont, too."

"I'm just surprised you're telling me officials inside Northern Ireland's capitol were interested in him."

Amanda shrugged. "Might help you find the last few pieces of the puzzle you're looking for."

Colleen turned the picture face down and shoved it back across the table. "Don't shit me," she said, frustration gripping the edges of her words. "I'm serious. Why are you showing me this?"

Amanda sipped her coffee, drawing in air to cool it. The sound was barely audible over the background din of coffee beans being ground and steam forcing milk into a froth. Her eyes roved each face over the brim of her cup as she took a second sip. "Off the record?"

The urge to storm out was tempered by a stronger urge to find out what the hell Amanda was talking about. "I haven't failed you yet, have I?"

Amanda sniffed. "No, but you're not as plugged in as you think you are."

"So give it to me. What am I missing?"

"Bishop Hughes is known for his studious neutrality and involvement in the peace talks between the U.K. and factions inside Northern Ireland that want one Ireland, not two. We noticed a change in communications, something we usually see when an organizational shakeup is in play or when an operation is underway. MI-5, the U.K.'s security service, alerted us that he's been in contact with a network in the States, and that network has been in direct contact with Wyeth."

"Wait a second. It's quite a leap to drop your focus from the Connaught clan to look at a guy known for neutrality and brokering peace deals, and worrying about who he's contacted and why." She stuffed back her impatience. "But we've worked together too long for me not to trust your instincts. Tell me more about his network."

"His contacts through the church are easy to track. Either he uses his office phone or home phone. He doesn't cover his tracks at all."

"Well, gee. What a shock that must be." Colleen didn't bother to hide her impatience. "A priest in Northern Ireland calling another priest in Boston. Boston's chock full of church-going Irishmen, remember? I'll bet no rational reason for contacts exists, like a family member checking on a loved one or a friendly chat. Please tell me you brought me here for more than that."

"Damn it, Colleen! Shut up and listen!" Amanda threw a large bite of muffin into her mouth and chased it with her coffee slurry. She darted a look around the café and sank deeper into her seat. "I'm sorry. No sleep. Long night. He's had numerous conversations with another priest who's connected with Blanton."

Colleen sat forward and looked at her friend. Early morning meetings at Norm's after an all-nighter was nothing new to them. Colleen had called Amanda in more times than she could count after a stakeout or long hours in the newsroom making deadlines. Amanda returned the favor by calling at any hour, insisting Colleen meet her. They had seen one another in any state of caffeine overload or withdrawal, on good and bad hair days. Today Amanda was coiled tight. The little muscles clenched around her eyes and mouth gave her a pinched appearance. Amanda didn't scare easily, but this was one of those rare days. "Okay, sorry for being dense. Blanton? Why do I know that name?"

"He's the Chaplain at Silvern. That's where Blanton has been in contact with Wyeth."

Colleen picked at the cardboard sleeve of her coffee cup. "He's a priest who checks in on the infirm. Hughes is a bishop."

"Archbishop now," Amanda corrected. "He just won a promo."

Colleen dismissed the update. "This is typical FBI this-is-the-house-that-Jack-built bullshit. So Hughes talked to the guy who talked to Blanton. Don't you think such contact can be explained as normal within the ordinary conducting of business, whatever it is priests conduct as business?"

"Wyeth helped execute the Manchester bombing as proved by the pictures and affidavit. She's an experienced terrorist. After a number of phone calls back and forth between the then bishop's conduit and Blanton, Blanton took Wyeth to the West Roxbury home of Tommy Sullivan. We've been watching Tommy Sullivan for some time. His son was injured in a bombing four years ago. The father is an active member of the IRA. Inside sources are very clear that Mr. Sullivan's sympathies are firmly for unification at any cost."

"Yeah. And?"

"American involvement in the peace process is essential. President Clinton helped the process along considerably by having his picture taken with Gerry Adams in Belfast. Gerry Adams is the head of Sinn Fein, the political party advocating for unification."

Colleen circled her hand at the wrist, signaling Amanda to bypass the preliminaries and talk faster. "Sinn Fein's the mouth, IRA the brawn. They say they don't coordinate efforts, but ... I'm way ahead of you here."

"That handshake helped Sinn Fein gain legitimacy. No one has been able to prove coordination of political policy with violent attacks. Bishop Hughes frequents political meetings at Stormont and his church is patronized by active soldiers in the IRA."

"So, you're saying that Hughes has conversations with other priests, who then contact Blanton, who then speaks with known activists–"

"Not mere activists," Amanda snapped. "Terrorists."

Colleen's eyes narrowed. "Okay," she drawled, "with known terrorists? What are you not telling me?"

"I could lose my job by telling you this."

"Yeah, it's not the first time I've heard you say that, and you still have one. Okay, so spill it."

"So that whole handshake deal?" Amanda said, leaning over the table on her forearms, "That deal was started through political connections here. No one's been able to prove a connection between the violent actions of the IRA and Sinn Fein. If a connection is found to be with Bishop Hughes, then there is a chain of evidence and events that the U.S. has negotiated with a terrorist organization. That's in direct opposition to U.S. policy."

Colleen sank back in her chair. The pieces were falling into place. She liked them better when they were scattered. Someone wanted the bishop to take a fall. Someone? Connaught. "So let me see if I'm reading this correctly. You're saying that Bishop Kavan Hughes is the secret confidant who has been the conduit of information between Sinn Fein and the IRA. You're saying that his increased communications to the U.S. with known sympathizers and active participants in past bombings is indicative of him being guilty of aiding and abetting a criminal act. But here's what's wrong with that. Nothing has pointed to a criminal network involving the Church. Nada. Nothing."

"Yet."

The potential threat she had been too afraid to acknowledge became real. "Yet?" She felt her mouth dry.

"Concerns that a bombing may be in the active planning stages are rising. We've noticed an uptick in communications with known sympathizers. The fact that many of the communications center around or involve Wyeth is a deep concern to us, especially in light of the Olympic bombing."

"I have to stop you there. All intelligence indicates that the Centennial Park bombing was done by some crazy lone wolf guy with an ax to grind about pro-life, or something like that."

"But Wyeth was there. Her horses were transported there."

"Yeah? Well MMC had quite the corporate presence there, too. Connaught's companies supplied most of the security equipment from metal detectors to communications. Are you forgetting that? Come *on*, Amanda! Think! What are the odds that all of that is pure coincidence?"

"People get struck by lightning. That's not playing odds. That's just plain stupid luck."

"Maybe so. If you're focusing on Wyeth, you *have* to keep your focus on Connaught, too. You can't drop him out of the equation. What if his presence there was to test the U.S. response to an attack?" She thought of the trove of documents sitting at her feet. Sure Wyeth was involved, but focusing on her was like treating a hangnail when the patient was riddled with cancer. Colleen struggled to keep her voice from catching. Her friend had never been so stubborn before.

"Most of my job is to track down the bad guys after they do something bad." Amanda laced her fingers around her cup. "But if I get to stop a bad guy before they do something bad, that makes my job *awesome*."

Amanda's eyes tore a hole through Colleen's heart and head. Amanda was singing Colleen's song, but in the wrong key. "So, you're convinced that Wyeth is the mastermind?"

"Her mother was a revolutionary. Wyeth is a disenfranchised loner with known connections to organized crime. Yeah, she might not be the mastermind, but something's up. It's not only the chatter that's been on the increase. We know arms shipments and explosives are on the move. I have to stop whatever has started before something horrible happens."

Everything Colleen wanted was at her fingertips, including adding the mainstream public interest catnip that a powerful bishop fathered a child with a known revolutionary. The proof was close, and closing the evidence gap on Wyeth and proving her to be an active terrorist was within Colleen's grasp. All she had to do was clench her fist around the brass ring and pull.

What stopped her? Connaught. Her reporter's instinct told her if she printed all she knew on Wyeth, the inroads she had made into exposing Connaught would dry up. And printing an unsubstantiated rumor that Hughes was the father would only serve to help Connaught.

Colleen would need either a first person confession or a DNA test to go live with that tidbit.

Connaught came from a long line of masterminds and had power. Wyeth had nothing. If Connaught supporters saw an opportunity to throw an innocent under the bus to protect themselves and curry favor with the head honcho at the same time, then nothing would stop them from lying, and Colleen didn't want to publish lies. Exposing Wyeth as a wayward-misfit-turned-terrorist was too easy, and adding the possibility that the bishop was her father was too good to be true. The reporters' adage? If it's too good to be true, it probably isn't.

But still. The facts dotted her path like a breadcrumb trail and she felt like Gretel standing in the heat of the witch's oven.

If she moved forward as Amanda wanted, she was helping Connaught carve his new identity as the good guy struggling to do the right thing. She wanted to take both Wyeth and Connaught down and needed her facts loaded in the chamber before she pulled the trigger. If the bishop was collateral damage, that wasn't her problem.

Doubt tugged at her. Amanda had all of the information Colleen had, probably more. "What more do you know about Hughes?"

Amanda rolled her eyes. "Nothing. Only what I told you. In his diocese in Belfast, he's loved like a rock star."

"You checked out his past?"

"Of course," she snapped. "Belfast native. Great student. Trusted community leader."

"Exposing him would derail the peace process and spark violence. Who does that serve? Who wins in that situation?" Colleen looked at her reflection in the mirror. Dark circles shadowed her eyes and her hair could have used a wash. The crowd in the coffee shop started to thin. Must be close to nine o'clock and the beginning of work. She pushed her fatigue aside. Exposing Wyeth and keeping Connaught on the back burner did not make sense. "Who wins?" she pressed. She knew the answer. She knew Amanda knew it, too.

Amanda started to shove her wrappers and coffee cup into her empty muffin bag. "Look. I wanted to do you a favor. If you're not interested in what I have to say, then screw you. That whole rich-heiress-turns-thug thing is *exactly* where you were headed when you first connected with the uncle."

"With her mind-control boyfriend in the mix, remember? You're the one who helped me formulate that theory."

"It was just a fucking theory." Amanda spat out the words.

"Slow down, will you?" Colleen said in a tone she hoped would calm her friend enough to get the conversation on a better track. "I get it. You want Wyeth front and center because of the connection to Hughes and because she was taken to meet with Tommy Sullivan's family. Combined with the chatter you've heard, you think an attack of some sort is in the active planning stages."

"Yes. The amount of evidence stockpiling against Wyeth internally is overwhelming. And I think the event is going to be soon so all resources have to be dedicated to Wyeth and not Connaught."

"Soon? Why?"

Amanda shrugged. "Hunch."

"Hunch my ass." Colleen sucked back the words. This was Amanda, the girl who took revenge on Colleen's elementary school nemesis by pouring maple syrup in the girl's wellies. This was Amanda, the girl who stood shoulder-to-shoulder with Colleen on the playground when the class bully threatened to deck her after she witnessed him filch the math teacher's wallet. Amanda didn't hold back when she spotted a wrong being committed. She was the one who clocked the bully with her lunch box and sat on him until the teacher arrived. Colleen continued, voice lowered. "You're blowing smoke up my ass. Your focus doesn't make sense."

Amanda glared. "You've got what you need to make it make sense."

"Who got to you?"

Too many years of tight scrapes and close calls made it impossible for Amanda to hide her fear behind professional duties. Amanda screwed her eyes shut as she spoke. "Just play it out my way, Colleen. I got my superiors on board with this strategy. C'mon, damn it. You want to play it this way, too. I just need you to go along."

Colleen reached across the table and gripped Amanda's hands in her own. "We've gotten out of tough spots before. I can help you."

Amanda blinked rapidly, eyes rimmed red. "Not like this."

"Just give me something to work with," she pleaded. "C'mon. We got this." A confident tone failed to match her words.

Amanda looked up at the ceiling, shaking her head in a mental battle. Her shoulders sank. "There's someone on the inside."

The reason for Amanda's irrational laxness on Connaught became clear. Someone was pulling strings from behind the curtain. "Whoa, like a Connaught mole inside the FBI?" Colleen waited. The coffee and bagel crowd thinned to one old man by the door hunched around a steaming cup. The potbellied clerk from behind the counter began to wipe down tables and straighten chairs.

"That's just it. I heard something about Magnus' death."

"Wait. Magnus' death? I thought that was signed, sealed, and delivered as natural causes."

Amanda ground the heels of her hands into her eye sockets. "When I asked more questions, things . . . things . . ."

Colleen finished her sentence. "Things got weird."

"Hey!" They looked up at a greasy T-shirt pulled tight over a huge gut. "Either of you ladies see who was sitting over there?" He jerked his thumb in the direction of a booth by the door.

"No," Amanda replied. "Why?"

"They left their backpack."

Colleen met Amanda's eyes for only a split second before she grabbed the strap hanging on her knee with one hand and with the other yanked Amanda out of her chair, diving for the narrow hallway leading to the restrooms and kitchen. Amanda's hand was ripped from her grasp as the table toppled over and chairs scattered. Colleen had no time to decipher the sounds before her eardrums, chest, and head compressed from the shockwave. Heat raced up her legs seconds before she realized flames were taking hold of the floorboards and walls.

A scream cut short. A yell of warning morphed to a yowl of pain. Dust and pieces of wood fell around her, joined by thuds of something soft. She didn't have time to be sickened by the reality.

"This way! Out the back!" Her face scraped along the dirty floor as she crawled army-style toward the voice. The roar of flames over her head grew louder. One sharp turn left, another right. The air cooled. Her bag caught on something and trapped her from moving forward. She stopped and tugged hard to free it. The bag moved an inch. Then two.

"Come on! Hurry!" The voice was closer. The roar continued to build. With one jerk, something gave way and she rolled forward. Someone grabbed her by the back of the collar and pulled her to her feet. A door flew open and two hands shoved her out to the alley.

She stumbled out to the morning air and stood, weaving, on wobbly legs. The employee from behind the counter held the door open, yelling back inside. Gray smoke billowed around him.

The man emerged out the door, greasy T-shirt replaced by charred skin. Rivers of blood spilled from holes gouged from flying debris. He held his hands up to his head. Smoke rose from where his scalp used to be. He staggered forward one step, stumbling over at his feet. His knees buckled.

With a *whoosh,* a blast of flame rushed out the door, throwing both men to the pavement. Remains of Norm and his doughnut shop scattered and fell like snowflakes.

It was over as fast as it had begun. The alley grew quiet except for the crackle of flames and the distant sound of sirens.

Colleen's brain struggled to process the flood of information. Physically, no searing pain demanded attention. No burned flesh. No broken bones. Emotionally was another story. She was numb. The reality that Amanda was dead would be dealt with later, after she had time to get even.

Connaught. Michael Fucking Connaught. And Wyeth. Jessica Fucking Wyeth.

She looked at the flames and blocked the upwelling of grief that was about to overwhelm her. Papers fluttered at her feet. Some burning, others singed and covered with soot. She slapped out the flames and retrieved as many as she could, swallowing back the puke that threatened to spill as she untangled her bag from Norm's motionless and burned feet.

Before she would sleep, before she would grieve or feel shock, terror, and revulsion, she would look into the eyes of Wyeth and declare her revenge.

Silvern Rehabilitation Hospital
Boston, Massachusetts

LIGHTS IN CAMBRIDGE winked on as the sky streaked with reds and oranges at the closure of another fall day. Jessica looked out over North Station, trying to focus on the beauty, but a restless urge gnawed at her. Silvern's routine lulled her into a state of suspended life. Nothing happened within its walls except words relearned and independence rekindled. Milestones, perhaps, but the calm troubled her. She had been told that convalescence in a still and controlled environment was beneficial for someone healing from a traumatic brain injury.

Stuttering speech and twitchy mobility evidenced scrambled motor connections, and her problem solving skills and linear thinking were disrupted as well. Rather than being patient with the healing process and the inherent boredom that comes from waiting, she felt the pressure of stillness build around her as if the silence of the city thrummed with a backing track of jungle drums.

"Three more weeks." Father Blanton answered a question not asked.

"Hmm?" She rolled her chair to face him.

"William said he'd have his home wheelchair accessible and ready for you in three weeks. Silvern agreed you can have a bed as long as you need. Most people leave because their insurance stops covering their costs. You're, er, not in that situation."

"Yeah."

"It was good of you to pay for the renovations and offer William a very generous monthly stipend. He seemed bewildered, but quite tickled."

"And?"

"And he was more than ready to sign the confidentiality agreement Declan had prepared, especially with Declan standing over him. Seems he finally figured out the legal costs associated with trying to change the fact you are his brother's rightful beneficiary. He decided against fraud proceedings too, not that he got much farther than rattling his saber by interviewing scumbag lawyers."

"Declan?"

He glanced at his watch and shrugged. "He was supposed to be here."

That wasn't what she asked and she was confused by his answer. Was she making the right decision to move into William's home? She masked her faulty thinking with determined action. Plowing ahead on a course of action was easier than questioning herself. Doing so would expose more broken connections. William was the only link to her past, to a time when Sunday suppers were filled with laughter and she was a big sister. His visits were rare, but he knew her and had memories of Gus, Bridget, Margaret, Jim, and Erin. He linked her to a time before her life went to hell. It was the only decision that felt remotely safe, but no place was without risk and the complexity overwhelmed her. Jessica huffed and returned to looking out the window signaling their conversation was over.

He hesitated. "Well, I'm heading home. Good night."

She listened to his retreating steps. When she was sure he wouldn't return on some forgotten errand, she stretched her back and lifted her legs off the footrests, straightening one at a time and suspending it in front of her until her thigh burned and sweat moistened her brow. Focusing on her physical improvement was easier than filtering through scrambled thought connections. Either she could lift her leg or she couldn't. Either she strengthened her muscles or she didn't. Determining to ride again was simple. Deciding to walk when her body became capable was so much easier than deciding to live.

Her decision to live held by a gossamer thread. The life she wanted to claim was one in the full light of day, not shaded by fear or shadowed with threat. Embracing her past could liberate or kill, and she didn't trust herself to accurately weigh her options. Regardless, she had to muddle forward.

Three weeks. She had three more weeks of playing possum before she would be forced to make a move. Crystal-clear thinking wasn't needed to know she'd rather drink bleach than live with that dirtball of a pseudo uncle, but trying to manage in a world void of logic and anchors was dizzying. And terrifying. Fear made her question every-thing. Worse than questioning everyone around her was the fear that maybe her injuries were permanent. Maybe the doctors' hopes for a modest recovery were too overblown. Maybe she really couldn't walk on her own again without leg braces or a cane. Maybe she really couldn't live independently again.

Maybe Declan wasn't a loyal soldier.

Maybe Declan was too loyal.

She had been wrong before and her heart couldn't bear to be wrong again.

A rattle of carts in the hallway said dinner trays were being re-moved as the evening shifted to settling patients for the night. Order-lies and nurses hurried from one room to the next, helping patients into beds. A rustle at her door didn't surprise her. Who it was did.

A petite woman walked to the door of her room. Her bobbed hair was windblown and wild, her clothes dirty and disheveled. She car-ried a canvas bag of some kind—filthy and soot-covered with what looked to be half-burned papers shoved inside.

"Jessica? I'm Colleen Shaunessy-Carillo, reporter with the *Boston Globe*." Although her face was less familiar, her name struck a chord. Colleen—the bane of Michael's existence. His harshest criticism of the Fourth Estate was levied with Colleen's name at the center of it. Electra spoke of her in better terms. Colleen's tenacity was appealing if it worked for you, daunting if not.

Jessica drew in a centering breath. The time had come to face the press without Electra's guidance. But this encounter happened too soon. Three weeks too soon to be exact. Jessica wanted to be more independent before she began to answer questions. No. No. No. She was wrong. She shouldn't answer any questions without Declan to guide her. No. That wasn't right either. Declan was Michael's counsel, not hers, and he couldn't be trusted to protect her or her interests.

Her torment must have been visible in her expressions. "Miss Wy-eth? Jessica? Are you all right?"

Damn it! As much as she craved being independent again and making her own decisions, she wanted someone to assure her she was doing the right thing. Like a child learning to ride a bike, she needed an extra set of wheels. She knew she was going to tell the truth and hoped that people believed her.

"Y-yes."

"I want to talk about the Connaughts."

Jessica drew in a sharp gasp. "Who? Why?" She watched as something flashed behind Colleen's expression. Her one gift from her injury ignited. The animal instinct to watch for the moment of attack to be ready to flee is buried deep within the human brain. Fight or flight, friend or foe decisions were made in less time than it took a heart to beat.

Colleen appeared poised to attack, but something stopped her. Jessica could only hope that some part of Colleen's brain assessed Jessica as not a predator?

Jessica squeezed her eyes shut, concentrating on forcing connections to fire in a sluggish brain. Artifice needed energy and clarity to form and thrive. Jessica had limited reserves of both. One point was clear; no amount of fear or threat would make her protect Michael or talk about Kavan.

She held up her hand, stopping Colleen from answering until she could formulate a sentence. "E-Electra said sh-she was wrong. Y-ou were right a-about M-Michael."

The canvas bag dropped to the floor. "Jessica. You know who I am, right?"

Jessica nodded her head. "Reporter. *Globe.*"

Colleen thumped back against the doorjamb. Her hands shook as she pinched the bridge of her nose. "Do you know what you've just said?"

"You were right about Michael."

"Ooh, shit shit shit," Colleen muttered under her breath. "Can I sit down?"

Jessica wheeled her chair to the side of the bed and motioned for Colleen to sit in the big easy chair by the window. With one kick, Colleen shoved her bag beside the chair and sat down.

Jessica watched Colleen arrange a workspace with shaking hands. Colleen was far from her friend, but was she an enemy? All Jessica knew how to do was to tell her truth as best as she could and let Colleen be the judge. After that? She didn't have an answer.

Colleen grabbed a pad of paper and pen. She wagged a voice recorder in the air and set it on the arm of the chair after getting a nod of agreement from Jessica. Glinting with fresh tears, her eyes narrowed as she spoke. "I want to be clear. This conversation is being recorded. I'm investigating Connaught connections to organized crime as well as your involvement with his organization."

"I didn't know."

"What didn't you know?"

"Everything."

The stars were in full bloom by the time they finished their conversation. Papers covered the bed and floor, sorted by date with newly scrawled notes on top. Soot and dirt smeared the bedspread. Through a combination of nods, jumbled sentences, grimaces, and tears, Jessica did what she had long contemplated. Not being a party to Michael's schemes was an easy decision. Not being involved in syndicates and not accepting his money for her rehabilitation were hardly decisions at all. She followed her instincts and her inner compass of what was good and bad.

With her magnetic north scrambled, she hoped she conveyed shock at being duped rather than vengeance at being the woman scorned. Either way, she exposed the underbelly of the Connaught clan and with that action, sealed her death sentence.

Colleen snapped her notepad shut—her favorite one with a pen sketch of the *Globe's* building and the paper's logo underneath. She gathered up papers and recorder, shoved everything into her bag, and hoisted the bulging canvas under her arm. The only thing missing was a double shot of whiskey. She'd treat herself to that after she filed her story.

"You're sure about this?" she asked, poised to leave. She didn't want to have doubts, but what unfolded in her conversation with Jessica threw her convictions into a thrasher. An investigative reporter is trained to report the facts and follow their trail to the truth.

She had confronted Jessica with everything she could.

Bridget? Truth emerged only a few months ago. The secret that she was Jessica's biological mother should have died with her. No radicalizing conversations ever occurred between mother and daughter.

Gibraltar? Sex-filled vacation. Jessica even blushed at the mention of it.

Ireland? The horse training gig was an excuse to research family roots.

Manchester? Not her idea to go, but her horse needed her training expertise.

Belfast? Traveled there to learn more about her mother from people who knew her.

Michael? She thought they were in love, but he abandoned her when she needed him most. The pain bled from Jessica's eyes.

What had Max warned Colleen about? He warned her to keep her opinion out of her stories and to follow the facts, even if that meant taking a U-turn.

Colleen tried one last volley.

"That affidavit casts your story in deep doubt. It's the one piece of evidence that acts like a decoding ring. With it, your willing involvement with the bombing is proven." Colleen spoke the words with bluster, waving a copy in the air, proof of all unspeakable things. She didn't say that without it, Jessica's story had a chance of being believed. She left that for fate.

"Tim lied."

With those two words, spoken without a tinge of guile, doubt crept into Colleen's heart.

"He . . . he," Jessica's face screwed up as she struggled to find the words. She rammed her fingertips into her temple, eyes searching the ceiling as if the word she sought would be written in its tiles. "He's . . . *wrong!*" Her skin reddened with effort.

"Yeah. Right. He lied. Got it." Colleen watched as Jessica pressed the heels of her hands into her eyes, struggling.

"No. No! He lied, yes, but he . . . he's *autistic!*" Jessica sank with relief at finally getting the word out.

Colleen shrugged. "Yeah. So?"

Jessica struggled to say more. "M-Michael used him. Manipulated. Tim wouldn't understand how he lied or what he signed."

What little Colleen knew of legal documents, she knew you had to be of sound mind to swear out a statement or have documents proving that the disability did not impact your judgment or your ability to discern truth from fiction. With Jessica's revelation about Tim, the affidavit's strength failed. More doubt entered where certainty should have reigned.

Years of experience interviewing sources for her stories trained her ability to suss out a lie or a fact hidden. Reading Jessica was challenging, as Colleen didn't know where her injury started or a deception began. Was the hesitation between words and sentences a clue to a falsehood being crafted or was it simply a brain trying to force synapses to work?

As the hours unfolded, Colleen became more and more convinced that Jessica spoke the truth, a tale she didn't expect to hear. She had expected Jessica to waver in the face of the documents Colleen spread before her. Colleen lobbed one fact after another to prove Jessica's culpability and close ties with Michael, leaving no room for questions. Colleen expected Jessica's silence and with it proof of her loyalty to Michael. The facts supported it. Colleen's suspicions that another narrative existed evolved into an epiphany.

Jessica did something no loyal soldier would do. She unfolded the layers of Connaught enterprises and exposed its ugly underbelly by supplying as many names, dates, and places as she could. In doing so, she became the solid source Colleen needed to publish the series of articles she had been sitting on for far too long.

When Jessica's story goes live, two things will happen—Michael Connaught and his businesses will burst into flames and a vicious battle of survival will ensue. She was a dead reporter walking.

Lost in thought, she strode down the hall to the elevators, colliding with an orderly pushing a food tray cart. Papers scattered.

"Watch it!" she snapped, squatting to her knees and sweeping the pages toward her with her hands.

The orderly used his booted toe to slide a few wayward sheets out from under the cart. "Watch it yourself," he grunted. He held a handful of singed papers up to her, dangling them just out of her reach. He towered over her. Bleached white scrubs pulled over a shirt and jeans. The tightly stretched fabric showed his dirty clothes beneath. He eyed her bag, then Colleen. "Rough day?"

"Slightly," she sighed.

"Heard there was an explosion in a coffee place in Southie." He handed her the pad of notes.

Colleen didn't know which was more irritating, his stench or his smirk. She snatched the papers out of his hand as the elevator chimed. "Go ahead." She motioned with her head toward the empty elevator. Sharing a ride with overripe food trays and a smelly worker could wait. "I forgot something."

"Sure you did," he said, grinning to show teeth in desperate need of a cleaning. He shrugged. "Suit yourself." He pushed the cart aside with an outstretched arm. He must have had a bad day, too, for his forearm was colored by deep reds and hues of a bruise. He entered the elevator with one stride. The doors slipped closed.

She waited a few seconds before pressing the down call button, jabbing it several times as if doing so would make the car's trip down to the lobby and back up again go faster. She crossed her arms in front of her, hugging the bag as close as she could to her chest. A corner of a page of her notes caught her eye. She bent down to pick it up, pushed the cart to the side, and froze.

Why was the cart still there if the orderly was clearing the rooms for the night?

She closed her eyes and replayed the encounter in her head and couldn't believe how stupid she had been. Jeans, T-shirt, and even boots weren't enough to snap her to life. She was so engrossed in her own thoughts she failed to recognize the orderly from the standoff with Declan. In one shuddering breath, another detail sharpened into focus.

The arm he used to push back the cart wasn't bruised. What she saw were the vibrant colors of tattoos showing a shamrock encircled by a rose.

She rushed to the nurses' station and stood on her tiptoes to peer over the counter. "Did you see the orderly who was just here?"

A nurse, with perfectly coifed white hair, looked up over a pair of glasses perched at the end of her nose. Her ID lanyard proudly proclaimed "MILDRED Silvern's Finest—20 years." A series of buttons and stickers studded the perimeter of her nametag. "Excuse me? Orderly?"

Colleen gestured toward the cart. "Yeah. He was clearing the dinner trays or something. That's his cart."

Mildred used two hands to steady herself on the desk as she stood and craned her neck toward where Colleen pointed. She sat down with an irritated sigh and reached for the phone. "No. I didn't see him, but that cart should have been cleared hours ago." She punched a few numbers in. "It's Millie on five. Have you seen Peter? He was supposed to clear the carts." There was a pause. "No? Well, send somebody else up. I want to button down the floor for the night." She hung up with a barely controlled slam of the receiver.

"Peter?" Colleen asked. "Big guy? Ugly teeth?"

Mildred's chuckle triggered a burst of coughs. "Peter? Big? The only thing big about Peter is his smile. He's got pearly whites that'd put a Cheshire cat to shame."

The hallway's speakers chimed at the same time Mildred's phone rang. She started to talk, then stopped mid-sentence and listened. She put her hand over the mouthpiece. "When did you see that orderly? How long ago?" she barked.

Colleen could feel the hair follicles on her arms and scalp constrict. "Five minutes. Ten max."

"The guy you described was hanging around your friend's room. I've seen him before. He used to work here, but he quit. Not sure why. Looked like he wanted to visit, but was waiting for you to leave. He was content just to hang out by the door. I thought he gave up and left. You sure he was an orderly?"

"He was wearing white scrubs and pushing a cart, so I guessed he was." She cocked her head. "He was there? At the door? How long?"

The person on the other end of the phone demanded Mildred's attention. Mildred held up her hand, shushing Colleen, and pressed the phone to her ear, cupping her hand over the mouthpiece. "Oh my God! Peter? The walk-in refrigerator? Did he slip?" Mildred's eyebrows shot up her forehead as she gave a small gasp. "It might work in his favor if the cold kept the swelling down! How long to do you think he was lying there?" She paused, face furrowed with concern. "I have someone here who may know something. I'll keep her here until someone can talk to her."

"What's going on? What happened to Peter?"

Mildred adopted the authoritative demeanor reserved for keeping the public calm in the face of chaos. "Nothing. Please stay here." The intercom continued to chime. The hallways started to fill with nurses and others, faces of each closed with professional fear, mouths pressed to straight lines.

Colleen sank back to her feet. "Oh, shit. Shit. *Shit*," she muttered. Amanda's death proved that Connaught's network would stop at nothing to prevent connections from being exposed. Colleen had one shot at getting even.

Protecting Jessica became as important as protecting her precious documents. And herself.

She turned toward Jessica's room.

"Wait. Where are you going?" Mildred demanded as she peered down over the desk.

Colleen flashed her most disarming smile. "My friend," she said with a thrust of her thumb toward Jessica's room, "I don't want her to be concerned. I'm going to stay with her. Okay?"

Mildred started to say something when her phone rang again. "Fine. Don't leave. Security is on their way up to talk with you."

Colleen had a moment's hesitation as she balanced reporting the story against *becoming* the story—but only a moment's. She swiped a coat off the rack and rushed into Jessica's room. "We've got to get out of here. *Now*. Someone overheard our conversation. We're both in danger."

Jessica didn't move. "Who? How?"

Colleen held the jacket up. "An orderly, but . . ." She glanced at the clock. "I'll explain it all, but we've got to *move*."

"Big guy. Yellow teeth?"

Colleen nodded and looked at her. "Can you walk? Sorry, I mean, can you . . . you . . . Ah, *shit!*" She gripped her hair with her hand.

Jessica pointed to the door. "Lounge."

"Lounge?" She started to protest then remembered passing the large room on the way up from the parking garage. She pulled the wheelchair beside Jessica, helping her settle into the seat. Next, she grabbed a blanket, and tucked it in, careful to cover Jessica's jeans. She looked around the room for shoes. Finding only a pair of boots, she yanked shearling slippers off Jessica's feet and shoved the boots on. She covered Jessica's shoulders with another throw, and wheeled Jessica out the door and into the hallway.

"Just taking her to the lounge," she said, smiling at Mildred who was too engaged with talking on the phone to notice them. Colleen kept her speed slow and steady as she walked down the corridor toward the lounge. Two nurses stood by the abandoned cart, clucking concern in soft voices. The elevator doors opened to an empty car. Colleen pushed Jessica inside and allowed herself one long exhale only after the doors slid shut behind them.

It took every measure of patience to walk to her car, but once there, Colleen stopped in confusion. Jammed with fast food wrappers, boxes of papers, and clothing for whatever weather New England decided to throw at her, Colleen's car had room for a driver. Passengers did not merit a thought. And a wheelchair? Forget about it.

She opened the passenger side door and shoveled an armload of bags and empty coffee cups onto the pavement. A shadow darkening the seat made her jump.

"Whooaa," she said, looking up at Jessica.

Jessica held on to the doorframe as she tossed the blanket into the car. She shoved her wheelchair against the wall.

Colleen's thoughts were in a whirlwind.

If she could lie about walking, what else could she lie about?

Jessica had Colleen persuaded she was merely an innocent pawn in the game of international terrorism. It almost worked, but when she saw Jessica push her wheelchair away and lower herself into the car, her concerns surfaced again.

As swayed as she was by Jessica's story, her doubts remained. Jessica did not speak the whole truth. Something else stayed buried. Something else had drawn Jessica to Northern Ireland. Michael's pull on Jessica had been strong, but it wasn't strong enough for Jessica to put herself at risk for him. So why did she go to Belfast? Each time she tried to talk to Jessica about her father, Jessica's face closed. A clue came when she pulled out a picture of the bishop. Jessica flushed and worked her mouth as if holding back something she wanted to say. Colleen terminated the interview figuring she had time to get the truth of the story behind the bishop. First, she determined to focus on Michael.

"Where?" Jessica asked as Colleen pulled out of the garage.

"I need to write and file this story. The safest place for me will be the *Globe's* offices."

"And me?"

She didn't answer. "That orderly back there–"

"Brendan" Jessica said, giving the devil a name.

"Brendan. You know him?"

"Abusive pig." Jessica pulled her jacket tighter around her.

Colleen recognized that abused women used the same motion when they didn't want to speak of the horrors experienced at the hands of their abusers. She understood immediately.

"Okay. Brendan overheard everything we talked about. He's no doubt raised the alarm. We don't have a lot of time before someone puts our heads in their crosshairs and pulls the trigger."

Jessica nodded in sad agreement. "No one leaves alive." She stared out the window. "I'm his decoy."

Colleen pulled out on Causeway Street and drove past North Station. The evening rush hour was over. With no game scheduled at the Garden, the streets were almost empty.

She pulled into an alley. Staring straight ahead, she gripped the steering wheel and peered up the street.

"Okay. I'm not a cat, so I don't know how many lives I have left. I must have lost eight today, easy." She tried to laugh at her joke, but the sound came out hollow and chopped. "I'm nervous about bringing you back to the *Globe* with me. I'd rather find a place for you, but you've got to be straight with me. You're not telling me everything you know, and right now, neither one of us can afford any bullshit."

Jessica looked at her, blue eyes two spheres of calm.

Colleen took a deep breath. "I don't understand why, and I need to. Why did Michael turn on you? More importantly, why are you still alive? There's more of a reason you're alive than just you being a convenient decoy to take the fall for the Manchester bombing. So, you take the focus away from him for as long as it takes to file charges and convict you of that attack. Then what? I'm sorry, there's more to why he's keeping you on a short leash."

"His uncle turned his heart."

"Listen, sister," Colleen blurted, "What Michael Connaught is doing to you no honorable man would do. Turning his heart had nothing to do with it."

Jessica worked her mouth. Colleen's reporter instincts buzzed. Her source was ready to dish. All she had to do was provide assurances.

"Listen. I protect my sources, okay? What you say will be off the record." Colleen watched as the storm of indecision gathered behind Jessica's brow. She scarcely breathed as she waited.

Jessica huffed with disbelief. "Protect?" She shook her head as if knowing some information could never be hidden once it was exposed. She shuddered as the storm raged.

Colleen sat quietly, counting the moments before she could press one last time. "I'll do everything I can to protect you and the information you provide. Knowing everything is the only way I can protect you.

A tear escaped the corner of Jessica's eye. "My father is the bishop."

"Oooh," Colleen exhaled through puffed cheeks. She pressed her forehead to the steering wheel. In the world of geopolitics and profits, the paternity of Bishop Kavan Hughes was worth dying for—either to protect it from discovery or to expose it.

Michael was keeping Jessica in check by using her father as ransom. The explosion of news surrounding any arrest of Jessica would be the perfect time to reveal the bishop's paternity. No amount of politicking or statesmanship would keep the news out of the world press nor keep coalitions from imploding. Factions would split. Violence would rage in the streets. Connaught's companies stood to reap millions in sales of weapons and supplying all the needs of war.

Dangling Jessica in a noose of false accusations would take the immediate focus off Connaught. Exposing the bishop ensured her silence and provided insurance that inquiries into a terrorist network would lead far away from Michael Connaught.

"I've got to file this story," Colleen said as she pulled back onto the street. "You're coming with me because . . ." Her voice trailed. No other choice existed. "The *Globe's* offices are only a couple of miles from here. We'll be safe there."

She made her way to Congress Street, deciding to take the highway back to Morrissey Boulevard in Dorchester. She passed Faneuil Hall. The stores had closed and bars had announced "last call." Only a few pedestrians walked the streets. She began writing her story in her head.

"Being followed." Jessica sat up straight and pointed at her sideview mirror. She dropped the visor open and used the mirror to look behind them. "Circle around. See if they stay."

Colleen took a left and headed back the direction they had come. She glanced anxiously in her mirrors.

"Still there!" Jessica said. "Can you lose them?"

In the second it took to nod yes, the back windshield spidered with a bullet hole. Colleen downshifted and braked, spinning the car down a street and weaving back toward the highway. A car came at them head on, then skidded to a halt sideways, blocking their path. Another car approached from the right, blocking escape routes to the south. The only route open was through the Callahan tunnel and north.

The brightly lit tunnel was empty except for one yellow cab. Colleen floored the accelerator, passing the cab, and then pulled into its lane. Two sets of headlights raced up behind the cab.

"Hang on." She slammed on the brakes. The cab's horn blared as it plowed into the back of her car. The force of the impact snapped their heads backward and the cars fishtailed across the lanes. She threw her car into third gear and hit the gas. The cab remained motionless in the middle of the tunnel, steam rising from its crumpled hood. With no room to avoid the wreck, the other cars plowed into the tunnel's walls. Men used open car doors to shield themselves as they shot at Colleen and Jessica. Colleen watched in terror as one man scrambled to the top of his car and pointed a rifle at them. Bullets ricocheted around them. Glass and metal broke and chipped around them. Colleen screamed.

Her car lurched to the right. It bounced off the side of the wall before she was able to straighten it. The sound of grinding metal was joined by a *thut thut thut* of a blown tire.

The bottom of the tunnel flattened out, and then rose. The car leaned and swayed as she rocked the steering wheel, narrowly avoiding hitting the guardrail as they passed the entrance to Logan Airport.

"Oh, God!" Colleen held her hand up to her throat. Blood pulsed between her fingers in time with her beating heart. "I'm in trouble."

Her head sagged forward, then lurched to the side as she struggled for consciousness. She pulled the car off of Route 1A, zigzagged down narrow streets, and rolled to a stop in a dead zone between street lights.

She could feel her blood cool as it ran over her hand and down her arm. Each beat of her panicked heart pushed more of her life away. Gravity increased its pull tenfold as she raised her head to look at Jessica.

"Don't," she said, stopping Jessica's attempts to stop the bleeding. A hard coldness of reality ebbed in from the edges, and along with it an odd calm. "Take the bag. Everything's there." Her chest ached with the effort to fill her lungs. "Get recorder." The seconds it took for Jessica to place the recorder in Colleen's hands felt like days. Colleen's hands shook as she pressed the record button.

"Th-this is Colleen Shaunessy-Carillo. I ... I've been shot. Jessica Wyeth ... innocent. Framed. Being used. Amanda Boch killed be-because she found an informant inside. St-stopped inquiries into Magnus Connaught's death. Not ... not natural ... murder." She panted as her breath ran out.

She felt warm hands smooth along her cheeks as they guided her head to rest against the seat. Enough light shone from the dashboard to illuminate Jessica's face. Tracks of tears shone against mottled skin.

"Was it Michael? Was it Michael who called you to say I was coming back?"

Colleen wanted to laugh at the tinny sound of Jessica's voice, but the effort was too great. "M-Michael? No. The old guy. Liam."

Why did Jessica make that sound? Like a strangled gasp? She couldn't figure it out and she didn't care. She cared less and less.

"It's soon," Colleen coughed.

"No. You're okay. I'll get help." Panic creased Jessica's words.

She wanted to say more, but knew the time had passed. "Something's planned. Connaught." She stopped and panted between phrases. "A shipment. Gonna be soon."

"When? Where?"

She closed her eyes, marshalling her strength for one last sentence.

"Go. Get papers to *Globe*. Max. He'll know what to do." Numb fingers fumbled as she pressed the recorder into Jessica's hands. She hesitated. Was there more? Was this it?

Thoughts thickened and slowed.

What more was there?
"Puhl . . . puhl . . . it . . . zer. . ."
She put the strap of her bag into Jessica's shaking hand.

Jessica couldn't stop her hands from trembling as she reached over Colleen's motionless body. She pulled the lever to recline the seat and was sickened by the gurgle that bubbled from Colleen's neck. The sound was identical to Gus' last breath and she nearly fainted at the shockwave of memory it triggered. She killed the lights and switched off the ignition. The engine ticked and dogs barked. A sound of sirens in the distance focused her thoughts.

What could she do? She could wait, but for who? Tension nagged at her temples as she tried to make a decision. *Am I safe? Do I run?* Fact by fact she assessed where she was and why, the primal drive of survival unblunted by injury. The most likely people to find her were not the police. They would be focused on the wreck inside the tunnel and an irate cab driver. The only people who would know to look for her were the ones who chased them to begin with. *Move. Keep moving.*

Her hands were sticky with drying blood as she pawed through the rubbish at her feet and found a half-filled water bottle. She held it to Colleen's lips, pouring small amounts into her slack jaw. Water dribbled down Colleen's chin. Jessica refused to acknowledge what that meant. With shaking fingers, she felt for a pulse. Nothing. She closed her eyes and said a moment's prayer.

Information flooded her brain. The metallic smell of blood filled the car. Fast food wrappers lay strewn on the little used road.

Gripping the doorframe, she hoisted herself to her feet and balanced her weaving body on wobbling legs. Even an able-bodied soul would have shaken with the dose of adrenalin that rushed through her veins, but her legs vibrated with uncontrollable tremors.

Oh, God. Can I do this? Am I a fool? She released her grip and tested her world. Her knees buckled and she stopped herself from collapsing on the ground, face inches from the seat. She squeezed her eyes shut. *I've got to do this.*

The smell of blood, and something else? The roar of a jet overhead. The sight of Colleen's motionless body. The taste of terror. She pressed her fists to her eyes and sifted through her senses.

A sound and familiar smell. The mix brought memories long buried to the surface. She knew of only one place where the smell of horses and the sounds of jets mingled. Suffolk Downs; the Thorough-bred racetrack where she spent many childhood hours.

Colleen had turned down a service entrance to the back stables. Dried leaves and rubbish tangled in the vine-encrusted mesh of the chain link fence. A gate, dented and bent from years of forced entry, sagged under the weight of a padlocked chain. Beyond the fence, tin roofs of the shed rows stretched out in darkened and rusted lines.

A few spotlights glowed toward the far end, hinting that any sta-bled horses were clustered in that area. Even in the dark, she still knew the place. A memory surfaced of darting in and out of barns, avoiding skittish horses and their grumpy grooms, squealing with delight as Gus pretended not to find her.

The weight of the bag pulled at her and she balanced herself against the hood of the car until she was sure she wouldn't fall. Her nights of practice at Silvern did not include carrying anything, and her legs and abdomen burned with the effort to remain upright. Her feet caught and stubbed on the ground, unfamiliar with anything other than smooth linoleum. Legs splayed for balance, she staggered and tripped toward the gate.

Sweat drenched her shirt by the time she shoved the bag through the underbrush onto a weed-filled path. The chain link clanked and groaned from her weight as she forced her way through. She emerged in an area that was half memory, half dream. Her head ached with the effort to categorize and process where to go and what to do next.

She needed rest.

Shelter out of sight. Get time to think safely.

Off-season. Few horses wintered at Suffolk Downs. Owners had shipped any horse of merit to race in warmer climates. A bare, grime-covered light bulb shed an anemic pallor over the entrance of one row. Long lines of stalls opened to a covered corridor. The top halves of a few doors were open, as if waiting for a horse to poke out its head.

She avoided the rusted cans and papers as she made her way to a stall. The door creaked open, alerting a dog in the distance. Once thick with straw and shavings, only a padded mat now covered the floor. She wedged herself into the far corner and sank to the ground, flipping the collar of her coat up and hugging it closed across her chest.

Colleen was dead. Because of her. And Electra. Maybe it was her turn.

Terror should have crept into the passages of her heart at the thought, but euphoria seeped in instead. She walked. She understood. She acted on her own. The months of hiding inside herself had had a dual effect. She had fooled the outside world, but a side effect was that she had fooled herself as well. Why? How did euphoria take hold?

Because she had told her truth to someone who had been her enemy and the truth won. She didn't have to hide behind a lie. She could stand alone. And stand proud.

She could protect Kavan by living her truth in the same way he had protected her.

She curled up into a ball and drifted off to sleep.

Silvern Rehabilitation Hospital
Boston, Massachusetts

DECLAN WAS AWARE of how the air shimmered around him as he parked his car at Silvern. Late at night, the garage was normally empty of visitors and daytime traffic, but this night was different. Police cars prowled the lot and streets. Groups of people clustered together in hunched worry.

His stomach sank as the elevator doors opened on Jessica's floor. Nurses bustled. Uniformed policemen stood next to the nurses' station and heads turned as he approached.

"Where's your friend?" Mildred asked, rushing to Declan's side as soon as he came into sight.

Declan didn't need to ask any questions. The buzzing feeling in his gut told him everything he needed to know. "What are you talking about? She's here."

"No, she's not." A police officer in the black uniform of the Boston force joined them. "We were hoping you'd be able to tell us."

Declan was aware of eyes on him as he answered the question. "Is all of this because a patient wandered off? What's going on?"

"An orderly was found unconscious in the kitchen freezer. He had been hit over the head. The woman who visited Jessica tonight may have seen something, but she left before anyone could talk to her. She took Miss Wyeth with her."

"Woman? What woman? What was her name?"

Mildred bristled. "How am I supposed to know the name of every visitor? She was a petite little thing with black bobbed hair and a messenger bag three times her size. Miss Wyeth knew her. They talked for quite some time."

That damned reporter. The buzzing in his gut increased a notch to feel like a swarm of bees. "What happened just before they left?"

"Nothing," Mildred evaded with a quick look at the police officer.

"Try again," Declan growled.

Mildred shifted under his glare. "That orderly, the one with bad teeth you complained about, hung out in the corridor and eaves-dropped on their conversation. After I heard someone was hurt in the deep freeze, I don't know where anyone went. That's when Miss Wyeth and her friend disappeared."

Any hopes he had to find a way to keep Jessica alive and Michael contained evaporated. He pushed his way past the nurses into Jessi-ca's room. The wheelchair was gone. So were her jeans, boots, and jacket.

The officer stepped in front of him as he turned toward the eleva-tors. "We'd like to ask you a few questions."

Declan surveyed the halls. Uniformed officers took notes from hospital personnel. "I don't know anything useful." He smiled, flash-ing his teeth.

"We'll be the judge of that. All information is important. Won't take long."

Declan shoved his business card into the officer's hand. "I'm local. Call me at that number and I'll answer any questions you have. I got-ta go."

The elevator doors slid open. Declan ducked behind a pillar as Baxter stepped out. He stole a glance at the unfolding scene.

"Holy Fucking Christ," Baxter ranted as he pushed his way into Jessica's room. Crimson crescents bloomed up his cheeks with such ferocity that Declan mused Baxter would bleed out if he cut himself shaving.

"She's gone? You mean to tell me Jessica Wyeth is *gone*?" Baxter yelled at Mildred. Declan jabbed the elevator button. The chimes sounded as Declan heard him say, "I gambled my career on her not being a flight risk and you're telling me she slipped out of here?"

"She's been off campus before. She'll come back."

"It's one fucking thirty in the morning. What are the odds she stepped out for coffee?" Baxter was too intent upon focusing his rage on the head nurse to notice the elevator's arrival.

Mildred stammered, intimidated into silence.

"I'll have your fucking head for this," Baxter said.

Alone in the elevator as he descended, Declan leaned his back against the wall, closed his eyes, and breathed, counting to ten on each inhale and exhale.

After the third breath, he opened his eyes.

"Game on," he said as he loped back to his car.

Suffolk Downs Racetrack
East Boston, Massachusetts

THE SOUNDS OF the stable sifted into her light sleep. Horses snorted and chuffed as they waited patiently for daybreak and for the morning routine to begin. Those were the sounds of comfort, not alarm.

Gravel crunched. A dog whimpered. She stirred.

Light flooded the stall, making it impossible to focus on the blurry form that weaved and bobbed in front of her.

A booted foot kicked her legs.

"Whadiya doin' here?" The voice was constricted. Too high pitched to be a man, too resonant for a woman. Young? Afraid.

Jessica opened her eyes slowly, careful not to move suddenly. Light silhouetted a compact figure. The quilted vest under his grimy barn coat did little to bulk up his frame. A few wisps of ginger-colored beard poked out from his chin. A knit cap was pulled over his brow. He held a shovel over his head, ready.

"You hearin' me? How'd you get in?" The dog at his feet gave an excited yip and stayed at his side.

She blinked and shifted herself upright. "Back gate. I shimmied through. I'm sorry. I . . . I . . . needed a place to hide."

Green eyes narrowed. The shovel hovered. "Hide? Who from? Why?"

"From some really bad people. They," she hesitated, wondering how to get him to help her. "They want what's in this bag."

"I don't want nothing to do with no drugs," he said.

"No. No drugs." She held her palms up, then slowly moved one hand to flip open the top flap. "Go ahead. Look inside."

He cocked his head, unsure of the offer. The dog shoved his snout inside, hoping for a treat. "What is all that?"

Jessica faltered. Before she spoke, she sorted through the sounds of the stables. No sirens. No urgent voices. Colleen must not have been discovered. "Documents. Letters. They belong, um, *belonged* to a reporter from the *Boston Globe.*"

"Why do you have them?"

She raised her head and swept her hair off her face. "Ever hear of Wyeth's Worldwind Farms?"

The shovel raised an inch. He leaned over and peered at her. Keeping the shovel aloft, he used his other hand to feel inside the bag. He pulled out a photograph of Jim Wyeth standing with a group of people in the winners' circle with a horse and a jockey mounted on its back. The jockey's silks bore the colors and logo of Worldwind Farm. "They used to race here," he said. "They were banned from racing when officials discovered their horses were drugged."

"Worldwind didn't drug."

His eyes narrowed. "Yeah? And?" The shovel lowered.

She forced her speech to be clear and fluid and enunciated each word carefully. "The people who did are the ones who want these documents never to be published."

He placed the shovel on the ground. "Do you know Gus Adams?" he probed.

Hearing Gus' name didn't surprise her. Anyone connected with the racetrack would know him. Gus was a legend. "Did," she corrected. "I did know him. Scrappy Irishman if ever there was one. I loved Gus Adams as a father."

He nodded as if she had passed a secret test. "And?"

Jessica blinked back tears. "He'd never harm a horse."

"Gus gave me my first job when I promised to finish high school, then saw to it I worked for another farm. Never understood why I couldn't work for Worldwind 'til I heard 'bout the doping scandal. I didn't believe a word of it. Gus was all about the animal. Word here was the Irish Mafia killed him to keep him quiet. He kept me away from all that." He reached out his hand to help her to her feet. She fumbled. "You hurt?" he asked, looking at her blood encrusted hands.

She leaned her weight on him as she struggled for balance. "The reporter who gave this to me is dead."

Face level with his, she could feel his manner change as recognition set in. "You're that Wyeth chick!"

She bit her lower lip. Her heart pounded.

"Wait. The reporter is dead?"

She had nowhere to turn. Either he would help her or not. "I need your help. I've got to get this to her colleagues. She was afraid that if it got into anyone else's hands, the truth would die along with her."

He hesitated. "You need to call the cops."

Did she? Who else could she turn to? If she didn't call the police, would he become suspicious and not help her? "There's a priest. Father Blanton. I need to call him. He and I can talk with the cops together." Seeing his doubt, she implored, "Please."

He mulled this over for a moment, then nodded. "M'name's Tyler. I owe Gus, and anything I can do to bring down the skeeves who killed him is good by me. You good to walk? There's a phone in the barn office a few rows over."

He gripped her elbow on one side and she used his shovel as a cane on the other as they made slow progress through the yards. The shed rows covered an area big enough to stable more than seven hundred horses. Tyler's office was toward the center. Low-lying clouds glowed amber with ambient light from nearby neighborhoods. Extended arms of hot walkers, like spines of a broken umbrella against the night sky, waited for the next carousel of sweat-slicked horses. Another jet roared overhead. A tinge of salty brine blended with horse and hay. The ocean was near.

She was grateful for the meager warmth of the office and for the offer of a stale doughnut. Tout sheets, training logs, and gear catalogs littered the top of an ancient wooden desk. Green lights flashed on a security panel. The dog curled up at the foot of a cot, blankets and sheets thrown into a rumpled pile from Tyler's hasty departure.

She kept her voice steady as she spoke with Father Blanton, telling him only that she needed him and was afraid. She stumbled on what to say when he asked for Colleen. "They shot her," was her only response. Tyler's stare made her squirm.

While they waited, they talked. She kept the conversation on horses. He was impressed she was back to riding so soon after her injury.

"People 'round here lived on every detail of your story. I heard you were never going to walk again."

He was so earnest. She liked him. "Yeah. I heard that, too."

He spoke of his dream to have his own string of horses and why he picked up the odd night as the barn watchman to supplement his wages. He retrained horses not suitable for racing rather than see them sold for slaughter. The money he made from selling horses he retrained covered their upkeep, barely. One mare, Glama Queen, was his joy. "Been seeing what she can do aside from run straight and fast. She's a thinker and can fly, too. Loves the challenge. Bet she's gonna make me enough to buy a proper stable of my own."

She watched him shift his weight from foot to foot, keeping himself between her and the door. The dog placed its face on his paws, eyes following Tyler's every move. She tried to stay calm, but dread inched up on her with each passing minute. Was she doing the right thing to wait for Father Blanton? Should she have called the police first? Tyler seemed okay with her decision, so it must be okay, but how could she be sure? She needed to make one decision at a time. *Don't get overwhelmed. Step by step.*

A light on the control panel began to blink red. An alarm beeped.

Tyler read the screen. "Someone's come through the back fence near where you entered." He punched a few buttons and surveyed the monitors. "And someone else has come in through the side. See here?" He pointed at the monitor to a male figure moving up the shed row. Even the grainy image was clear enough to see that the man clasped a gun in both hands in front of his chest as he walked with his back to the walls. At each door and corner, he paused, then pointed his gun inside the area, searching. Tyler clicked through other images. "They've got the service entrances covered. I see at least three cars."

Tyler spoke over his shoulder as he reached for the phone. "I'm done waitin'. I'm calling the cops." As soon as he picked up the phone, the lights went out. He tapped on the switch hook with the phone held up to his ear. "Line's dead, too." He grabbed her arm and started to run out the door.

She pulled her arm out of his grasp. "Go without me. I ... I can't run."

"Those guys will be here soon enough. You can't stay."

She pushed the bag into his arms. "Get this to the *Globe*."

Gray light came through the window. She could see his black silhouette as he turned his head and leaned back to look out the door. "Wait here." The dog bounded up to follow him and Tyler raised his palm even with the dog's nose. "Stay."

The dog gave one yip in frustration and lay on its belly, head facing the door.

A few minutes later she heard the familiar sound of hooves grinding on dirt. Tyler stood with two horses.

He spoke in a whisper. "They're coming from the other side. We can go out though the track exit, then circle around through the back. I know a way out. You sure you can ride?" He waited until she nodded. "Good. These two don't race anymore, but still have some game." He rubbed their necks with obvious pride.

"Leave that," he said, reaching for the messenger bag.

Jessica clutched the bag to her chest, confused. What if she let it go and someone else found it? Her painful and slow progress to the stable was enough to convince her she shouldn't ride an animal unknown to her while carrying the bag. She had a hard enough time maintaining her own balance.

"No. You." She pushed the bag into his arms. When he hesitated, she pleaded. "Please. It's everything."

He grabbed the bag, tested its weight, and pulled the strap over his head so it hung on his body diagonally.

Then he hoisted her up and watched in the experienced horseman's way to make sure a new rider communicated well with the horse. He waited until her horse was calm before he swung himself up on the other.

"You don't have to tell Glama much to get her moving," Tyler said, referring to the mare Jessica rode. He brought his finger to his lips and motioned for her to follow.

They began at a walk, but the horses had other plans. The horses skittered and danced, bodies moving sideways as much as forward, primed for the unexpected adventure. Their necks arched and they worked the bits in their mouths.

He kept them to the side of the paths, where the dirt was less firmly packed and muffled the sound of the hooves. Jessica counted passing three shed rows before she became aware of a large expanse opening before them.

The track at Suffolk Downs was a one-mile dirt track with a turf track inside the oval. As soon as the horses turned the corner, they fought for their heads, leaning on the bits. The force pulled Jessica's arms forward and upper body off balance. She tightened her core and willed herself on.

Shouts came from behind the barns. More voices joined. One shot rang out.

"*Goddammit!*" Tyler yelled. "You ready?" He didn't wait for a response before he set off at a gallop.

Jessica tensed. Fear fired synapses in her damaged brain and scrambled her ability to control her body. Muscles clenched and twitched causing her arms to pull and release on reins and legs to kick and squeeze. The normal routes of communicating with the horse lost in the static of injury.

Glama tossed her head and pinned her ears back showing her confusion. Jessica could not stop her own body from signaling fear and knew the mare intuited her signals that a predator was near. Glama knew only one thing to do once her own survival mechanism was triggered. Tyler and his horse were four strides ahead before Jessica freed Glama's mouth from a tight grip on the bit, but once released, Glama accelerated. She flattened her body over Glama's neck, wrapped her hands in flying mane, and tried to clear her mind of everything.

Jessica listened to the pounding hooves ahead of her and guided Glama to follow. Glama's legs churned at the earth. Clots of dirt flew up. Along with the four-beat sound of their gallop was the sickening *thwip thwip* of bullets striking the track around them.

"Stay to my left flank," Tyler yelled. "Keep her a head behind."

With each stride, Glama's body coiled and released under Jessica. The mare's neck pumped forward as her legs and chest surged them over the ground. Jessica positioned Glama and could feel, more than see, Tyler at her right shoulder. He used his horse's body to steer them away from the grandstands, toward the back stretch.

"There's a gap in the brush and a low fence," he yelled. "Gather her up to shorten her stride. She's good for at least a four foot jump."

No time to think or adjust. Jessica clenched her stomach muscles, shifted her weight back and increased pressure on Glama's mouth by increasing tension on the reins. The mare responded first by lowering her head, fighting Jessica's grip.

Think three jumps ahead and you'll work as one with your horse. Gus' words pounded a mantra in her head.

"*Heyo, horse.* I'm in control here." Jessica kept her voice strong and steady, using pressure on the reins to do the same. Instinct overrode broken circuitry. Muscles pulled her forward and legs gripped. Glama's head came up and her stride shortened in time to gather and launch over the fence. The sound of hooves stopped as their flight began. For one moment, they hung together, suspended only by trust. The jump arched, then fell. The sound of hooves pounding the earth began again. Instantly, thick brush and brambles ripped at Jessica's legs and arms. Momentum kept her astride as they crashed through the underbrush.

Leaves and branches scattered as they emerged under a street-light. Houses in the working class neighborhood sat silent and dark as a chorus of dogs began to bark. Tyler turned left, using the body of his big gelding to cut off Glama, forcing the mare to slow. He headed to a park, avoiding swings dangling from a play structure and turned wide around a tubular slide, yellow plastic nearly glowing in the dark.

The sound of squealing tires and an engine accelerating made him whip his head around. He leaned over, grabbed Glama's bridle, and pulled them to a stop behind the cement dugout of a little league field.

"What are you doing?" Jessica yelled, turning to see where the car was.

Tyler pulled the bag up over his head and put it on Jessica. He took off his belt and used it to secure the bag to Jessica's back. "This should keep the bag steady. I've been watching you ride. If it's centered, you'll be fine." He pointed down a street. "Go down that street, bang a right, then left. You'll hit the beach. Once on the beach, open this baby up," he said, patting Glama's neck, "and head north. The police have a station on the beach. Big brick building. Can't miss it." The sound of screeching tires neared. "Trust me. By the time you get there, they'll be looking for you."

"What are you doing?" She adjusted the balance of the bag. Lights on porches and in bedrooms popped on. Owners began yelling at dogs.

Tyler looked up the street. "Stay to the backyards. I'll keep to the streets and make 'em think I'm heading back to the main gate. Go!"

A shower of sparks cascaded off a nearby jungle gym and puffs of concrete from bullets missing their mark and hitting the wall behind them convinced her. Tyler galloped across the baseball diamond and disappeared behind a soccer goal. The car spun around and followed him. Jessica drilled her leg into Glama's side, cuing the horse's haunches to spin around, lessening the need to pull hard on the reins. Horse and rider fused. They were off.

Keeping to the backyards meant she didn't risk Glama's fine legs on hard pavement. The well-tended lawns offered the perfect footing for Glama's hooves. Shadows of houses loomed ahead. Glama cantered with an easy stride while Jessica acclimated to the bag on her back and the terrain.

A porch light turned on. The door flew open, and a dog barreled out of the house and down the steps, yipping a high-pitched bark, its path sure to bring it under Glama's hooves. Either the dog was going to be trampled or it would snarl in Glama's legs and horse and rider would fall. She could feel Glama begin to panic and shy away from the dog when a brown streak flashed ahead. Tyler's dog catapulted across her path and barrel-rolled over the intruder. Shocked yelps filled the air. Something popped in the distance. Gunshots?

More lights flashed on. The night air filled with shouts and shocked cries.

"What the fuck is that?"

"Somebody call the freaking cops!"

"Wicked cool! Ma? There's a horse in our yard!"

She reached the pavement and turned right. The air cooled as she neared the ocean. Glama veered at sheets flapping on a clothes line. The horse's sudden change in direction shifted the bag violently to the side and nearly unseated her.

Ahead, a man in boxers stood in the center of his backyard, waving his arms.

"Stop! Hold up!"

Jessica could feel Glama falter. The horse had no basis of trust in Jessica and indecision telegraphed through the horse's body and into Jessica's. With one voice, Jessica murmured, "We've got this. You're safe with me." Glama's ears flicked back, listening. Her stride lengthened.

The man leapt to the side as they blasted past and leapt over a picket fence. They landed in a yard dominated by the hulk of an above-ground pool. Glama headed for the gap between the pool and the house.

Three teens clamored onto a porch, each pushing the other to be the first down the steps. Their Saturday night plans suddenly changed.

"Fuckin' A, man. Get outta my way!"

"Holy Fucking Christ. A horse!"

"You kiddin' me? You'll get trampled!"

"Grab 'em!"

They ran toward Glama, arms flailing. Glama swerved, desperate to avoid the tangle of bodies. Her back hooves slipped, plunging her haunches into the side of the pool.

Water sloshed over the pool's dented enclosure. The pressure of the escaping water crushed the side, further imploding the structure, releasing the pool's contents in one massive rush. The tidal wave swept the three teens down their driveway, their screams a mix of shock and awe.

A few more strides and the earth changed from dirt and grass to sand.

Using the race horse's instincts, Jessica put her arms forward.

"Go."

And Glama flew.

Salt spray stung her face as they streaked up the beach. Glama's hooves barely made a sound as Jessica kept to the firm sand where the waves shrank back from the ebbing tide.

The white beach stretched ahead of them—a line of houses on one side and the black waters of the ocean on the other. The band of sand offered the perfect home stretch. The night was cold but the air above the ocean was warmed from the current. Ghostly wisps of fog hovered above the waves and glowed from the reflected lights, waving them on, applauding. The apparitions rose and fell with gentle sighs.

Jessica's fingers and toes burned with life as her muscles began to shake from exertion. Her balance shifted. The bag pulled.

Houses gave way to a long wall that separated the road from the beach. Glama surged ahead, strides exploding over the sand.

Jessica fought to control her shaking muscles. Throbs of pain locked her fingers in Glama's mane. She started to slip off-center.

A car roared up the road. Brakes screeched as it fishtailed to a stop. Pops. Bursts of sand erupted around her.

More gunshots. Shouts.

Her muscles battled for balance, but the duration of exertion was too much. The bag pulled her backwards into the sand. She bounced once and tumbled over, dragged along by Glama as the horse panicked and fought for her freedom. Sand ground into her mouth and eyes. The bag acted as an anchor and the reins ripped out of her hands. Gravity held her in place like a turtle on its back.

Bullets whined and pocked around her. She waited for the searing pain, wondering how long it would take before one ripped through her skin. Her thoughts were on Glama, running free up the beach, as she looked up at the sky, amazed that the night had cleared and wishing the stars were stronger in their battle against street lights. She closed her eyes, committing the moment to memory.

She was calm when hands yanked at her, pulling on her coat and clothes, and remained ragdoll limp as she was forced to balance. Her legs buckled under her weight.

"Stop shittin' around. You're no more a cripple than I am."

Hands pulled her collar upward and gave her a shake, making her head rattle. She commanded her legs to go underneath her and push. After a few attempts, she was able to lock her knees and balance, suspended by the grip on her coat.

Sirens echoed off the sides of buildings, chopping their cries into vibrato. She waited.

A volley of gunshots crescendoed then stopped. Her knees sagged again.

"You hurt?"

Was she? She shook her head.

"I don't know your game, but you're not foolin' me. No one can ride a horse like that and not stand up. Open your eyes."

She hadn't realized her eyes were closed. Opening them meant opening to a new reality, to a world where guilt and innocence were relative. She kept her eyes closed for one last deep breath, savoring the ocean air.

She blinked her eyes open.

Free from her rider, Glama barreled up the beach. The horse's body was a black smudge against the foggy night. Red and blue lights flashed on the jumble of marked and unmarked police cars lined up along the road at least a mile ahead. Dark shapes of onlookers emerged from the mist, arms crossed in front and hunched from cold. The shock of seeing a horse galloping free drew their attention.

No one noticed Jessica.

Except Brendan.

He propped her onto her feet as if jamming a post into the ground and shook her again when her knees buckled. His breath billowed out of him as he panted. Peppermint mingled with his typical stench. The smell turned her stomach.

He shoved her forward to a waiting car. "Get a move on."

Her legs refused to obey. Her feet dragged and tripped in the sand. The activity of the last hours was more than her body had experienced in the past weeks.

"I can't!" she exclaimed. "I'm too tired."

Something hard pressed into her ribs. A gun? "Walk," he said.

The command to move her legs forward was met with shaking muscles and a cold sweat. Her nervous system ignited in red hot pain. Lightning struck deep inside her brain and down her body. Her vision tunneled with flashes of blue-white light. She cried out and fell.

More hands grabbed her as Brendan was joined by another man. They half carried, half dragged her off the beach and shoved her into the back seat of the car.

She didn't know whether to laugh or cry. The protective catatonic cocoon that had been her safety net and oasis for months spun around her, demanding to lock her away from the world again.

Retreating into her inner reality would not protect her from the men who now drove like madmen through darkened neighborhoods. She willed her hearing to sharpen. The car decelerated and made two sharp turns. Five minutes. Seven max. The roar of a jet overhead shook her core. They stopped. Someone got out of the car. A massive door slid on its tracks. The car moved forward before it stopped again. The large door slammed shut.

"Get up."

Hands pulled at her jacket and dragged her out of the car.

She opened her eyes to see they had entered an airplane hangar. A cavernous roof arched above her. Crates and boxes of different sizes lined the perimeter.

Brendan sat her down on a stack of pallets and looked at her with a mixture of professional resolve and admiration.

"I gotta admit, you had me believing you'd never walk again," he said, shaking his head with disbelief. "Jokes on me, I guess. I should've known you could fool anyone."

"I'm. Not."

"No? Well you had Michael fooled you loved him and I can only guess the angle you had goin' with his lawyer. Then I heard you talk to that reporter. I gotta say, I should've killed you when I could have covered my tracks with 'natural causes.'"

The driver of the car, a moose of a man in a Patriots sweatshirt and Red Sox baseball cap, stood beside him. "How long're we gonna wait here?"

"Not sure. Could be a long one. Grab a coffee, will you?" He looked at her. "Cream and sugar?"

Was he serious? "Fuck you," she said. As her eyes adjusted to the light, she felt her brain chug to observe and parse what was around her. They were toward the front of the building, close to the side. Banks of fluorescent lights hung from the ceiling. Most were turned off. Little light from the night sky filtered through the row of windows that capped the walls. She could just make out the outline of ceiling joists soaring upward into the gloom.

Each end of the building had spotlights and massive sliding doors large enough for a modest-sized aircraft to enter. A private jet sat inside. Jessica's heart skipped a beat as she searched for the MMC logo on its tail.

"You killed Colleen," Jessica said, struggling to her feet. Her legs shook in protest. She stopped trying to stand and sat with a thump on a pile of pallets.

Brendan shrugged. "Tough break. I couldn't let you get your story out. Me and Tiny here," he said, jerking his thumb toward his partner, "would be out of a job."

"Police roadblock. Aren't you worried the other cars were caught?" she asked, fishing for information.

"Nah. Our boys are good. No worries there."

Her heart sank. "What is this place? Why am I here?"

"You don't know?" Brendan asked, genuinely surprised. "Well, I'm not going to be the one to tell you."

His smug manner made her want to launch at him and scratch his eyes out.

"Here," he said, tossing a shipping blanket to her. "Get some rest. It's going to be a long day."

She curled into a ball. Within minutes she fell into the dreamless sleep of the damned.

When she awoke, light flooded in from the windows. The angle of the shadows on the floor hinted at late afternoon. The smell of strong coffee and food made her stomach growl.

"Here. Take this." A steaming to-go cup was placed in her hands.

Jessica pushed herself upright; eyes squeezed shut to block the pain in her stiffened muscles. She opened them and gasped.

"Good to see you, Jessica."

All thought left her as she looked into Michael's eyes.

The man she saw wasn't the Michael she believed had tipped off Colleen. With Colleen's dying breath, Jessica had learned that the man she had fallen in love with hadn't betrayed her to the paparazzi she loathed. She saw the man who used every resource he had to give her the best horses and the best care. In one dizzying moment, every fiber of her being wanted to fall into his arms and be embraced by his world.

351

Logan Airport
Boston, Massachusetts

THE MUSCLES IN Declan's jaw pulsed with each clench as he watched Michael wrap Jessica's hands around the coffee cup and brush a strand of her hair off her cheek. Brendan and Tiny, disinterested or unaware of the unfolding drama, sat on crates with a picnic of fast food between them.

The look of abject shock on Jessica's face gratified him.

"What! M-Michael?" Jessica sputtered and coffee spilled. "Now? You're here *now*? Where were you when I needed you?" Her voice strained with the struggle for control.

Michael reached over and coiled his fingers in her hair beside her face, reaching his mouth toward hers.

Declan kept a smile from his face as she pulled away.

"I couldn't come, Jessica, you know that." Michael lowered his hands. "It was your choice not to leave the U.S. when you had the chance in Louisville."

"You call that a choice? What would have happened next? Run more?"

"You would have been safe."

"I would have been damned. I needed distance from you, your uncle, and . . . and . . . all this." Her eyes scanned the hangar.

"I never lost touch with you. I knew how you were, who you saw, and what you did every day. I . . . *couldn't* be here."

"Why are you here now?"

The whine of a jet engine drowned their conversation as a second jet arrived, the MMC logo on its tail plainly visible. A ground crew hoisted hoses from a fuel tanker. Smaller vehicles darted between the aircraft. A side door, the size of a typical garage door, opened on the side of the building. One box truck, with "Branchwood Caskets" painted on its side, entered. Jessica and Michael watched in silence as conversation was impossible over the din.

Declan used the distraction to inch closer. After a few minutes of activity, the engine was cut. Men shouted. A loading platform was raised up to the jet's fuselage.

A smile of satisfaction grew on Michael's face. "When Declan told me you were missing, I couldn't stand it any longer. I came as soon as possible. He made the arrangements and assured me that as long as I don't clear in through customs and stay on airport property, I'm safe. I had to be here to help find you."

Jessica's expression told Declan all he needed to know when she heard his name. He pulled himself further back into the shadows.

"Why now?" Her eyes blazed with hate and hurt. "It's been *m-months.*"

"I learned my uncle had had a stroke the day I saw you off at the Belfast airport." Was that a shimmer of tears in Michael's eyes?

"That's a lie! He called Colleen and got the reporters to hound me."

Michael shook his head slowly and wiped his eyes with a knuckle. "I know. He knew the hell it would create and called to spite you."

"I never did anything to him," she stressed, incredulous.

An air of resignation surrounded Michael. "Maybe it was the strain he put on himself, but he had the stroke later that day."

"You should have told me."

"I knew all of my communications were being monitored, so it was best I never contacted you. Plus, my uncle needed my care."

"*I* needed you!" she sobbed.

"I surrounded you with the best people and did everything I could for you," he said as he reached to embrace her. "I love you."

Jessica scrabbled backward away from his grasp. "No. *No.* I don't know what this is, but it's not love."

"I need you."

Declan watched emotions pass over her face. He wanted to step forward, to end her confusion and move events along, but thought better than to stop a conversation that needed to be had.

"Need? You *need* me? For what? To divert attention from all this?" She thrust her chin in the direction of the box truck and jets. "You used me to ... to ... " Jessica's face darkened with the expressions Declan had grown to know when a storm of words was swirling inside her head and jamming together before they could emerge from her mouth. Declan wanted to finish her sentence for her and sucked his lips closed.

Michael tried to take her hands in his and Jessica pushed him away. Angered at being rebuffed, he overpowered her. A lethal look darkened his eyes as he easily grabbed both of her hands in one of his and used the other to force her mouth to his.

Declan's muscles coiled and he flexed his hands in preparation to attack, but Jessica freed her hand and slapped Michael across the face.

The slap stopped Michael's assault. "You have a choice," he said, rubbing his cheek. "You can live a life surrounded by the best horses and ride in the world's most elite events. I can provide you with everything you could possibly want."

"You don't know what I want," Jessica said, eyes blazing.

"Yeah, I do." He stood up and leaned over her, the threat and dominance in his posture clear. "You want to protect your father."

Jessica gasped. "M-Michael. Don't say it."

"If you do not help me, I will expose your father as the lying pig that he is. I will testify that you and your father have been actively involved in the planning and execution of terrorist attacks here and in the U.K. Everything is in place to have you spend the rest of your life in a Supermax prison somewhere in the middle of Colorado."

Her eyes narrowed. "Go ahead. Bring it on. I-I'm innocent."

He chuckled. "Exactly what I thought you'd say. If you're not worried about yourself, then your father should be your concern. Have you heard? He's an Archbishop now. There's even more at stake if he's exposed as a rebel-fucking shill."

"Michael. Don't."

"You have no idea the bubble my wealth creates. Money buys passage and silence, and the tools of war can be delivered without the slog of paperwork required to exit and enter countries. The kind of wealth my family has creates a world where borders are no more than lines on a map. And you? You provide a needed distraction and Declan's been a great help to me."

On cue, Declan stepped from the shadows. Jessica's shock pained him. He kept his eyes averted. "You give me too much credit," he said.

"Nonsense. You're the one who figured out the international flight refueling angle. Like with people, Customs rarely bothers with cargo from flights that are merely stopping in a country rather than entering. Using my private fleet of corporate jets provides an implicit level of protection that cargo won't be monitored," Michael said, rubbing his thumb and fingers together in front of his face to imply bribery. He motioned toward the two jets at the end of the hanger. Men scurried like ants to transfer freight.

"And your Uncle Liam perfected it with one last piece of assurance," Declan said. "You feared the pattern of 2100's arms shipments would eventually be discovered and needed a fail-safe way to operate outside of international law."

Michael glowed with satisfaction—the star student had mastered the lesson. He finished Declan's explanation. "If a correlation between the travels of MMC's fleet of private jets and armed civil unrest was made, connections back to my money would follow. I needed a decoy." He raised his eyes and looked at Jessica.

"Just one question for you," Declan said, cocking his head to the side. "Just when did you realize that Jessica, with her horses traveling to international events with all of the gear and crates required, was the perfect woman for you?" He knew the answer, but knew Jessica needed to hear it.

"My father hated your family and my uncle hated you," Michael said, keeping his eyes on Jessica's. "I loved you from the moment I laid eyes on you. Then? I didn't know what direction my life was going to take, but it was my uncle who knew that you'd be perfect. He began to encourage me to dream." He turned to Declan. "My father blocked me from expanding our business to its full potential. I had to make sure he'd stay out of our way."

Declan raised an eyebrow. "'Make sure'? How far did you go to 'make sure' your father stayed out of your way?"

Michael stared at him. "You're the only one who ever figured it out. I thought I'd have to kill you for your silence, but you've been very loyal."

"Say it. Say the words," Declan challenged. "Go ahead. You've nothing to fear. Show us who you are."

"I killed my father so I could run the companies without his interference," Michael boasted.

Jessica shrank back, repulsed.

Declan's lips tightened in a rueful smile. "All I had were suspicions and a few empty air canisters, but it's good to know I was right."

Michael nodded with satisfaction and returned his attention to Jessica. "Once I learned from you that your father wanted to remain in the priesthood, I knew I had the leverage I needed. He's quite a guy," he said, rubbing a spot on his jaw. "International reach, too."

Michael searched Jessica's face as he spoke. "Two jets landed at Louisville the day you returned to the States. One held you and the other a new form of gelignite en route to South America. By calling reporters, my uncle used your fame and ensured only you received attention. Oh, the explosive?" he continued with obvious pride, "A cell of the IRA in Ohio refined the formula and manufactured the gelignite. Very profitable. Few people know of the cell's existence and even fewer people know that the Catholic Church has a major presence there. A few hours in a truck got the shipment to Louisville. There was so much attention on you, no one gave the small crate so much as a passing glance. When my jet landed in Grand Cayman, that decoy woman drew attention away from my operation again. Perfect. From there, it was easy to coordinate the final transport to South America. If anyone had suspected anything, any investigation would have hinted at Church involvement."

Declan felt his stomach drop seeing the panic in Jessica's eyes as she spoke. "I'm innocent. You don't need my father." Her eyes implored him to believe her. He counted to twenty as he inhaled, willing sweat not to bead on his brow.

"You think you can prove your innocence?" Michael called over his shoulder. "Brendan? Bring it here."

Brendan approached them, wiping the remnants of his meal on his sleeve.

"Hey. I want to get out of here. I got to the girl before the cops did, so, as far as I see it, my job's done." He belched. "Next crew's arrived. All these guys running around'll draw attention, so I'm gonna go, but I want to make sure I get that bonus."

Brendan placed the messenger bag in the middle of the floor.

"Everything you need to prove your innocence has been removed and is safe," Michael said with a nod toward Declan. "Oh, right. And everything needed to tear down my organization is still in there." He turned to Brendan. "Go ahead."

Brendan grabbed a red fuel container and poured its contents over the bag.

Michael held a lighter up in his hand and looked at Jessica. "One last chance. Work with me, Jessica. Together we can accomplish so much."

Jessica's voice was strong and steady as she spoke. "I will not become a terrorist."

A moment's conflict flickered behind Michael's brow. "I really don't want to hurt you, but I know the good I can do."

"What, by p-planting bombs in shopping malls? By p-providing explosives to anti-government rebels? You're a m-monster," she sobbed. "I will protect my father until I die." Tears pooled in her eyes. "If I work with you, would you keep my father a secret? Would you swear to protect him as well as any other of your assets?" She covered her nose to avoid the stench of the fuel-soaked bag.

One corner of his mouth pulled upward in a smile. "You can bet your life on it."

"I don't believe you."

Flames whooshed to life as Michael lit the bag and papers on fire. "Without any proof, who's going to believe you over me?"

The sound of diesel engines revving up overpowered their conversation.

Declan glanced at his watch. Three o'clock. Perfect. He put his hand up to protect his face against the heat of the flames.

Jessica glared at him as the smoke alarm sounded and lights began to flash over the exits.

Shouting erupted. People began to run in all directions. Two men ran up to Michael and placed themselves as human shields. One in front. The other behind. They rushed, hunched together as a single unit, away from the commotion.

All the doors flew open at once. An army sectioned in teams of eight poured through each door. In seconds, dozens of armed agents flooded the interior. Rifles pointed in every direction.

Multiple voices shouted, "FBI! Hands up! Get on your knees! Hands where I can see them."

Gun shots sounded.

Declan launched his body at Jessica, throwing her to the ground and covering her body with his own. He placed his mouth by her ear. "Lie face down. Hands above your head. Don't move or you will be shot. Do you understand?"

He waited until she nodded her head before he stood and emptied the contents of a fire extinguisher on the flaming pile of papers. He looked up. Michael was being pulled by his bodyguards behind a cluster of crates. Was that a trap door in the shadow? Jessica's disappearance had forced him to bring Michael to the States before he could thoroughly map the building. Was there a door? Where did it lead to? He recalled no exit point and he'd come too far and had too much at stake to be wrong now. He started after them when a group of agents, clad in black S.W.A.T gear emblazoned with A.T.F. across their backs, descended on him and pointed a rifle at his nose.

"Hands where I can see them. Lie down slowly. Don't move." One rifle remained trained on him. He was aware of other agents disappearing behind the crates.

Declan slowly lowered himself to his belly making sure to keep his hands visible and steady. Shadows moved across the floor in all directions. Men shouted orders. Others yelled in fear. The cacophony lasted minutes, then died down.

He turned his head to look at Jessica. A woman officer, armed with a rifle and wearing a Kevlar vest stood over her. He allowed his lips to crease with a smile as he saw 2100's logo. The irony didn't escape him.

"Name?" The officer said.

"Wyeth. Jessica Wyeth."

"Well, Jessica Wyeth," the officer replied as she zip-cuffed Jessica's hands behind her back, "You have the right to remain silent."

Revere Police Station
Revere, Massachusetts

JESSICA PRESSED HER back against the cinderblock wall of the holding cell. Other women netted in the raid were processed at other stations, leaving her cell uncrowded. A luxury. One woman lay along the bench, mouth agape and snoring. Jessica could smell the alcohol from across the cell. Another girl, wearing a Revere High School sweatshirt hugged her knees to her chest. Bloodshot eyes rimmed in black stared at a spot on the floor. Fingers, with nails bitten to the nub, open and closed on the arms of her shirt in a way that reminded Jessica of LeeAnne. A pang of longing for the days on Electra's farm ran through her.

Sunlight from the emerging day crisscrossed the filthy floor with a rosy hue. Voices echoed along the halls, tumbling over one another and blurring individual conversations. Certain words emerged distinct and emphatic.

"Wyeth."

"Threat."

"Terrorist."

"Danger."

"Flight risk."

The station was a hive of activity and she could only listen to the shouts and curses as those arrested were booked and processed. The upswing of energy when word spread she was part of the raid's haul bothered her. Information overwhelmed her and her temples throbbed trying to make sense of it all.

Over twenty men were rounded up, including Declan, but she heard nothing about Michael. Declan's expression as they zip-cuffed him, was as unreadable as ever, but Jessica thought she saw a brief smile of satisfaction. She laughed when they offered her one phone call. Who the hell was she supposed to reach out to?

Holding cells at area police stations were at their breaking point. As soon as the courts opened in the morning, everyone taken in the raid would be formally booked. Some would be released on bail. The less fortunate or connected would be transported to other facilities where ribbons of barbed wire would surround them rather than a neighborhood. The prospect of bail for her was dim in light of looming federal charges.

She dragged and stumbled over her feet when two Revere officers, one man and one woman, half escorted and half lugged her into a separate room. The interrogation room was furnished with a long wooden table and three chairs. Her stomach sank as Agent Baxter entered.

"We never did get our chance to chat while you were in Kentucky," he said, placing a cup of steaming coffee in front of her and tossing a handful of creamers and sugars down.

She willed the color from rising in her cheeks by pushing out her abdomen and breathing deeply. "We tried, remember? Scheduling difficulties." She straightened her legs and winced as pins and needles attacked her feet. "B-besides, it's not like I haven't b-been easy to find."

Baxter splayed an array of papers on the table, turning a photo of a woman toward Jessica.

"This is Agent Amanda Boch."

The name sounded familiar. She cocked her head. "Amanda?"

Baxter leaned in. "Do you know anything about her?"

Did she? "I don't . . . I don't think so."

Baxter sat back in his chair and opened his arms in a welcoming gesture. "You can tell me anything, you know." He grinned.

"Amanda? Boch? I . . . think . . ." She stopped her stammer mid-sentence as lessons from her conversation with Declan in Electra's garden surfaced. She had emerged into a world of criminals and relative truths. Her reality no longer mattered. She waited, a marionette on loose strings.

"I want a lawyer."

Baxter's grin dimmed. "Lawyer? You don't want me to think you're hiding anything, do you?"

She glared at him. "Think what you w-want."

"I'll tell you what I think," Baxter said, leaning over her, his jowls glowing. "I think you're the cause of this agent's death. She was killed because she was zeroing in on you. The reporter's death is on you, too. Two women with the balls to go after you are dead." His voice cracked as he looked at Amanda's picture. "I will do whatever it takes to make sure you never walk free again. You want to talk with a lawyer? Fine. Talk all you want, but it's all lies coming out of your mouth. Anyone who can fake an injury like you did will say whatever it takes to connive and manipulate. You disgust me."

He put a picture of Colleen's messenger bag on to the table. "Everything I need to know is right here. Boys in the lab are going to have a time piecing things together, but this is the stuff agents' dreams are made of." The messenger bag looked how Jessica felt—battered, used, and burned. He placed another paper down. Colleen's illegible scrawl filled every line. "That reporter laid it all out right here. Radicalized by your mother. Trained by operatives in Northern Ireland," his voice trailed. "What a smoke screen you had going. I was putting the pieces together all wrong. Everything makes sense now. Combined with what Agent Boch had on you, these documents seal your fate."

Jessica blanched. "The recorder! Where is Colleen's voice recorder? And the notebook?"

Baxter smirked and tapped the picture with his index finger. "Recorder? Notebook? Nothing like that in here at all."

A knock on the door startled her. Baxter opened it, annoyed at the interruption.

"Who are you?" he demanded.

"I'm Miss Wyeth's attorney, Brooks Carter. I wish to speak with my client in private." A drawl lengthened his words and softened their edge, but his steel was no less evident.

Jessica tried to hide her shock at seeing Brooks. Her mind swam with fatigue. She would have been relieved at anyone coming to her assistance, but Electra's attorney? His swept bangs and cleft chin left no doubt he was the man Electra trusted with her life. She stared at the impeccable charcoal suit, blue shirt, and red and gold striped Rep tie, and shining wingtips. His coifed and impeccable appearance stood in sharp contrast to the grime covered cinderblock walls.

Baxter's cheeks reached a new level of red. "It's up to her to decide to speak with me or not. I was just being friendly."

"Don't play me as an ass," Brooks snapped. He straightened his back as if remembering his Southern manners. "There's no need to take any more of your time, friendly or not." He placed his briefcase on the table. "You can go."

Baxter turned to Jessica. "I'll be at your arraignment Monday morning. The minor charges will be for trespass, destruction of property, and endangering the public. The more interesting charges will be for accessory to murder, conspiracy, smuggling, fraud, and so much more." He didn't hide his glee. "The prosecutor will argue for no bail and there's not a court in the U.S. that would grant it to a suspected terrorist. You're looking at an undetermined time at Framingham prison while your trial is being prepared."

"What? No horse theft charges?" Brooks drawled, looking decidedly bored as he polished his already shining cufflink.

Baxter snarled. "A stablehand vouched for her. No theft." He gathered up his papers and left, slamming the door behind him.

Too many thoughts and emotions battled to be expressed. Was she relieved? Terrified? Jessica pressed her fists to her head. "I don't understand." She looked at him. "None of it is true. How can all of this go away?" Jessica wanted to be comforted at seeing him, but the way Brooks stood erect in the room and checked his watch set her on edge.

"Miss Wyeth, it is my pleasure to be here," he said, his manner softening as he sat across from her. "You have some powerful people who are determined to cause you trouble. Fortunately, you have some folks who want to help you, too."

"Help? I've got no one."

His eyebrows shot up his forehead. "I beg to differ on that, Miss."

"Why are you here? Who called you?"

"I'm here because Miss Electra's last instructions to me were to do everything I can to help you."

"Oh, Electra," Jessica moaned, a fresh wave of sadness washed over her. "She's gone."

"Yes, ma'am," Brooks said, taking a respect-filled moment to allow Jessica to gather herself, "but I do have some information for you first." He retrieved a yellow legal pad amid a stack of papers from his briefcase.

"What about this arraignment? And b-bail? Is it true that I'm stuck here?" Her cloak of defiance dropped, leaving her panic exposed.

Brooks shook his head in bewilderment. "You really have no idea what's gone on here, do you?"

"That agent! He said I'll never get out of here."

Brooks sighed. "Poor Agent Baxter. I don't blame him for being blinded by anger at Agent Boch's death. He's been so busy hoping he had a career-making case on his hands, he refused to see what was happening outside of his silo. No matter, he'll get the notoriety he was hoping for, but not for what he thought."

The events of the past day snowballed into a wall of exhaustion. Her muscles, tossed and thrashed from her brutal escape and ride, inflamed and stiffened. She hugged herself against the aches.

Brooks reached across the table and grabbed her hand. "Sweet lord, you're a wreck. We need to skip the pleasantries and get you out of here." He stood up and pressed the intercom button by the door. "We need to get out now."

What was he doing? If being released was as easy as pressing a button, the legal profession would be starved for cash. A roar of voices rose from the other side of the door.

"Wait, you're a corporate attorney not a criminal defense one, right? I d-don't think my getting out is that easy," she said, trying to put the pieces together.

The door opened and Father Blanton entered pushing a wheelchair. His ring of hair was disheveled and a day's stubble shadowed his face. "Lord have mercy on my soul. My prayers have been answered. How are you? Can you walk?" he asked. He maneuvered the chair beside Jessica's seat and locked the wheels. A faint scent of coffee enveloped him.

Before she could respond, Declan walked in, skin and eyes bright. He moved as if he wanted to brush Father Blanton away to rush to her side, but he hesitated and dropped his hands to his thighs. "Are you alright? I haven't been given any information on how you are."

Jessica blinked and rattled her head as if doing so would help make sense of what was happening. "What are you doing here? I saw you arrested!"

Declan and Brooks looked at one another. Brooks shrugged and Declan spoke. "You did it, Jessica. You're free. No more suspicions. No more Connaughts and all of their enterprises. You're done."

Outside the door, men and women in uniform craned their necks to witness the unbelievable.

"Michael and most of his key personnel were rounded up and arrested in the airport raid. We could not have done that without your help," Declan said. "For months, Northern Ireland had refused to extradite him. The longer he remained untouchable, the stronger his network became. The only way we could arrest him was to get him on U.S. soil."

Brooks nodded in agreement. "You and Electra dissolved your interests just in time. The Rose was blooming."

"And it needed to be pulled out by the roots. The timing had to be right." Declan rubbed his forehead in a motion that brought Jessica's attention to his drawn cheeks covered with stubble. Although animated with excitement, exhaustion was just below his surface. "I have to say your escape with Colleen threw my plans askew, but it proved to be an opportunity. Nothing motivates Michael like protecting his assets, and he insisted on coming to Boston to help locate you. Once he was here, the rest was easy. We mobilized the raid when his entire Boston crew was in the hangar. Hard to play innocent when you're shipping guns, explosives, and money in caskets."

"But, but you're his attorney! You worked for him," Father Blanton exclaimed,

Declan smiled and extended his hand as if in introduction at a first meeting. "Declan Cleary, Federal Bureau of Investigation Special Agent."

Jessica and Father Blanton gasped. Brooks gave a Mona Lisa smile.

"I was recruited by the FBI when I was in law school. They knew of my connection to the Connaught family from my summers at Ballyronan. It took a lot of assurance on their part that my dual identity would only be known to two superiors inside the Bureau, and Agent Baxter was not one of them." He smiled and looked out the door at the crowd of faces. "I'd say he's finding out right about now. Anyway, the law firm I worked for had been a conduit for the Connaught organization. It wasn't long before I was placed inside."

"But you treated me like I was . . . was chattel!" she shouted.

"You were," he said, eyes downcast. "Connaught's chattel, and I thought you were a willing participant in Michael's plans. He and his uncle were very good at constructing a world where you looked guilty. My orders were to take Michael down, and if you were part of the process, so be it."

She shuddered at knowing what could have been.

Brooks broke in. "Mr. Cleary and I wrestled quite a bit when I started untangling Electra's interests from Michael's involvement. I believe that's when he began to see you were being used in a larger scheme. At first, nothing I did weakened his opinion you were a radical in the making, but–"

"But people who are injured and fighting for their lives don't have the energy or the mental resources to lie." Declan started to reach out as if to touch her, and then stopped. "Oh, and one other thing," he said, visibly hiding his pleasure. "I had Colleen's recorder in my pocket and recorded Michael's entire conversation with you in the hangar. It's all there, Jessica. Colleen's documentation and research is stellar. Michael's confession to Magnus' murder, the conspiracy to implicate you, everything is there."

"And now we need to get you out of here and back to Silvern to get you checked out," Brooks said, moving to help her get into the wheelchair.

Declan nodded. "Definitely—with a few extra officers on duty at Silvern. You think you were hounded by the press before? You have no idea what's waiting for you. You can rejoin the world when you're ready." He moved beside the wheelchair. "Come on, let me help you sit."

"No," Jessica said, pressing her palms on the table and pushing herself to her feet. "I'm walking out of here on my own."

Father Blanton offered his arm as support and Declan stood on the other side of her.

As she hesitated at the door of the interrogation room, a hush settled over the crowd. A sea of blue and black uniforms parted, with arm patches showing departments from Revere and Boston. Plainclothes detectives and agents stood behind them. She was vaguely aware of Baxter pressing himself against the back wall, eyes glowing in his beet-colored face.

The quiet scared her. How many times had she been paraded in front of a crowd or dangled as bait? Years of survival taught her to fear the authorities when she had secrets to hide and people to protect. Her heart burned with longing to change events, but she knew regardless of what she did from this moment on, that it was only a matter of time before Kavan's story became grist for the infotainment mill. All that she had struggled to prevent would unfold in headlines across the world.

Father Blanton must have felt her concern. "Don't worry," is all he said.

"It's okay. We got this," Declan said as he gave her elbow more support.

She moved a shaking step forward. Then another.

The crowd erupted with applause.

"Way to go!"

"Awesome! Couldn't've done it without ya!"

The sounds shrank as she focused on moving forward, willing her knees not to buckle.

April 1997
Brandywine Farm

JESSICA PULLED WINO up to a trot from an easy canter. The early spring day's air was heavy and fragrant from the mignonette flowers Electra's gardeners had cultivated around the border of the cross-country course. Dew had burned off and the day promised to be hot, reminding her of mid-summer days in Hamilton. The rolling pastures, crisscrossed by miles of black fencing, felt welcoming and familiar, yet not quite like home.

Maybe, in time, she would feel her roots grip her soul to this place. For now, she would just be.

She took her feet out of the stirrups and dangled her legs at Wino's sides, alternately pushing her heels down and straightening her legs to strengthen and stretch her muscles. The pins and needles feeling of rolling her ankles in little circles gave her a moment's joy in the simple beauty of movement. Wino flicked an ear back at the sound of her sigh.

"Easy, babe. Just walk yourself out and cool down," she said, reaching forward to pat Wino's sweat-streaked neck. "It's back to the barn for you." She watched a black horse and its rider launch over a double oxer, change leads, and barrel up a hill, and made a mental note to raise the height of the jump for the coming week's training.

She stopped outside of the barn and drew in a deep breath to prepare to dismount. Leaning forward, she pulled her right leg over Wino's rump and turned so her stomach was on the saddle. Then she slowly lowered herself to her feet using her arms to balance against Wino until her thigh muscles stopped buzzing. Wino's tail flicked and an ear tipped cautiously backward, but the horse didn't fidget as Jessica drew up the stirrups and brought the reins over his head.

"You're looking great out there. Need help?" LeeAnne walked forward to take the reins. She wore jeans with a brightly colored floral shirt, one hand-chosen by her from Electra's closet at Jessica's insistence. She placed her hand under Wino's chest. "Still a bit warm. I'll walk him before I hose him down."

Jessica looked at the line of earrings surrounded by a mass of jet black hair pulled back in an uneven ponytail. Gone were the tortured cornrows and the shaved head. LeeAnne's hair, not yet long enough to be completely captured in an elastic band, was held out of her face with a pink headband. Pale white scars tracked across LeeAnne's inner forearms. Gone were the crusted red lines, and her eyes were free from the thick bands of black that had encircled them last summer. Something pressed against Jessica's thigh and she looked down to see Ginger, tail wagging in greeting.

"Well, good morning to you, too!" Jessica laughed and gave Ginger the demanded ear rub and back scratch. She straightened. "Thanks, LeeAnne. Who's up next?"

LeeAnne ran a halter up the reins and over Wino's head and slipped the bridle off. "Carolyn's up on Kilkea next, and Nancy is finishing up on Gapman on the cross-country course. They look good, don't you think? Rolex shouldn't be too tough."

"I'm not worried about cross-country for them, it's dressage they need work on. Margi's here to coach later, right?"

"Yeah," LeeAnne answered. "She comes around four and the horses will be rested by then. I think that just leaves Foxfire for you. He's in his stall with the saddle on. Just needs a bridle. You can manage?"

Jessica flashed a smirk. "I think I can handle a bridle just fine." She started to walk toward the barn and stopped. "Thanks, LeeAnne. I appreciate your help, but I want to make sure you have time for your homework."

LeeAnne called over her shoulder as she walked away with Wino. "Yeah, I know. I know. 'Let me do it.' 'Don't baby me.' 'I've got to do things on my *own*,'" she said in a mock whining tone. "Whatever. We have work to do and not all day to do it. Just moving things along so I have time to study." She snapped her fingers and Ginger bounded after her. "Oh, some guy is in the barn waiting to see you."

Jessica walked across the courtyard to the barn, forcing her gait to be steady, and willing her left foot not to drag her big toe. Her walk was slow and purposeful. The slight rise of the hill challenged her and she put all of her concentration on the mechanics of her stride.

Place heel. Roll foot forward to ball. Push with toes. Lift with knee. Extend from hip. Place heel.

"You're doing great. Amazing to see you."

Was that a burr inflecting the words? The interior of the barn was dark. She looked up and saw a figure silhouetted against the sunlight flooding the opposite end of the barn. Tall. Fit.

She blinked to adjust her eyes but didn't need to see to know who he was. She could feel the pull with every fiber of her being.

"Dad!" She rushed forward, almost stumbling.

Kavan caught her elbows. "Easy there, child." He held her at arms' length, eyes shimmering with emotion. He searched her face. "Father in heaven. You're even more the image of your mother."

She let herself be enveloped in his hug and felt his presence seep into her, filling crevices and mending wounds. Her face pressed into his shoulder. A faint scent of incense clung to him. He didn't move or shift in that uncomfortable way that would hint she was overstaying her welcome. He held her without impatience as she cried herself empty of the confusion that had haunted her.

She wiped her nose with the back of her hand and brushed tears from her cheek. Only when he patted his pockets and produced a neatly folded hanky did Jessica notice he was dressed in buff-colored trousers and a casual shirt. She fingered the blue cotton. "Oh, this." Her voice faded. "No cassock. You ... you're not ..." Fresh tears welled. "It's my fault. I'm so sorry."

"Nonsense, child. It's me who should be saying my sorries to you, but there's no looking back, only forward." Kavan placed his finger-tips under her chin and lifted her face to look her in the eye. "The moment I received your invitation, I've been looking forward to being here with you. It took more than a wee bit of time to tie up loose ends in my life, but I'm here now." He made a show of surveying the barn and over the pastures. "It's wonderful to see your home. Show me around?"

The maelstrom that had been their lives seemed reflected in the flecks of dust that swirled and flickered in the shafts of sunlight. The past months had brought change that neither could stop and both had predicted. He linked his arm through hers. "Come on, Brooks is waiting up at the house," he said.

Jessica left instructions for Foxfire to be ridden by another rider and crooked her arm into Kavan's as they walked across the drive-way. Brooks' red Jaguar convertible, with wire spoke wheels, was parked in the shade of the live oak. He waved to them from the veranda, his royal blue shirt and white pants the perfect attire for a morning visit.

Jessica smiled to herself and focused on the details of the moment, knowing that the sweetness of life was in savoring the simple details. She no longer yearned for the salt-tinged air of seaside gallops on the beach near her childhood home, nor did she long for the earthen smell of peat from her mother's home. Bougainvillea and pine marked where she would now live. As herself. Without disguise.

But could stepping into Electra's void ever feel like home? Maybe, in time.

For now, she could wait and relearn what an uncomplicated life is supposed to feel like.

"Ah, the lady of the manor," Brooks said as they approached, raising a coffee mug in salute. "Electra knew what she was doing when she made sure Brandywine went to you. I've never seen you look so happy or the farm so busy. Amazing." He reached over and shook Kavan's hand in greeting. "Your Excellency. Good to see you again."

Kavan shook his head. "Kavan, please," he said, correcting. "Technically, I'm on sabbatical, but it's confusing, yes?"

Jessica pulled a rocking chair forward, making a grouping of three. The woven seat creaked as she sat. "I'm glad you're taking your time to decide and didn't renounce your vows completely. All of this has been so . . . so . . ." Words failed her.

"I spent my life helping men decide the trajectory of their lives, but when it came to managing my own, I was at a loss. I'm going to give myself the gift of time and not force a decision. I feel more at peace now."

His words echoed in her heart. She wondered if he knew how closely their souls aligned. She smiled. "Me too. No more lies."

Kavan's gaze looked beyond her eyes as if he had a clear view to her most private thoughts. No artifice would stand between him and the essence of who she was. His aquamarine eyes could harden to cold stone, but today they warmed Jessica with trust and security.

Instead of lamenting her past, she began to cherish it. All she had been through—and all Kavan had given—sweetened these simple moments.

The late morning activity hummed. Sounds of saws and hammers from the new barn and residence being built mixed with laughter and bits of conversation. Stablehands, in jeans and polo shirts, and riders, in breeches and boots, led horses or carried buckets. An older woman, with graying hair and a loose-fitting shirt, stood in the barn's doorway directing horses to the barn to be groomed and tacked or turned out into the paddocks.

"She's new?" Brooks asked.

Jessica followed his eyes. "Yeah. Mandy Hogan, from Windrush. Her experience running a hippotherapy and therapeutic riding center fit with Electra's vision. Did you know? Mandy has family in the next county and moving here was perfect for her." She stretched her legs and rubbed the knots from her thighs. "Mandy's as good with the horses as Margi is with the girls. I should have known Electra had most of the plans in place when I first met LeeAnne." She beamed. "LeeAnne is studying for her degree in social work. Did she tell you?"

Kavan poured water from a waiting pitcher. Lemon slices and ice cubes clattered into his glass. "I've missed a few pieces here and there. Fill me in."

Brooks warmed to the conversation. "Electra Lavielle had a dream to fill Brandywine with children. When she had none of her own, she set about creating a haven for young girls and women who were abused or had challenging home lives." He looked at Jessica with raised eyebrows. "You quickly became her first choice to run the farm, but she didn't have a chance to ask you before ..." He looked away and swallowed.

He inhaled a steadying breath and continued. "She had a network of mentors already in place to help with the emotional component of working with young women at risk. Eventually, she would have liked to offer more adaptive riding programs to handle physical as well as emotional and behavioral needs, but I think she'd be very happy with what you're doing, keeping the focus on the women while having the goal be competition."

Jessica picked at the rocker's wicker, remembering another time when she sat with Electra. The threads of that conversation wove into the scene she saw today. Each of the grooms, riders, and groundskeepers were women dedicated to helping one another.

After a final week at Silvern, Jessica came directly to Brandywine and considered the improvements to Williams' townhome to be a final separating of ways "gift." William was thrilled to have a freshly renovated home without the burden of worrying about her, and wept with relief at being released from caring for her. At Brandywine, Jessica found all the help she needed to continue with her rehabilitation.

"I'm entering Gapman and Breezy into Rolex, but am not expecting too much. Gapman's training started too late to really prepare him for it and Breezy's dressage passes look like a drunken sailor on a heaving ship. My new horse, Glama Queen, has a lot of potential, but is very green. I think my competition days are behind me, but I can still train."

Kavan laced his fingers through hers. She felt his thoughts. *'Tis a miracle you can do as much as you do.*

She also felt his pain. He teetered as a man in a crisis of faith. The revelation of his paternity did not explode into the world in violent uprisings as she had feared. He had unfolded his truth to the men and women at risk of being betrayed by *how* they learned about his past, not that he *had* one. In the months since he first met Jessica in secret, he had worked steadily to bring the leaders of rebellion and government into his confidence. The combustible mix of shock and betrayal that would have ignited with an ill-timed exposé in a newspaper was defused with his personal confession to them and an apology for being supremely human. In a testament to the respect he had nurtured throughout his career, no arms were raised in uprising, only in embrace.

The casualty of his truth was not measured in riots, burned buildings, or dead bodies, but in Kavan requesting to be laicized by voluntarily giving up his clerical state. Jessica did not understand all the details, but learned that an archbishop from Africa spoke to the Pope on Kavan's behalf. By being laicized, rather than fully renouncing his oath to the Church, Kavan would be welcomed back into his full role in the future without any additional ordination or ceremony—if he so chose.

"I've only seen the jump races at Cheltenham and Aintree, which you say is like the cross-country event here in Kentucky at Rolex. I'm looking forward to seeing these other events you've spoken of. The, um, what do you say? Ah! Yes! Grand Prix jumping and dressage," he said, pursing his lips like a nervous schoolboy. "I won't be underfoot living here?"

"No, Dad. Never." She paused, savoring his preferred title. "In fact, I don't think I could take on this adventure without you. I'm good with being able to judge horses, but people? Not so much. I know you'll be able to help the girls to forgive themselves for what's happened to them." Her eyes prickled with tears and she blinked them away. She could speak about what was in the hearts and minds of many of the women on the farm, but when it came to her own, she faltered.

In that unspoken and unbreakable bond between father and daughter, she felt his acceptance as he rubbed her arm in response. "Give it time, Jess. Forgiveness is all around you. When you're ready to accept it, it's already there. Waiting."

Instead of crying, she surprised herself with a laugh. "Spoken like a true *Father*," she said, teasing. "I think the last of your boxes arrived yesterday. Is there anything more?"

"No. Everything has been shipped here or is in storage," Brooks said as he grabbed some papers from his briefcase. "I've seen to the sublet of his flat in Belfast. He's all yours for the next year. Just in time too, I see. You're going to need support after you testify at Michael's hearings."

"I can help her with that."

Jessica startled to see Declan standing at the door. His normally guarded and unreadable eyes gleamed in the morning light. A slight tan colored his pale skin. The lines around his mouth had almost disappeared and his tightly cropped hair had grown out, softening his look.

Jessica used her arms to push herself to her feet to give Declan a peck on the cheek in greeting. She stepped back, just out of his reach. "Declan! You're early," she said, smiling.

"Declan? Declan Cleary?" Kavan stood up and embraced him. "Pleasure to finally meet you, sir."

Jessica blinked in surprise. "Wait. You two know each other?"

"In a manner of speaking, yes. We've spoken, just never met," Kavan said, pumping Declan's hand. He lowered his voice. "I owe a debt of gratitude to you."

"I've heard it said that the Lord works in mysterious ways," Declan laughed, face glowing with genuine warmth. "I'm glad I passed muster with your colleagues here in the States. I have to say, when your network first made contact with me in Atlanta, the dual nature of my job did make things interesting, but getting to know you helped me put the pieces together faster." He continued shaking Kavan's hand and used the other to grip Kavan's shoulder. The two men stopped speaking and a lifetime of meaning filled the silence between them.

Catching himself, Declan stepped backward, embarrassed, and spoke to Brooks. "I brought the papers we discussed."

She looked at Brooks. "You two have business? You can use the Bridge if you'd like," she said, her face creased with a stab of sorrow wishing it was Electra who invited them to the Bridge and not her. The stab was not as sharp as it had been, a fact she noted as progress.

The grief would always be with her, but the pain lessened as time moved on.

Brooks bowed his head in understanding. "Nothing that can't wait for later. If you don't mind, I'd like to sit in on hearing what's going on with Michael."

Declan pulled another chair up to the group. "He's not going anywhere for quite a while. As you know, the court deemed him a flight risk and refused him bail. The judge pulled his passport for extra insurance. All of his assets have been frozen both here and abroad. He'll go to trial on a myriad of charges."

"It would be so much easier if he could be prosecuted on one charge, but supporting terrorism isn't that easy to prove," Brooks said, warming to having lawyer shop talk with Declan.

"True enough. He'll be prosecuted on tax evasion, racketeering, fraud, customs violations and more." Declan looked at Jessica. "You'll be asked to testify about how he used his private fleet of jets to bypass customs for international shipments and how he used charitable purposes as a cover for funneling money to illegal ones."

She nodded. "And Magnus' murder?"

"The murder trial will be separate and won't involve you at all."

The morning heated to afternoon. What had begun as four isolated individuals blended into one family with a friendship at its core. Mandy strolled up and chatted, helping herself to water and a cookie. After remarking on the heat of the day and the weather forecast for the coming week, she grabbed a piece of fruit before returning to the barns. LeeAnne approached and stood on the walkway, but did not ascend the steps as she updated Jessica on the day's training. She scuffed her toe into the ground when Jessica tried to draw her into small talk. Her relief was visible as she gave her good-byes with a promise to study. The afternoon's dressage trainer and riders arrived and the orchestrated events of a well-managed farm played out under Jessica's watchful eye.

The afternoon faded into evening and the air freshened before taking on the dew of night. Brooks tapped his head in salute as he sped off in his sports car and Kavan used the quiet of the day to take a stroll on the grounds and unpack his belongings in his suite of rooms.

Jessica and Declan settled into a comfortable silence as the cicadas started to chorus. In an unconscious rhythm, they rocked in unison while the sky turned from shades of blues to pinks.

"You're welcome to stay in the guest house," Jessica said. She felt his eyes on her, but trained hers to follow the fence line to the horizon. Black and brown figures of grazing horses dotted the pastures. The grey body of Blue Jeep stood in stark relief against the fresh spring grass.

"Thanks anyway, but I have a room in town at the inn." He stood and offered his hand to help her up. They started to walk toward his car. "Tomorrow morning Brooks and I will go over more of the contracts Michael and Electra had together. He's using an abundance of caution to make sure nothing ties back to you. He's a good attorney. I can see why Electra trusted him."

"Yeah," she said, voice faint.

"You've come a long way," he said, and waited for a response. When none was offered, he continued. "Are you sure you want to make the trip to Boston? I can arrange for your deposition to be done down here."

"No. I'm okay. I need to go. Are you saying your raid wasn't such a clean sweep after all?" she teased.

He scoffed lightheartedly. "Anyone in Michael's organization who wasn't rounded up at the airport is probably hunkered down so tight they won't even risk so much as a parking ticket for the foreseeable future."

"I heard you received honors for a successful operation. Congratulations. I mean it, really. That's great."

"It could not have happened without you. You know that."

"I know. You did what you had to do. You got the bad guys and cleaned the streets. Good job. Really," she said, voice flat despite trying to sound upbeat. In her head, she knew telling the truth of all she knew about Michael, his uncle, and their operations was the right thing to do. Her heart was taking more time to catch up.

"I think you know me well enough by now that I don't do anything half way."

The open button of his shirt exposed the smooth skin of the hollow of his neck. She wanted to press her face against his chest and breathe in his scent while he kissed and stroked her hair. She wanted to feel his masculine arms embrace her. She wanted to feel those things while enveloped in a cocoon of complete trust.

Something must have changed in her expression as he reached for her. She could feel the heat of their bodies meet in the cool evening air.

His eyes, once black and unreadable, warmed to velvet. His skin grew moist as he brushed his fingers against hers. She saw his neck muscles tighten with a swallow.

"Jessica," he began searching the horizon as if the right words to say could be found there. "The weeks I spent watching you struggle to find a way to recover, even as you were terrified of what would happen when you did, showed me who you are. I had started out believing you were Michael's shill, but quickly learned otherwise; but I couldn't break my cover."

"I heard everything you ever said, even when you thought I couldn't."

"I figured as much. So, then, I guess it's not that hard for you to know I mean it when I say I want to give us a try."

His declaration was nothing new to her. Brooks had told her to expect as much, saying Declan looked for reasons to meet in Perc. She envied Declan's ability to look inside of himself and state what he wanted.

"I know," she responded, "but I'm not anywhere near being able to do that."

"Because of Michael?"

She tried to answer the question, but didn't know how. "Partly, but mostly because of me. I don't trust my judgment. I fell in love with a man who had a heart that could change. I don't question his love for me, but somewhere along the line I fell to second place. He and I met, what, less than two years ago? My life had been turned on its head and I thought I needed someone to anchor me. And this," she said looking out over the barns and pastures, "this is all so new that I need time to just be."

"He's in jail because of what he did. You have nothing to do with his problems."

"I know, but I thought a person just knew if another person was good or bad. I didn't know I had fallen under the spell of a murderer. I can't trust myself."

"Don't be too hard on yourself. You met Michael when he was struggling to own his family's legacy and bend it toward good. He tried."

She nodded slowly, remembering. "His uncle knew it was only a matter of time before Michael succumbed."

"I don't think he succumbed as much as he realized he couldn't lead two lives. Michael and I had many conversations about how he could untangle the web of corporations his father created. I thought my undercover work was going to be fruitless, but I couldn't understand why he didn't take advantage of Magnus' death by making a clean break from his father's criminal activities. Once I uncovered Magnus' murder, I understood his bigger game and how that involved you."

"I'm not hiding anymore. All my cards are face up. There's no more game to play. My private life is public entertainment and my father's career was destroyed because of me."

"Enough of that talk. I won't be hearing you bash yourself up."

They turned to see Kavan striding toward them across the driveway.

"My life was built on my decisions, and I won't be hearin' you take credit for God's plan." Kavan's skin was flushed from his brisk walk. An air of contentment surrounded him. "How can you doubt or blame yourself because life's events brought you to this moment?"

Jessica used Kavan's arrival to step away from Declan. He started to reach out to stop her, then let his arms fall to his side with a sigh.

Kavan's eyes narrowed and looked from his daughter to Declan and back. Jessica could feel his thoughts and squirmed at being so exposed.

"From my perch, I see my daughter living on a farm of her dreams in a life filled with meaning. Your work with the women here will heal you as well as them, and the fact I can be a part of this satisfies me in a way I couldn't have imagined for myself. And for you," he said, turning to Declan, "there'll be no more staying at the inn for you. There's a guest house going begging and you should consider it your home away from home."

Jessica started to protest, then stopped. Kavan had stepped in to her life and grabbed the brass ring of fatherhood. She had someone who understood her past and present, and cared enough about her to open up her future.

She could feel her cheeks heat and kept her eyes downcast. "It would be nice if you stayed."

"Okay. I will," Declan said in a soft voice.

Kavan waited a beat before he stepped forward and linked Jessica's arm and motioned for Declan to follow. He brought them back to the veranda.

"Tomorrow, I'd love it if you could find a suitable horse for me to ride. I can only go so far on foot and there's much to see," he said, looking out over the distant Pine Mountains silhouetted by the setting sun. "Now then, what about those mint juleps I've heard you Yanks talk so much about?"

Jessica laughed. "It's made with Kentucky bourbon, not Irish whiskey."

"Ah, well, the sacrifices one must make to get along in the world," Kavan said, beaming. "Just bourbon's in the glass?" he asked, expression hopeful.

"Electra liked to make hers with sweet tea and extra mint," she replied, turning to enter the house. "I'll make a pitcher."

Declan placed his hand on her arm. "Relax with your dad. I've got this." He walked to the kitchen.

Kavan didn't hide his pleasure at watching Declan. "He's a good man, Jess."

The creak of wicker didn't cover the sound of her sigh. She let the chorus of cicadas answer for her.

ABOUT THE AUTHOR

CONNIE JOHNSON HAMBLEY writes high-concept thrillers featuring remarkable women entangled in modern-day crimes. Growing up on a dairy farm in New York meant she had plenty of space to daydream and ride one of her six horses. All would have been idyllic if an arsonist hadn't torched her family's barn. Bucolic bubble burst, she began to steadfastly plot her revenge against bad guys—real and imagined—and received her law degree from Vermont Law School.

Connie moved to Boston and wrote for *Bloomberg Business-Week*, *Nature* and other wonky outlets, but she craved to create stories with vivid characters and worlds were the good guys win, eventually. Her suspense novels force the reader to reconcile the blurred edges between good and evil. *The Charity* earned reader praise and *The Troubles,* won Best Fiction at the Equus Film Festival in New York City. Her short story, *Giving Voice*, won acceptance in *New England's Best Crime Stories: Windward*, published by Level Best Books. She keeps horses in her life by volunteering as a horse handler at Windrush Farm, a therapeutic riding center located in Massachusetts. Connie is a board member and a featured speaker of the New England chapter of Sisters in Crime.

Learn more at:

www.conniejohnsonhambley.com

Twitter: @conniehambley

CPSIA information can be obtained
at www.ICGtesting.com
Printed in the USA
LVHW110909180522
718906LV00019B/1179